"...the narrative puts its mea~
of living flesh on the dry bones of
skeletonized history...Schoonover's
best effort to date."
-Chicago Sunday Tribune

"Picaresque, romantic recreation of
history..."
-Kirkus Book Reviews

"A real contribution to the history
of Spain and the Spanish people...
recommended for pubic school and
university libraries"
-Library Journal

"...unfurled in swatches of bright
color and sound sentiments, you will
like 'The Queen's Cross.' "
-Saturday Review

QUEEN'S CROSS

BY

LAWRENCE SCHOONOVER

TO MY DAUGHTER

ELIZABETH

ISBN 13: 978-0-9760867-4-1
LC: 2008929381

MEDIEVAL EUROPE

SCOTLAND

SCANDINAVIAN STATES

MUSCOVY

ENGLAND

LOW COUNTRIES

LITHUANIA

HOLY ROMAN EMPIRE

FRANCE

HUNGARY

SPAIN

ITALIAN STATES

OTTOMAN EMPIRE

PORTUGAL

MUSLIM CALIPHATES AND KINGDOMS

EGYPT

© CARTE ROUGE

SPAIN & WESTERN MEDITERRANEAN

FRANCE

NAVARRE

ITALIAN STATES

Valladolid

Saragossa

PORTUGAL

CASTILE

ARAGON

Rome

Lisbon

Toledo

Barcelona

Seville

Cadiz

Granada

SICILY

Malaga

Tripoli

MOORISH KINGDOMS

© CARTE ROUGE

CHAPTER 1

THE provincial town of Arevalo was in no way distinguished; it was not a suitable residence for a queen. The walls of the alcazar, the principal fortress of the place, were in disrepair. The iron bars at the window slits, which should have been smart with paint, were weak with rust. The castle gardens suffered from lack of care, for the queen had lost her taste for flowers and in any event her meager pension, irregularly paid, could not support an adequate staff.

Yet the countryside was pleasant and healthful. The wheat fields, stretching in all directions, shone and undulated like a golden sea to wash the foot of the long low line of hills that rose on either horizon. The purple-flowered saffron, an herb indispensable to Castilian cookery, impregnated the clear air with a sweet aromatic perfume that would have impressed a traveler, had there been any, as exotic.

Midway between the line of distant hills that bounded the little valley, which was intensely farmed, like all fortuitously fertile spots in Old Castile, the Adaja River slowly meandered among the peasant farms. Here the stream was gentle; but that did not mean that a few miles to the north or south it might not change character completely, to become a rocky torrent, or perhaps a swamp, since nothing in Spanish terrain is ever reliable and only the unexpected can be predicted with certainty.

The best thing about the river, as far as the queen was concerned, was that it supplied an abundance of cheap fish for Wednesdays and Fridays every week of the year. During the long season of Lent, which she observed more strictly than most people during the present reign, there was uninterrupted fish for forty days, including Sunday, which even her chaplain said was self-denial better suited to a cloister than a Dowager Queen in retirement. The truculent governor

1

of the castle, an old soldier, portly, red-faced and irreverent, regarded the river as a necessary evil, since it kept the moat well sluiced and sweet, a much neglected consideration in castle sanitation: hilltop castles always had foul moats and the grandees who inhabited them were often mysteriously sick; riverside castles seemed to make for health. Don Pedro de Bobadilla had a face full of long-healed scars; his wrists and ankles still showed marks where Moorish fetters had bitten into the flesh. He had married late, and he indulged his young daughter to a degree that scandalized the queen. "It was bad enough when you let her ride a horse instead of a mule, which is proper and ladylike," she had once scolded him, "for now the Infanta insists on a horse too." And it was not in her heart to deny the princess a horse. Had not Joan of Arc ridden horses? "But it has come to my ears that your bold Beatriz went swimming in the moat last night, naked as a fish! Is the report true?"

"Your Highness, it was very dark, very hot. I whipped her soundly for that. But she wasn't naked, I swear."

The queen had said, "Any repetition of such a performance will bring about your instant dismissal from my service. Remember."

There would be no repetition, the governor had sworn, and offered to whip Doña Beatriz again for setting a bad example to the Infanta. But the queen's anger had passed quickly. The governor would not have whipped the girl again anyhow, and he was not concerned with losing his position—who else loved the widowed consort of the late king so much that he was willing to donate his services? She forgot the incident and lapsed again into the mild and dreamy melancholy that was now habitual with her. It seemed to her little suite of retainers that exertion fatigued her more and more every year, and that she dwelt more and more in the past when she was Queen of Castile and León, when the old king was still alive, before the hated "Dowager" had fastened itself upon her title like an incubus.

The Dowager Queen was still an important person, however, because of her two children, for if the present King Henry should beget no heirs—and in twelve years, first with one consort, then with an other, none had been born—then her son, Don Alfonso, would inherit the crown.

Safety, safety above all, had guided her to Arevalo, for beyond the wheat and saffron fields in the valley of the Adaja, beyond the rim of purple hills, lay vast reaches of bare and rocky wilderness for many miles in all directions. Here was the safety of isolation, here was the safety of the king's forgetfulness; here she could live unmolested in her lengthening widowhood and bring up her children in decency and dignity away from the court of her stepson, Henry IV, whom history would call with inelegance "Henry the Impotent." There was much at the court of King Henry to cause anxiety to the mother of the lad who might be king and the green-eyed girl who was next after him in the line of succession and might be queen. When, at irregular intervals, a messenger from the capital would arrive with her allowance she would hide Don Alfonso, lest it be noted that he was frail, and Doña Isabella, lest it be noted that she was already almost a woman. Neither would be safe at the court in Valladolid.

King Henry, when he remembered the Dowager Queen at all, would sometimes send her or the children a gift. Hers might be a cheap tortoise-shell comb, though she never wore combs in her hair any more. Doña Isabella's was likely to be a book of lurid love poems, which the queen would order burned. Don Alfonso's as a rule consisted of cast-off clothing which one of the foppish courtiers at Valladolid had discarded because it was all of six months out of style. The Dowager Queen would order it destroyed. Long, gaily colored cloaks smacked of the flowing robes of the Moors, heretical, alien. Don Alfonso would go back to his short threadbare cloak, intensely black, intensely Spanish.

3

Once in a burst of generosity the king had actually sent the heir presumptive a bottle of perfume with a gushy little note that it was the latest thing at court: rustic Arevalo must not stand in the way of a prince's acquiring polish, which, said the king, was very, very important in princes. Don Alfonso never saw the odd gift. The Dowager Queen unstoppered the bottle, sniffed with distaste and recognized the Moorish product. She dropped it into the moat. It happened to strike a rock at the base of the castle wall. It shattered, and for many days the breezes that drifted over the battlements were full of a lingering perfume of musk and jasmine and roses. Was it possible, the Dowager Queen asked herself in dismay, that men at Henry's court perfumed themselves? Santiago! Why?

It was not, of course, fashionable to visit the Dowager Queen, even to pay one's respects on the anniversary of the late king's death. But not all men in Spain perfumed themselves and some remembered her in her better days with affection. One, a Fray Tomás, made a point of visiting her regularly, four times a year. The monks under his care were satisfied to see him depart, for his discipline was extremely strict. Yet they called his visits an act of charity, since no possible benefit could accrue to him from any attention to the widowed queen; and they noted that he, who would never allow them the luxury of a mule, was just as severe with himself, for he would walk the entire thirty miles to Arevalo unattended through wild and dangerous country without so much as a morsel of bread on his person. Fray Tomás seemed equally oblivious of heat, cold, hunger, fatigue and the wild beasts that lurked in the wastelands between Segovia and Arevalo.

It would greatly have amused him had anyone said, "Fray Tomás, you are a saint, living in a dream, forgetful of the world and leaving all things to God." That was a lazy mystical way, the way of the stylites who had lived on the tops of pillars in Egypt, waiting for ravens to feed them. The day of the stylites was long since past. Spain in 1462 was not the Egypt of the patristic age. Spain and Fray Tomás, who was Spanish above all else, were intensely practical. He walked because walking would set a good example, because he was young and strong and could well endure it. He took no food because he was accustomed to fasting—he could not remember the taste of meat, which he had not eaten in more than ten years—and chronic hunger in the midst of plenty was so habitual that it passed unnoticed. As for the beasts—boars, bears, wildcats—he carried a heavy staff. He felt himself by no means under special protection, and if they had attacked him he would simply have bashed out their brains. For beasts, like devils and heathens, were cowards at heart, you could rout them by a bold attack; they were formidable only if you were unalert.

Fray Tomás came by these traits honestly, for he was a scion of an ancient Castilian house whose ancestors had fought the Moors. At thirty he was prior of the Dominican monastery of Santa Cruz in Segovia. He administered it superbly, considered it a trust from God and coveted no greater advancement in the Church, though his uncle was a cardinal and could easily have secured preferment for him. But his uncle resided in Rome; Fray Tomás might have been required to leave Spain, and to him that would have been an early taste of purgatory.

His conscience had pricked him at first because of the pleasure he took in the long invigorating walk. The way led by twisting forest paths where his sandals in his sturdy stride stirred up the fragrance of fallen pine needles, then into a bare and treeless upland full of tumbled rocks and prickly growth, across the valley of the Eresma, where there was a bridge much in need of repair in the present reign, and by nightfall into the purple hills from which the alcazar of Arevalo was visible, small and dark amid the geometric design of crop lands and fallow fields of the peasants. He

5

reproached himself with a Moor-like sensuality for dwelling with pleasure too long on the beauty of Spain, though he could not help loving his country, and there was nothing in his vows that required him to prefer the ugly to the beautiful. But it always eased his conscience to devote himself to instructing the Infantes whenever he visited the Dowager Queen.

He belonged to an Order with a special care for education. There were Dominicans teaching the young in every country of Europe, and beyond Europe in Russia; and beyond Russia in far-off Persia, India, China, all over the great round world. Through their far-flung missions the Dominicans had amassed an immense practical knowledge of geography.

It was natural for him to teach, and the children looked forward to his visits because he was better informed than their regular tutors and he made things simple to understand. Like a child himself he saw the world in sharply contrasting blacks and whites, without qualification—as black as his mantle, as white as his habit. He was tall of stature, his chin had a determined thrust, his voice was harsh and his appearance was somewhat formidable to the young prince and princess.

Once, while he was speaking with pride and enthusiasm of the distant missions, Isabella asked excitedly, "Is there not great danger that the missionaries may venture too far in their travels, Fray Tomás?"

"No distance is too far to reach the heathen, *mi princesa.*"

"But will they not fall off the edge of the world?" Fray Tomás hesitated only a moment. To a merchant he would have answered, "No ship has ever fallen off yet." To a philosopher he would have answered, "The earth's shadow on the moon during an eclipse is round." To a university student at Salamanca he would have snapped, "Reread your Aristotle, young man; for shame!" But these were not arguments that boys and girls understood. So first he spoke with ponderous authority, in Latin: *"Mundi formam omnes fere consentiunt rotundam esse"* translating it at once, since he knew that royalty did not speak Latin, "'It is generally conceded that the shape of the world is round.' Those are the words of the Holy Father himself, Pope Pius II." And then he closed the matter with an argument that their young minds could grasp: "Only a few ignorant sailors still fear to sail on the ships that carry our holy faith to distant lands. Only a wicked or stupid man would contend that the earth is flat as a pancake. Can water rest on top of a pancake? No, it would run right off. And so it is with the earth. If the earth were flat, all the water in all the seas would have spilled over the edge long ages ago. But Spain is surrounded by sea, and so is every other country."

Fray Tomás was not really interested in the rotundity of the earth; he was merely a little concerned lest the prince or princess, some day in a position of power, might hesitate to send out seaborne missions for the propagation of the Christian faith. Far closer to his heart was Spain and her troubles, especially the Moorish kingdom of Granada that fastened itself like a leech on the rich and beautiful Andalusian plains.

"Never forget that Spain is shaped like a shield. The very map of this blessed land is a picture of Spanish destiny, which is nothing less than to stand like a shield, protecting not only ourselves but also the whole of Christian Europe against the unspeakable evil of the Moors."

Thus it was that Spain had always stood, Fray Tomás said, throughout seven long dark centuries when at times it had seemed that the Cross might fall forever before the Crescent, as infidel hordes swept up to the very foothills of the Pyrenees. But the Spaniards had never surrendered. From their mountains in the Asturias the hardy ancestors of the prince and princess had slowly pushed back the turbaned invader ever farther towards the south.

But there, in recent years, the crusade had faltered. The lower part of the shield was still defiled by the Moorish Kingdom of Granada, insolent and rich with a population of three million infidels.

When would another Spanish sovereign arise to complete the Reconquest and hurl them back into Africa?

It seemed to Fray Tomás that nowadays Spanish kings were all too apt to accept them as equals, particularly King Henry. But he did not say so, since it was his duty to teach, not to stir up discord between the king and the heir presumptive. Unity was his theme. Don Alfonso listened, his young mouth resolute. So did his sister, the Infanta.

"I'll help you, Alfonso. I'll marry Portugal—or Aragón. Then the Christians will be twice as strong."

"When you marry, little sister, you must follow your heart. I shall take care of Granada, Io el Rey! That is a man's job."

Fray Tomás overheard the whispered remarks, but did not reprove the youngsters. He thanked God for their high spirits.

"Next time I shall touch on the neighboring kingdoms of Portugal and Aragón." He smiled, since Isabella, at least, already showed signs of political maturity. "It is true that the three Christian nations ought to be one, in order that Spain may stand united against the infidels."

Retracing his steps to Segovia he composed his next lecture in his neat and orderly mind, hoping that his lessons might serve in some small way for the greater glory of Spain and the humbling of the Moors, He did not flatter himself that history would remember him, though he supposed that the name of his uncle, the cardinal, might be noted in a line or two by the pens of the chroniclers. He seldom thought of his own name, which was Tomás de Torquemada.

It was not to be his lot to deliver the next lecture. When next he walked from Segovia to Arevalo the little castle was tightly shut. Only after he had knocked and shouted several minutes did a small grilled wicket open in one of the sally ports of the massive gate.

"Go away," the guard scowled,

"Kindly inform the Queen Dowager that Fray Tomás is here."

"She receives no visitors."

He would have slammed the wicket in his face, but Fray Tomás thrust his staff through the bars. "I do not recognize you, good guard; perhaps you do not recognize me. I am Fray Tomás de Torquemada, prior of Santa Cruz in Segovia. I call as usual to pay my respects to the Dowager Queen and Instruct the Infantes. Inform Her Highness that I am here."

"You are quick with your staff, señor prior, more like a caballero with a lance." He was peering behind Fray Tomás suspiciously. "If you are truly a prior, where are your companions, your almoner, your escort, your mounts?"

"I came alone, and I walked."

The guard shook his head, unconvinced, but he said, "One moment, señor prior," and turned, muttering to himself, "they told me to expect peasant customs in the provinces." The wicket shut and Fray Tomás heard bolts being thrown.

Shortly Don Pedro de Bobadilla appeared, his face curiously pinched and his scars more prominent than usual. He shouldered the guard aside and threw open the gate. "Ten thousand pardons, your reverence. The men are all new here, all spoiled, all suspicious, all very courtly mannered, as you see. They are under orders from the king himself to admit no one. Enter, enter—and bless this house as you have never blessed it before. It needs blessing."

"The children are ill?"

"They are gone, everybody is gone, all the old guards, my wife, even my daughter, the apple of my eye, my little Beatriz."

"Where to?"

"To Valladolid and the court, to be brought up like court

9

ladies and learn how to bend the knee to the new heiress to the throne. An escort came a week ago and took them away." Don Pedro spat. "The captain said, 'Here's a pretty red rose to keep the white rose company!' and pinched my Beatriz' cheek, which never knew a man's touch till now. The horrid shame of it! But I could do nothing. Then off they galloped, all the gay shining escort, in long cloaks. There were even some noble Moors in colored turbans to give the cavalcade a touch of elegance."

"Softly, Don Pedro" It seemed to Fray Tomás that the guard was eyeing the governor sharply; he might be a spy, though from whom and for what purpose Fray Tomás could only conjecture. "We had better speak privately."

"I do not care what happens now."

"The Dowager Queen cares."

"Alas, the poor queen is beyond caring for anything."

"Not dead!"

"Worse!"

"This will need explaining, my friend."

It was quickly explained in the governor's private apartments, away from prying eyes and inquisitive ears.

A week ago a flying herald had galloped to the gate and shouted imperiously for admittance. Then, in the presence of the governor, the Dowager Queen, the Infantes and all the assembled personnel of the castle, he had unrolled a parchment engrossed in royal purple and gold and proclaimed:

> *Io, el Rey*—I, the King: Be it known
> to you that by the grace of God this
> Tuesday just past, the Queen, Doña
> Juana, our dear and well-beloved
> spouse, was delivered of a daughter,
> Juana, Infanta of Spain and heiress to
> our double crown of Castile and Leon

and to all the Seignories, towns, estates, titles and honors appertaining thereto; the which hath already in the Cortes been acknowledged and confirmed by the noble dukes, counts, marques, lords and other grandees of the seventeen cities composing the said Cortes of these our realms. And this we make known to you that you, with us, may thank God and rejoice, and tender your homage and fealty to the said princess Juana, our daughter and heiress. *Io, el Rey.*

Hard on the heels of the herald came the escort, for Henry the Impotent, having at last disproved the mocking title by which he had been known for so long, was wasting no time. Don Alfonso, no longer the heir presumptive, and Isabella must appear publicly in Valladolid and do homage to the new Infanta, lest there be any doubt in anyone's mind that the children of the Dowager Queen were now thrust aside and excluded from their inheritance. It was the further will of the king, the captain of the escort said, that they be brought forthwith to live at court, permanently. There, he said, their education would be broadened—

"There is no doubt of that," Fray Tomas said sadly.

—and their welfare and guidance undertaken by the king himself, whom "all loyal subjects were encouraged to salute as Henry the Liberal," according to the captain.

"Liberal in every sense," grumbled Bobadilla. "Do you know, reverend prior, how the gossip runs with respect to the Princess Juana, whom he fatuously calls his daughter?"

"I permit no gossip in my monastery, Don Pedro."

"It is whispered," the governor said, lowering his voice and glancing over his shoulder, "that the Princess Juana is not the daughter of the king. The queen has taken a lover, the same fine handsome wolf of a captain who headed the escort, Don Beltran de la Cueva, who pinched my Beatriz' cheeks. Already there are some at the court who call the new 'heiress' La Beltraneja, daughter of Don Beltran, though of course they dare not raise their voices."

"But you seem to have heard of it."

"From one of the Moors."

"A mother knows the father of her child," Fray Tomás said. "Except perhaps in the most abandoned of circumstances. What does the queen say to this gossip?"

"Oh, the queen, the queen! What would she say? She says it's King Henry's, of course. By one wicked act, no doubt enjoyable to both of them, she quiets the gossip about the king—very largely, anyhow; she establishes complete dominion over his weak womanish character; and she strengthens enormously her own power, since any queen is doubly strong when she becomes mother of a future queen. Oh, she has every reason to say, nay, to protest, that the new princess is the king's."

"And the king?"

"Is perfectly delighted."

"Not jealous of Don Beltran?"

"On the contrary. He goes out of his way to honor him. Immediately after the queen gave birth he gave Don Beltran a new title, the Count of Ledesma—'for distinguished services to the Crown', if you please. So read the proclamation." The governor smirked. Fray Tomás did not even smile.

"Spain, Spain! This holy land that once was proud to be known as the seminary of all Christian virtues! Home of the knightly Orders of Campostella, Calatrava, Alcantara, whose warlike caballeros sought no higher honor on earth than to fall fighting against the Moors and win a martyr's crown in heaven! Whose kings were known as 'the bold', 'the wise', 'the good', and one, 'the saint'! Poor Spain, now fallen so low that her king is scoffed at—El Impotente! More than gossip gives credence to that epithet, since he could not have married his present giddy queen had not the Church set aside his first

12

marriage, *por impotencia.* The word *respectiva,* I grant you, was added, but that was pure charity, since its meaning is ambiguous. No one doubted where the fault lay. Spain is fallen on hard days, mi amigo, when a Spanish king consorts with the enemy and adds the heathen Moor to his court to give a touch of elegance."

"There were young women in the cavalcade, your reverence, all gay and laughing, to attend the Princess Isabella: bold, pretty creatures on little white mules in costly gold and crimson trappings. They were dressed in low-cut gowns without sleeves, showing their bare arms; some girdled their breasts with leather thongs from crossbows, so that the silk clung tight as skin, some had borrowed turbans from the Moors and wore them jauntily, some went shamelessly bareheaded; one carried a sword, one a dagger in her tight girdle; all painted their lips and darkened their eyelids; and—you will not believe this— when the wind blew, their skirts were so short that I saw their naked thighs, painted too. Cosmetics applied over the entire body! What will become of my child?"

"What will become of Spain, with a court so iniquitous?" The governor was silent.

"And the Dowager Queen whose children have been snatched from her?"

"I fear she is mad," the governor said. "She has always been melancholy, but something snapped in her mind when this new sorrow came upon her. She sits all day in a dark corner of her chamber, staring straight ahead of her, speaking to no one."

"Let me see her, Don Pedro."

"It is a forlorn hope, Fray Tomás. Don Beltran saw her and talked at length. But he told me afterwards, 'No use asking *her* to swear the oath of fealty. She doesn't know what she's doing.' That's why he left her here."

"Still, I must see her."

But the Dowager Queen did not recognize Fray Tomás. She sat in her chair in the shadows, rocking herself back and

13

forth with an odd and endless motion, her hands lying limp in her lap, empty, open and motionless. If only she had wrung them—or wept—or blinked her eyes! Fray Tomás shook his head and sighed hopelessly. She did not greet him, nor did she bid him farewell when he left.

Yet she had not quite remained speechless; a spark of her once strong mind still glowed, like the flicker in one last ember before the fire dies and darkness closes in forever. Once, with a tremor of the helpless hands, she had muttered, "Impotent, impotent as a Moorish eunuch," and once, "There will be factions, there will be factions, there will be factions."

Pondering the last cryptic words, Fray Tomás felt his heart uplifted, not, God knew, at the prospect of factions in Spain, with one faction favoring La Beltraneja and one Don Alfonso. Indeed, he prayed fervently that no such factions would form, for that might mean civil war, and civil war would mean the continued existence of the Kingdom of Granada at the tip of the shield.

But he knew his Spanish countrymen. Factions *would* form. "Let them be just strong enough," he prayed, "to protect Don Alfonso and Doña Isabella." He thought of those jugglers at fairs in Segovia at harvest time: they walked on tight ropes over the heads of the breathless crowds, carrying heavy staffs by the middle, which seemed to make the feat more difficult and actually made it easier.

When forces are equally balanced it is sometimes possible to walk a hazardous path without falling. God worked in wondrous, hidden ways.

CHAPTER 2

Don Beltran de la Cueva relaxed and hooked one long, superbly turned leg over the cushioned arm of the queen's most comfortable chair. His face was wind-burnt and still ruddy from the cold, He was fatigued; he loosened his sword belt and just succeeded in stifling a yawn.

Turning from her mirror the queen smiled at him over her shoulder. "A languid entrance for a caballero into a lady's apartment, Don Beltran. Are you tired?"

"A little."

"A cup of wine?"

"Do not call anyone just now."

"Nay, that is better. For that you shall have everything."

She set down the tiny rouge pot, carved like a jewel in bright green malachite, and the delicate little brush which she had been about to apply to her lips. She rose and went to one of the windows where, reaching in between the draperies and the casement, she took out a goblet, another, and a squat bottle of heavy dark-green glass.

"I cannot tell from your appreciative eyes," said the queen archly, decanting the liqueur with a soft, white, practiced hand, "whether it is the queen or the cordial that you desire most." As the goblets filled, a perfume of ripe peaches, hot in the summer sun of a decade past, suffused the already warm and perfumed air of the room.

Don Beltran sought to make a courtly reply suited to the temper of the times: "The heating qualities of wine and the heating qualities of women—"

She laughed. Her laugh was singularly deep and musical. "Do not go on, Beltran. The Marqués of Villena does it so much better. I said you should have everything."

She held the goblet to his lips and, when he had drunk, took a sip from the same place. Then she leaned over and

15

kissed him, the filmy lace of her gown slipping from her shoulder,

"I like your mouth when it's wet," he said, crushing hard against her lips.

She did not answer, her eyes closed, the long heavily blackened lashes brushing the white of her cheeks, relaxing against him.

"Everything. Always."

"So little to be so great a queen," he whispered into her hair.

"I will be great for you—and the Infanta."

"The prettiest black eyes in the world!"

"Prettier, blacker than Doña Beatriz de Bobadilla's?" The tone was teasing but there was a sharpness in it. She had heard how he had pinched Beatriz' cheek the very first time he set eyes on her.

"That child!"

"She is only in the awkward age, Beltran. One day I dare say she may be quite presentable, in spite of her low birth."

He touched her cheek with his big hard hand. "The fairest skin in all of Spain."

"Fairer than the Princess Isabella's? Everyone says she's the most beautiful girl who ever came to court. Don't you care for green eyes and golden hair, Don Beltran? You will be terribly out of style. Even the king—"

Don Beltran laughed. "The king, too?"

"Henry has a keen eye," the queen said dubiously, "No one loves color the way he does, and you've got to admit she is colorful."

"No one is colorful but my queen."

The shared goblet, the shared kiss, again the wet pressed lips.

"Nevertheless, I shall continue to torture myself with jealousy," she pouted.

There was a discreet scratching at the door of the chamber. The queen sat down again before her mirror, a sheet of rare Venetian crystal that reached to the floor. Don Beltran wiped his lips with the back of his hand. The queen took up her rouge brush again.

"You may enter," she called impatiently. Only one man would presume to disturb the queen of Spain when she was closeted with Don Beltran. That man would be the only one for whom both halves of a palace door would swing open. Lesser personages, in accordance with Spanish etiquette, the most minutely precise in the world, would enter by the single portal.

The noble page, with a peaches and cream complexion but a firm chin that gave it the lie, announced, "His Serene Highness, the King."

Henry the Liberal hesitated on the threshold, "Good evening, Ledesma. Juana, may I come in?"

She could not keep him out. Moreover she was bending every effort these days to present a picture of happy domesticity between herself and the king for the sake of the Infanta. One did not betray irritation in front of pages when the father of one's daughter, a fathership one worked endlessly to emphasize, entered one's chamber.

She shrugged her white bare shoulders and nodded to the king in her glass.

"Do not rise, Beltran, do not rise," he said, patting his wife's visitor familiarly on the back. "You have done me a great service today. You are always doing me services, bless your heart." Don Beltran relaxed again into the chair and the king walked over to the queen, who was now applying the brush skillfully to her full red mouth. The king's step was soft and quiet as a cat's as he walked; his velvet shoes were green and little jewels twinkled in the heels.

"You gave me so little time, Henry. I'm only half made up," she said petulantly, "and Don Beltran is terribly tired."

"It was a matter of importance or I should not have bothered you, my dear. I know he is fatigued. Riding all the way from Almazan in this cold! Poor boy! But I could trust no one else. No one is so perspicacious, no one is so intuitive as our dear count of Ledesma. Nay, no one else could have ridden so fast and so far—no one has the physique. A paladin! A Cid! A—"

"Oh, Henry, for goodness' sake. I quite appreciate Don Beltran's qualities."

"No doubt he told you why I sent him."

Neither answered. King Henry did not seem perturbed by the obvious fact that they must have been talking about themselves, nor did the twin goblets offend him.

"No? I see he did not. Then I shall have to later. But right now—" He held out what appeared to be a fluffy assortment of silks and velvets, lace and brocades. "—you simply must help me pick out some suitable gowns for Isabella."

"Good heavens, why? The child is quite suitably clothed as she is, modestly, warmly, soberly, becoming her age."

"She dresses like a frump, and so does her friend Beatriz. It just doesn't look right, I say. Do you think so, Beltran? Tell me honestly. Is it right for my sister and her chief lady in waiting to walk about dressed like a couple of Arevalo peasants? It makes them look ugly; people will think that the royal family are nothing but boors and rustics. Even the pages laugh at their gowns."

"Which of them?" the queen demanded.

One of them was Francisco de Vades, the youth who had just admitted the king. But for reasons of his own the king chose to be vague.

"Well, I just have a feeling that they laugh. After all, the pages are noble, well-bred, most beautifully mannered. Sensitive young men like that would surely laugh at frumpish, old-fashioned dresses when everybody else tries to keep abreast of the prettiest styles. Both girls could be pretty, especially Isabella. Just look at these! I've chosen a green gown for her, this one with the pearls. Beatriz, of course, ought to wear something red, with white around the throat, and, say, silver earrings—she can manage heavier accessories than Isabella because her coloring is so much stronger—and I think—" He riffled through the gowns till his heavily jeweled fingers lighted on a certain special one. "—This!" he said triumphantly. "The very thing to cut a figure at Fuentarabia next spring. Don't you think so, Juana? Don Beltran? Gorgeous?"

He laid the others aside, expertly as a sempstress, without wrinkling them, then held the gown against him to show how it would fit the princess, Don Beltran had difficulty controlling his features; the queen shot him a warning glance. One did not laugh at a king who, in theory at least, was an absolute monarch and the father of the Infanta.

"She will have to meet a dangerous autocrat, my dear. All of us must make a good impression on the king of France. In this my little sister will be a credit to the House of Trastamara. Don't you think so? Yes? No?" He smiled engagingly over the lacy bodice, his jeweled slippers mincing under the green silk folds of the skirt.

Queen Juana was not aware that there were plans afoot to meet the formidable Spider King, Louis of France, but she was vitally interested in anything that concerned the foreign relations of Spain and the future fortunes of the Infanta, her daughter, whose baby hand had been kissed in homage by all the grandees of the realm, including the Princess Isabella and Prince Alfonso. For though there had been much grumbling and many raised eyebrows, no one had yet dared openly question the child's legitimacy. Such a suspicion would have particularly revolted the innocent minds of the Dowager Queen's two children, Doña Isabella and Don Alfonso, whose inheritance the unexpected infant had usurped.

Looking at the seductively low-cut gown that the king was displaying, the queen compressed her full lips in disapproval. Doña Isabella was certainly not going to be permitted to appear in anything like *that!* She would turn the heads and steal the hearts of half the men at court, including Don Beltran.

"I think it is utterly out of the question for a girl of her youth," the queen said positively,

"Oh, I don't agree, don't agree at all," the king protested excitedly. "I pride myself on an art in these matters. Isabella has long since left behind the pudgy softness of girlhood—and when it isn't pudginess it's that dreadful angularity of the bones, which is just as bad, I must say. She is beautifully modeled, but who can tell under those frightful clothes that the Dowager Queen made her wear at Arevalo? Could there be better proof that my poor stepmother is crazy as a coot? When we meet the King of France—and that will be an important state affair, my dear—Isabella must look like the radiant princess she is, mature, regal, with a bosom made, simply *made*, to pin orders on. Eh, Beltran, you rogue?"

The queen leveled her flashing black eyes on Don Beltran, who read in them, "If you dare to agree! If you *dare!*"

"Your Highness," the uncomfortable caballero replied, "*I* suppose I do not think of the Princess Isabella in quite that light. To me she remains merely a sweet child, Your Highness's little sister."

"I expected more awareness from you, of all people, Beltran. Perhaps I am wrong. But I did think I was right this time, just for once."

He did not drop the matter entirely. "The Marqués of Villena assures me that we must make a splendid impression on the French king, or he will never decide in our favor." He pronounced the name of Villena with emphasis, glancing from the queen to Don Beltran, to let the words sink in, to remind them that Villena, the old favorite, had not yet been completely replaced by Don Beltran, the new.

It was the Aragonese rebels again, the king explained. The neighboring kingdom of Aragón occupied the Mediterranean shore of the Spanish peninsula, just as the kingdom of Portugal occupied the Atlantic. Between them, high, dry, isolated, lay Castile, as rugged in terrain as Castilians were ragged in character, differing in every respect from the maritime kingdoms on the flanks of the Spanish shield. Kingdoms that lay along the seas were always turbulent and tolerant, open to seaborne infection of ideas by reason of their trade with foreign states. East of Aragón across the Mediterranean lay Italy, drunk with a ferment of intellect and neo-paganism that men had begun to call the Renaissance. West of Portugal of course lay nothing but the mysterious Atlantic; but to the south of her loomed a dark and forbidding continent, Africa, home of the Moors, down whose shores for years past the ships of the Portuguese had been probing ever farther and farther, bringing back fortunes in gold and ivory and Negro slaves, a new and unchristian but immensely profitable source of wealth.

In the king's dissertation both Don Beltran and the queen recognized the mind of the Marqués of Villena. Henry never troubled to inform himself about matters of state. The couple was uneasy. Villena was an enemy. It was awkward that he could still make himself powerful with the king. They looked at each other with understanding: whatever Villena hoped to accomplish by dressing Isabella in a seductive gown must be thwarted. The queen smiled to herself. And what a plausible explanation to give Don Beltran! Before the king half-finished his speech Isabella was doomed to the drab garb her mother had prescribed at Arevalo.

The king continued.

The turbulent Aragonese had been in a state of periodic rebellion for many months, A group of their leaders had appealed to Castile for help against their king.

"I gave them a little help on the sly," said the king, "to keep things stirred up, thus embarrassing my good cousin John and that son of his, who fights like a demon, a miracle in a lad so young."

"Who is he?" the queen asked.

"The son? His name is Ferdinand."

"How old is he?"

"Exactly the age of Isabella."

21

"But you say Isabella is a woman, full blown, mature, God knows what all you said. Now you admit how young she really is. Out of your own mouth you contradict yourself."

"Men and women mature at different ages, my dear queen. Isabella is a woman, Don Ferdinand of Aragón is just a lad."

The queen let it pass.

"It is most important that Louis of France meet, admire and like Isabella," the king said.

"If you are planning a seduction," Don Beltran observed, "I doubt if Isabella or any woman could tempt him stark naked. He isn't the type."

"Beltran!" the queen snapped. It was not to her liking that Don Beltran should entertain mental pictures of Isabella in the nude.

"My lord of Ledesma," said the king, flushing pink as a girl, "we are speaking of my sister."

"I meant no offense, Your Highness," Beltran said hastily.

"Of course not, Beltran. Your truant tongue. Your completely masculine mind. It's one of the most fascinating things about you. Yes, Juana? No? But yes, of course, I forgive you, dear boy. No, no, there is nothing so crass in the wind. Villena suggests, and I quite agree with him, that Castile must make a great show of wealth and power."

The Castilian forces, fighting on the side of the rebels against the crown of Aragón, had so embarrassed King John that he had called on France for help and complained that Henry of Castile was an aggressor and invited Louis to act as arbiter in the dispute. Since Louis had agreed, Henry had to agree or bring down the massed might of the French king's armies against him. Now the trick was to make a magnificent appearance at Fuentarabia, where the arbitration would be held, and to that end the Marqués of Villena had decided that there should be not one, no, not one drab woman in the Castilian entourage.

"Why not just leave her behind?" the queen suggested.

The king seemed prepared for the question. Villena must have primed him adroitly. "The French king has an extremely suspicious mind and would certainly wonder why I had excluded a member of my own family who stands third in the line of succession: quite likely he would suspect that I had poisoned her."

There were times, the queen thought darkly, when poison could be a most useful tool of diplomacy.

"Who would harm the child, Henry? Who would even harm Don Alfonso, who stands second?"

"Why 'even', my dear?"

"Your Highness always twists my most innocent remarks against me," she pouted. "I simply meant that Alfonso is even younger than Isabella."

Don Beltran remarked, "Villena vastly misreads the character of the French king if he has suggested to Your Highness that a display of magnificence on the part of Castile will influence the arbitration in our favor. Villena imposes upon Your Highness, because he believes riches should be flaunted, but Louis of France would simply sneer, 'If the Castilians have money to throw away I will decide in favor of Aragón, lest Castile grow too powerful.' He believes in dividing and conquering, balancing the power of his neighbors one against another, so that his own voice is always predominant," The queen agreed. "What will he think if he sees Isabella dressed in jewels and costly lace? To say nothing of the impropriety of that dress—he is reputed to be a great prude."

"Remember, Your Highness, I have seen the French king," Don Beltran said. Beltran did not care what Isabella wore, but if Villena was for the green dress, he was against it. "His Most Christian Majesty dresses like one of his own peasants, all patches and rags."

"Isabella must certainly not outshine the queen of France," the queen added positively. "No woman would stand for that."

"True, true," Henry said, his confidence shaken. "It is difficult to make up my mind when good friends like Villena and Ledesma advise me so differently, How was the French herald garbed in Almazan, Don Beltran?"

"Like a pauper, Your Highness." Beltran knew that that was not quite true. The herald who had met him and delivered the French king's offer of arbitration, a document with which Beltran had spurred back with all speed to the king, had been clothed in a tabard of silver lilies on a ground of blue, well-worn and travel stained, no doubt, but by no means like a pauper's. But in the struggle for the king's favor it was always necessary to oppose the advice of the Marques of Villena; it would help to exaggerate the French herald's plainness.

The king sighed and took up the gown again, stroking it. "I cannot decide, I cannot decide," he murmured. "The matter of a good appearance is so terribly important and now I do not know which appearance is good, this beautiful gown or those—those flour sacks from Arevalo. What shall I do?"

He would go back to Villena, the queen knew, and Villena would have the last word. She would have to compromise.

"One of her young ladies might wear it, Henry; but believe me, it is not suitable for Isabella."

The king's face slowly brightened. "Upon my word, what a capital idea! Beatriz de Bobadilla shall wear it, eh, Beltran?"

"Excellent, Your Highness," Don Beltran replied.

The queen whispered hotly, "You don't have to be so enthusiastic!"

The whisper was injudiciously loud; the king heard it. "Sangre de Dios!" he cried in alarm, "Don't you two quarrel! I cannot risk that. Have you forgotten *our daughter,* Juana? Do you want factions in Spain?"

He turned on his jeweled heel and walked towards the

door with his curious quick catlike step, one foot before the other toe down, like a dancer on a tightrope. Perhaps he was.

A few paces before the door he clapped his hands twice. The double portals swung open, the page stepped swiftly aside and bowed the stiff low horizontal Castilian bow.

They heard the king say as the door closed, "Come sing to me, Francisco. I am weary with great affairs. My lute is in the cabinet."

Don Beltran made a face as if there were a bad odor in the room.

Queen Juana shrugged her shapely shoulders. "Who cares?"

CHAPTER 3

KING Louis of France was at Biarritz on the Côte
D'Argent, so called from the silvery mists that rose from
the crests of the long, lazy waves of the Bay of Biscay that
washed the beaches of the little fishing town. King Henry of
Castile was at San Sebastian in a similar frontier town across
the boundary marked by the Bidassoa River. King John of
Aragón waited upriver in Navarre, a kingdom in name but
smaller than many a county and actually a tiny buffer state
between the three nations, secure in its precarious integrity
(somewhat like Don Alfonso and Doña Isabella) because
of a balance of contending powers around her. This far the
three kings had traveled towards the rendezvous that would
arbitrate the dispute between Aragón and Castile. This far,
but no farther.

King Louis demanded that the two Spanish sovereigns
cross over the river to France since they were the disputants
and he was the arbiter, Neither Castile nor Aragón agreed.
King John objected that he had already traveled twenty leagues
and would travel no farther. King Henry, prompted by the
Marqués of Villena, objected that it would be incompatible
with Castilian dignity to parley outside the national territory
of Castile.

While the three sovereigns bickered over protocol,
the mild early spring of the Cantabrian riviera burst upon
the countryside and transformed it into a lush miracle of
beautiful greenery that was astonishing to anyone reared
in the rigorous uplands of Old Castile. Isabella and her
brother took long rides through the leafy woodlands and
emerald green fields of this delightful new country, hunting
occasionally. Sometimes they simply enjoyed the prospect
of endless rolling pasturelands which, it would seem, could
fatten enough cattle and sheep to feed the entire world.

Sometimes they would draw rein and listen politely while peasants or fishermen in scarlet breeches pulled off their odd circular berets and made what was probably a little speech of welcome in their utterly incomprehensible Basque tongue: Don Alfonso would nod and make some equally grave, equally incomprehensible reply in Castilian, and the princess would answer their friendliness with a flashing smile; and that, at least, they understood and returned with interest.

"A woman like you," her brother said with a courtliness beyond his youth, "could furnish up the alchemy to soften the pride of the three kings and break their silly stalemate."

"Alchemy is wicked—I *think*" Isabella said. "At least Fray Tomás used to say it was. He said gold was gold, lead was lead, Moors were Moors and Jews were Jews, and nothing can ever change into anything it isn't naturally, since that is the way God made the world."

"I don't believe him."

"Neither do I, at least not about the Jews and Moors. Because he also said that when they were baptized they were just as good as anyone else. Still, he is a very learned man,"

"Probably he only meant the alchemy that tries to change gold."

"Yes, that would certainly be wicked."

"Anyhow, I was talking about the alchemy of golden hair and a lady's smile."

"Please don't talk like Beltran and Villena, Alfonso."

"I swear I meant it, Isabella!" He was afraid he had offended her, but she laughed and smiled at him so warmly that all the eldersisterly reproach vanished.

"Let's gallop! I'll race you to the river!" She touched her heels to the mare's flanks and set off at a pace that set the pebbles flying behind the horse's hooves. He gained, but she beat him by a length.

"I had a headstart," she conceded, tossing back the hair that the wind had blown and tangled. She liked riding bareheaded and, in the easy-going atmosphere of the court, no one had ever reproved her except the queen, when Don Beltran was around.

At the bank of the Bidassoa they let the horses drink. It was a small stream that might have been forded at most seasons of the year, but now it was swollen by the snows that were still melting in the Pyrenees mountains. In the midst of the stream there was a small island, a few acres dotted with tall oak and chestnut trees and covered with a carpet of greensward so brilliant and young that it looked like a superb new tapestry.

"What a magnificent jousting field!" Don Alfonso said, surveying the large smooth areas of turf between the trees.

Isabella said, "What a velvet for a gown if they could weave it so soft and beautiful!" For a moment they let their eyes linger on the beauty of the islet. Then there was a rustling in the bushes along the river bank and a score of brilliantly colored pheasants, disturbed by their presence, rose into the air, their red and green and golden plumage shimmering with a curious metallic lustre.

The birds identified the island; Isabella suddenly realized how far she and her brother had wandered in their ride. They were close to the triple frontier of Navarre, Castile and France. She glanced anxiously at the sun, which was well past the meridian. Queen Juana would be furious again.

"We had best be getting back, Alfonso. The queen is almost as strict as Mother was."

Don Alfonso's face darkened. He did not like the queen. But as far as Isabella was concerned he had to admit that she had proved herself a watchful protectress, forbidding her to be alone with any male but her own brother. Isabella had a suspicion that Queen Juana would have been satisfied if the dresses she prescribed had looked positively dowdy, but she was grateful to stand in the background among surroundings that had shocked her at first by their levity, and she did not protest. Neither, of course, did her brother, since brothers never do. In obscurity, she was safe. Alfonso sensed it though he did not analyze it; and he had felt free to spend much time with one of the great lords of the court, Don Alfonso Carrillo, the premier prelate of Castile, Archbishop of Toledo, a gruff, bluff, booming giant of a man, a mixture of warrior and priest. This old-fashioned ecclesiastic was at ease in armor or vestments and sometimes wore both at the same time like the fighting churchmen of the old Crusades. Carrillo had taken a fancy to the lad and spoke of attaching him to his suite. The primate was one of King Henry's chief negotiators in the coming arbitration.

As they retraced their steps Isabella said, "Will you do something for me, Alfonso? Do not suggest it as coming from me because all these great statesmen would laugh at a girl, but you are the king's brother, a man, and they will not laugh at you. Tell Carrillo that you think the Isle of Pheasants is the place for the three kings to meet, because none of them will lose dignity there. An island in the middle of a river doesn't belong to anybody."

Within a few weeks the spot where the Infantes had watered their horses presented a brilliantly changed aspect, and the Isle of Pheasants was famous. The birds deserted it, driven away by the sudden invasion of thousands of human beings. The plenipotentiaries had met, agreed with the Archbishop of Toledo that the little island, so providentially situated at the junction of the three frontiers, would satisfy all the exacting demands of protocol. The Isle of Pheasants was gravely internationalized for the purposes of the parley.

The three kings and their escorts had converged upon it from three sides, each in a separate kingdom, each separated from the neutral island by a short distance of shallow water that horses could easily ford. There was no town in the vicinity but tent cities arose on the river banks, full of the noise of barking dogs and neighing horses and sentries shouting in French, Castilian and Catalan and even the guttural cries of the Arabic of Granada, for King Henry had brought his Moorish guard, to the utter disgust of the French. Full also of the smells of holiday wine being broached and of Guipúzcoa cider from the orchards of the Basques hereabouts, whose warning that it was heady and treacherous could not be understood. And full of the mingled smells of cooking to the rear of the camps where carcasses of beeves and wild boars and deer with the antlers still on roasted on giant spits all day over pits of glowing embers. And the less appetizing, but ordinary and acceptable smells of garbage being thrown into the river and horses' hooves burning as blacksmiths shod them with spiked shoes suitable for a tournament.

For protocol also demanded a friendly passage at arms in addition to the feasting to put everyone in good spirits before the serious business of arbitration; and for this a tilting field had been staked out on the Isle of Pheasants, marked by spears from which fluttered—in exactly equal proportion, none higher than another—the banners of Castile, of France and of Aragón. The profusion of brightly colored flags, each with its proud long history, each with its jealous heraldic significance, mingling in friendly closeness, augured well for the success of the parley.

In equally friendly closeness the sovereigns sat in the shade of a cloth-of-gold pavilion during the running of the lists, the only occasion that Isabella and Alfonso were permitted on the island. It seemed to the princess that the French king must be very short of funds, for he and all his suite were dressed in homespun and often he cast a greedy eye (or perhaps it was scornful) on the costly canopy that King Henry had provided. She did not know, as Louis did to a penny, the state of the Castilian treasury. King Louis had not brought his queen though John of Aragón had his, a hard-faced woman many years his junior; and of course King Henry had his: Queen Juana was Queen of Love and Beauty and would bestow the prize on the knight she adjudged to have borne himself most honorably in the lists. Sometimes such decisions were difficult, especially in international combats when every precaution had to be taken lest somebody get hurt and the game degenerate into a serious international incident. Coronal heads must be used on the spears, thus changing the lethal point to a relatively harmless pad. Swords were of silvered whalebone. And, lest the charging horses crash head-on, a stout timber barrier ran the length of the field separating the horsemen, forcing them to cross lances above it. Nevertheless, the game could be rough, and Don Beltran, with the queen's colors streaming from his helm, hugging the barrier at a tremendous gallop, succeeded in unhorsing a French opponent on the other side, an almost unheard-of feat of dexterity and strength.

Queen Juana thrust aside the flowers and scroll of poetry that were to have been the prize. Impulsively she stripped off a garter and placed it, all perfume and love knots, on the brawny right arm of the man who had wrought such a prodigy. King Louis seemed to be more interested in the fact that the French knight, having been raised to his feet by his squires, could walk off the field, but the incident of the garter had not escaped him, for his thin lips were twisted into a smile that was very close to a sneer. King John of Aragón, though he was well over sixty and supposed to be suffering from cataracts on both eyes, leaned forward, reaching for a pair of glasses that hung on a chain on his breast among his orders. The Queen of Castile wore stockings of Moorish silk, on legs that belonged in a Moorish harem!

"By God!" he muttered.

His queen frowned and whispered something in his ear.

"I know I'm here on business," he replied in a hearty whisper that anyone could hear.

"He wouldn't have unhorsed our son," the queen said proudly.

Queen Juana answered diplomatically, "It was agreed that royalty should not participate in the sports for fear of accidents. And Prince Ferdinand is still really too young, don't you think?"

"The Catalan rebels have reason to fear him," King John

said stoutly.

"Far too young," the Queen of Aragón agreed.

In the background the Archbishop of Toledo, who had cheered among the rest while the jousting was in progress, now lived up to the ecclesiastical cope that he wore during the negotiations and frowned mightily at the display which the Queen of Castile had just made of her legs.

In the background also Beatriz de Bobadilla plucked at Isabella's sleeve and whispered, "Somebody's been looking at you instead of the fighting. He hasn't even noticed my dress!"

Her brother warned in her other ear, "Don Ferdinand of Aragón has a roving eye."

Isabella did not turn to look, for the field was alive with workmen who rapidly broke up the sections of timber fence that divided the field and set them in new positions so that they formed a small circle directly in front of the royal pavilion. She steeled herself for something she had seen many times, something she supposed she was not yet old enough to enjoy quite so much as the grown-ups.

Something was about to happen in the fenced area before them, something that would cap the sport of the day and add a finishing touch to the pageants and feasting and merriment that had preceded the negotiations. Something stronger than bloodless fights with whalebone swords and blunted lances. Something that would serve a purpose akin to the coffee that Moors drank after a heavy supper, or brandy that Christians drank: something at once stimulating and soothing, after which the mind was clear and the emotions quiet, ready for sober state affairs.

The ape on horseback. A classic sport. It was quicker than bullfighting and hilariously funny.

A spirited white pony, white for a special reason, was led prancing into the arena. To its back, fastened by an iron belt to the saddle, was a big black foolish ape. Its arms and legs were free; its more-than-human feet gripped at the saddle girth with toes like fingers; its scarcely less-than-human face grimaced in fear. Then came the dogs, snapping and snarling, led on stout leather leashoo by men in leg armor, for the dogs were starved for the occasion. In the arena the man who was holding the horse's bridle hurled pepper into the ape's face, another handful into the pony's nostrils, and leapt over the fence. Simultaneously the dog tenders slipped the leashes of the dogs and jumped to safety. The ape screamed, the horse neighed piteously, rearing up and charging blindly among the dogs, which instantly attacked it viciously.

Now the reason for the white became apparent, since blood showed more vividly against it as the hounds leapt up and slashed their fangs again and again into the horse's flanks. Instinct drove him to try to protect himself by kicking; his hooves were spike-shod to better his chances; one lucky kick caught a dog in the belly and sent him sailing like a shot from a catapult over the barrier almost into the royal pavilion, where he fell dying, his intestines gushing out on the grass. But instinct also drove the other dogs to the horse's throat, which presently became red-wattled with hanging shreds of torn flesh. Shortly a critical vein was slashed, and his head went down. The dogs tore off his ears.

The baiting of the horse would have been sufficiently amusing in itself, since it was very like bull baiting, another popular sport. But the thing that made the ape-on-horseback so excruciatingly funny, so funny that the spectators laughed till their sides ached, laughed till tears streamed out of their eyes, was the absolutely fantastic behavior of the ape. He could not be unhorsed, no matter how quickly his mount reared and maneuvered to escape the dogs, because he was chained to the saddle. His feet, which at first had gripped the girth like an unskilled caballero's, had now been bitten. Maddened by pain he both kicked like a man and clutched like the ape he was, trying with bleeding feet to beat off the dogs or to catch them and strangle them. Meanwhile his arms flailed wildly about, tearing at the horse's mane, beating at the horse's neck and head, pounding the horse's rump or warding off with an upstretched arm the leaps of the dogs when at times they jumped clear over the horse's back. It was as if a horseman with four arms had suddenly gone wildly, aimlessly mad. The shrieking of the ape, high-pitched and human, the screams of the horse and the snarling of the dogs merged into a steady war of passion-begotten sound, and found a counterpart, from which it was almost indistinguishable, in shrieks of laughter and yells of encouragement from the spectators, now for the horse, now for the dogs, now for the ape, but always to kill, kill, kill, kill, kill!

King John of Aragón, holding his glasses close, was cheering for the ape: "Caballero! Caballero! God gave you four hands! Use them!" King Henry cheered the dogs. Queen Juana, Don Beltran now at her side, stared entranced at the scene, which was rapidly degenerating into a sea of blood, her breathing rapid, her breast straining against the crossed thongs on the bodice of her gown.

King Louis cheered none of the participants. When Isabella glanced at him she discovered with a start that his hard calculating eyes were staring straight into hers as if he could read her thoughts. He looked quickly away. She wondered what he thought she had been thinking; his face was softer than usual. She hoped she had not spoiled his sport, and she tried to appear animated.

She cheered the horse, but it went down at last. The dogs swarmed over it and tore out its throat. The ape, falling, was ripped to pieces. The game was over. The attendants threw huge chunks of meat into the arena to satisfy the appetites of the still voracious dogs. Later, when they were sleepy, the men would enter with sticks and whips and salvage those which could be used another time and destroy those which were too maimed to make another day's sport. Meanwhile the royal spectators in the cloth-of-gold pavilion rose and took leave of one another, congratulating King Henry on his entertainment.

King Henry's face was usually pallid, but now it appeared flushed, as if he had drunk too much wine. He left the field on the arm of his page. Singing could be heard from his tent long after sunset, the voice of Francisco de Valdes, accompanied by plaintive strains from the king's own lute plucked by the king's own hand.

Just before dawn when the watchfires were low and the tread of the sentries was heavy with fatigue, a figure bent over Isabella as she lay asleep and a hand was pressed firmly over her mouth. She started up, and a scream that would have brought the guards thundering to help her, half-formed in her throat, till she heard a well-known voice and recognized a friend.

"Beatriz! What a fright you gave me!"

"Hush, please, oh please! Not so loud!"

"But what is the matter?"

"There is a man in my tent."

Again it took all the strength of Beatriz de Bobadilla's hand to stifle the scream.

"No, no, you do not understand. I let him come in."

"Oh Beatriz, for shame!" She was close to tears. "My friend, my dear companion, the only one I can talk to! But it isn't your fault; it cannot be. You drank Basque cider at supper—I did not see you, but you must have. It is the fault of this suave, unwholesome country; the air is evil, perfumed, soft, like a wicked Moorish bath. Nay, you are here, you came to me, you are not dallying with your tempter. Come, let me get up! We will denounce the scoundrel and turn him over to the king. Flogging is too good for him. Thank God you thought better of the matter."

"The man in my tent is the page, Francisco de Valdes, and we must not turn him over to the king."

King Henry's attachment for his page was one of the juiciest tidbits of gossip around the court, but Beatriz was by no means sure that Isabella had heard the stories or understood them if she had heard. Certainly Beatriz had not mentioned them.

She tried to explain. "Valdes wants to act like a man. He would rather be tilting in the lists than singing to the king night and day. Everybody makes fun of him and calls him nasty names. He can't stand it any more."

"Names like 'sweetheart, señorita, little darling'?"

"I didn't know you knew."

"Alfonso told me; so did Padre de Coca."

Her brother and her chaplain. Apparently she had heard, inquired, and been informed. Isabella's education had progressed as rapidly as Beatriz' own, but not once had she gossiped with her best friend.

"Poor Henry, poor strange half-brother. It is witchcraft, or some foul Moorish curse. He should get rid of those wretched heathen companions."

"And I must get rid of the man in my tent! He wants to go over to Aragón."

"I don't blame him, Beatriz."

"He said this was the best chance he had ever had. He got as far as the river, but the sentries are thick there. One almost caught him; that was when he dodged into my tent. I *had* to help him, Isabella."

Isabella smiled in the darkness. "Of course you did. I understand. And now you're in trouble."

"Trouble! I'm in a mess. In the morning the servants will come to make up the bed and clean—and there will be Don Francisco. Trouble indeed. He can't go and he can't stay. I thought of a dress-"

"He's much too big."

"Anyhow, he refused."

"I agree that he cannot stay in your tent. But he can stay in mine."

"Oh no-"

"Till I get him a better disguise."

36

Quickly, quietly, Isabella dressed. She hurried; there remained at best another hour of darkness. There was only one disguise that would serve. At first she thought of her chaplain's hooded habit, but Padre de Coca traveled light and probably he had only one. Moreover, she was convinced that the good man would take a dim view of Valdes' impersonating a priest, no matter how laudable the end.

But there was her brother Alfonso, and his powerful friend Carrillo. If the primate of Castile did not have an extra monk's habit among all his vestments, copes, layman's clothing and spectacular suits of armor, who would? She threw a cloak around her and whispered to Beatriz, "Go back to your tent and wait for me."

"Don't do anything rash, Isabella. Oh dear, I shouldn't have let him in."

"Yes, you should. What I'm planning isn't wrong; what isn't wrong will prosper."

It was a saying she had picked up from her mother, the Dowager Queen, a sort of credo with her. Beatriz heard a sentry salute her respectfully, then tramp away as he accompanied her in the direction of Don Alfonso's tent, which adjoined the archbishop's. She slipped out in the dark and hurried to her own tent. One was lucky to have so faithful a friend as Isabella. One was lucky too, of course, to be a princess, whom guards did not question, though more than one lady had stealthily opened the flaps of her tent and disappeared for a space during the night while the cynical guards turned the other way.

In her tent she whispered hotly, "All I know is that you will spend the rest of the night with the princess, Santiago! If you so much as raise your voice or speak one improper word—"

"Nay, God bless Her Highness!"

No one much cared, certainly no one questioned the princess's indisposition next day, since it was the day of the parley and she was to be left behind. Queen Juana paused briefly at her tent to inquire after her, taking care not to disarrange her tiara as she peeked in.

"A headache," she announced to Don Beltran at her side. "Nothing but a little headache." She had no intention of permitting Beltran to enter, and quickly led him away.

The king was in a terrible pet. He had had his breakfast coffee as usual, one of his oddities since it was a Moorish drink; but Francisco had not appeared to wake him and serve it. Francisco de Valdes had disappeared.

"Everything's starting wrong," he complained, standing at the door, peering in peevishly, suspiciously. "This is an unlucky day. Nothing will go right, I feel it. My coffee was too strong, I'm all feverish and —and nobody can find my page. Dear God, suppose he fell into the river and drowned!"

"It's very shallow, Your Highness," Isabella said from her bed. "Do please come in—"

Doña Beatriz drew her breath in alarm, turned it into a cough and just succeeded in keeping her eyes from straying to Isabella's bed, where two large coverlets draped to the ground.

"—or remain outside, Your Highness, I'm afraid of the draft."

"True, true!" muttered the king, drawing back and closing the flap hurriedly. Doña Beatriz had coughed; Doña Isabella, covered up as she was, had obviously taken a chill. King Henry was not a man to hazard his health lightly.

"*You* didn't see Francisco, did you? A sentry reported that he took you to Alfonso's tent last night."

"I was wakeful. I felt uneasy. I spoke to Alfonso about a ride today, but I don't suppose we'll be able to take it now."

"No, no, I suppose not. It's better to stay in bed. Well, get well, Isabella. I'll send you a surgeon if I can find one. Pest! I can't even find Francisco. He's drowned, or somebody stole him. Santiago! How I shall whip him for upsetting me so. It will be a pleasure. With my own hands I'll whip him on his bare back; it will be a pleasure. Poor dear Francisco! I hope he's not drowned."

"I'm sure you'll find him," Isabella said. She breathed a prayer of thanks that no one, apparently, had noticed a tall dark figure of a monk slip into her tent just before sunrise. But if anyone had, she was quite prepared to say that she had asked for the services of a priest when she felt her sudden sickness come on during the night. It would have been a lie; she did not like to lie; but in one sense it would not have been a lie at all, for assuredly Carrillo had helped in the abduction of King Henry's page, and assuredly Carrillo was a priest.

Her brother Alfonso laughed heartily when he visited her later in the day, for he was left behind too while the great ones went to parley on the Isle of Pheasants.

"The archbishop scowled and spat and slapped his thigh and swore through a whole litany of saints. Then he swore by a pandemonium of devils. And then he produced the monk's habit. Today he told me a good deal more about Henry, things I can't repeat in front of ladies."

"Valdes knows them and I don't believe them," Isabella said.

"Sister, that is most enigmatic. Shouldn't he come out before he smothers?"

"Not till it's dark, I'm afraid."

"Are you all right, Valdes?" Don Alfonso asked.

The muffled grateful voice from the ground under the bed answered, "All right, thanks to God and Your Highness."

"There's scarcely a sentry left, Isabella. Everyone's on the island making a great display. No one would question a monk walking towards the forest," Don Alfonso persisted. He was ill at ease at the thought of his sister harboring a fugitive all day.

"They will tarry on the island till nightfall at least. Villena and Carrillo will talk endlessly; the queens will have to have their say, especially the Queen of Aragón, who seems a most forceful person. No, we have time, and at night we will be sure of success."

"I think *you* ought to be Castile's advocate," her brother said.

"You know I'll never rule Castile; you might have; I never."

"And you would have been my prime minister."

"Silly."

"Am I silly, Doña Beatriz?"

"She should be queen," Beatriz de Bobadilla said unequivocally.

To Francisco de Valdes, sweating and hopeful under the bed, their young uninhibited conversation made at least as good sense as the talk he heard day in and day out among the counselors of King Henry the Impotent.

"She should!" he agreed in a low voice, but it was muffled by the coverlets that hid him and no one heard.

On the Isle of Pheasants during the day the presentation of conflicting claims consumed interminable hours. The King of France listened politely, saying nothing. By sunset there were undoubtedly more speeches to come, but Louis XI, casting a weary eye at the failing light, cut the King of Aragón off in the middle of a sentence.

"I am happy that everyone is in agreement," he said sharply. His chancellor, as at a signal, handed him a large roll of parchment which had apparently been prepared before the parley began, for it was already engrossed in treaty form, lacking only the signatures of the high contracting parties. "It is always a delight when one can contribute to peace. I am, of course, particularly happy from a personal point of view that my own troops will not be involved in battle, neither against Castile—" he stared hard at King Henry, who dropped his eyes "—nor against Aragón." And he leveled his cold hard eyes at King John.

"But by God, Your Majesty, I am the aggrieved party.

King Henry sent troops to aid my rebellious subjects against me, his own cousin!"

"So he did, sir. And they have been rather successful against you. I was under the impression that that was why you first appealed to France."

"Which of us would Your Majesty fight?" the Queen of Aragón demanded, her face taut and angry.

"Why, Madame," the French king replied softly, "whichever of you refuses to sign."

The French army was the envy and fear of every king in Europe. Neither Aragón nor Castile wanted war with Louis.

King Henry bit his fingernails. King John glowered, But the French grand chancellor began to read the treaty, and little by little their faces relaxed. It was a masterpiece of the policy that had made King Louis famous, respected and feared. If it held any of the subterfuges, for which he was equally famous, they did not appear on the surface.

Everyone involved would win. Only neutral Navarre, which was not represented, lost anything. King Henry, as a successful invader to whom something was due, got a slice of territory which pushed the frontier of Castile to Estrella in Navarre and included that fortified town, in return for which he agreed to call back his soldiers and stop helping the Aragonese rebels. King John of Aragón, who had ancient claims on Navarre, agreed to let Castile have that portion. King John, relieved of the menace of the rebels, also received assurances from France that France would withdraw from some border cities about which France and Aragón had been disagreeing for years, a sore spot that had immobilized thousands of Aragonese troops. The French would simply withdraw. King Louis, for his part, agreed not to press his own substantial claims against Navarrese territory, which he possessed of ancient right no less than King John.

Thus, without cost to themselves, Castilian pride was satisfied, the King of Aragón once more sat securely on his throne; and an aura of friendliness, confirmed by a great feast which was also prepared in advance, descended upon the Isle of Pheasants. In the darkness Francisco de Valdes, having walked unchallenged to the river, weighted his monk's habit with a stone and swam across to the camp of the Aragonese.

Before the summer was out King Henry would discover that his proud new frontier was utterly indefensible and that the town of Estrella's fortifications faced both ways: the walls would be manned by indignant Navarrese and the gates would be slammed in his face. Everything would be just as it had been before, except that the rebels no longer menaced King John and the balance of power had been restored.

King Louis performed a graceful act for Isabella, who, Queen Juana had mentioned, was sick. He offered the services of his personal physician.

"It is not fitting for a man to attend an Infanta of Castile," Queen Juana had replied primly.

"Oh, I think it is, I think it is in this case," King Henry had answered. "She looked most alarmingly flushed and she was simply covered with blankets, simply covered. It might be a contagious fever."

"Madame," said the French king, "when you see my physician you will not think of him as a man. But he is extraordinarily competent." He was also one of Louis's most trusted spies.

The queen saw him and agreed that such a creature would cause no scandal. She wished all of Isabella's admirers were as ugly as the humpbacked physician, who, Louis said, was the Chevalier Olivier le Daim. His was the only elaborate garb in the entire French camp, with upturned points on his shoes so long that tasseled golden garters secured them under the knees,

Isabella received him in some alarm and confusion when he arrived the next day. He had with him a beautiful dog— she thought it might be, perhaps, a custom for hunting dogs to accompany French physicians when they made calls on the sick; this one was scarcely more than a puppy.

"I am really ever so much better, Señor le Daim."

He smiled, bowing very low. "It jumps to my eyes that Your Highness speaks truly," he said. "Now I need only report to my master that Your Highness's recovery is complete, for which, I assure Your Highness, he prayed all night long."

"Assure His Majesty that I am most grateful for his prayers," Isabella said. But she added, since the hunchback's eyes were full of amusement, "I was extremely ill last night, just the same."

"His Majesty knows that you had reason to be. His Majesty desired me to tell you—" he lowered his voice and glanced over his shoulder "—that a certain Spaniard swims marvelously well, but is careless when it comes to disposing of monkish apparel. It floats. I buried it. No one will know."

"His Majesty seems to be well informed," Isabella said doubtfully. "But I know nothing of these matters."

"Alas, then Your Highness will not understand the words I was commanded to add, namely, 'Valdes is safe in the suite of Prince Ferdinand of Aragón.'"

"It is always a pleasure to hear that anyone is safe, Señor le Daim." She was less and less at ease with the Frenchman.

But the Frenchman, hesitating only a moment, said in a serious voice, freighted with candor, "My master thought he read your heart at the disgusting spectacle of the ape-on-horseback, for he also likes animals. Frankly, I advised him against something that he commanded me to say, since I did not believe that a young woman could keep a secret. But my master is never wrong; your cautious answers uphold his infallible instinct about people. He said you were the greatest statesman at the Spanish court, He said that Your Highness will hear, at a future date, that the treaty signed last night stipulates the marriage of the Infanta Juana, whom some call La Beltraneja, to my master's brother, the great Duke of Guienne. My master commanded me to say that in his heart he wishes it were you, not the Princess Juana, and that he will work to that end."

It was a strange, left-handed proposal. She wondered why the French king would make it on the sly, with such confidence that she would keep it secret. Suddenly the suspicion struck her that he did not care if she kept it. He was reputed to like to stir up quarrels among his neighbors.

"I am not versed in politics, and I am far too young to think of marriage yet, Señor le Daim." She nodded slightly, and he knew he was dismissed.

"Before I go," the Frenchman said, "my master begs you to accept this little hound. He will grow up into a magnificent hunter."

Apparently the sinister French king also knew that she liked hunting. It was uncomfortable to be the object of so much and such accurate interest.

But the friendly little animal was sniffing at her slippers and wagging his tail. There would be no harm in accepting him and she did not wish to stand talking too long to the Frenchman.

"I am afraid I have nothing but thanks to give to His Majesty in return." She smiled, patting the head of the puppy, who promptly licked her hand, then tentatively took her fingers in his mouth and decided not to bite because they weren't food. Isabella laughed. "What is his name?"

The Frenchman was bowing himself away, "My master will be bounteously recompensed if you will call him Charles, which is the name of his brother, the Duke of Guienne."

Charles seemed a foolish name for a handsome puppy. So did Carlos, its Spanish counterpart.

"I'll call him Duke," she compromised, "and thank King Louis very much for me."

CHAPTER 4

AFTER the costly meeting on the Isle of Pheasants, which had placed a heavy burden on the Castilian treasury, a lengthy period of armed neutrality ensued between Isabella and her half-brother the king. She began to realize that a man is not necessarily harmless because he has little oddities of speech and effeminate manners. Sometimes such a man also possesses a woman's intuition.

Grieving over the loss of his favorite page, King Henry became morose and suspicious. He seemed to connect Francisco's disappearance somehow with Isabella, and often questioned her closely on her activities during that night when the sentry reported that she had visited the tent of her brother Alfonso. He would bring up the subject quite suddenly in the middle of a conversation about something else, seeking to catch her off her guard, as if he were looking for her to betray herself by an altered expression or the flicker of an eye. It was a constant strain, but it taught her self-control; she remained bland and calm under his most stealthy assaults.

Unable to confirm his suspicions, he banished her from the principal supper table and relegated her to the second table, which was one step lower than the king's. It was a sign of public displeasure in a court where nobles had been known to fight bitter private wars over an inch or two of difference in the elevation of the dais on which a table stood, or whether one ate one's supper seated in a chair with arms, without arms, or on a common bench.

Don Alfonso promptly deserted the royal table also and went to sit beside his sister. He was allowed to remain; the king declared that he had been thinking of bringing down the former heir presumptive a notch or two anyhow. In the first flush of his popularity upon the birth of the Infanta Juana, which was enhanced by his diplomatic success at the Isle of

45

Pheasants, King Henry felt himself very strong. He would have been perfectly happy but for the loss of Francisco de Valdes. He had replaced the page with the noble son of a Moorish potentate in Granada, but turbaned little Ahmed brewed the coffee too strong and sang with an Arabic accent which Henry found offensive.

The Archbishop of Toledo on his first appearance at court after the Isle of Pheasants, noting the public degradation of the Infantes, frowned and refused to sit at the royal table. He had actually taken a few steps towards Isabella and Alfonso when the king called him sharply back,

"What is this, my lord archbishop? Are you heading a faction against me? Do you wish it to be said that there is a king's party and a party for the children of the Dowager Queen? Sit down, sir!"

"*You* are dividing the kingdom, sire, not I, since you are dividing the royal family. If the Infantes may not sit at your table they may always sit at mine."

"Go ahead and take them. It will be a relief to get them out of my sight."

"May I?"

"It will be a relief."

But there were social objections to taking them both since Carrillo's establishment was almost exclusively male, composed of priests and soldiers.

"I will take Alfonso first," he said, sitting down. "Isabella is a woman and I shall have to make special arrangements for her. My household is not organized on a female basis."

"Put her in a convent. You of all people ought to be able to arrange that."

For obvious reasons the archbishop did not care to probe the cause of Henry's bitter resentment against Alfonso and Isabella.

"I do not think a convent would be wise. She evinces broad interests, a capacity for state affairs that would be wasted in a convent."

"I think a convent would be ideal," Queen Juana said, adding in her thoughts, "And the stricter the better!" Isabella was growing more striking every month, every week, almost every day. The minstrels had begun to look in the direction of the second table now when they entertained at supper. Queen Juana had recourse to the rouge pot more and more frequently to meet the threat to her own great beauty, which she realized with a pang of jealousy would fade in exactly the same proportion as the cool loveliness of Isabella's young womanhood grew into the warmer loveliness of womanhood full blown.

"You are not suggesting," King Henry said to the archbishop, "that you think Isabella will ever be queen!" He mimicked sing-song the nasal tone of a fishwife sneering at a competitor, "Nyah, nyah, she evinces broad interests, capacity for state affairs' does she. What broad interests, pray? What broad interests, my lord archbishop? Spiriting away handsome pages to enjoy lasciviously in the night and then have drowned in a river to hide her shame?"

"Henry!" warned the queen.

"What capacity for state affairs? What need has she for such a capacity?"

"Henry, I'll leave the table!" Queen Juana threatened.

The king succeeded in restraining himself. "No, no, please. I was only about to remark, my dear, that Isabella will never be forced to bear the burden of government. Already she stands third in the line of succession. Soon she will be fourth, because of a little burden that *you* bear, eh, Juana?"

"It is a little early to announce publicly," the queen murmured demurely, "but, yes, God will bless the House of Trastamara with another child."

The archbishop raised his eyebrows. "Indeed?" Beyond the second table, seated at the third, Don Beltran was gorging himself with meat. The House of Trastamara forsooth! "I congratulate Your Highness, and the proud father to be."

"Thank you," said King Henry. "This time it will be a

prince, with God's help, of course."

Queen Juana smiled over the tables to Don Beltran. "With God's help," she echoed piously.

The king said, "You will pray for a prince, my lord archbishop?"

"I will pray," said Carrillo, "for Castile."

"Same thing," said the king. His mood seemed to have lightened.

It was not lightened for long. The forces he sent to occupy his new city in Navarre discovered that a prolonged siege would be necessary to take the place he thought had been given to him by treaty, and he could not afford a siege. The army, unpaid and unprepared to fight, fell back to the old frontier on their own, without orders, and deserted. He sent out couriers with angry protests to Aragón, to France. King John replied that he had only relinquished a right to the city, not guaranteed to deliver it; and added slyly that he was sure that his good cousin in Castile would rejoice with him that the Aragonese rebels were now loyal and orderly. King Louis replied that he too had merely relinquished a right to Navarre, and mentioned that he would not at this time send a bill for the splendid feast on the Isle of Pheasants, which, since the island lay in ceded territory, was now properly chargeable to the treasury of Castile. King Henry fumed and bit his fingernails and whipped his Moorish page. The multiple indignities! To be threatened with a bill for entertainment, an entertainment that was part of an arbitration, an arbitration that was to give him a town, a town that his soldiers could not occupy because they had deserted, and deserted because he could not pay their wages! Round and round, caught in a vicious downward spiral of misfortune where one catastrophe begat the next. He cursed his empty treasury.

It was not his nature to practice economy, since he could not bear the thought of denying himself luxury. Therefore he blamed his advisors. Duped on all sides, he now broadened the scope of his anger to include not only Isabella and Don

Alfonso, who had spoiled his pleasure, but also his chief negotiators at the Isle of Pheasants, Archbishop Carrillo and the old court favorite, the Marqués of Villena.

Thus the factions grew wider apart and more clearly defined. Queen Juana and Don Beltran were delighted at the turn of events. There were soft words of self-congratulation between them. Villena and Carrillo lay under the king's displeasure! Their own star was in the ascendant! With undisputed power assured over the king, whom somebody would always dominate, all Castile would lie in the palm of their hands.

Quick to push an advantage, since the king was unstable, the queen resolved to confirm herself in that power. The method by which she schemed to accomplish her end was particularly congenial to her temper, since it would eliminate Isabella once and for all.

Queen Juana had been a Portuguese princess before she married Henry the Liberal and became Queen of Castile. Her brother was the King of Portugal, fat, rich, providentially a widower, and well into his middle age, which was of the flabby sort. Why not arrange a marriage between him and Isabella, who was young, it is true, but by no means too young to furnish her fat brother with heirs to the Portuguese throne? Disparity of age was no drawback to a royal marriage. Had not the treaty of the Isle of Pheasants destined the Duke of Guienne for little Juana Beltraneja, a man twenty years older than the child who was just learning to walk? And the queen derived a secret pleasure from the prospect of a bleak and loveless marriage for Isabella. How easily the arguments took shape in her mind! How plausible they were! Isabella was grave, high-minded, self-disciplined, calm, passionately devoted to Castile and sternly schooled by her mother (the old fool!) to venerate the ideal of kingship. Were not these the perfect prerequisites for a queen? Nor would it be anything unusual. The royal family of Castile had formed unions for centuries with the other two Christian kingdoms of the peninsula, now with Portugal, now with Aragón. There could be no political objection from Henry to his half-sister's marriage with Alfonso, "the African," of Portugal.

But there was more. The Portuguese king was as rich as King Henry was poor, by reason of the Portuguese-African trade. True, the Portuguese explorers had not yet found their way to the fabulous wealth of India in their efforts to sail around Africa, which seemed ever so much larger than anyone had expected. But African gold dust, ivory and apes (for the noble sport) and exotic woods and dyes, and above all shiploads of Negro slaves poured into Portuguese harbors and heaped gold into the coffers of Alfonso the African. He was not, of course, of African blood any more than the Scipio Africanus of ancient Roman times. It was merely a classic custom to call a king occasionally by a title that commemorated some foreign exploit: Alfonso the African of Portugal had once led an expedition against the Moors of Tunis, where his meager success had won him his glamorous title of honor.

Less compelling arguments than these would have convinced Henry the Impotent, who was anxious to get rid of Isabella and still grieving over the loss of Francisco. But Juana's crowning argument was the best of all.

"Once my brother sees Isabella he will beggar himself to possess her!"

"Do you think he will make me a settlement on her?"

"Such a settlement as you've never dreamed of! I know my brother. Castile's financial troubles will vanish."

"Now why didn't somebody think of this before!" he cried plaintively. "Nobody ever gives me a thought, I am never considered; I am of all the world's kings the most ill used, absolutely ill *used!* I'll send off a courier at once!"

"Not *too* fast, Henry, You must not throw her at him. Make him pant for her. Invite my brother the king to some likely place in Castile, Gibraltar for instance, where he can look across to Africa; the air is soft and romantic in the south. Call it the anniversary of his glorious African expedition. Join him there. Celebrate. Let him see Isabella; then make the offer while she is under his eyes. Let her wear that dress and we must teach her to drink more wine. But do not throw her at him or he will make you a smaller settlement."

"What a magnificent plan! Villena could never have thought of this."

"Neither Villena nor Carrillo. Only Don Beltran and I have your true interests at heart. Dear Henry!" She kissed him.

"Upon my word!" he remarked, his jeweled fingers to his lips. Then thoughtfully, "I suppose we ought to do that in public from time to time."

"Have I ever refused?"

"I was only thinking. I heard the whisper *La Beltraneja* again the other day. Some of Carrillo's and Villena's followers, I suppose."

"If Isabella were safely married, and if her brother—he's not robust, you know—there would be no more of these whispers."

"Oh no, Juana, I couldn't do away with the boy."

The queen shrugged. "No, I suppose not. That wouldn't be right, would it? The archbishop would surely disapprove."

"Anyhow, are you not going to give me a prince?"

"I promise, with God's help." She smiled. "Do remember, my dear, how much Don Beltran and I love you. Now don't you think you'd better go practice your lute or perhaps have some coffee? A maid is coming to give me my bath."

"I just don't *like* Ahmed," he grumbled, accepting his dismissal.

In the hall he happened to meet Don Beltran. "Do go see the queen!" he whispered excitedly. "She has just had the most fascinating inspiration."

CHAPTER 5

SPRING comes early in Gibraltar, and the early months of the year are dry, since everything in Spain is different: May and June, which elsewhere are wet, are in Gibraltar almost rainless. This, though little else, Queen Juana had known about The Rock when she suggested it as a likely spot for Alfonso the African to meet Isabella. Star-spangled nights were a certainty, with a honey-colored moon rising out of the Mediterranean, drenching the ancient towers of the Moorish castle with a warm romantic light. In such a light the fat Portuguese king would perhaps appear younger than he was, and perhaps it would work a magic on Isabella, who had not shown enthusiasm for the union.

No one indeed was well informed about Gibraltar. Neither King Henry nor King Alfonso had ever before set foot in the place, nor any of the elegant nobles who frequented their courts: it was a recent acquisition of one of Castile's most fiery and intractable noblemen, the Duke of Medina Sidonia, whose vast estates lay far to the south in Andalusia bordering on the Moorish frontier. Medina Sidonia, like frontiersmen living in any age close to the enemy, was fiercely independent, as quick to fight a private feud as a war with the national enemy. He possessed that other characteristic of rough and ready frontiersmen as well; he was almost pathetically eager to be just as cultured as the polite inhabitants of the capital. His private army had wrested Gibraltar from the Moors less than two years before. When he heard that two kings and a princess were to honor his new possession with a visit he was beside himself with joy and engaged a tutor to help him eliminate the worst of the solecisms of his Andalusian dialect.

His hospitality was lavish.

Medina Sidonia formed at once the usual opinion of

Henry the Impotent, but shrugged it off with a smile. So be it. As long as such a weakling sat on the throne of Castile the duke need never fear that his overlord would curtail his own absolute power over his enormous Andalusian estates, where he ruled with almost regal authority. He curled his lip at Henry's Moorish page. Moors were not fashionable here in the south where the Reconquest was still a reality.

"We never honor the infidel hereabouts, Your Highness," he ventured to say to the king.

"My dear duke, I do not like Ahmed at all, not at *all*. But I lost my favorite page and nobody else can brew me my coffee. Perhaps you have someone. It would be a most welcome gift. Yes? No?"

Medina Sidonia did not care for Moorish coffee; and Gibraltar, it seemed to him, should already have constituted a most welcome gift to the king, who had neglected to thank him for it.

The duke replied that he, his house and all his possessions were the property of his liegelord the king of Castile, kissing (as the formula went in speech) the king's hands and feet.

"Oh dear," said the king, for of all Castile's polite phrases this was the most empty and meaningless. Perhaps he should have brought the queen to charm a good page out of this rustic grandee; he must have many likely lads in his service. But Queen Juana had stayed behind for reasons of her own, something connected with Isabella's brother, who, the queen said, was too frail to undertake the long journey.

Isabella had ridden the whole way, scorning a litter, scorning a mule, scorning even a side saddle. The frontiersman in Medina Sidonia might have preferred a pale princess in a litter, but he could also admire a princess who could ride a horse sixty-five leagues with a seat like a caballero's and arrive fresh and radiant at the end of her journey.

Instructed by Henry, who had been instructed by Juana, Medina Sidonia conducted the royal visitors on a tour of the Moorish castle, then arranged (as the sun was sinking) to leave Isabella and her royal suitor alone in each other's company while the rest of the party withdrew out of earshot but not—quite—out of sight, for the sake of propriety. Everyone knew the purport of the meeting: Portugal had signified his willingness to marry the Castilian princess and all that remained was Isabella's formal acceptance of her king and her crown. When, as the queen had put it, he began to pant for her, Portugal's settlement, already generous, could be hoisted to the breaking point. No one, knowing Isabella, doubted that Alfonso the African would pant, and pay. Nor did anyone doubt that Isabella would accept him, for she had not, in fact, actually refused. Every string of her heart had been skillfully played upon: her duty as a princess, who ought never to think of herself; her patriotism; the advantages of lasting peace with Portugal; but above all the strengthening of Castile and the presentation of a united front against the Moors.

Medina Sidonia, noting that her cheek was pale under her healthy tan, had taken her aside on a pretext of explaining the machicolation of one of the fortress's walls, through which boiling pitch and molten lead could be hurled down on the heads of attackers, "Will you accept the king of Portugal, *mi princesa?* By God, you need not if you do not want to!" The duke of Medina Sidonia could muster an armed force almost the equal of Henry's own, and far more loyal.

"I wish to do what is right, my lord duke; may God instruct my heart."

"Amen," said the duke. "But I will pray that He does not instruct you to throw it away."

"Many have advised me to accept him, for the good of the state."

"The good of the state! What about the good of Isabella, Infanta of Castile?" His honest eyes flashed. It was on the tip of his lawless tongue to blurt out that only ugly royal princesses ought to be sacrificed for political ends, and that if King Henry wished to secure his kingdom he ought to fight for it.

"On the other hand," Isabella smiled, "certain others have advised me to refuse the king."

"Good! And if Henry the Im—I mean, the Liberal, goes into a tantrum over your refusal, come to me. The lances that took Gibraltar are not afraid of the king!"

"No, friend, I should not wish to be cause for factions against my brother the king."

"Half-brother," Medina Sidonia muttered.

"But still the king, sir! Do not forget that."

Alfonso the African presented himself on a rampart overlooking the sea. In the distance, a smudge on the darkening horizon, the coast of Africa could be seen. Dutifully Isabella had put on the daring gown, but she had thrown a light cloak over the nakedness of her shoulders on the excuse that the evening breeze was chilly. She had not dared affront King Henry by sewing a piece of lace into the deep décolletage of the bodice, though that had been her first thought.

But she wore on her bosom a jeweled cross, that the sacred symbol might seem to whisper, "For shame!" if Alfonso the African's eyes should stare too fixedly.

The Portuguese king was a swarthy man; in his youth he must have been handsome, a sort of male counterpart of Queen Juana's dark beauty. But Juana was much younger than her brother; in him Isabella saw the ultimate shipwreck of Juana's charm: the full pouting lips grown pendulous in middle age, the plump curves of youth fallen flabby with years of good living and self-indulgence.

The king's hand, into which he took hers as he bent to kiss it, was hairy, moist. She struggled to keep her composure at the unexpected shock of the contact, standing poised and regal, forcing a smile. But in a sudden wild instant of fancy she saw herself leaping from the battlement, hurling herself upon the jagged rocks below. She thrust the unworthy thought from her, that coward's way, way of the impious, the damned. She shivered involuntarily.

"Cold, little princess?" With a heavy proprietary hand he drew her cloak closer around her shoulders.

"A little," she said. "I thank Your Highness."

In the distance King Henry, spying on them, hissed, "The old fool's covering her up! He's blind as the King of Aragón!"

Isabella had seen his appraising glance travel her up and down, from the silver net on her tawny hair to the tips of her silver slippers; she knew he was not blind. She was glad her shoulders were covered now.

He was dimly aware of the figure he might cut in the eyes of a girl almost the same age as his own son. He had quickly noticed her little shudder and he could not reasonably blame it on a chill in the air, which patently did not exist. There had been no welcome in her grave wide eyes, looking at him so forthrightly; no coquetry, no calculated downward glances; only disturbing flecks of luminous green in those honest eyes, like lightning whose power could not yet be measured. The Castilian Infanta had unsuspected depths.

The sun set, a full moon rose, and the sea that had been carpeted with gold was now carpeted with silver; but the magic of the wondrous evening wrought a more potent spell on Alfonso the African than on Isabella. He swore to himself he would never give her up. Time would cure that little shudder of hers—perhaps she was only in awe of him. He would cling to that hope.

Remembering that she was fatherless, young and deprived of a mother, since the unfortunate Dowager Queen was so far advanced in dementia that she did not recognize her own children, the Portuguese king cleverly offered himself as her protector: old enough to serve as a father, tender as a mother, and, in addition, still young enough to be a loving husband, who would deny her nothing. What was void in her life he promised to fill; what was insecure he promised to make safe; and as for a husband's love, how much better to marry a mature man who had already proved himself competent in that respect!

"There is much in what you say, Your Highness; but it is hard to grasp all in a breath."

"There is time, *mi princesa*. I do not hurry you."

He dwelt on his African adventure, hoping that she would love him for the war he had fought. He had led a fleet of warships into the Mediterranean and attacked the Moors of Tunis in their ancient African homeland. True, he had sailed away without conquering any territory, but he had struck terror into the hearts of the infidels and brought back much booty.

"I wonder that Your Highness traveled so far to seek the Moor," Isabella said, "when three million of them remain on Spanish soil."

He could not admit that a quick raid in a flagship was more comfortable, more spectacular and far more certain of success than a long and tedious war over impassable mountains. He was ashamed to confess that he was past the age when a violent assault on a walled city would appeal to him. One chafed painfully in the saddle when one's thighs were as substantial as Alfonso the African's.

"It was a matter of strategy," he said pompously. "Strike at the roots, that is my policy; then let the branches wither. "

It might have been good strategy seven centuries earlier, Isabella knew; but Granada was now more important than the African homeland. And Granada was in Spain.

"A princess would not understand war," the king said.

But most of all he spoke of the personal benefits to Isabella if she would accept him: a wardrobe of seven hundred gowns, with jewels to match each costume; mirrors from floor to ceiling, not only of silver but of gold—had Isabella ever seen a glass mirror backed with pure gold? A most wondrous invention, imported from the Republic of Venice, costly beyond telling, but less than her due! An army of personal servants, butlers, fruiterers, confectioners, ladies in waiting, maids for the bath, maids to curl the hair, maids to paint the fingernails, minstrels to sing her to sleep at night, minstrels to sing her awake in the morning, Moorish slaves for a bodyguard, if she shared King Henry's predilection for their colorful turbans; Negro slaves if she preferred—the newest, most amusing fashion in Christendom.

Isabella was not opposed to slavery for prisoners of war, since countless Christians were groaning in Moorish dungeons, starving, dragging their three-hundred-pound chains. Pedro de Bobadilla, father of her dearest friend, still bore the marks of Moorish cruelty. But the notion of slavery because one's skin was black was new to her.

"There are no Negro slaves in Castile," she said doubtfully.

"Portugal started it," Alfonso said proudly. "It is extremely fashionable, worthy of a queen. One day the custom will sweep the world."

"Are they Christian?"

"Never did a race espouse Christianity so enthusiastically! No, *mi princesa,* set your mind at rest in that respect."

"Then why are they slaves?"

Alfonso plodded on to other things, for he had marshaled all his arguments. The greatest advantage of all was the Portuguese crown. Who would refuse a crown, ancient, honorable, rich, and, above all, ready! He reminded her that she was third in the line of succession for the crown of Castile; nay, probably fourth by now, since Queen Juana's time was past its term and a herald might be expected at any hour announcing the birth of another Infante or Infanta of Castile.

"From the bottom of my heart I wish her well in her travail."

He thought he was making progress; he patted her shoulder. He touched with some smugness on the generosity of the settlement he was prepared to make if she would accept him. "I suppose that the annals of Castile will show few instances of so much gold pouring into the treasury on the marriage of an Infanta. That is the measure of my love, Isabella. Your brother the king will lack nothing henceforth."

"I am sure it will be a great comfort for him to be able to pay his soldiers," Isabella said thoughtlessly.

The king's face changed. "What did you say?"

"If I marry you, he can pay his troops."

"Just who suggested that, *mi princesa?* Or did you think of it yourself?" His whole manner had suddenly altered. He eyed her with a look that might be respect, might be suspicion. He had certainly stepped back a pace.

"It is an honest debt," she said. Somehow she must have let slip a secret, a secret that displeased the Portuguese king. Both Carrillo and Villena had stressed to her the importance of paying the troops. She had assumed that such payment was a matter of common knowledge, and it was one of the reasons she had not publicly refused to consider the marriage. "If Henry had been able to pay them they would not have deserted in Navarre."

And Castile would suddenly possess a formidable standing army, a potential threat to Portugal! Alfonso had expected King Henry to squander the settlement on personal pleasures as usual. That would have pleased him. But not this. The price of the princess might be too high.

"I had not supposed that my dear cousin of Castile would employ the profits of his sister's marriage for so warlike an end," Alfonso said. "Such moneys, from such a joyous event, ought to be expended in happier things, celebrations, tourneys, entertainments, feasting, all the good things that I know my dear cousin enjoys. Someone has advised him very ill. It cannot be Juana or that good fellow Don Beltran. Is it Villena? Carrillo?"

It made her feel dirty to be made the medium of

exchange that would furnish funds to tempt further her too-easily tempted halfbrother. "I think a prince's first duty is always to pay his troops," she said with conviction. The green lightnings in her level look were bright.

"So it is Villena, it is Carrillo," he said in a low thwarted voice. He was silent for a moment.

"Wouldn't you pay your troops first?" She had a disturbing way of asking unanswerable questions.

"I had not expected our meeting to deal with these matters." His tone was disconsolate. He had hoped for an announcement of the betrothal tomorrow. His court poet had already written some admirable verses in commemoration of the event. But not even for Isabella would he personally raise the specter of a mighty Castilian army to threaten himself. He had expected to extend his influence, not diminish it.

"I hope I have said nothing to displease Your Highness. I only told the truth. I think I shall always tell the truth."

"It would simplify things if everybody did," he said shrugging. She was slipping out of his grasp, a sweet cup snatched away before he could taste it. He was far from pleased; but he certainly was enlightened, "You are either a most guileless child," he said, bowing very low, "or the most consummate statesman I have ever been worsted by." The settlement had fallen to zero. He would have her cheap or not at all.

His kiss at parting was formal, his lips scarcely brushing the back of her hand, their fingertips scarcely touching. "I beg you to consider my suit, Isabella. And I, of course, must consider the details of the marriage contract, which seem to require some clarification. That, I believe, may take time. But as I said in the beginning, I do not hurry you. Meanwhile, it would not be fair for you to tell anyone that you had refused me out of hand."

She knew he was asking her to save his face, while the negotiations, no doubt, started over again from the beginning, on a different basis. She complied willingly; she too had been enlightened by the interview; she felt a sense of relief, as if a reprieve had come from a clement monarch to a condemned criminal.

"Indeed I cannot refuse you, Don Alfonso, for that does not lie wholly with me since before an Infanta of Castile can marry, the Cortes of the realm must assemble and concur in her choice. Is that not so?"

The king smiled ruefully. "And who told you that, little princess? Nay, I know. Carrillo again, wasn't it?"

'I'm sure it's a law." Isabella smiled.

He sighed; he knew it was a law; he knew too that Henry the Impotent would not dare call the Cortes, which would demand that he pay his debts. It would have been so pleasant to have got her cheap! "By all means, let us respect the law."

The group around King Henry when they returned were sternfaced and solemn; King Henry's cheeks were wet with tears that streamed down unheeded and dripped from his chin, which was trembling.

"Oh come now, good cousin." Alfonso the African laughed. "Do not take it so to heart. She didn't entirely say no. Things will just take a little longer to work out, especially," he added sternly, "the little matter of that settlement."

"Oh?"

Obviously Henry did not understand.

"It will have to be revised in more realistic terms, applicable to the situation."

"Situation?"

A dusty herald stood in the shadows behind the king. Isabella touched Alfonso's arm and whispered, "He isn't crying about us. He wasn't close enough to hear. I think he's had bad news. Be kind to him."

"More realistic settlement?" King Henry blinked wildly about, blinded by sudden torchlight as a group of Portuguese retainers formed about Alfonso to escort him to his quarters. "Oh no, not another blow today!" He seemed to grasp some of the import of Alfonso's words. "Settlement dead. Son dead. I am ill used, *ill used,* by Heaven itself! I cannot bear it!" He turned and fled weeping from the castle battlement. The assembled notables who had come to witness the first meeting of Alfonso the African and Isabella broke up in indecorous confusion.

Isabella found herself on the arm of Medina Sidonia, whose jaw was set like granite. "What did he mean, *son dead,* señor duke?"

"Queen Juana has just borne him, or somebody, a dead boy. Don Beltran de la Cueva is said to be weeping his handsome eyes out at her bedside."

She snatched away her arm, "For shame for that! Have you no heart? If you have no heart, have you no manners?"

He shrugged. "None of the one, I'm afraid; maybe a little of the other." They walked some time in silence in the direction of her apartments. "What did King Henry mean by *no settlement?*" he asked.

He would find out anyhow. Everybody would know. "Portugal does not think I'm worth a Castilian army's wages," she replied.

Medina Sidonia grinned. "Good girl! You could not have planned it better."

"I did not plan it at all. But I'm glad of the way it turned out. No one is insulted."

At the door of her apartment he said, "The king will set out for the north tomorrow at dawn. You don't have to go with him if you don't want to, you know. My house and all I possess—hang it all, princess, I cannot mouth the courtly words. Stay here and let me take care of you."

"Poor Juana. She has been good to me. She needs friends now."

Medina Sidonia grinned again, less pleasantly, "Ask Beatriz de Bobadilla about poor Juana, and your brother."

Isabella looked at him, her eyes wide with alarm and uncertainty. "The Infante was slightly ill; the queen, who of course could not travel anyway, stayed behind to nurse him. What does Beatriz know that is hidden from me?"

"Maybe she just learned. I'm afraid you'll have to ask Señorita de Bobadilla. I wasn't meant to hear, I suppose. She was cursing like a trooper."

"What did you hear? Everything! Please!"

"I heard that Queen Juana is a whoring bitch, and a poisoner to boot; and that the devil deserves a candle for bringing her bastard stillborn into the world. Beatriz is a good brave girl."

Isabella gasped. Words like that, in times of great stress, sometimes tumbled out of the garrison-bred daughter of the old Moorish fighter who was governor of the castle at Arevalo.

The door opened. Beatriz was in riding habit. She was in a state of extreme agitation.

CHAPTER 6

"DEAR Beatriz! My dear, impractical, impulsive friend! Did you really delude yourself that we could help my poor brother by stealing out alone, unattended, in the dead of night? Did you imagine for one instant that Henry would let us go? And if he should, could we find our way through sixty leagues of mountains and forests? And if, by chance, we should manage all that, by what miracle could two girls pull down the walls of the citadel of Madrid?"

Having brought Beatriz to some realization of the difficulties, Isabella promptly lost the clear-thinking self-possession that had strengthened her all through the trying day. She flung herself on the bed and buried her face in the pillows, sobbing convulsively. "He's dead! I know he's dead! Juana murdered him!"

It was Beatriz' turn to comfort her friend. "Let us cling to the hope that he is out of danger by now, princess. Carrillo has soldiers."

But Isabella would not be comforted and did not sleep that night. Over and over the words of Medina Sidonia came to her in a nightmare: Queen Juana is a whoring bitch and a poisoner to boot, and the devil deserves a candle for bringing her bastard stillborn into the world.

Clearly, Queen Juana, sick with the loss of a male heir and desperate at the prospect of a growing faction of great nobles who doubted the legitimacy of little Beltraneja, had made an attempt on the life of the prince whom everyone acknowledged as a legitimate scion of the royal house of Trastamara, Isabella's brother, Don Alfonso. Hastily, sketchily, the herald who had stood in the shadows on the battlement during Isabella's interview with the king of Portugal, had whispered all he knew into Beatriz' ear: immediately after the birth of Queen Juana's dead child a squad of footmen had arrested Don Alfonso, purporting to act in King Henry's name, and imprisoned him in the alcazar at Madrid, a little town in a wildly wooded region known only for the game and the outlaws that lived in the dark surrounding forests of eucalyptus and pine. There, first, she had starved him; then sent him a sumptuous meal.

"But the princess's hunting dog, Duke, had also been shut up with the prince," the herald said, "and the prince, moved by compassion, let the dog eat first." The animal went into convulsions and shortly died in agony.

"But the rest of the herald's report was encouraging," Beatriz said, and repeated the assurance again and again all during the long march up from Andalusia. "You have friends, dear Isabella, friends like the herald, where you would least expect to find a friend, since he is a king's man; as well as friends who are far more powerful," and she would tell how Don Alfonso had managed to bribe or persuade one of the alcazar guards to carry a plea for help to Archbishop Carrillo. "Carrillo has always adored you and loves Alfonso like a son, He will send his soldiers. The king will not dare oppose the Primate of Castile. It would mean civil war."

"A civil war in such a cause would be a just war," Isabella said. The green lightnings in her eyes were flashing. "Poor brother prince! Poor half-brother king! But the queen must be mad!" Then weeping again, "Ay de mi Castilla!"

The threat of civil war edged closer as the cavalcade made its way northward. It could be felt in the air; it could be sensed in the attitude of the people, who sometimes lined the route to cheer feebly, more often stood in sullen silence, eyeing the long line of horsemen and grandees with a hostility that they did not trouble to conceal. Some towns shut their gates in King Henry's face and refused him admittance, an unpardonable insult to Spanish pride, an overt act of rebellion to a Castilian king. King Henry's only response, in the absence of his queen to advise him, was to sulk, to give the rebellious towns a wide berth and to scold his half-sister. "It's all your fault. You're plotting against me. Everyone is against me."

"If you will permit me to see my brother, if only to make certain that he still lives, I will prove to Your Highness that I am loyal to the Crown."

But the king looked uncertain, muttering suspiciously, "No, no, you shall not go to Madrid," as if he were afraid of what she would find there. He doubled the guard around her and Beatriz. It was significant that the guards were Moors. "I have ordered these gentlemen to keep an eye on you and your friend," he said unpleasantly. "And if you try to escape from their protection I have given them license to hold you by any means, any means at all, my dear sister. I hope you understand."

Isabella lifted her chin in a brave little gesture of confidence that she did not feel. Even Beatriz, usually so brash and daring, rode closer to her after that. It was the first time Isabella had known Beatriz to be afraid. They were now completely cut off from the other female members of the cavalcade, like prisoners, surrounded by the pampered, turbaned, alien guards, whose manners were as elegant as the whispered stories about them were sinister and strange. These were the privileged infidels whom Henry (to add a touch of color to his court) permitted to carry into Castile the harem customs of pagan Granada. It was notorious, and it was true that the dark and comely aliens—for Henry would have none who were not comely—had only to express a liking for a Castilian girl and the Castilian king would try to oblige. If she were highly placed, pressure would be brought upon her to be pleasant to the noble representative of a peaceful neighboring kingdom; if she were a commoner she would simply disappear, and outraged fathers and weeping mothers appealed in vain to the king, who denied everything, or the courts, which could do nothing, for the return of the girls. That Henry would permit such license against an Infanta of Castile Isabella could not quite believe, but she was afraid for Beatriz. In his present wild and wretched mood King Henry was totally unpredictable.

Meanwhile the daily, too intimate contact with the Moors, who even glanced into her tent at night, was one long culminating insult that grew increasingly difficult to bear. There was a breaking point for even the youngest, strongest, healthiest nerves. Isabella found herself unable to tell whether the flashing smiles of her swarthy guards were lascivious leers when a breeze exposed her ankles, or whether they were grins of amusement at her obvious embarrassment.

One night, as she was praying, the guard outside her tent pulled aside the door flap and stuck in his turbaned head. Isabella turned her face, white with outrage.

"Have you no decency?"

Beatriz, however, jumped up from her knees and hurled a pitcher of water at him, with a word of reproach that would have done justice to an artilleryman. The pitcher happened to be of earthenware, and it happened to be cracked. It broke against his face, and a jagged shard cut him painfully on the cheek.

By what seemed a miracle of unlikelihood, his expression did not change; he paid no attention to pain, blood or the water that drenched his bright silk robes. He continued to smile his unfathomable Eastern smile: "I implore your pardon, Your Highness; it is wrong to intrude when one is at prayer to God. The king instructed me to tell you that a herald has arrived from Archbishop Carrillo with a message that your brother, Don Alfonso, is no longer in Madrid but now enjoys the best of health in the archiepiscopal palace in Toledo. The king wished me to stress that Don Alfonso is well."

"I thank God, who has answered my prayers," Isabella breathed. "Carrillo marched upon Madrid?"

"With half the king's own army, and liberated the Infante," the Moor replied, still smiling. "So many Castilians prefer your brother to the king." Division in the king's army was nothing to a Moor; nay, it was excellent for Granada, which welcomed division in Castile no less than did Portugal.

Repentant, Beatriz tore a strip from her skirt and rushed over to wipe the blood from the cut in the Moor's cheek. "I am terribly, terribly sorry! I thought you were peeping at us."

He shrugged. "It isn't deep and it doesn't hurt; but if it were and if it did, what would that matter? We have a proverb, 'What Allah wills, will be; what He willeth not, will not be.' Before old Adam drew a breath it was foreordained, alas, that a cracked pitcher should smash into my face, flung by the rosy-fingered, moon-faced Señorita de Bobadilla. Señorita, I kiss your hands and feet. Your Highness, your devoted servant," and with surprising dignity, drenched as he was, he bowed himself backwards through the door of the tent. Isabella sighed; she would never understand the Moors.

The good news of Don Alfonso's safety softened her mood. But Beatriz, musing on the Moor's words, was indignant.

"Moon-faced, forsooth!" she sputtered, "Isabella, am I moonfaced?"

Kneeling again in a prayer of thanks, Isabella paused to laugh softly. "It's only a quirk of their tongue, Beatriz. In Moorish, to be moon-faced is to be surpassingly beautiful."

The way to Valladolid lay through the valley of the Adaja. It would have been normal and reasonable, in a kingdom less divided, to stop and refresh themselves at Arevalo. But Arevalo was one of the towns that refused admittance to the king. His flag no longer flew from the castle that had been Isabella's home for so long, the home where her mother still lived in darkness, the home where Pedro de Bobadilla was still governor. In place of the royal standard the flags of a host of rebellious grandees flaunted the wind, defying King Henry the Impotent. The drawbridge was up. No trumpet of welcome sounded. Armed men patrolled the ramparts.

"We could make a bolt for it!" Beatriz whispered tensely. "Father would let *us* in."

Isabella looked at her sadly. "You know better than that."

"No, Father would not let us in," Beatriz admitted. "Not even if we could break out of this ring of idolators."

The guard with the cut cheek smiled. "Señorita de Bobadilla, that is one thing, at least, that we are not." and, addressing himself to Isabella, "I beg Your Highness to counsel the moon-faced lady to do nothing rash. The king is in a peculiar mood!" He nodded his brightgreen turban to the spot where Henry had drawn rein and was talking to an esquire, who suddenly ran to a packhorse and pulled the king's helmet out of a velvet saddle bag. "It would be dangerous and foolish if some unexpected act on the part of the lady were to precipitate an engagement with the castle here and now."

Glaring at the castle, the king put his helmet on his head, took it off, polished it with his sleeve, put it on again—then took it off and, bursting into tears, called for a litter, in which he rode like a woman or a very sick man for the rest of the day.

He was heard to say, "I have endured such insults as no King of Castile has ever endured before." No one replied, but the sneers on the faces of the Moors made even Isabella wince.

Insulted the king had been, but not as he was to be. That would come at Medina del Campo, a scant day's ride from the capital.

Medina del Campo sat like a great gray rock on the great gray plateau which constitutes the rugged heartland of Old Castile, "old" because it was the first great province to be wrested from the Moors in the early centuries of the Reconquest, a perennial crusade not yet at an end. None but the native-born could love its wind-swept, sunscorched, treeless vastness. Isabella loved it intensely, with a fierce

Spanish love: for the bleakness was gold in the sunlight, green trees did grow in the river valleys, there was grass on the steppe-like plain for sheep that bore the finest, softest wool in Christendom, bringing prosperity to cities like Medina del Campo; and the stubborn earth could be made fruitful by the industry of peasants as hardy and stubborn as the earth itself.

The earth was always close, and at night the stars were close also, jewelled points of colored fire an armstretch up in the crystal air. Close, too, was God, since heaven and earth were so near to each other in the uplands of Old Castile: close and real and very personal. There was none of the mystic in Isabella. She had seen a church in a village through which the cavalcade had passed where the image of the Crucified had been taken down from its cross and laid on a bier on a quilted peasant blanket. The agonized head, crowned with the crown of thorns, rested on an eiderdown pillow. A naive, but very natural act of kindness which Isabella could understand.

The gates of Medina del Campo were open, but it was the openness of a place too contemptuous to defend itself. An army of the greatest lords of the kingdom occupied the city and spilled out in a long array of tents onto the surrounding plain. Among the host of heraldic banners that floated over the tents and snapped from poles on the walls were those of Archbishop Carrillo, the Marqués of Villena, Isabella's brother, and—a new one—the formidable standard of Don Fadrique de Henriquez, Admiral of Castile. Such was the magnitude of the faction now allied against the king. Don Fadrique was an international figure; he could quarter on his shield not only the castles of Castile and the lions of León, but the crimson bars of Aragón also. He was not, of course, an Aragonian; but his daughter had married the Aragonian king and thus he was grandfather to young Prince Ferdinand, who would one day be King of Aragón. Such a man wielded immense power. In his litter King Henry groaned. No doubt the insurgents would demand that he abdicate. He withdrew the Moorish guards and ordered them to an inconspicuous place in the rear. He assured Isabella that he had asked them to attend her only for her protection.

"In view of the hostility of your friends," he said petulantly, "I could trust only my Moors to be unswervingly faithful. Concede that they were attentive and well-mannered."

"I think they tried to be, Henry. But I do not like them and I cannot understand them. And if my friends are hostile it is not I who made them so."

"You shall see your brother at once, of course. I do not know how you heard the ugly, traitorous rumors that the queen had poisoned him."

Isabella did not tell him how she had heard.

"As if my pretty little Juana would do such a thing! False, lying, villainous tongues. Do not give ear to them. Do not desert me, Isabella; do not hate me; I need you, Isabella. The rebels yonder are going to ask me to step down. I will not give up the throne. Never!"

"I do not join them, if that is their demand."

"I am the king. Am I not the king?"

"Assuredly, Henry!"

"Am I not the only king?"

"There can be but one king."

"Will you support me if they ask me to step down?"

"Of course I will."

"To step down—in favor of your brother?"

Isabella did not hesitate. "Even if they ask you to step down in favor of Alfonso. But are you sure that that is what they want? There has been no parley."

"Oh, I do not know, I do not know. But I'm sure that is what they want. What else could they want? There will be a parley, and that will be what they want. Oh dear, oh dear, oh *dear!*"

She met her brother at once; no obstacle was put in her way. The king, now joined by Queen Juana, was at great

71

pains to be charming to the Infantes, Don Alfonso and Doña Isabella. She found herself wondering what, in the swirling currents of political faction, had happened to make her a personage of such importance. And as for her brother, he was treated with such deference that it almost seemed as if he, not Henry, were the king. He was inclined to treat his late imprisonment as something of a joke.

"Perhaps the queen was a bit desperate when she found out what was in the wind. The only casualty was poor Duke."

"It could have been you."

"At any rate I was released, thanks to Carrillo and Don Fadrique. You have heard the great news?"

"Only that you are alive and well. How I prayed God for that. The rest does not matter."

"Oh, but it does! King Henry has a bitter cup to drink tomorrow, for tomorrow he will sign a document that sets aside La Beltraneja and restores me to the succession!" He squared his shoulders; he looked very proud and competent. How quickly the little brother of Arevalo had grown into man's estate.

"If only poor Mother could understand this wonderful thing. How happy she would be."

"Always take care of her, Alfonso."

"Always. I promise."

"Is it certain that the king will sign?"

Alfonso laughed. "He has no choice."

The king signed, and the Concord of Medina del Campo became famous throughout Europe in a matter of weeks. Never had a king so humbled himself. The language of the document was sharp: sins and injustices and tyrannies had grown up during his reign such as never before had been known in Castile. He had surrounded himself with infidels; he had squandered the public treasure; his courts did not enforce the laws. "The thing that makes us weep drops of blood—" so went the language of the Concord—"is to see Your Highness dominated by the Count of Ledesma, Don Beltran de la Cueva," and the Concord demanded his instant dismissal from court and from all his rich political posts.

In insulting proximity there came the bald statement, "Doña Juana, the so-called Infanta, is not your daughter." King Henry, in signing, publicly branded his queen as an adulteress, his daughter as a bastard.

But there was more. It concerned Alfonso and Isabella. For the tranquility of the realm and in the interests of justice, Don Alfonso was named and acknowledged Prince of the Asturias, heir to the throne. As for Isabella, the Concord "begged and required" that no marriage should be forced upon her without the consent of the three estates of the realm.

"What does Queen Juana say to all this?" Isabella asked.

Alfonso looked thoughtful. "Now that is a peculiar thing, sister. The queen affects to be perfectly satisfied with the entire arrangement."

Isabella wondered.

CHAPTER 7

WITH the king humbled so abjectly, the army of insurgents melted away to their own estates and their own affairs. Don Beltran disappeared; the Moors disappeared. Everyone went to church regularly. The queen used less rouge. Never had she been so charming; never, indeed, had she labored so hard to appear charming, especially to Isabella, whom she now needed. And since the court was now decent and safe, even Carrillo conceded that here was the right and proper place of residence for the sister of the heir to the throne.

"I would rather come with you and Alfonso," Isabella said.

"My dear girl, what would a princess do among all my priests and warriors?"

"I do not dislike priests or warriors."

Carrillo chuckled. "Nor would they dislike you; nay, I am afraid you would prove a distraction that would work a great detriment to their duties. Better to stay here, *mi princesa,* at the heart of things where there are other ladies. Remember, one day, perhaps soon, you will marry. I must not permit you to hide yourself in Toledo; no eligible princes are likely to make their way to my celibate barracks of a household." He shrugged and laughed. "I am informed by those who are expert in these matters that when a man seeks a bride he is in no mood for cathedral incense or for the odor of harness leather, which seem to hang over my establishment: he is in a mood for the fragrance of perfume, which he will find at court—though I am happy to say there is somewhat less of it now than there was."

Isabella smiled. What a mixture of courtier, caballero and prelate the archbishop was.

She stayed. But she did not feel quite so easy in her mind

74

as Carrillo. Queen Juana, these days, was too good to be true.

Most of King Henry's subjects were thoroughly contemptuous of him. Many others simply pitied him. A few, however, moved by self-interest or respect for the office of the king, still clove to him, and these constituted his party. "After all," they would say, "he never really hurt anybody." To such as these it was a source of considerable comfort that his demeanor grew cheerful and confident after the signing of the Concord of Medina del Campo. The discord that had all but erupted into civil war seemed to have been composed; the dark clouds had passed, and with them their threat of storm.

King Henry, now reunited with his queen and taking his strength from her, could afford to look cheerful and confident. She had shown him a way to recoup all his loss of power and prestige. There was a way to win back the Marqués of Villena. There was a way to win back the army. There was a way out of the slough of dishonor into which the Concord of Medina del Campo had plunged him.

That way was the marriage of Isabella. A very special and statesmanlike marriage.

"The terms of the Concord stipulate that no marriage shall be forced upon her," the king said nervously, his lip unsteady.

Queen Juana's voice was sharp, her cheek pale. Don Beltran had been away many weeks; she scarcely cared what she said. "In God's name, Henry, for once, only for once, be a man! Dare a little. Do a little. Do not forever be scuttling into corners like a cockroach! Who will know that Isabella had to be—well, let us call it 'persuaded' into the marriage? Isabella has a normal healthy appetite. Let her fast, let her fast for a while, and I think she will find herself quite hungry, even for Don Pedro."

"Fasting didn't work on her brother."

"That was an entirely different circumstance," Queen Juana said primly. "How was I to know the fish was spoiled?"

"There is certainly no harm in a little fasting," King Henry said, "and it might indeed go far toward winning her over to Don Pedro. But wouldn't she renounce him afterwards?"

"By the time she is fed—" the queen began.

"You phrase things so *roughly*, my dear!"

"It is a rough world; it is a rough kingdom; it needs a rough ruler. I phrase things as they are. But for your sensitive ear, Henry, let us say that by the time she is permitted to break her fast she shall have entered irrevocably into the holy state of matrimony. For if I know Don Pedro Giron, he will consummate the union once, twice, thrice, a dozen times over, before he lets her sit down to the wedding feast—"

"Juana, Juana, *please!*"

"Sensitive ear again, Henry? Pray, what is wrong with consummating a marriage? It's a sacrament, isn't it? Isn't Isabella always mooning over everything religious, always reading her prayerbook, always praying, always going to church?"

"I was only thinking—I mean to say, this Pedro Giron, what an active man!"

"Oh. Yes, of course. That is what you *would* mean, isn't it?"

"Good gracious me!"

"We were speaking of Isabella, Henry, Do you suppose for one instant that she would renounce a husband after that?"

"No. No, positively not. Not Isabella." He paused, smiled, "What a beautiful plan! So remarkably feasible. Why, it's even respectable. It is, isn't it? Don Pedro isn't as bad as they say, is he?"

Queen Juana shrugged. "Suppose he were? But I'm sure he isn't."

The king said oddly, "Actually, Juana, he *couldn't* be.

Nobody could."

Don Pedro Giron, old and far as the king of Portugal, was one of the richest and most envied grandees of Castile. His military power was unique: he occupied the exalted position of Grand Master of the Knights of Calatrava, a military order founded in the early days of the Reconquest to fight the Moors and now three hundred years old. The rules of the order were monkish in origin, since professed monks were the original knights: austere in discipline, celibate in their private lives, eating meat only thrice a week, preserving silence at table, they slept and prayed girded with the sword, ready for instant battle.

The city of Calatrava, once on the Moorish frontier, had long since been incorporated into Castile, and through the centuries professed monks had ceased to join the order. Warrior-priests like Archbishop Carrillo were an oddity nowadays, respected and honored indeed, but as a fond and wistful anachronism. Through the centuries too had come a relaxation of the strict original rules: members could marry if dispensed from their vows, and dispensation, at least for officers, was easy to get; meat could be eaten anytime and in any quantity, as the gross body of the Grand Master was eloquent witness. And poverty was no longer considered a virtue: the order was fabulously wealthy. Over its great treasure the Grand Master held absolute sway, accountable neither to his council nor to his king. The common members of the order, though their discipline might have appeared lax to the ancient founders, were the best fighters in Castile. For them the Grand Master's word was law even against the king himself.

During King Henry's reign corruption in the state was working downward from the top. Thus the great body of the knights *was* strict, loyal and well behaved. Only the top was rotten. Don Pedro Giron owed his position entirely to that slippery old court favorite, the Marqués of Villena. They were brothers.

The known facts about Don Pedro were simple and unpleasant: he was sensual, gluttonous, slothful, vain; as ugly and stupid as his brother, the Marqués, was elegant and sly.

The whispered stories about him were unappetizingly like the stories about the Moors, whose decadent vices he was known to have shared and improved upon.

Such a man King Henry now wooed with the dazzling prospect of marriage to such a princess as Isabella. For by gaining Don Pedro over to his side, the king would gain back his powerful brother, the Marqués, and all the staunch knights of the great Calatrava Order, their towns, castles, estates and enormous revenues.

"My dear," repeated the king, "it is a beautiful plan."

"And then," the queen said, her color rising, "you can safely repudiate this silly Concord of Medina del Campo."

"Of course I can."

"And Don Beltran shall come back to court, where he belongs."

"Of course," said the king absently. "But upon my word, Juana, from your description I should expect *you* to want the Grand Master."

"You idiot, she can *marry* the pig, I can't. I'm married to you."

Softly at first, in a persuasive manner, Queen Juana broached the subject to Isabella: at the age of seventeen one was already ripe for marriage, nay, if one were a princess, almost overripe, if the truth were faced squarely, since a princess's duties were always heavier than an ordinary woman's, involving high policies of state, and thrust early upon one.

"I have always been willing to do my duty." Isabella smiled. She was blushing slightly, a little breathless. Marriage of itself was not repugnant. She wondered whom they had chosen for her this time. She was well schooled in the tradition of her duties, and accepted them; she was prepared to demand very little for herself—but wistfully she thought what a blessing it would be if the chosen prince could be someone not too old, not too unattractive, someone whom some day she could learn to love; but most of all, a prince who could learn to love her. It was increasingly notorious among European royalty—a sign of the degenerate times—that they deserted their mistresses and bastards only long enough to make a state marriage, and then went back to their mistresses. She had hoped she would be the lucky exception.

"Who is he, Your Highness?"

Beatriz, more skeptical, said boldly, "Isabella doesn't have to take him, you know. She can't be forced. The Concord."

That was no way to talk to Queen Juana. Angrily she blurted out, "He is Don Pedro Giron, Grand Master of Calatrava. One could hardly do better."

"But—is he not vowed to celibacy?" Isabella asked.

"His vow is already dispensed."

"He has been approached? Everyone knows? I was not consulted?"

"Naturally some arrangements have had to be made: proclamations, invitations, dozens of gowns to be designed and made up, the decoration of the cathedral—my dear child, you do not think that you are to be hurried into this, do you? You still have a week at least."

Isabella's face went white; Giron's reputation was known to her.

The queen was prepared for refusal; she had schemed how to handle that. But she was not prepared for what Beatriz did.

Black eyes flashing, Beatriz jumped to her feet. In an unexpected gesture that was destined to become famous beyond the confines of palace gossip, to spread throughout the kingdom and eventually to find itself at the tip of every chronicler's pen and gain for itself a permanent place in the annals of King Henry's miserable reign, the impulsive girl drew a hidden dagger from her breast and flashed it before Queen Juana's eyes. "God will never permit such an outrage," she cried. "And neither will I!"

Queen Juana took to her heels. Since Beatriz did not actually stab her, she recovered sufficient composure to hurl back at them from the door, "You'll think better of Don Pedro when you get hungry!"

Immediately the room filled with guards. The Moors must have been quietly filtering back to court, another ominous sign. One great leering hulk of an infidel pawed at Beatriz' bosom for hidden daggers, holding a hairy hand over her mouth to stifle her screams, till Isabella cried, "For shame!" and to Beatriz, "Please, please do not make things worse than they already are!"

The Moor shrugged. "I cannot risk a poignard in my back while we conduct Your Highness and this tigress to a place of retirement. Those are the king's orders."

Isabella took Beatriz by the hand; helplessly they suffered themselves to be led away. From the cheerful lighted royal apartments they were taken to a tower room, barred, draughty, and absolutely devoid of furniture of any kind. They heard the heavy bolts thrown. They heard the slippered feet of the Moors pad softly down the flagstoned hall, fainter and fainter into the distance, till another door grated shut, leaving them in silence and darkness.

Isabella said in a voice that was eerie and hollow in the emptiness of the room, "Dear God, let me die of starvation before I marry Don Pedro!"

Beatriz wept uncontrollably, sought Isabella in the darkness and huddled close to her, finding her kneeling. "It is my fault, my terrible fault! I should have been silent and let you agree—or pretend to."

"But I'll never agree, Beatriz."

Beatriz did not want to die. Next day, and the next, no one appeared at the door of their prison; not to bring them a stub of a candle, not to bring them a morsel of food, not even to give them water to drink. Even condemned criminals were provided with water.

"Won't you call, and pretend to agree?" Beatriz begged.

Isabella called. But it was only to beg for Beatriz' release. The distant door creaked softly; they were watched. But it was not the plea that Queen Juana expected; the door closed again, and nothing happened.

Then suddenly, on the morning of the third day, everything changed: food, water, servants, every comfort appeared in a rush.

Something had happened, something that the minstrels would put to music as they sang before generations of Spanish grandees when the supper boards of the great hall were cleared and fires crackled on castle hearths and the travails of Isabella were remembered. "Legend, legend!" the polite and sophisticated gentlemen of a later age would protest, "A *far* too facile coincidence!" But to Isabella and Beatriz, living the simple truth, it was the triumph of hope and prayer. The justice of God, or the Devil collecting his due, had intervened in the life of Don Pedro Giron. And ended it.

He had already set out from his castle at Almagro, with perfumed wax on his pointed black mustache, with a new velvet suit and a roistering retinue of boon drinking companions. So great was their enthusiasm and so urgent the desire of Don Pedro that three blooded warhorses did duty as pack mules to carry the loads of wine with greater speed. There were trumpets and laughter; hooves thundered and gaudy pennons snapped in the wind. With rough jests and bawdy jokes, such as traditionally follow a bridegroom, the Master of Calatrava came to Villarubia. "A few more short hours," they shouted. "Do not founder your mount!"

"We will go on tonight, and just see if I won't," he replied.

"Nay, stop and refresh yourself, to be the more valiant in the combat of love!"

"Are you suggesting that I need to be restored?" And much of the same. But he stopped.

During the night he became violently, suddenly ill. There was a choking sensation about his throat; it was almost impossible to expand his lungs. When he did manage to fill them, coughing and wheezing painfully, the breath did not strengthen him. It was as if invisible bony fingers were circling and constricting his throat. He gasped in a strangled voice that someone was garrotting him.

A reputable physician treated him; there was no improvement. He lingered the clock around and then closed his eyes and, cursing, died. His many titles and great estates not connected with the Order passed to his three bastard sons. Very soon the news reached Valladolid and put an end to Isabella's imprisonment.

The Grand Master's death had instant repercussions throughout Europe. In France King Louis XI grinned and nodded approval: "To poison an enemy at such a distance is a great art. The little Spaniard will bear watching." In England Richard of York, with his withered arm and his monstrous ambitions, murmured, "What a princess to aid me to beat my way to the British throne, if I could contrive to wed her!" In Portugal, King Alfonso was vexed: "I'd never have suspected such depths, I must marry her after all, before she gets too powerful." Such was the reputation of the court of King Henry the Impotent and such was the character of fifteenth-century royalty. Yet the reputable physician, signing the death warrant as was prescribed by law, stated clearly that the Grand Master had died of an acute inflammation of the throat, which had struck inward and developed into a quinsy, which was prevalent in the district that year and which had carried off many, both great and small.

Only in Aragón did no one smirk or suspect foul play, and there old King John said to his son, "Ferdinand, what did you think of the Castilian Infanta that time when you watched her during the sport of the ape-on-horseback?"

"Sir, she had a bewitching back."

"I'd empty half my coffers to get her to turn around," his father mused, He had always desired a union with Castile.

"So would I, Sir!"

Chance, in the sudden death of Don Pedro, coupled with cynical miscalculation of Isabella's fortitude, now conspired to destroy Queen Juana's schemes and King Henry's futile hopes. The whole realm was plunged into bewildering confusion, for even as royal heralds were shouting the glad tidings that the Infanta would marry the Grand Master of Calatrava, rebel heralds were spurring in every direction with the news that the Grand Master was dead and that the Infanta was a prisoner in the palace.

The late insurgents once more sprang to arms, not only in defense of Isabella but also because the news of her marriage was coupled with a statement that the Concord of Medina del Campo was now, of course, a dead letter. This meant the return of Don Beltran to court, the restoration of La Beltraneja to the succession, the return of the Moors to favor and a continuance of all the old abuses. In short, everything was to be just as it had been before.

This time there was bloodshed.

Late in August the insurgents met the king's army at Olmedo. Rebel and royal forces were approximately equal. From his camp Archbishop Carrillo sent a herald with a solemn old-fashioned défi to Don Beltran, assuring him that now indeed his time had come, since no less than forty caballeros had personally sworn his death. Don Beltran, superb animal of a man, sent back the same messenger with a minute description of his dress, to help them find him in the melee of battle: let them look for a tall knight on a white stallion, with gray and silver armor, and the queen's green sleeve for a favor on his helm.

Isabella's brother, though his armor bore heavily on his spare frail frame, fought bravely. Yet he would have gone down many times had not Archbishop Carrillo, conspicuous in a scarlet cope with its white embroidered cross thrown over his cuirass of Toledo steel, come roaring bull-voiced and formidable on a high chestnut warhorse, cleaving a path through the host whenever the crush around the lad looked too dangerous, for Alfonso, of course, was an object of special attention. Throughout the day Don Beltran, in a display of valor that would have set the queen swooning for love, his silvergray armor now crimsoned with the blood of his sworn destroyers, set an example of gallant butchery that rallied the king's men again and again, till the sun went down and the two armies drew apart for pure fatigue. None of the principals were killed. King Henry, indeed, had fled the field and hidden in a farmhouse.

Carrillo, nursing a wounded arm, sent a scouting party after him when the battle had ended by mutual consent for the night. King Henry buried himself in a haycock and could not be found.

Next day the casualties proved heavier than expected, and the battle was not resumed. Both sides left the field with their dead and their wounded, with drums beating and trumpets trumpeting paeans of victory.

When it had become apparent that civil war was at last inevitable Queen Juana had fled with La Beltraneja to Segovia, a city of singular strength. With her, under heavy guard, went Isabella, half-hostage, half-guest. War was the business of men.

There were now two kings in Castile, since the "victorious" insurgents had irrevocably repudiated King Henry by fighting against him.

There remained only to crown King Alfonso, Isabella's brother.

His coronation was a sorry affair.

CHAPTER 8

AVILA, scene of Alfonso's coronation, was a city girt round by a granite wall studded with eighty-six watchtowers, the very archetype of the image that springs to mind at the words "castle in Spain." Geoffrey Chaucer had already written "Thou shalt make castles in Spayne, and drem of joye...." and given thereby a new phrase to the forming English language. But he wrote as a foreigner, in a foggy faraway northern isle. To him the image was rosy and insubstantial, wrapped in the misty quality of a dream that would vanish.

To Isabella, who knew the city well, castles in Spain were as common and beloved as mutton in Chaucer's England, in no way insubstantial. The walls of Avila were not rosy, but solid and gray, quarried from the heartrock of the Gredos mountains that loomed in the distance against the sky.

Yet there was a dreamlike quality about her brother's coronation. To a princess reared to respect the sanctity of the throne, in spite of its occupant, there were aspects of a nightmare in the events which now took place at Avila.

Outside the city on the plain where there was room for the crowds to gather and watch, Archbishop Carrillo and the insurgents had erected a great wooden platform, elevated so all could see. On it a throne was reared, and on the throne, crowned, sceptered, girt with the sword of state, sat the effigy of King Henry IV of Castile. Though his crown was tinsel, his jewels paste, his sword mere painted wood and his body made of straw, the lifeless scarecrow represented the king, and some of the peasants who had gathered to watch the spectacle pulled off their caps.

A band of drummers beat a dead march on muffled drums. One by one the leaders of the rebels approached the effigy; one by one they tore off the insignia of royalty and threw them into the dust: the sword of state, that had not protected the state; the sceptre of power that he had abused; the crown that he had proved unworthy to wear. Then with a furious beating of drums to signify the anger of his subjects the image itself was cast down from the platform. A shout of triumph went up from the rebel nobles; most of the common people were quick to join, but a few of the slower-witted groaned audibly.

Then Isabella's brother mounted the vacant throne, to the fanfare of trumpets, and even those who had groaned found voice to cheer the lad against whom no evil had ever been spoken, whose claim to the throne was acknowledged by all, whose whole life lay ahead of him and from whom so much could be expected. The scarecrow on the ground was forgotten; everyone now cheered, and King Alfonso was escorted in triumph back to Avila.

Isabella, in the alcazar at Segovia, heard of these things at second hand, and her first word at the news was a sorrowful "Ay de mi Castilla!"

In a more orderly state the existence of two kings would have demanded a settlement: one or the other would have been crushed. But Castile had not been orderly for years. The momentum of chaos is strong, and disorder can be lived in if one is used to it. Now that Alfonso was crowned—and bearing in mind that the battle of Olmedo had not been such a glorious victory after all—the insurgents lost some of their enthusiasm and the civil war was not resumed. In its place there sprang up countless little private wars, neighbor against neighbor, castle against castle, all over the kingdom. The roads were unsafe. Outlaws banded together in the forests. The peasantry was listless, since who knew whether what was sowed could be harvested, and what was harvested could be kept—or would it be stolen by the lord of the castle a league away? There were rumors of plague. There was intrigue and shifting from one side to the other among the great nobles. The nation paused.

In Avila Alfonso begged the Archbishop, "Sir, is my sister forever to remain prisoner in Segovia?"

"Lad, lad," the troubled prelate replied," she isn't a prisoner. Not exactly, anyhow. We cannot strike till we are a little stronger."

"I propose to lead an army against Segovia at once!"

"Hm-m," reflected Carrillo, rubbing his chin with his big coarse hand. "I don't say the army wouldn't follow you, lad. But you and they would all die. Segovia is impregnable."

Its citadel was the strongest in Spain. Its ancient walls were Roman work, and the imperial Romans had built for the ages.

Tears of anger and chagrin glinted in King Alfonso's eyes, but he fought them back. Carrillo threw a heavy arm over his slender shoulders. "Don't take it so to heart, little Highness. Your sister is doubly and trebly safe. All she will suffer is a little anxiety and boredom, as women always suffer in war. But safe."

"I do not share Your Reverence's complacency," Alfonso said.

Carrillo's laughter boomed. "Then I must instruct you. Item: if we cannot force Segovia, nobody can; so you need not fear that the place will be plundered by some neighboring grandee in a local disturbance. Item: strong as it is, the city will fall of itself once our party is big enough to overawe the king. They will simply open the gates. Item: the one sure way for Henry to unite our party against himself is for him to harm Isabella. Spaniards become marvelously vexed when beautiful princesses are murdered. Henry knows that; he will avoid such a tactical blunder."

Alfonso shivered as if he were cold. "Yet Queen Juana tried to poison me."

"Believe me, Alfonso, I know more of this wicked world than you do, and the death of your sister, whom I love as I do you, is not the direction toward which the evil state of the realm now tends. She will be guarded more closely than

Henry's treasure—all that remains of it—which everyone knows he has transferred to Segovia for safekeeping. I wish I had it." His bantering mood had grown grave and wistful. He was too proud to admit that the funds of the rebel faction were low.

"I respect your wisdom, sir, but I cannot rest till Isabella is beyond the reach of Queen Juana."

"Patience, lad; the right is on our side, and the right will win, with the help of prayer—and rather a great deal of money." His voice trailed off, musing. "I can get funds from the Grand Rabbi; he's more than half a Christian anyhow. I can get funds from Isaac Abrabanel; he's unsalvageable religiously, but he is worried about some massacres of his people since these outbreaks of the plague."

"The Jews will back my cause?"

"The good ones will, the bad ones won't, just like the Christians. And why not? The Grand Rabbi hates what Henry has done to this land. Abrabanel's interests are centered more on his people, but if I drop a word that my preachers have my leave to preach a sermon or two reminding fanatics that the Jews don't really poison wells and bring on the plague, no doubt he'll make a contribution to the cause."

"Don't they always preach that, if that is the truth?"

The Archbishop said, "They preach the Gospel. I never allow them to meddle in politics unless I have to."

Alfonso looked at Carrillo's arm, which was still in its sling. "I thank God, sir, that *you* meddled in politics. If these Jews will help, I shall thank God for them too."

Carrillo said gently, "You will be a good king. Remember, they are not all bad, and none of them is as bad as the Moors. I am sometimes chided by zealots like Torquemada, the sainted prior of Santa Cruz, who believe that my views are too liberal—he would call them lax. But a brave Jewish soldier is the Governor of King Henry's alcazar in Segovia, guarding the king's treasure as if it were his own. And a Jewish surgeon has just removed the cataracts that were blinding the eyes of old King John of Aragón, restoring his sight like a youth's of twenty. No, no, there is good in them, and much ability. Though we should never relax our efforts to convert them, naturally."

How simple the lessons of Torquemada, compared with the lessons in statecraft that Alfonso was having to learn as king!

"And I think Don Fadrique could contribute," the archbishop continued. "Don Fadrique, Grand Admiral of Castile. Perhaps he can loosen the purse strings of his grandson Ferdinand over in Aragón. You must get to know Ferdinand, Alfonso; he handles the finances for his father. Ferdinand is a subtle prince, with a statesmanlike head on his shoulders. But stingy! Splendor of God, so stingy! Louis of France is a spendthrift compared with the crown prince of Aragón!"

Thus the archbishop, marshalling his funds as coolly as he marshaled his soldiers in battle.

"And then I shall lead the army against Segovia?"

"I promise. And I shall be with you."

"Will it be soon?"

"I am almost as impatient as you." For Carrillo's logical itemization of the factors that worked for Isabella's safety were more convincing in his mind than in his heart. With Queen Juana nothing was logical.

Yet she possessed a keen instinct for self-preservation. Over the scent of her perfume she sniffed the political wind, and sensed the menace in it. On the surface at least, she was polite, almost deferential, to her hostage; and her solicitude extended to Beatriz. The best apartment in the great old castle was set aside for their use, with a suite of high-born ladies in waiting to serve them. Never had Isabella lived so luxuriously. They were not permitted outside the castle walls, however.

"In troubled times," Queen Juana said, helplessly shrugging her beautiful shoulders, "what can mere women do? The king would never forgive me if I permitted his half-sister to travel, with the roads so dangerous."

Beatriz said with pleasant impertinence, "The king will soon make the roads safe for his *sister.*"

Juana flushed angrily. "You know very well which king I meant."

Even Isabella smiled.

The summer days were long and hot, the nights oppressive and full of the noise of sentries' shouts and the tramp of soldiers' feet on the granite battlements. It seemed to Isabella, who seldom drank wine, that the water from the castle well was bitter, and she looked wistfully at the mighty old Roman aqueduct that brought to the rest of the city the limpid waters of the Rio Frío, down from the Sierra Fuenfria to the south. The mountains looked pure and close and clean. There were frequent comings and goings of heralds, but they all wore King Henry's livery. Juana said they brought no political news, and since her attitude remained the same, Isabella believed her. Presumably the stalemate continued. Summer wore on towards fall and the blue-green of the Guadarrama Mountains went leaden in hue as the vegetation parched and died.

Beatriz walked on the battlements restlessly, black eyes, black hair, black mood and black looks for the guards, who refused to answer her questions, any questions at all, though they always saluted her respectfully. Then when she had passed, they would chuckle and wink and nudge one another in the ribs: "Would you give a day's pay for a night with her?" "A year's!." "You wouldn't last a year." "Who'd last an hour with a panther?" "Who'd care?" "But what an hour!" For the guards too were bored and uninformed of what went on in the outside world.

On a sultry day, in a particularly sultry mood, Beatriz overstepped the only restriction that Juana had put on their movements within the castle. She stopped at the door of the great square keep, and entered. The keep was the highest and strongest structure of the castle, a massive tower of masonry, virtually a castle within a castle, round which the rest of the fortress had been built. All else might fall, but if the keep could be held there still was hope. When the keep was reduced, then indeed, like a man stricken through the heart, the castle was lost.

Beatriz did not enter the forbidden door unopposed. A scar-faced veteran of a guard looked down on her from a head's vantage of stature and rasped, "You cannot come in here, young lady," What Beatriz said, in a crisp, clear, unmistakable voice, took his breath away. She reached out with both hands and pushed him vigorously aside, so that his armor clanked against the stone of the wall. She was past him in a trice.

"By God's five glorious wounds," the astonished man swore, "I never before heard a lady use that word!" He peered into the shadowy interior of the keep, but Beatriz had disappeared. "So much the worse for her." He shrugged. Then he smiled. There were few women in this part of the alcazar and Beatriz had lightened an otherwise tedious tour of duty. Nor did he fear for the Governor's safety. There were other guards inside, and one lone girl, no matter how vigorous her tongue or her arm, could scarcely be construed as a danger to the king's treasure. She'd soon come flying out, that she would.

She walked through a dark hall, her skirts rustling with the impatience of her steps. She passed a series of heavy oaken doors securely locked and chained with ponderous iron chains. Behind her, like the entrance to a tunnel, the brilliantly sunlit door grew small and golden in the distance. It was as if she were in a prison underground, though she realized she was actually in a tower. Some of the defiance went out of her manner. She felt hemmed in, she wanted open space around her again; but she did not go back. When she came to a steep flight of stairs at the end of the corridor she lifted her skirts and hurriedly mounted them, toward the sunlight above. The stairway was long and windowless, without a rail, made for fighting men who had no fear of heights. She hugged the wall.

Suddenly the stairway ended on the highest floor of the tower, just under the roof, and here the aspect of things was less grim, for she found herself at the door of a spacious apartment with many windows, narrow indeed, and barred, fighting windows; but they let in the light. There were weapons and armor about, stacked iron cauldrons, piles of cannon balls of stone and iron. It was a functional part of the castle, not usually lived in; but it had been made livable, even luxurious. There were thick Moorish carpets on the floor, paintings on the wall, wax candles in sconces, a great brass brazier in which charcoal could be burned in winter to warm the room. There were also a bed and, oddly, a small dining table, just big enough for one. The bed was a hard folding cot, such as soldiers used in camp. By contrast, the table was set with a silver plate, a silver goblet, a crystal decanter, a silver spoon and, astonishingly, one of the strange new forks that fastidious people were beginning to use to convey food to their mouths at mealtime instead of using their fingers like everybody else. The custom was said to have originated in Italy, like so many other queer notions. Most Spaniards maintained that the Italians must have very dirty hands if they were afraid to handle their own food. Beatriz had never seen a fork before, though she had heard rumors that they existed. Here, it seemed, one was actually employed— perhaps whoever lived in the tower was expecting a lady. She glanced at the uninviting army cot. No, hardly a lady.

A thoroughly masculine voice with tremendous authority in it said, "To what good turn of fortune am I indebted for the honor of a visit from the Señorita de Bobadilla? I was not informed that Queen Juana had changed her standing order."

Beatriz wheeled about; her skirts billowed out like a dancer's with the speed of her sudden, frightened motion, and brushed the velvetshod legs of the man who was standing so close that she had felt his breath on her neck when he spoke.

"I thought I was alone," she gasped.

"And I thought I was," he answered, bowing formally, not too low. "How pleasant to have in common that we are both wrong." He was big and dark, with a student's face that was curiously at variance with his capable soldierly hands; and his hands seemed at variance with themselves, since they were clean as a monk's and there was an ink spot on the right one. Beatriz no longer felt bored.

She dropped him a curtsey (no deeper than his bow) and smiled, "You seem to know me, señor, yet I have not the honor of knowing you; and I thought I had met all the men in the castle."

"I am Andrés de Cabrera," he said.

"You, the governor of this alcazar?"

"Who places himself at your service, Señorita de Bobadilla."

"But—but I assumed the governor was ill, since I never saw him in the great hall at supper."

He paused. Perhaps he was a woman-hater and resented the influx of queens, infantas and high-born ladies in waiting into his castle. Yet he did not look like a woman-hater; it seemed to Beatriz that he was eyeing her with exceptional appreciation, and she was used to being eyed appreciatively. She lowered her glance; she was not returning the usual look with her usual lack of interest. "I am perfectly well, señorita. Not ill at all."

"And I supposed you would be a much older man," she said. "My father is governor of an alcazar. At Arevalo."

"I know. Don Pedro de Bobadilla is honored in his charge and in his daughter."

Beatriz said inquisitively, "The castle of Don Andrés de Cabrera is far handsomer, and Don Andrés' daughter, if he has one, must be so too."

"I suppose I shall never know till I have one, señorita, and I shall never have one till I have a wife." He smiled slightly. "It has been a pleasure to answer your personal questions."

Beatriz colored. "I didn't mean to pry, truly I didn't. I was interested. Are you dismissing me?"

"The queen will be furious. You shouldn't come here. Old Sanchez at the door is a gossipy soul; he will tell everybody how a girl overcame him, first with a word, then with a frontal charge that pinned him against the wall."

Beatriz' color deepened. "You heard what I said?"

"Alas—" the governor grinned—"I did, señorita."

"He made me so angry. I'm terribly ashamed. But how did you hear?"

He crooked his ink-stained finger. "Come. I'll show you."

He led her to a place where the wall of the apartment curved outward; here the floor was built to overhang the outer wall of the tower. A trapdoor in the floor was open. The sheer, clear, unobstructed drop was sixty feet. Beatriz was familiar with the common machicolation of castles, which enabled the defenders to pour boiling oil and molten lead on the heads of attackers, and had recognized the iron cauldrons in which the deathly rain was heated; but she had never seen such a big drop-hole as this.

"Since it is just above the main gate of the keep, it has to be big," Cabrera explained. "I often open it to get a little fresh air on these hot days; I happened to see you vanquish my guard."

"Do you always live in the tower?"

"I have the honor of making my usual quarters available to the Infanta, and to you."

Beatriz approached the gaping hole and peered down. Cabrera caught her firmly by the arm and steadied her. "Careful now!" He spoke sharply as to a mischievous child.

Beatriz let him draw her away. "I'm terrified of heights," she admitted, "but I wanted to see."

"I'd better close it," he said. "If there should be an accident I might just as well throw myself down after you."

To anyone else Beatriz would have quipped, "Would you care if I fell?" but she did not feel like bantering and flirting with the governor, whose clean-chiseled features were grim. Obviously, his solicitude was based on something serious.

"I do not understand, Don Andrés."

"If King Alfonso wins the war he will hang me for not taking care of his sister's dearest friend. If King Henry wins he will hang me for letting an enemy spy on his treasure house. And there you have it, señorita. Your presence here is embarrassing, though I find that I do not wish to dismiss you."

"I shall go at once, Don Andrés."

The governor said, "I closed the trapdoor, didn't I? Must you go?"

"I shouldn't even have come. I knew Queen Juana's orders, but I was irritable and bored and angry at being a prisoner."

"I thank God you did come," he said.

"Anyhow, I'll be late for supper if I stay."

He did not answer.

"Why does the governor of the castle never eat with the queen, Don Andrés?"

He hesitated. Then, "Let me show you the portrait of my father, señorita." He took her to one of the paintings that hung against the rough stone wall of the apartment. It was superbly to the life, the almost speaking image of an elderly Castilian grandee wearing the ministerial chain of office, but with the long untrimmed beard of an Old Testament patriarch. Over his shoulders was draped the tallith, with its long blue fringe, the mantle worn by the Jew at prayer from the time of the Wilderness.

"He was a minister of finance to the late King Juan during the last reign," Cabrera said. "He died before I was born and my mother, a Christian, brought me up in the true faith. But Queen Juana insists that I am a Jew, and Queen Juana, of course, does not eat with Jews." His voice was icily correct.

It was a new theory to Beatriz. "But blood doesn't make you a Jew." She was suddenly afraid that Isabella might think it would. "Blood doesn't make you anything. Almost everybody, even the Marques of Villena, has Jewish blood in him if you go back far enough."

"I suspect there's a lot of Moorish blood among some of our great families, too, especially in the south. It would be remarkable if there were not, after their seven hundred years' sojourn in Spain. As for me, my Christianity does not, perhaps, go back far enough to satisfy the queen."

It was enough to satisfy Beatriz de Bobadilla; she said as much with her usual forthrightness. Don Andrés flushed beet-red with gratitude. He grasped her hand and kissed it. "Mi señorita, I kiss your hand—"

She did not withdraw it though his kiss was far from the casual brush of the lips that courtesy dictated. It was warm as an embrace; she felt the warmth in her own lips.

"—and if I were not an extremely self-disciplined man," he added with a smile, "I would kiss your feet also, thus acting out in very truth, 'Os beso las manos y los pies.'"

Beatriz had never thought of anyone actually doing it, "It is a strange and foolish expression," she said. "But very nice."

"Once it was very accurate, señorita. It came from the Moors, like so much, both good and bad: for Moorish slaves still kiss their masters' hands and feet."

Beatriz said, "I do not know; I am not a student, señor governor," and touched the inkstain on his hand, smiling. The little gesture gave her an opportunity to disengage their hands; Andrés de Cabrera, apparently, was disposed to hold hers through the supper hour.

"Oh, the ink." He laughed. "Besides guarding King Henry's treasure I must also make a weekly accounting of it, though he never asks to see my books. As I say, I am an extremely self-disciplined man."

"I shouldn't suppose there'd be much left," Beatriz said. "The way he lives, and the amounts he squanders."

The governor looked at her oddly. "You would make a most beautiful and dangerous spy, señorita."

"By God's truth," she replied, "it is nothing to me whether King Henry has one maravedí or a hundred million! I have lived at his court and seen how prodigal he is, and how stupidly he manages, and I spoke my mind as I always do. I do not care a fig if the coffers behind those chained doors are empty or full."

"Yes," said the governor, "that's where he keeps it."

"I wasn't asking."

"But I don't mind telling, since no one but the king shall ever enter as long as the governor of this castle lives."

"Don Andrés, Don Andrés, I am not a spy. I should not have entered the keep at all except that I was weary with endless confinement and worried for Isabella, who grows paler and sadder every day. Though she never complains. Is she never to be released? I care nothing for myself."

The governor said, "I would ten thousand times rather release her than you."

"I would ten thousand times rather you did, Don Andrés."

"For love of the princess, your friend?"

He was asking too much, too soon. Yet it was a measure of his loneliness, despite his great office.

"Will it suffice if I answer, 'For love of a friend'?"

"God bless you for that, señorita!" It would suffice. For the time being.

They walked down the stairs of the castle keep, which this time seemed to Beatriz only one story high, Don Andrés holding her arm and walking on the outside close to the dizzy drop of the unrailed steps. "Have a care!" she warned, drawing him closer to her, away from the peril.

The governor said, "I would they had built them narrower."

At the lowest level where the door of the tunnel, golden in the light of the sinking sun, grew larger as they approached, he said, "Shall I see you again, Beatriz?"

The dropping of the formal "señorita" was unexpected, but not unpleasant. "Not in the tower, Don Andrés. I might steal."

"You have already stolen, Beatriz: stolen something that neither King Henry nor I can command."

"It is very late, mi amigo."

He did not quicken his slow deliberate step, yet he was thinking at a furious pace. "No, not in the tower. I will not permit you to visit the sleeping quarters of a man."

Proprietary already? Beatriz wondered. But it was how a good man ought to feel, unless he meant to toy with her.

"I sometimes pray Matins in the chapel," he said. "Queen Juana seldom prays at all, and never at midnight. I can feel at ease at my devotions when her scornful eyes are not hurling 'Jew' at me."

At the door of the keep old Sanchez' cuirass clanked again against the battlement, this time because he stepped back in astonishment when Beatriz and the governor came out, her hand resting familiarly on his arm like a lady with her lord.

"The Señorita de Bobadilla lost her way," said Cabrera sternly, "and entered the keep by mistake."

The guard's face leered with gross and eloquent understanding,

"Keep a civil tongue in your head!" snapped the governor.

"But I didn't say nothing, governor, nothing at all!"

"See that you don't, if you expect to keep your post."

"Si, si, señor gobernador! 'Fore God, not a word."

"You quieted *him*" Beatriz whispered.

"Oh no," Don Andrés said simply. "You can never quiet

a gossip. But now his gossip will be the truth."

"The truth?"

"He will say that I love you with all my heart and soul."

"He will?"

"He will say that I want Beatriz de Bobadilla to be my wife."

"Your wife?"

"He will have us married in a week."

"Oh no, Don Andrés, please not in a week. Not so soon. Isabella would be scandalized."

"I count it no treason to my king to reveal that Princess Isabella will not be a guest in this castle a week from today."

Now it happened, as a matter of course so natural as to be inevitable, that Isabella also prayed Matins occasionally. She, whose father had died when she was only two, whose mother's understanding had withered before she entered her teens, had learned early to pray. There was no one else to hear. And God, who was close to all Spaniards, seemed especially close and near to the Castilian Infanta. To Him she had taken her little troubles when she was little. With her growth had grown her faith, and now that she was no longer little the habit of prayer was strong and the comfort of prayer was great in the greater troubles that she sensed—she did not yet know for certain—were pressing against the castle walls from the outside world of men and war. There had been a flurry of galloping couriers in the past few days. Queen Juana was distant and secretive. Beatriz had been alternately radiant and morose, and extremely uncommunicative, for Beatriz. Even the weather was wrong.

On a night that should have been crisp and cool, but when a dank unseasonable mist hung over the battlements, shutting off the view of the mountains, imprisoning the stale smells of kitchens and stables like a miasma, she rose from her bed and slipped into her dress and went to the chapel to pray. She tiptoed out of the room, not wishing to wake Beatriz. At the door of the chapel she paused. Beatriz and the governor were kneeling side by side. Her hand was on his arm and they were conversing, their faces very close, in an undertone that was soft, earnest and full of understanding.

The perplexing thing was not that a young man and woman should meet in a church. People met often in churches when services were not being offered, to gossip, to rest, or merely to pass the time of day and munch nuts and sweetmeats in one another's company. Even plays were put on in churches with costumes, scenery and musical accompaniment, to great groanings from the spectators when the saint actor was in peril and unrestrained whoops of applause when the sinner actor fell into the smoking jaws of the monstrous scenic devil while thunders of hell beat out from the biggest drum that could be procured in the village. No, the perplexing thing was not the meeting, since the governor, self-effacing though he was, was a man and would inevitably be attracted to Beatriz. The perplexing thing was why a man in his position, whose attention would be a favor, had been at such pains to be secretive. This looked like an assignation of a pair of guilty lovers.

Isabella walked back to her apartment, frowning. Beatriz needed a talking to, and if Beatriz would not listen she decided to speak to the governor himself.

Shortly Beatriz tiptoed in, her face rosy, her shoes in her hand, to find the candles lit and Isabella looking at her reproachfully, with the blue-green lightnings asmoulder in her eyes and ready to blaze.

"*Maria Santísima!* I thought you were asleep," Beatriz said.

"I am not."

"But you *were* asleep, and now you are dressed."

"One dresses to go to the chapel to pray."

"Did-did you *go?*"

"Yes. And I came back."

Beatriz sat down miserably on her bed, bright tears brimming in her black eyes. "Alas, then you saw us. How dreadful it must have looked. But he is the governor, vuestra alteza." She almost never called Isabella *Your Highness.*

"I know el señor Gobernador Don Andrés de Cabrera by sight. Since he has never had the courtesy to present himself, not even in his capacity as my jailor, I have not desired to know him better."

"Oh, but I know him so well. Please believe me; he is the dearest, most chivalrous of men."

"I could see that you thought him dear; chivalrous he is not."

Now the big bright tears welled over the long lashes and traced two sad little courses that glistened wet in the candlelight on Beatriz' cheeks, from which all the color was suddenly gone. She was pale with something deeper than guilt, which Beatriz might have brazened out.

"I love him so much," she sobbed. "He wants to marry me; I yearn to marry him."

Isabella softened. Marriage was an entirely different matter. "Then why in the world be so furtive? Must you always create the wrong impression?"

"I was afraid of what you would think."

Isabella put her arm around her shoulders and hugged her affectionately. "Dear friend, have I ever said I did not wish you to marry, close as you are to me, much as I love you? I am not a sovereign or a parent; I cannot command you. I would not if I could. Did you suppose perhaps that I would accuse you of deserting me by marrying my jailor?"

"I was just afraid of what you would think."

"Nothing could make me happier than your happy marriage. But not to this handsome mysterious governor, who tempts a lady into a holy place for a secret meeting. No, no Beatriz; not to him. He is hiding some secret guilt or he would declare his love in the full light of day, not hide it in a shadowy chapel at midnight."

Beatriz said spiritedly, "His guilty secret is only that he wishes to stay away from Queen Juana, who calls him a

Jew."

Isabella said soberly, "Is he a Jew?"

"Queen Juana says so. His father was a Jew."

"No, no, not his father, not his mother. Is *he* a Jew?"

"His mother was a Christian all her life, and Andrés was baptized when he was three days old. She raised him in the true faith, and Andrés has never swerved from it. I love him, and I know."

Isabella said, "Why then, you silly goose, he isn't a Jew!"

"Queen Juana says he is because his father was, and his forefathers before him. She says it's in the blood, and so she will not eat with him."

Isabella could laugh gaily when things made no sense to her. "She's worse than Fray Torquemada. The worst he ever said was "They never change, even when they pretend to, ' and that was when he was teaching Alfonso and me to beware of converts who convert only for gain and prestige, 'crypto-Jews' he called them, who secretly practice their wicked religion. That makes them hypocrites, liars, lapsed heretics, subject to the laws; there is nothing worse than a liar. But Jews who staunchly remain Jews are not punished."

Beatriz said, "The queen is scornful, Andrés is sensitive—and I didn't know how you felt about these things. Some people think like Queen Juana."

Isabella laughed again. "What a senseless world it would be if everybody thought like her! Blood and forefathers, indeed! What a mixture they make us! I have Plantagenet blood; does that make me English? I have Capetian blood; does that make me French? My forefather Louis IX of France is a canonized saint; does that make me a saint? My great-great-grandfather Henry of Trastamara was a bastard; does that make me a bastard? No, no, Beatriz, we are what *we* are. Andrés de Cabrera is not a Jew just because his poor father was."

Beatriz said, "I think that you are an angel," and Isabella

felt her hand suddenly grasped, kissed impulsively and wet with tears.

Beatriz' outbursts of emotion sometimes embarrassed Isabella; she rose and patted her friend's hair, which was tousled and mussed by now. "Go to sleep, Beatriz. I shall pray to God to bless you and your love."

But Beatriz had another fear and did not go to sleep immediately. Not all of the whispered conversation in the chapel between her and the governor had been about themselves, she said. Some of it had concerned the bitter water from the castle well.

"I told Andrés that you did not like the water here and asked if there were not some light wine in the cellars that would be more palatable."

"The queen has been pressing wine on me, too, Beatriz."

"I told him that. He grew very thoughtful."

"She always did, of course, but more so lately than usual, it has seemed. I had tried to hide my dislike of the water, but she must have guessed. But any water is better than the strong vintages she drinks. If the governor has some light wine I'll be thankful for it."

Beatriz looked at her oddly. "He doesn't want you to drink wine; he was quite positive; he virtually forbade it."

"Forbade it?"

"And to me, too."

Isabella smiled. "It is a small matter to me, but it will be amusing to see you, Beatriz, on a diet of water!"

"I'm afraid it is more than a small matter, Isabella. Andrés is King Henry's man—alas, I cannot change his stubborn loyalty—but he muttered something about not wanting a dead bride and a dead princess on his hands when the army comes. That is all he would say, and I think he was sorry for saying even that much. Then he said he would have fresh water from the aqueduct in the city delivered every day for our use. 'And see that you drink nothing else!' he said."

Isabella thought of her brother, thought of the dead dog. It is difficult to poison water; it is relatively simple to put a massive dose of poison into heavy wine, which hides its color and blankets its taste.

The governor had not identified which army was marching on Segovia, but there was no need to. Patently it was not friendly to Queen Juana or it would never have driven her to renewal of such desperate expedients. The mystery of the recent spate of couriers was now clear.

In Avila the boy king Alfonso had given Archbishop Carrillo no rest, pestering him night and day, first begging and finally commanding that they march forthwith to liberate his sister.

"Little Highness," Carrillo replied, "learn that you cannot spur a starveling horse. Money is coming in every day; the Grand Rabbi has already contributed; Ferdinand of Aragón makes great promises, but is slow in delivery as usual; and Isaac Abrabanel has made a token payment. The money will come, lad, the money will come. But these things take time."

"Your Reverence, my time is running out."

Alfonso's eyes were feverishly bright, though Carrillo's physician said he had no fever and diagnosed his complaint as a humoral imbalance, where the element of heat had gained ascendancy over the element of cold, as often happens in young men. This condition was aggravated by the unseasonably hot and humid weather, by certain malign planetary configurations and by the patient's understandable anxiety over his sister.

Copious bleeding had done no good, however. The physician then suggested twice-daily bleeding. Carrillo would not permit that. On which the physician clucked his tongue and shook his head and declared, "Since Your Reverence cannot see your way clear to avail yourself of my science, no one can say how soon His Highness will be in need of Your Reverence's prayers," and withdrew with a grave face.

Alarmed by the physician's disclaimer, Carrillo permitted the double bleeding, but Alfonso, already frail, now grew so pale of cheek that at length he forbade any bleeding at all.

Carrillo was equally alarmed by Alfonso's remark, "My time is running out," which might mean so much. Carrillo was always disturbed by mystical remarks that seemed to foretell the future, since one never could tell whether they stemmed from a sickness or from the angels. Both were extremely disconcerting to a practical man. At such times the archbishop became most at ease when he girt on his sword and mounted his favorite black charger and threw himself into action.

"You will never be satisfied till we march," he grumbled, "so march we shall. It will be better than broodings and bleedings. But *ojalá,* that I had ten thousand men and some siege guns!" Yet he bore in mind that all the money King Henry had was locked up in Segovia's alcazar, and he tried to persuade himself that the burning in King Alfonso's eyes came from the angels.

To Cabrera's disgust the city of Segovia offered no resistance to the army. He said some hard things to Beatriz about Torquemada, the prior of Santa Cruz, who went out of his monastery in full ecclesiastical procession with his monks and preached a sermon in the public square, forbidding the shedding of Christian blood.

Isabella sighed, "Since this is war and, worse, a civil war, I suppose that for once good Fray Tomás does not know where his duty lies and will not take sides. Nothing is black and white in politics."

They saw the army advance and camp within bowshot of the castle walls. From the battlements Isabella could make out the features of her brother as he stood before his tent, over which flew the black castle of Castile and the red lion of León, and the figure of the archbishop before a tent flying the banner with a great green cross.

The governor glowered. "They have no guns. I have.

They are mad."

"Por Dios, if you fire," Beatriz threatened, "I swear that I will—"

"Knife me, thou tigress?" He smiled. "I have heard about your knife. Or push me over the wall, like old Sanchez?"

Beatriz sobbed into her handkerchief. "I never knifed anybody, and I didn't push Sanchez over the wall. But I swear I will never marry you if you fire."

"My mission is to defend the king's treasure, not to attack. But if they attack me I will fire. I do not think they will. These walls are proof against a force twice the size of this."

"Does it pose no danger at all to the castle?"

"None at all, my dear."

"But wouldn't it be very uncomfortable living here during a siege?"

"Oh probably. There would be shortage of food in time, minor danger from falling arrows, catapult missiles crashing down once in a while, crossbow bolts making it awkward on the walls, all the usual things."

"Will there be casualties?"

"There are bound to be a few, but I'll take care of you."

"I wasn't thinking of myself. I was only afraid you might represent this formidable force to the queen as absolutely harmless. As I see it, there are going to be wounds, death and intolerable inconveniences. You are an honorable man; you never lie. Even Isabella admires your fidelity to King Henry, though he is against her. Can you truthfully tell Queen Juana that she is in no danger?"

Cabrera exploded with laughter. "Dear girl, you are not only a tigress, you are a diplomat. I had already decided what to do with the princess, and the lukewarm temper of the city proves that I was right. Now I know what to do with the queen—and glad I shall be to be rid of the smell of her. Beatriz, my beautiful diplomat, this force looks more formidable to me every minute! There will be a parley; there always is. Then I shall give Queen Juana my shuddering estimate of this mighty host."

There was a parley on neutral ground just outside the gate of the alcazar, since none of the principals would put themselves in the power of the others for fear of being held hostage. Alfonso, as king, demanded the instant surrender of the fortress and an oath of homage from his vassal the governor. The governor demanded the instant dismissal of the rebel army and oaths of homage to King Henry. But these were mere civilities, the traditional showing of feudal teeth in accordance with custom which nobody took seriously. With expressions of mutual esteem and protestations of their own invincibility they withdrew, agreeing to meet again on the morrow. Then, the amenities over, the real haggling would begin.

During the night Andrés de Cabrera sought audience with the queen and reported with perfect honesty that the rebels had marched without opposition through the city of Segovia, up to the very citadel. True, the castle was strong, but it was not provisioned for a prolonged siege and no one knew when, if ever, King Henry would march to its relief. Meanwhile the townspeople were apathetic; no aid could be expected from that source. And he did not minimize the element of personal danger to which everyone in the castle would be subjected when the stones and javelins began to fly. He could promise her security only in quarters deep underground at the bottom of the keep, and he told her that vinegar was already boiling in the kitchens to kill the lice and chase out the rats.

Queen Juana's reaction was quick. She saw herself deprived of light, air, freedom of motion and entertainment, doomed to an indefinite stay in a damp, unwholesome dungeon like a criminal. The prospect stifled her. Knowing her husband she did not count on a speedy release.

She flew into a tantrum, abusing the governor, cursing Alfonso, spitting obscenities against King Henry; and ended by sobbing violently, soiling her handkerchief with dark eye cosmetic, demanding some means of escape.

"An escort of soldiers would be suspect, Your Highness. We are surrounded. But I can arrange for the cart of the water carriers to take you through the lines. In a day you will rejoin your husband, in the safety of Valladolid, surrounded by his loyal caballeros, the Marqués of Villena, the valiant Don Beltran de la Cueva, and all the rest."

Queen Juana eyed him malevolently, wondering if he had known how strongly the mention of Don Beltran, from whom she had been separated so long, would weigh with her. But the governor's handsome features remained perfectly bland and respectful.

That night the water carriers' cart carried an unaccustomed burden back to the city and beyond the mountains, away from the sore spot of war.

Next day the parley was renewed in earnest. The archbishop was disposed to demand at least expenses for his forces; Cabrera refused him a single maravedí. "That is one subject I will not discuss with Your Reverence; my cannon will speak for me." King Alfonso's demands were moderate in the extreme: he demanded only the person of his sister and her friend.

"In the absence of the Queen," the Governor smiled, "who did not take the princess with her when she suddenly decided to go elsewhere, I do not consider that I am under orders to keep Doña Isabella in custody."

Carrillo shouted, "Queen Juana is gone? Santiago, but I wanted her."

"I conceive it my mission, Your Reverence, to guard the king's treasure," the Governor said with elegant sarcasm.

"King's treasure, forsooth!" the archbishop grumbled. "Don Beltran's!"

"Someone's, assuredly. In any case, she is gone."

Carrillo knew he could not have got her anyhow.

"I am impatient to return," Alfonso said. "When will my

sister and Beatriz be released?"

"Her Highness is at liberty to depart at any time. As for the Señorita de Bobadilla—perhaps you had better ask her. I should like her to remain."

"Oh no, none of that," the archbishop thundered. "No hostages, Don Andrés."

But Alfonso had caught the softness in the governor's tone.

"Wait a moment, Your Reverence." He smiled.

The governor said, "Doña Beatriz has done me the honor to consent to become my wife. It would not be proper for her to leave after that."

Statesmanlike thoughts went racing through Archbishop Carrillo's mind. Here was a heaven-sent opportunity to install permanently the best friend Isabella had squarely in the house of the king's able and honest treasurer, where she would influence him and win him softly over to the right side in a languid civil war. Had he schemed and brought to pass such a maneuver it would have been a feat of national significance. But God, and young hearts, had accomplished it in that mysterious manner which works so slyly for good where it is least expected, confounding the devious wisdom of diplomats and glorifying history with its thousand unlikelihoods that cynics can never quite believe.

Carrillo was astonished and delighted, but he could hardly believe it himself. Somehow he must make sure that Cabrera meant what he said, that he was not, after all, deceiving her with promises and actually holding her hostage.

"Señor gobernador," he declared, offering his hand, "let me congratulate you. I should be happy to officiate at the union of this good girl with a man of your integrity. I am prepared to do so at once."

Cabrera, overwhelmed, knelt and kissed the archiepiscopal ring. "That the Primate of Spain should so honor me, whose father was a Jew!"

"Tut, tut, man. The fathers of half the Holy Apostles were

Jews." The banns, the triple announcements in churches, all the delays that ordinary people experienced before they could marry, Carrillo dispensed and swept away with a wave of his hand. He married the daughter of the governor of the alcazar at Arevalo to the governor of the alcazar at Segovia that same day; and that same day the rebel army decamped, with Isabella and King Alfonso, brother and sister, reunited.

The reunion was short-lived. Despite all the efforts of the best physicians in Castile, despite renewed bleedings doubled and redoubled, despite huge draughts of bulls' blood, despite infusions of bezoar from the gut of goats, despite elixir of unicorn's horn, despite blistering poultices applied to his flesh and chicken feathers burnt in the sickroom to purify the air, and despite the heartfelt prayers of half a sorrowing nation, King Alfonso died. He never reigned. The only crown he ever wore was tinsel, on the vega of Avila in a travesty of a coronation. In his coffin it was remarked that his hair was the same golden hue as his sister's, who kept vigil beside him in death.

There was now no prince of royal blood to lead the rebel lords.

Of one accord they turned to the stricken Isabella and offered her the crown.

CHAPTER 9

ISABELLA now found herself a figure of international importance. The memory of Joan of Arc was still fresh in the minds of the older generation of statesmen. Grave gray heads turned thoughtful in many a European chancellery at the prospect of another girl of equal piety, greater beauty and amazing personal magnetism placing herself at the head of an army, uniting a nation. Dispatches were torn open with impatient hands, and candles burned far into the night as sharp intellects scrutinized the latest news from Spain. And many statesmen, especially Louis of France, whose life work was foreign chaos, concluded that she must be murdered, married or warred against if she did in Castile what Joan of Arc had done in France. Meanwhile they watched and waited.

In Valladolid King Henry wept, and even Queen Juana, shaken by her recent flight, lost confidence. In the streets of her own capital no one cheered and many grandees of the court openly wore mourning to honor the stainless memory of the dead King Alfonso.

"I've got to appease her," King Henry said.

Queen Juana readily agreed. "You can always retract whatever you promise. The temper of the people may change." At the same time in Avila, in a scene that was painful to her followers, Isabella refused the proffered crown.

Carrillo was appalled. The Grand Admiral entreated her with tears in his eyes. The rebel grandees were dismayed.

"But your brother did not refuse!" Carrillo pleaded.

"My brother was a man, with a man's conscience, which is more complex. He did what was right for him, and I must do what is right for me. I am not a statesman. All I know is that King Henry is my father's son and received his crown in unquestioned succession from the King my father. As long as Henry lives I will not war against him."

And no grumbling of the factious lords would shake her. They learned the lesson of her deep devotion to legitimate rule, but they gained no leader in their civil war.

"It would be most unwise to tell King Henry of your weak decision," Carrillo said sternly.

"I doubt if you'd let me tell, my lord archbishop. I am always a hostage of one side or the other."

"I could wish that you were a man, *mi princesa,*" he said. "Or at least that you had a husband to make your decisions. But do not reproach me with harsh words like 'hostage'. I meant only what I said, not a jot more: it *would* be unwise, it would be disastrous for the realm, to surrender completely to Henry, who is in a position where he must compromise, even if we sue for peace, as now we must."

"Peace is my constant prayer. I could not serve the cause of peace by warring against the legitimate king. I will lead no factions."

Carrillo wavered. He thought of the temptation on the pinnacle of the temple, of the temptation in the wilderness, of the temptation on the high mountain. "Let me pray that you are guided aright and that your instinct is sound." The archbishop was gaining a new measure of the Castilian Infanta. Crowns are not easily or often rejected.

But the rightness of Isabella's decision was soon manifested in a startlingly practical manner. Not only the rebels sued for peace; King Henry also sued for peace. The couriers with invitations to the parley actually passed enroute.

The meeting was amiable, and Isabella gained more than a dozen battles would have gained her. King Henry granted general amnesty to all the rebel lords, both great and small, and their followers down to the last war-weary footsoldier.

He acknowledged her Princess of the Asturias, heiress to the double crown of Castile and León, though to do so he excluded little Beltraneja and for the second time implicitly branded his queen as an adulteress.

Isabella was present at the parley. "And I must not be

constrained in my choice of a husband, when I come to marry," she stipulated. "I must be free to choose him without interference."

Forthwith the unheard-of demand was incorporated into the treaty. Henry incontinently threw away one of the most valuable and generally accepted rights of kings, to arrange the marriage of an heir.

She asked no more. But Carrillo did. Was not the Princess of the Asturias to be maintained in a state conformable with the dignity of an heiress to the crown?

The revenues of the cities of Avila, Buete and Medina del Campo, Molina, Olmedo, Ubeda and Escalona were set aside for her. Carrillo smiled to himself. With Beatriz now mistress in the castle at Segovia that was *one* article, at least, of the treaty that would be kept to the letter.

In a splendid ceremony of investiture at Valladolid, which everyone contrasted with the sorry spectacle of her brother's coronation, rebel and loyal lords alike competed to be first to kiss her hand and swear her their oaths, while bells rang from the church towers, bonfires blazed in the streets and the common people cheered themselves hoarse for love of the princess who had brought them peace. In a gesture that Isabella disliked, but that he insisted upon as if humiliation were queerly pleasant to him, King Henry himself walked on foot leading a snow-white mule on which she rode to a luxurious residence that had been set aside for her.

Round her there gathered a sober court of all that were best in the kingdom. Even the Marqués of Villena, with his scented hair and pearl earrings, would sometimes present himself, to pay his respects and incidentally to spy out the strength of her following. It was strong; it was healthy. And he would ask himself how anybody could be cheerful, as everyone obviously was, without the fortune tellers, the palm readers, the acrobats and dancers and magicians and necromancers, the love affairs and drinking bouts and gambling games that furnished amusement in King Henry's court.

Had Isabella been ugly and old, had she been crooked in body or mind or as loose as the worst of the women that disgraced the court of the king, still she would have had suitors. For she wore a coronet and one day she would wear a crown. But the statesmen in the chancelleries of Europe found themselves confronted with a phenomenon that happens once in a century: here was a princess of unquestioned right to a throne, the throne of a great nation that was rich in natural wealth and a glorious history of valor—did not Spain still stand as a buffer state against the Moors, protecting all Europe? —the throne of the politest nation in Christendom and only now temporarily in eclipse because of a king whose weaknesses were probably mental. This once-in-a-century woman, far from being ugly and ancient, was eighteen years old and so lovely to behold that her beauty seemed a work of supererogation on the part of the angels. Nor was she soft or weak or easily tempted. With a shake of her head she had refused a crown, and brought peace where before there was civil war.

The matrimonial mills in the great European chancelleries began to grind at a furious pace. Even from faraway England there came an offer of marriage. Young Richard, the duke of York, sent an emissary asking for her hand. "My master," the emissary hinted, "is destined for greatness in England. True, there is a minor civil disturbance in my island home, but that will pass, and it is not too much to hope that one day Richard's duchess will be England's queen."

Isabella heard him out with dignity, but she did not encourage him. Everyone knew that the "minor disturbance" was the disastrous civil War of the Roses that had torn at the vitals of England for years and would probably continue for years. She warned him that the Castilian cortes, which she patiently explained was the same as the English parliament, would probably not wish the heiress of the Castilian throne to leave Castile for residence in so dangerous and distant a country as England.

King Louis XI of France also sent an emissary headed by a cardinal. He was extremely well-informed, as were all Louis's ambassadors. "This Englishman, Richard of York, is a cripple with a withered arm, Your Highness, a bloodthirsty man with a wicked heart, who will blast your personal life and involve Castile in foul and endless wars. How much more pleasing to God and my master would be a union with the Duc de Guienne, my master's brother, your good and powerful neighbor to the north of the Pyrenees. The Duc de Guienne is such a gentle man!"

She heard the French cardinal out too. There was much logic in what he said. France was the most powerful nation in Europe, so powerful that Castile might become a mere French province if she should accept. She was rather afraid of the French king, and she knew very little about the Duc de Guienne. Yet she did not flatly reject him. Indeed she could not, for Carrillo too was pressing a marriage upon her. So were the Marqués of Villena, and King Henry and Queen Juana and the Grand Admiral, though to different princes and for different reasons.

And Beatriz! Who wrote from Segovia that she was divinely happy with her Don Andrés, adding in a mixed-up happy way, "What a burden virginity is to a girl!"

Things were simple for Beatriz, who had seen her caballero face to face and married him for love. Beatriz did not have to negotiate at a distance, through foreign emissaries, for foreign princes. Once the ambassadors' missions were accomplished *their* duties were at an end, and no doubt they would be given an order or an estate for their pains. But Isabella would have to live with the prince in the terrible intimacy of marriage, to share his bed and bear his children. All her life long.

Alfonso of Portugal, older and fatter than ever, also sent an emissary, who was also a cardinal, also a persuasive advocate. "Once Your Highness thwarted my master's love, on a beautiful night at Gibraltar, by warning that King Henry was planning to pay his troops with funds from my master's generous dowry. But all that is changed now; only my master's love has not changed, Nay, if it has changed, it has changed for the better, like the dowry, since both have grown."

King Henry, Queen Juana and the Marqués of Villena strongly favored the Portuguese marriage, which would get Isabella permanently out of the kingdom and dissipate her following. For Isabella to refuse was doubly difficult: she was loath to leave her beloved Castile, yet she knew that Portuguese and Castilian Infantas often married across the border and tradition was strong with her. On more personal grounds the aging king filled her with dread, but she could not tell the cardinal that.

"Is there not some impediment in our kinship, Your Eminence? We are cousins."

The cardinal was well prepared. "No more, Your Highness, than in your kinship with your cousin Ferdinand of Aragón. True, the Church prohibits marriage within the fourth degree of kinship, but the Holy Father can always grant a dispensation."

Isabella sighed. The reigning Pope Paul had considered her brother a rebel when the civil war had set him up as a rival king in Castile; no doubt he considered her a rebel too. No doubt he would grant her a dispensation to marry Alfonso of Portugal if Portugal and King Henry asked for it. But she doubted very much if he would grant one for her to marry Ferdinand. And Ferdinand was also wooing her.

"Negotiations with Rome always take time, do they not?" Isabella asked.

"Sometimes they can be expedited," the Portuguese cardinal replied.

"Pray, do not press the matter, Your Eminence. I want everything done with decorum."

"My master has waited a long time, vuestra alteza."

In this cold and complex political game, with its distressing crosscurrents, which she had to play alone, where her love of country was involved and her body was the pawn, she envied

Beatriz. But there was a stubborn streak in Isabella. Princess or no princess, she too had a right to happiness!

Very secretly, unknown even to Carrillo, she sent her chaplain, Alonso de Coca, across the Pyrenees to Bordeaux in Guienne. There, from a distance, he observed the person whom the French emissary had described as "such a gentle man."

The chaplain's report was instructive. "The brother of the French king is a feeble effeminate prince with rheumy, watery eyes, and so languid of body that he cannot support the weight of armor like other caballeros, but goes about in a cloth-of-silver coat to simulate the same, an eccentricity which causes great amusement here in Bordeaux. His legs are spindly and bent almost to deformity." And the chaplain added with a sally of wit, "I know not what sort of man appeals to a lady's eyes, but the Duc must have found favor with one, at least, since he daily is seen in the company of his mistress, a great fat woman named Madame de Montsoreau."

On the chaplain's return Isabella sent him to Saragossa in Aragón. If one had to employ agents one had better do a good job and employ trustworthy ones.

From Segovia the chaplain reported in a vein that at first caused Isabella to smile. Good Padre de Coca must have acted in his younger days as one of those scribes who wrote letters for the vast number of illiterate persons, by no means confined to the lower classes, who occasionally found themselves required to put their thoughts on paper. Many a needy divinity student eked out his slender purse in this way, and often the missives were love letters.

"Prince Ferdinand," wrote Padre de Coca, "is in all things a most excellent caballero, straight of limb and tall of stature, with the carriage of a king. He is strong in the lists, where he disports himself whenever no serious fighting is at hand; though recently his fighting has been in deadly earnest, the Catalans being restless again. He admires all manly sports, riding and hunting indefatigably, especially wild boars; and playing at pelota, in which he greatly excels. Often, I regret to say, he relaxes by playing cards; but I hasten to add that he plays only for the skill of the game, to outwit his opponent, never to gamble. He is most cautious in the spending of money.

"He is abstemious in food and drink, the plainest of viands sufficing, and water his favorite beverage. His speech is persuasive and pleasant, and I believe that a certain harshness in his voice may come from long shouting of commands in the field. His forehead is high, his nose most nobly long, his hair crisp and wavy, reddish in hue. His eyes are blue and calm. His chin, which is clean shaven, is determined. There are no spots or sores on his skin and he bathes so frequently as to cause comment, at least once a week. But this is probably owing to his active manner of life and is in no wise effeminate.

"He is assiduous in the practice of religion, making his communion often and fasting. His father the king holds him in great affection, and he him. So do the ladies.

"In dress he is sober, in manners restrained.

"Temperate is the word for Prince Ferdinand in all things save ambition for power, which I do not conceive to be a sin in princes of our dark age when civil strife so lamentably pervades all nations.

"Were I the earthly father instead of the ghostly father to Your Highness, how I should pray for Your Highness's union with such a caballero!"

Slowly the enthusiasm of Padre de Coca communicated itself to Isabella. She read it over and over, wanting to believe every word of it. It was almost too good to be true. And how it contrasted with what she knew of her other suitors! "If Ferdinand of Aragón is half the pAragón painted by my chaplain's pen, which almost seems bewitched, I am blessed above all other princesses!"

Archbishop Carrillo and the Grand Admiral, Ferdinand's grandfather, had long favored Ferdinand, stressing the benefits that would accrue to both kingdoms if Castile and Aragón should unite, as they would when Henry the Impotent and old King John of Aragón should die. On their deaths Isabella would succeed to the crown of Castile, Ferdinand to the crown of Aragón. But there would be one throne, one kingdom, *Spain!* Their children would be kings and queens of Spain. The very title rang with majesty! Politically, economically and militarily the benefits of the great territorial amalgamation were inestimable. The new Spain would rival France in organic unity and power.

Now, to the great delight of Carrillo and the Grand Admiral, Isabella told them she would accept Ferdinand. At once they drew up the complicated marriage contract that tradition required when royalty married. It was a marvel of statecraft, very long and full of checks and balances, since it had to protect and delimit the rights of both countries, lest Castile think itself subject to Aragón or Aragón to Castile.

Then Isabella forthrightly made public her decision.

Immediately everything went wrong.

King Louis of France, who abhorred unity anywhere but in his own realm, quickly sent money and soldiers to aid the rebel Catalans in Aragón. "That will keep young Ferdinand out of the marriage bed for a while, and, with luck, get him killed in battle!"

King Henry, strengthened by the interval of peace, fearful of adding all Aragón to Isabella's following and frustrated in his attempts to get her out of the kingdom, whined that Carrillo had used him ill, *ill;* Queen Juana sobbed and threatened; the Marqués of Villena called Carrillo traitor and sent soldiers to arrest him.

Caught unaware, the archbishop was forced into hiding, to try to reassemble the late rebel lords. The Grand Admiral withdrew to his own estates.

Thinking Isabella now deserted, King Henry appeared and demanded that she instantly disavow her acceptance of Ferdinand and signify to the Portuguese embassy which was still in Valladolid, that she would marry Alfonso of Portugal. She refused.

"I did not hesitate to imprison your brother," he said, "and I shall not hesitate to imprison you. In the morning my Moorish guard will have the honor to escort you to the alcazar at Madrid if you do not obey me," and he padded out in his jeweled slippers, quaking with the temerity of the ultimatum he had just screwed up courage to deliver.

She still refused, and said her prayers, and went to bed.

During the night a young nobleman, Gutierre de Cardenas, majordomo of Isabella's little court and a devoted follower, muffled to the eyes in a long black cloak, spurred out of Valladolid with the marriage contract concealed in his breast and set his horse's head toward Aragón.

In the morning the soldiers came to arrest Isabella. But they could not get through the crowds. The news had leaked out. The streets were milling with townspeople who had risen spontaneously and leaderless, seizing on any weapons that came to hand—pikes, old swords, peasant scythes, butchers' knives and meat cleavers—arming themselves in defense of the princess who had brought them peace and who had been promised by solemn treaty that she could marry anyone she chose. Isabella could scarcely believe her eyes. The amazing reaction of the people was true because she saw it happening, but it was more like a scene in a miracle play or some wildly unlikely song that the minstrels sang.

King Henry quickly countermanded the order for her arrest, and protested that he had sent the soldiers only for her protection.

But Valladolid was no longer safe. She prayed that God would speed her courier to Ferdinand, and Ferdinand back to her.

CHAPTER 10

GUTIERRE De Cardenas made his way through a countryside swarming with the king's partisans. The border between Castile and Aragón was defended by a line of grim castles; and the castles were chiefly owned by various members of the great Mendoza family, a clan traditionally loyal to the Crown, hence hostile to Isabella. Cardenas was forced to avoid the larger towns and travel by unfrequented circuitous routes, a factor that delayed him. But had he been careless or unlucky, had he been arrested and searched and the marriage contract discovered, his delay would have been longer, perhaps permanent. After Isabella's innocent declaration of her intention the Marqués of Villena, Queen Juana and, of course, King Henry the Impotent were in no mood to trifle.

Beyond the bleak and desolate region of the frontier he entered the kingdom of Aragón and descended into the fertile valley of the Ebro. Here the fierce cutting winds of the cruel Castilian upland lost much of the October chill. He sensed, though still far off, the mellowing magic of the warm blue Mediterranean Sea. No Spaniard, bred in the frigid winters and scorching summers of Old Castile, could ever pass into Aragón without sniffing the balmier breeze with suspicion, convinced in his heart that the breed of men in this land, like its climate, was made of stuff less stern than Castilians, full of soft wiles like the Aragonian weather, amiable, seductive, sensuous. Treacherous. And so thought Gutierre de Cardenas, loosening his cloak about his throat. But he was in friendly territory now; he no longer feared arrest and he took the shortest, fastest way.

He supposed himself unexpected. It was gratifying to find a welcome at Saragossa, the capital; the city gates swung open as for a visiting prince at the name of Isabella of Castile.

It was gratifying to have an officer conduct him at once to the very gates of the palace; and he reasoned that Aragón, so long and wistfully hopeful for Isabella's marriage with their crown prince, was merely at pains to be courteous to any courier of hers. A few minutes later he was to discover that he was not quite unexpected. Messengers from Carrillo and the Grand Admiral had already preceded him, from towns closer to the border.

At the palace gate a young man in court dress, obviously attached to the royal household, smiled, extended his hand and addressed him in pure Castilian, wholly free from the slightly nasal twang of the Spanish spoken by the Aragonese: "I am Francisco de Valdes, Your Excellency, to serve God, Your Excellency and your mistress, Her Highness Doña Isabella." Valdes' face had an open, friendly look and his handgrip was firm.

"I am Gutierre de Cardenas, though scarcely an Excellency," he said. "I bear a private message from Her Highness."

"Anyone from Her Highness is an Excellency, Don Gutierre. The king, Prince Ferdinand, the queen, the council, everyone is awaiting you."

"Me?"

"They supposed it would be Her Highness' major-domo. They have prayed for your safe arrival, and so have I, whom once Her Highness saved from a slavery worse than the Moors'. Would Your Excellency follow me?"

Travel-stained and weary as he was, he was conducted at once to an audience chamber; and there he was asked to sit, actually to sit, in the presence of two crowned heads and one that would wear a crown, a free and easy etiquette that would never have been countenanced in Castile, not even in the loose and irregular court of King Henry. Cardenas was ill at ease, but immensely flattered.

King John eyed him shrewdly with his keen and newly restored vision. "Isabella sent you a good man, Ferdinand.

122

Rides hard, by God. I like to see saddle sweat on a man's breeches."

"John, for goodness' sake!" the queen said. Cardenas colored up to his ears.

"Well, I do."

Ferdinand, standing behind his father's chair, said quietly, "Don Gutierre could do with a cup of wine, Father. A man gets thirsty in the saddle, and no one has given him even a moment to change and refresh himself."

"Couldn't wait to hear what he had to say, son; couldn't wait. Well, lad, out with it. Will Isabella have my boy?"

"Sir—I—I—have some papers—"

The queen sent a page scurrying off for wine. "And some fruit, Don Gutierre? A chicken?"

Was he going to be asked to eat with royalty, too?

"A cup of wine would be most welcome, madame."

"Wine for everybody!" the king said loudly, and instantly corrected himself. "Oh no, not for the prince. Never touches it."

"I think I should like to join Don Gutierre in a cup of wine, sir."

"Eh?"

"Yes."

"Then the day of miracles is still with us indeed."

The queen herself poured the wine from a glass decanter into Cardenas' goblet, which also was glass, clear as a diamond and paper thin. Aragón looked towards the East, towards Venice and the distant reaches of the Mediterranean, towards Constantinople (now so lamentably fallen to the Turks and renamed Istanbul) the city that had first taught the Venetians to make glass. The wine was native Spanish, but the glass partook of the same exotic and slightly suspicious luxuriousness that characterized the Aragonian weather.

Having honored the guest by filling his goblet, the queen gave the wine to a page, who filled the other goblets. King John downed his with hearty relish; Ferdinand sipped.

"Well?" said the king.

"Couriers from Archbishop Carrillo and the Grand Admiral have already notified us of the Infanta's publicly proclaimed decision," Ferdinand said, "as well as the other good news, namely, the regathering of the great lords whom King Henry so basely brands as rebels."

"I wanted to hear it from his own lips, Ferdinand."

"It is true, Your Highness, that Doña Isabella, my mistress, has done me the honor to permit me to act as courier for this great and good news, entrusting me with her marriage contract, drawn up in proper form by the greatest lords, lay and ecclesiastical, of Castile."

He produced it.

"She hasn't got all the greatest lords," King John said practically. "But she's got the best. Except for the Mendozas, of course."

Ferdinand held out his hand for the parchment, which King John was carefully unrolling.

"Nay, lad, not so fast. I am still the king, and my eyes are good again since that Jew surgeon of mine couched them."

"A Christian could have done as well," Ferdinand said.

"And I'd have been blind as a bat. No thank you," the king said, reading rapidly. Having scanned the long marriage contract he passed it to Ferdinand. "It looks all right. Sign it."

Ferdinand ran his eye down the long list of provisions, politely phrased, but startling in their content.

His face did not change, but he said, "Don Gutierre has ridden a great way and is very fatigued. Would it not be courteous to let him withdraw for a while?"

"I'm afraid I brought only the clothes on my back," Cardenas said. "I came alone."

"Francisco will give you a suit of mine," Ferdinand said pleasantly. "I should say you and I are about of a size."

And now he was going to wear the crown prince's clothing!

The queen raised her eyebrows a trifle at such an honor, but King John chuckled. He knew the suit would be threadbare, but it was always good to see Ferdinand's thrifty diplomacy at work: Ferdinand wanted to talk about the contract without offense to the touchy Castilian envoy. Castilians were always touchy.

At the door Francisco de Valdes whispered excitedly to Cardenas, "Let me tell you about a remarkable occurrence on the Isle of Pheasants, when the Infanta spirited me out of the service of Henry of Castile." And before he had changed into Ferdinand's doublet and hose, which were threadbare indeed, but still a prince's, Gutierre de Cardenas learned more of the courage that, even in her youth, had run so deep in Isabella.

Behind the closed door of the audience chamber Ferdinand said harshly, "This contract deprives me of all authority over my future subjects—"

"Not all, Ferdinand. Not all, by any means."

"—and all authority over my future wife!"

King John looked slyly at his queen. "As for that, thou son of my loins, you but share the fate of us all who take on the joys and responsibilities of matrimony."

"And high time, too," snapped the queen. Ferdinand shrugged it off.

"Listen," he said, quoting the document. "I must live in Castile, and not leave the realm without her permission."

"She will be the 'Queen Proprietress' of the realm. It is a usual stipulation," the king said.

"I must alienate no crown property."

"Would you want to? It will be your own property. More than my kingdoms of Aragón and Sicily combined."

"I must make no civil, military or ecclesiastical appointments without her consent."

"She will consent, lad, if they are just ones. That stipulation is full of Castilian fear. They are afraid you will replace Castilians with Aragonians in posts of honor."

"I must eject no nobles from their estates—"

"Isabella will eject them if they don't behave."

"—and try to get back all Aragonian estates now in dispute on the frontier and restore them to Castile!"

"Nay, that *is* a bad one. But who can enforce all the clauses in a marriage contract? Who has the power to, once you come to rule? Nobody!"

Ferdinand nodded. "True, true; that is most certainly true," he said softly. "I need not live up to all this."

"It's not at all a bad contract," King John said. "You undertake to war against the Moors. That you will like! And Granada will make you rich as Midas, once you take it."

"Once I take it."

"You will take it," the queen said proudly. "You will always take anything you want. You are my son."

"Mine too," King John said. "Don't forget that; I fancy I could still break a spear in the lists." And to Ferdinand, "Note that both you and Isabella will sign all ordinances—does that sound as if she wants to rule alone? Note that she provides you with an enormous revenue for your personal expenses, more than a Queen of Castile ever did before for her consort, and you needn't account for a maravedí of it to her or anyone else. That is unheard-of generosity in a Castilian."

"True, the allotment to the consort is generous. I'd never need it all; I'd use it against the Moors."

The king said, "The awkward provisions—which can always be sidestepped—are not directed against Aragón. They are merely inserted by Carrillo, a consummate statesman, to allay Castilian fears, to unite the country behind you and your princess, and to placate the nobles, especially the Mendozas, who object to your marriage. And when you come to rule," the old king said, his lifelong dream shining in his eyes, "then, *then* Spain will be one, as God meant her to be!"

Ambition alone, and confidence that the awkward

provisions could indeed be sidestepped, would have impelled Ferdinand to reach for the pen to sign. But the queen reminded him, "Don't you love her, Ferdinand? It seems to me that I have heard you express yourself at times that you did."

King John laughed. "I once heard him express himself to the effect that the Infanta has a most beautiful backside."

"John, don't be vulgar!"

"I said," said Ferdinand, "that Isabella has a most beautiful back, which she kept turned to me during an ape-on-horseback entertainment."

"Same thing," said the king.

"John, please."

"Oh very well, my dear."

"I was extremely drawn to her beauty, I have always felt love in my heart for her," Ferdinand said soberly, "though it seems many years ago, and I did not know in what direction my marital duty would lead me."

"You make it sound very dismal." The queen smiled. "It wasn't that long ago, and she's prettier than ever now."

"And your marital duty, my lad," the king said, "leads straight to her bed."

The queen lowered her eyes. Ferdinand grinned, signed, "That, sire, is no heavy duty."

"If we must speak of beds," the queen said distastefully, "let me warn you, son, that you must give up completely that *woman* of yours."

"Naturally, madame. She means nothing to me."

"I'll make provision for her somewhere," King John said amiably. "I'll send her back quietly to Italy, marry her to some nice Calabrian caballero."

"I am afraid, sire," Ferdinand said, flushing, "that she may present something of a problem for quite a while. I regret to confess—" he looked shamefacedly at his mother "—that my friend, the Duchess of Eboli, presented me with a son four days ago."

"*What!*" shouted the king.

"You treat it somewhat coolly, Ferdinand," the queen said.

"I had intended to break this news gently, little by little, to spare you the force of its shock. Unfortunately, the arrival of the Castilian courier forces me to pour it all out at once."

"Like the filth of a chamberpot from a casement pouring down on my head!" the king roared.

"Softly, softly, my husband," the queen replied. But there was no softness in her tense, low voice. Her accusing eyes were fastened directly upon the king. "Does Your Highness forget the Duke of Villahermosa?"

"That was years ago, years ago!" sputtered the king. "Times were different, and I was young. The Duke of Villahermosa is now a respectable peer, a valiant caballero, a distinguished fighter, one of the props of my throne."

"Nevertheless, he is Ferdinand's bastard half-brother, and I never said a word, John, never once."

"This is different," the king said weakly.

The queen replied, "For wives it is always the same."

"I was very young."

"So is Ferdinand. Will you acknowledge the child, Ferdinand?"

"He is mine, and I will acknowledge him."

"You are a good man," said his mother softly. "A good man can make one mistake. But do not acknowledge your bastard at once, Ferdinand. Confession is good for the soul, but it should be delayed while greater things are afoot. Isabella would not understand a thing like this just now."

King John, recovering somewhat, thundered, "Isabella is the biggest prude in Christendom, and if you blurt out this—this unfortunate little business—you will ruin forever the last best hope of union for the Spanish crowns!"

"Isabella will love, then Isabella will learn," the queen said; and this time the king heard the softness in her tone and saw, with keen eyes that thanked her, the smile on her lips as she looked at him across the room, across a lifetime of love.

"We will take care of your friend and your child," the queen said. "Very quietly. When he is older you shall acknowledge him."

"I surely did not mean to imply that my acknowledgment would come now, madame. I will do it only when I am strong in Castile. It would be most impolitic to acknowledge the infant now. And, of course, he may not live."

Her son unquestionably could treat things coolly.

It was fortunate that Ferdinand possessed a cool head. The Aragonian treasury was low. The Spider King of France was threatening the northern provinces and encouraging the Catalan rebels in the south.

"Our soldiers are busy," King John said, his brow furrowed with troubles. "I can spare you scarcely a decent guard of honor for your entry into Castile."

Ferdinand replied, "I do not plan to enter Castile at the head of a powerful escort of 'foreigners'. The future king of Castile must not come as a conqueror. Meanwhile my bride is beleaguered in her own palace at Valladolid. That first!"

He dispatched a flying herald to the Duke of Medina Sidonia in Andalusia with a signed copy of the marriage contract and an inflammatory letter ostensibly lamenting the divisions in Castile which rendered King Henry's and Isabella's following *equally powerless*. Ferdinand's letter was admirably calculated to remind Medina Sidonia that now was the time to improve his own personal fortunes. "So?" said the Duke of Medina Sidonia, swallowing the bait. "Weaker than ever in the capital? I always did like Isabella!" And he seized the opportunity to make private war on his neighbor, the Marqués of Cadiz, whom he always fought whenever the central authority was especially incompetent. Andalusia flamed up with civil strife again.

Bewildered, the Marqués of Villena and King Henry

marched south to try to put down the discord. Queen Juana with her rouge pots and wounded pride fled to the safety of Villena's alcazar at Madrid, indignant and bored with a life that was developing into one perpetual series of flights. Yet Isabella did nothing but pray! Who was fighting her battles for her?

In Saragossa Ferdinand smiled craftily. "For the moment, at least, the pressure is off Isabella. Have I not done well, my father?"

"Admirably," said the old king hesitantly, for Ferdinand had a certain twinkle in his hard blue eyes. "What is it you want? You always want something when you look like that."

"I was merely wondering, sire, whether I am properly equipped to woo so exalted a princess as the *heiress proprietress* to the double crown of Castile and León."

"It seems to me that you have pretty well demonstrated your equipment, son. That Eboli woman."

"If my mother were listening, sir, assuredly she would say, 'Do not be vulgar'. I refer to my title. You too have a double crown."

King John sighed, smiled. "Oh very well, very well. I have lived out nearly four-score years; time will claim us all in time; take what you want; no doubt you are right; if I cannot give you money or soldiers I can at least give you honors. What shall it be?"

"I should be infinitely better equipped if I wore a crown."

"Not Aragón! No lad, not that; not yet."

"Sicily, sire."

"I was afraid you would ask for Aragón. That would be too soon. I am not yet in my grave."

"Your Highness is in the golden prime of life; and if my prayers can aught avail before the throne of heaven, Your Highness shall sit secure on your own for many years to come."

"If I had your tongue I should not be beset by enemies in my old age. Take it, Ferdinand. Take the crown of Sicily It is ancient and honored; honor it always. It is also a bit precarious."

"I will honor it! And I will secure it!"

"Take it, take it!"

The great chancelleries of Europe soon learned and noted with quickening interest that Ferdinand of Aragón was suddenly a king, a young man to be taken seriously, crowned with the crown of Sicily, a diadem refulgent with bloody glory won in the Crusades and one that still could be formidable.

There remained the irritating factor of Isabella's tender conscience. "She refused the King of Portugal on grounds of kinship," Gutierre de Cardenas had said. "She fears a protracted delay from the Roman court before a dispensation can be procured to marry Prince Ferdinand, who is also a close relative."

"Does she now!" King John said pleasantly. "Put such fears out of your mind, Don Gutierre. All that was taken care of long since."

"Was it?" Ferdinand asked.

"Do you doubt me, your own father?" King John demanded.

"In nothing, sire." Ferdinand smiled. But this, he thought silently, should prove instructive.

"Then do not doubt me now. Once married, if I may so express myself, knowing my son, the damage will be done and no power under heaven would separate husband and wife. The world will be confronted with a *fait accompli*. All will give way before it; Aragón and Castile will be one flesh and one kingdom. Henry and Henry's faction will wither like a frostbitten flower."

Cardenas said, "She will never marry without the blessing of the Church."

131

"Nor will she have to," King John said.

It seemed to Cardenas next morning that things could happen with astonishing swiftness in Aragón. With every outward manifestation of reverence King John produced a scroll of parchment that swept away in the twinkling of an eye all impediment to the projected marriage: it was a bull of dispensation signed by the supreme authority of Christendom, the Pope, permitting Ferdinand of Aragón to marry *anyone* related to him within the fourth degree of kinship. The document was convincing to Cardenas, not only because few monarchs would have the effrontery to forge a communication from the Holy See but also because the leaden seals were almost impossible to counterfeit.

King John said plausibly, "One of the great difficulties among us royal families is that we are all very closely related. I took the precaution some years ago of procuring a dispensation for just such a contingency as has now arisen. An angel must have guided me!"

Ferdinand's face was gravely expressionless. If he was smiling inwardly nothing showed on the surface. The seals were unquestionably genuine; but then, many papal bulls came from Rome. It would not be impossible to transfer them from one piece of parchment to another.

"You will note," King John said, "that there is a blank space for the name of the bride. Candidly I avow, though my son and I have never considered anyone seriously except Isabella, that there just might have arisen a situation—had she died, which all the saints forbid!—where Prince Ferdinand might have had to marry another princess. But another princess too, as I mentioned, would very likely fall within the prohibited degree of relationship. Do you follow me, Don Gutierre?"

"Perfectly, Your Highness."

"Nay, you look skeptical!"

"Your Highness, I protest—"

132

"Perhaps you think we plan to use this bull more than once!" With a firm hand he penned in the name, *Isabella of Trastamara, Infanta of Castile.* "The ink is ineradicable, Don Gutierre," he said accusingly.

It was not only ineradicable. Ferdinand noted that it exactly matched the ink of the Holy Roman Chancery, a remarkable coincidence.

"Your Highness, such an unworthy suspicion never crossed my mind!"

"Then you will not be surprised that the Holy Father who signed this bull is not Paul II now gloriously reigning in Rome but the late pontiff of blessed memory, Pope Pius II."

Cardenas crossed himself. "I am not skeptical, Your Highness. It would of necessity be the late Pope Pius, since Your Highness received it some years ago."

It would indeed of necessity be Pius, Ferdinand knew. The present Pope favored King Henry!

"If anyone dared to be skeptical," Cardenas said, anxious to clear himself, "the seal of the late pontiff alone would be convincing, to say nothing of the blank space reserved for the lady's name and the well-known Chancery Script in which the bull is written."

"Ha! You noticed that? That shows you are a scholar as well as a gentleman. A wonderful invention of the sainted Eugenius IV, this Chancery Script!"

Cardenas had not known that it was Eugenius IV who had substituted a swift new cursive hand beautifully legible for the stiff old-fashioned Gothic in the diplomatic correspondence of the Holy See. Ferdinand suspected that his father had not known it yesterday.

King John carefully sprinkled fine white sand over Isabella's name, to dry the ink and keep it from blotting when the scroll was rolled again. He turned to Ferdinand, addressing him first by the royal title to which he was now entitled as King of Sicily. "I have done what I could to smooth Your Highness's way, to Castile and to your bride."

133

Then, embracing him affectionately, "God bless you and keep you, dear son, till we meet again—if we do. Fare safely, fare swiftly, farewell. And beware of Mendoza castles!"

Ferdinand said thoughtfully, "I have been thinking about that."

That night there rode out of Saragossa not one but two parties of horsemen. The first, which took the fastest, shortest route, leading straight through the principal cities, was a group of nondescript merchants with cheap kitchenware rattling in shoddy chests strapped to the backs of mangy, spavined nags. The other, which rode on richly caparisoned mounts, wore the dress of noble caballeros and went by cowpaths and byways and obscure circuitous routes, especially in the vicinity of the Mendoza castles, which Ferdinand would logically be expected to avoid, thus making themselves only the more conspicuous to any of King Henry's spies who might be lurking on the frontier on the lookout for the unwelcome prince.

Indeed, the leader of this handsome band still wore Prince Ferdinand's doublet and hose.

CHAPTER 11

THE sleepy guards on the Castilian frontier, whose duty it was to watch for smuggled Eastern treasures—for pepper and purple dye, for ivory and coffee and jade—peered into the traveling chests of the Aragonese merchants and languidly let them pass, A few cheap pots and pans were not worth haggling over, even for a bribe. "I do not see why one must travel at night to trade *this* trash," the guard said.

The leader of the merchant group said, "We need the daylight hours for selling. These days it's hard enough to scrape up a few maravedíes for food, let alone drink."

"God's truth," the guard agreed.

The servant who was leading the horses across the border said, "Señor guard, the inns are much cheaper at night when no further travelers are expected."

"Speak when you're spoken to!" the senior merchant said roughly.

"I beg your worship's pardon," the servant said humbly. He realized at once that he should not have spoken; the habit of command is hard to break.

The guard waved them on, with a parting sour word, "You could teach that apprentice of yours some decent manners."

Out of earshot the senior merchant said, "A thousand pardons, Your Highness. You simply don't sound like an apprentice when you talk. I was afraid he would look into the chests."

Ferdinand said severely, "I was afraid you were going to give him a gratuity. As for the chests, he was far too sleepy to look for the double bottom." On further reflection, a little later, he admitted, "No, Francisco, you were right, I should have held my tongue even if you had parted with a coin."

They pushed on at a steady pace, not sparing the horses.

Spavin is not a fatal disease in horses; it is not a disease at all; it is the gnarled remains of old straining, showing itself in bony excrescences on the shanks of the beasts, rendering them wondrously ugly and worthless for sale, but by no means incapacitating them. And these were carefully chosen, well-fed and rested for the journey.

"With luck we'll reach Osma tonight," Valdes said.

The night was cold and clear; the stars were close, and a biting wind cut across the high Castilian plateau. In the starlight the region was wild and rough, sparsely dotted with rock-strewn peasant farms. But there was a crystalline quality in the atmosphere that exhilarated Ferdinand, even though it nipped at his bones: this was the stern hard land, tierra de cantos y santos, the land of stones and saints, where nothing came in half-measure.

This was the land where Valdes and Cardenas had been born: Valdes, whom Isabella had smuggled out of King Henry's service, but who now was guiding him back into King Henry's kingdom, where assuredly King Henry would find an excuse to clap him into a dungeon, if nothing worse. And Cardenas, whom he had planned to trick into wearing his princely apparel—and had not had to. When Cardenas learned he was to head a decoy group of caballeros, he himself had made the suggestion, laughing gaily as if the dangerous impersonation merely added zest to the adventure. He had said, "I shall act in every way as I think Your Highness would act, except that I shall run away if we are attacked, and thus lead them further astray!" Ferdinand's own mind was practical and analytic; it disturbed him not to be able to define with precision the quality in Isabella that evoked such devotion. One should know one's wife, to know how to handle her. What made her followers love her so? Not beauty alone. The Duchess of Eboli was extremely beautiful, and he did not love her very much; never did really, though she had been pleasant company on that flying trip to his father's domains in Italy, and then the minx had got pregnant and followed him back to Aragón. Well, that would be covered up. Till he was strong in Castile, this land of stones and saints. But, he thought, "This same stern land that bred Isabella and Valdes and Cardenas has also bred King Henry and the slippery old Marqués of Villena. It can be managed." Patience. He would be strong in Castile.

It was midnight when the little party drew rein to breathe their sweaty horses for the first time. Some had begun to limp, the halfhealed tendons in their legs protesting against the long hard ride.

Black against the skyline, blotting out the fiery stars in a grim rectangular pattern that shot up unexpected turrets, there loomed a castle. No light shone from it, nor from the small village that clustered around its base.

"Yonder is Osama," Valdes said in a low voice, as if he were afraid the wind would blow his words across the distance and sound an alert.

"The place is friendly to Doña Isabella," Ferdinand said, "and so is the Count of Trevino, master of the castle, if I am to believe the couriers from Carrillo and the Grand Admiral." He had to believe someone. They drove the weary horses apace.

Ferdinand patted his horse's neck. "You poor beast, you have served me faithfully in pain. If you get well I shall present you to Trevino; if not, I promise to have you shot instead of letting them slit your throat." The horse, perhaps sighting the distant castle and hoping for rest, limped a little faster, down the long last mile of his painful journey. Shortly they clattered over the cobblestones of the castle courtyard.

Valdes shouted, then Ferdinand joined with the trumpet voice that so often had carried above the tumult of battle to rally his men; but there was no answering halloo from the battlements, which seemed deserted. The night was dark and hostile as before, and Ferdinand was tired and cold. And hungry, since he had refused to stop even for food since nightfall.

Impatiently he led them to the main gate and hammered against it with the hilt of his sword. Above him loomed the sheer height of the keep, with its menacing system of overhanging watchtowers where sentinels were, or should be, posted. "You, up there! Open up and let me in! I am Prince Ferdinand of Aragón!"

A sentinel, roused from a comfortable sleep in the watchtower, shouted angrily down, "So you're Prince Ferdinand of Aragón, are you? Well, I am the Holy Roman Emperor, and here's a present for You!"

There was a whoosh in the air, and down came hurtling a rock from a drop-hole in the watchtower; it was big enough to have crushed three men, had they been standing shoulder to shoulder. It narrowly missed the prince as it crashed into the courtyard, striking sparks from the cobbles.

Ferdinand sprang back and let fly a litany of curses as only a Spaniard can curse, starting with God the Father and exhausting his breath long before he had exhausted the catalogue of saints. Had good Padre de Coca heard him at that moment he would have warned Isabella, "Temperate is not *always* the word for Prince Ferdinand. His rages can be violent in the extreme."

Valdes and his companions joined their shouts to his, protesting that he was not only Prince Ferdinand of Aragón but also the King of Sicily and that this was a sorry way to welcome a reigning monarch. There was a steely noise from the inner court and the running of mailed feet, as if guards were gathering.

Ferdinand laughed, his temper quickly under control, "The fools think they are being attacked."

Some minutes passed. He could hear the battlements being manned, crossbows being wound taut, their ratchets clicking; presumably more rocks were being readied at drop-holes in the barbicans. Presently a little wicket was cautiously opened in the main gate, torchlight began to shine through the iron grating and a voice called, "Let him who says he is

138

the prince step forward and be recognized."

"That is an Aragonian," Ferdinand said, and strode up confidently to the wicket

The face beyond the bars, well out of reach of a dagger thrust, suddenly changed. "Sangre de Dios, it is the prince! You were reported at Calahorra!"

"This is where I am," Ferdinand said calmly.

There was a flurry of activity inside, the thumping of heavy timber thwarts thrown down in haste, the metallic sounds of iron bolts unlocking as the ponderous machinery that secured the main gate was set in motion to open it.

"At Calahorra?" Ferdinand mused. Apparently he had been recognized in the vicinity of the strongest of the Mendoza castles, the seat of the Bishop himself, titular head of the powerful family of royalists. Faithful Cardenas! He hoped he had got through. But privately he condemned such rashness. It was chivalrous; it was selfless devotion of the highest order; but Cardenas was not acting in all things as Prince Ferdinand would have acted. A smaller Mendoza castle would have sufficed.

The great gate swung wide. The group of merchants found itself safe behind strong stone walls for the first time since leaving Saragossa.

Shortly the Count of Trevino came forward to meet his guest, full of apologies, full of good news. "An inexcusable blunder, Your Highness!"

Ferdinand smiled. "Not at all, mi primo." Trevino flushed with pleasure at the title, which he did not deserve. A Castilian king would have addressed only a grandee as "my cousin"; a lesser noble had to be satisfied with mi pariente, my kinsman. "The sentinel did only his duty, since I am at Calahorra."

"We surely did not expect Your Highness."

"A princely cavalcade left by another route; my merchants and I came by the high way."

Trevino laughed heartily. "Yet I suspect even Cardenas is

safe. King Henry is still in the south, or at least he is supposed to be. It's hard to tell where anybody is these days. And the countryside is quiet. My watchman says he thought you were a gang of—I implore Your Highness's indulgence—robbers!"

"Fortunately one of your men, a border dweller by his speech, recognized me."

"I hope Your Highness will not hold it against the man that he entered the service of a Castilian," Trevino said uncomfortably. "The fellow came to me with a story of a barren farm that he said would not support his family—"

"I too am changing countries, in a way," Ferdinand said. "I shall not blame another for doing what I myself am doing. Before I go I shall give him a florin for the good service he rendered me."

Francisco de Valdes could hardly believe his ears; but before Ferdinand left he did give the man a florin. He had no intention of permitting his reputation for stinginess to take root in Castile.

It was good news that King Henry was still in the south; it was good news that Trevino had a strong guard of trustworthy knights to escort him to Valladolid.

Clean, fed, dressed in new apparel, mounted like a prince and completely refreshed by five short hours of sleep, Ferdinand set out at dawn, to the surprise and chagrin of all the caballeros whose powers of recuperation did not equal his own, which were tremendous. The pots and pans and spavined horses he gave to the Count of Trevino with many flattering expressions of esteem, calling him mi primo and inviting him to the wedding.

In Valladolid, where Isabella had proclaimed her decision to marry him, where the common people had rioted in the streets when King Henry opposed him, he was greeted by swarms of cheering citizens, dressed as for a fiesta. They had proclaimed their own holiday, and as the richly mounted cavalcade slowly progressed through the streets, with caballeros flying their colorful heraldic banners and the mingled standards of Castile and Aragón fluttering and kissing each other atop gilded spears, the crowds strained for a glimpse of the king-prince whom their beloved Infanta loved and whom they too wanted a chance to love.

Nodding and smiling to right and left, waving a friendly hand in a fawn-colored glove, riding his high charger with soldierly skill, he presented as startling a contrast as could be imagined to Henry the Impotent. That day were scurrilous placards nailed to King Henry's palace gate, and illiterate obscenities chalked on his palace walls, while the people sang wildly to Ferdinand,

> *Flores de Aragón*
> *Dentro in Castilla, son!*
> *Pendón de Aragón!*
> *Pendón de Aragón!*

It would have reddened King Henry's pasty face to hear Ferdinand and his companions welcomed into Castile as the "flowers of Aragón." It would have infuriated the Marqués of Villena to hear Castilians hailing the standard of Aragón, pendón de Aragón, as if it were already their own. Ferdinand was stealing their hearts, as he had stolen Isabella's—from a distance of a hundred leagues. A formidable man.

Not everybody cheered. Some Royalists furtively left the streets and disappeared. Couriers sped off to the south. King Henry and the Marqués of Villena spurred home towards their seduced and precarious capital, leaving Medina Sidonia and the Marqués of Cadiz to continue their disastrous feuds in Andalusia.

Before she set eyes on the man she was to marry Isabella heard crowds cheering him in the streets. Her little court was clustered around her. Beatriz had come up from Segovia; Cardenas and his caballeros on their fast horses had got safely home. Men wore their swords and jeweled orders, women their richest velvets and finest silks; the room was brilliant in the steady clear light of pure-wax candles glittering on ancestral jewels in a treasure of lace headdresses. Isabella stood straight and regal, her copper hair gold in the golden light, the green very prominent in her eyes, that were big with excitement. Only outwardly was she calm.

"It is a happy omen that the people cheer him," Beatriz said.

Isabella whispered, "Is my coif straight? Should I have put on a little rouge after all, just as you said? I feel pale as a ghost. How shall I be sure which one is the prince?"

"Cardenas knows," Beatriz replied.

Isabella laughed softly, unsteadily. "What an awkward thing if I should mistake one of the others for him!"

Her cheeks were indeed too pale, Beatriz thought. "Perhaps just a *little* rouge—"

"Nay, then I should look like Queen Juana," Isabella said. And now she was blushing.

"There is plenty of time," Beatriz said soothingly. "He will go to the archbishop first and meet his grandfather there." For Ferdinand's grandfather, the Grand Admiral, as well as Archbishop Carrillo had regathered their forces and boldly returned to Valladolid to take up their residence.

"I wish they would hurry," Isabella said, but checked herself, "nay, that is wanton," and blushed redder than ever.

Beatriz said, *"Mi princesa,* you are lovelier than an angel!" in a tone so freighted with unfeigned admiration that Isabella wanted to hug her.

"I hope Carrillo will have news from Rome," Isabella said anxiously. "He has seemed somewhat evasive on that subject."

Beatriz said comfortingly, "Surely the dispensation has arrived by now. Perhaps he wants to surprise you."

"At the last moment? That would be unkind, unlike him."

"He is always so busy with his soldiers."

Isabella nodded doubtfully, "That is most true, and they

are most important. But the dispensation gives me nightmares, Beatriz. The Holy Father was not friendly to my brother; how can I hope he will be friendly to me?"

"The archbishop will manage." But Beatriz did not feel the confidence that she tried to impart. Her husband, still staunchly loyal to King Henry, had not thought the Pope would comply.

"I am afraid I must sound most unmaidenly in a hurry."

Beatriz smiled, "Ferdinand would be delighted to hear you say that."

"For shame, Beatriz! He mustn't!"

Outside there was a new burst of cheering, and the clattering of many horses over the cobbles; the flickering of torches shone through the leaded panes of the casements.

"He must have heard you," Beatriz said impishly. "At any rate, he's here."

The doors opened, Carrillo and the Grand Admiral entered, followed by the Aragonian caballeros, who were now in court dress, which they wore with more ease than the disguises they had so recently put off and in which the shabby "merchants" were no longer recognizable. Everyone was smiling, the Grand Admiral's eyes were misty with emotion, and it seemed to Isabella that Carrillo had never worn so complacent an expression. Perhaps the news had come from Rome; perhaps he had planned to surprise her. He certainly looked sly.

But among the richly dressed and handsome young men she could not quite be sure which one was Ferdinand. One of them looked familiar. Tentatively she directed a hesitant smile at him.

"No, no, Your Highness," Cardenas prompted her in a whisper. "That is Francisco de Valdes." Isabella remembered now. Of course! The Isle of Pheasants, the page she had secreted in her tent, nay, actually in her bed. The deep blush which followed the memory was not at all out of place under the circumstances. Every Aragonian's eyes lighted up in tribute,

Ferdinand's included, who muttered under his breath, "Maria Santísima! They did not exaggerate when they said she was beautiful."

Cardenas continued, softly, hurriedly, "Ese es! Ese es! The fair one with the high forehead!" In his excitement ese es, ese es—"that is he! that is he!"—half-whispered, half-hissed, tumbled out of his mouth like the two letters "SS", spoken rapidly.

Isabella whispered her thanks, and resolved one day to show her gratitude. He had spared her an embarrassing moment and probably stopped many gay stories at her expense at their source. Shortly the shield of Gutierre de Cardenas would begin to display a new device, the blazoned letters "SS", for him and his House forever, as long as a Cardenas should draw breath in Spain. In a similar moment of embarrassment, Isabella remembered, a lady's dropped garter had become a badge of honor in England.

Ferdinand, flanked by his white-haired jubilant grandfather, who happened to be ridiculously short of stature, and Archbishop Carrillo, whom he topped by half a head, advanced smiling, unhesitating, to where she stood.

For a moment they paused and looked at each other, while the two great statesmen beside him, Isabella supposed, made little speeches of introduction.

"I should have forgiven you if you had taken one of my ladies for me," Isabella said, a trifle guilty in her conscience at her own misapprehension.

Ferdinand kissed her hand; his hand was firm and hard, holding hers; his lips were pleasantly warm. "Your Highness," he said, "I was told that I had only to present myself to the most beautiful woman in Castile, and she would be Isabella. Had they said 'in the world' they would not have told more than the truth."

Things, thought the Grand Admiral, were going very well indeed, for he knew his grandson: Ferdinand was simply bewitched. Carrillo beamed; Isabella had never looked more radiantly happy.

Prompted by the statesmen, the courtiers and attendants faded away. There was business aplenty to transact after the first half-hour of small talk while the young people made each other's acquaintance. Isabella had no mental reservations, Ferdinand none; yet it seemed to them both that their elders were hurrying the interview.

"Youth," admonished the Grand Admiral, "is not aware that old enemies know how to cram a year of scheming tricks into the hour that youth forgets."

"I must marry you two at once," Carrillo said flatly.

"What?" Isabella asked mildly, through a veil of Ferdinand's pleasant, flattering words.

Ferdinand laughed. "At least let me make my bride the gifts I smuggled across the border. There was a double bottom in the chests that carried my pots and pans." It would have been boorish to mention values but, with a joke about smuggling valuables over the border and outwitting the customs guards, he was able to put a price on the gifts he had brought Isabella. The Grand Admiral was amazed; King John of Aragón had beggared himself for his son.

There was a coronet of emeralds and diamonds—green was for golden hair, Ferdinand said, whose glory only diamonds could outshine, value 20,000 florins. A magnificent necklace composed of laced strands of balas rubies, Eastern work from Badakhshan, a district near Samarkand, where the only true balas came from, hence the name, value 40,000 florins. Skillfully, if gently, he placed it around her neck and clasped the clasp. Isabella held her breath, her hand at her throat: no man had ever *dressed* her before. Then her breath came again in a sort of sigh—for after all—after all—

But there had been more in the merchants' chests: a sapphire brooch—was he going to pin it on her breast? Delicately, he did not —value 2000 florins; a diamond ring of his mother's, whose worth he said not even a customs guard could have estimated, because it was priceless with love.

Suddenly the Grand Admiral remembered something. All this treasure was in pawn to a group of Valencia bankers; King John had pledged it as a security for a loan to pay his troops to put down the restless Catalans. What it had cost the doughty old king, in promises, threats and cajolery, to repossess it from the coffers of the pawnbrokers, the Grand Admiral could only conjecture. But King John had gone to even greater lengths, he suspected, in the matter of the papal dispensation. "Never," he thought, "had a prince so devoted a father! May he prove worthy of him."

It seemed that he might. For there was another treasure from the double bottom of the chests, the fruit of Ferdinand's own stubborn thrift and unrelenting fiscal management: 8000 florins in pure minted gold, each coin full weight, unclipped; he had inspected each one, he said, and he knew. The velvet bags that held the gold were heavy.

Isabella knew the usefulness of money and admired jewels like any other beautiful work of art, but looking at him she said with perfect candor, "Far more than the gifts, I shall cherish the giver." There was yet one gift more. Ferdinand drew from his breast a little iron cross, shiny and worn with ages of handling but totally unadorned, awkwardly fashioned, a little twisted, as if the rough man who had made it had worked in secret with no previous skill at such things. It hung from a delicate golden chain of modern workmanship and no great value. It was, he said, wrought from one of the Nails. It had been venerated for centuries at the Hagia Sophia in Constantinople; and when that great church, with the mighty Eastern Empire, had fallen, it had passed into the hands of the Turk. The Turkish Emperor had sent it to his father, King John of Aragón. Now it was Isabella's.

Even the Grand Admiral crossed himself. Of course, it was notoriously a part of Mohammed the Conqueror's foreign policy to make such gifts to the Christian kings of Europe, since they were worthless to him and Westerners valued them extravagantly.

And there had sprung up an enormous traffic in spurious Eastern relics after Constantinople's fall. But a gift from the Grand Turk himself might be presumed to be genuine, at least in the eyes of the Eastern Church.

Isabella handled it reverently. "When I die," she murmured, "I shall build a cathedral to enshrine this holy thing; and while I live, it shall seal my love."

CHAPTER 12

AS soon as Ferdinand had presented the last of his gifts Archbishop Carrillo repeated, "You two must marry at once. I am prepared to perform the ceremony this very night."

Isabella frowned slightly. "Why tonight, Your Reverence? Why this haste, which is unseemly in you and unmaidenly in *me?*"

Carrillo was a man of action, a throwback to a rougher age of chivalry. A bride, he said, might legitimately give up her maidenly thoughts on her wedding night, a tactless remark that deepened Isabella's frown. He was impatient of delays and covetous of quick results even when no emergency existed to justify them. At this moment, however, an emergency certainly did exist. He told her some news that his couriers had brought, startling news: King Henry and the Marqués of Villena were approaching the capital by forced marches with all the troops they had taken with them into the south. They had sworn to prevent her marriage by force of arms.

"But he has repeatedly sworn that I was free to choose my own husband!" Isabella said.

Carrillo said, "Henry is a liar."

"The king blows this way and that," said the Grand Admiral, "like a weathercock. He always did and he always will. If he returns before you marry Ferdinand he may very well succeed in separating you permanently. But if you marry at once there will be nothing he can do about it, and he may even be friendly."

Isabella looked unhappily at Ferdinand. "I did so want everything done with decency and decorum."

Ferdinand smiled. "Since the wind seems to set in the direction of haste," he said, "so be it! Marry us tonight, Your

Reverence, if the lady will have me; it's an ill wind that blows no good to someone, for it simply hastens my happiness."

"I will have you, mi señor," Isabella replied softly. The words could have meant either "My lord" or "my husband." "If the archbishop has received a favorable reply from Rome. And if we may wait at least until morning. I will not have it said that Isabella of Castile flung herself into her marriage bed like a gypsy woman, panting and unprepared by prayer!"

That was the first time Ferdinand saw the green eyes flash, and the first time he sensed beneath her exquisitely feminine exterior a strength of character deep as the granite roots of her own Castilian mountains.

The look of complacency returned to Carrillo's face. "The reply from Rome," he muttered. "Ah yes, the dispensation. My own representations at the court of the Holy Father have not as yet borne fruit, owing, no doubt, to his long illness and perhaps a misunderstanding of your late brother's activities. In fact, I had begun to wonder whether we might not better rely on my own primatial authority, since there are many precedents for such action in early Church history. I grant you that things have tightened up considerably in recent centuries. Fortunately I shall not have to assert the ancient prerogatives which probably still attach to my office. King John of Aragón, by remarkable foresight, obtained a dispensation years ago from the late Pope Pius II."

"I have it here," the Grand Admiral said amiably. "Would you like to read it?"

Isabella looked into the grave and trusted faces of her advisors and the handsome face she already knew and loved of the man she was about to marry. The only Latin she knew was the Latin of her habitual prayers. *"Benedicta, tu"* she murmured, *"in mulieribus";* blessed art thou among women. All had been miraculously arranged. She did not look at or question the dispensation; she could not have read it if she had.

Carrillo warned, "My latest courier reports that the king

149

is very close. I should feel infinitely easier in my mind if tonight—after all, what difference does a few hours make—"

"Tomorrow," Isabella said firmly.

"Oh very well." Carrillo shrugged. "But you are taking a wholly unnecessary risk, and I cannot for the life of me see why."

"My lord archbishop," Isabella said with a smile, but with unmistakable irony, "it may be that you did not have the good fortune to be born a woman."

"Neither did I," said Ferdinand, and from him the remark was wholly acceptable.

All that night the great cathedral of Valladolid, which was still in the process of construction, rang with the noise of workmen's hammers covering the scaffolding with velvet, draping banners and tapestries over areas of the masonry that were raw and unplastered. Isabella could hear, or thought she could hear, the faraway sounds as she lay wakeful on her bed, full of strange thoughts; and the strangest of all was the thought that tomorrow night a husband would share that bed. Yet why was it strange, since it had happened ever since Mother Eve shared hers with Adam in the Garden? And when one came to examine the matter, one was married far longer than one was a maid. It was borne in upon her how young she still was, how little of her life she had lived. In a few years it would probably seem perfectly natural to be married. There would be children; she would try to be a good mother. One day she would be Queen; she would try to be a wise queen. Husbands were said to be trying at times; she would try to be a good wife. They were always going off to war and the brave ones, like Ferdinand, often got killed. She saw in her shadowy chamber the spectre of widowhood, like her mother's, years of sadness, loneliness. Why such black thoughts, tonight of all nights? Padre de Coca had said he was temperate. "Dear God," she prayed, "increase his temperance within him, that he may plan his battles shrewdly, and keep him safe when he goes to war."

Perhaps the great stillness of the night was responsible for her somber mood. The healthy wind that usually blew, filling the air with a complex of sounds that the ear did not hear, had fallen to dead unnatural calm. Without the wind it was queerly warm, almost oppressive, though she could see her breath in her bedchamber as usual. That at least was natural on this unnatural night. Through the dead air, as if magnified, she heard the snarling of Valladolid's scavenger dogs in the streets, the slow tramp and melancholy calls of watchmen in their rounds and, yes, unquestionably, the thudding of workmen's hammers in the cathedral, hollow and muffled by distance like spirit hammers underground. And every hour she heard the church bells, louder than she had ever heard them before and curiously speeded up, as if the hours were following too closely upon another, as if time were compressed.

Towards morning she drifted off into a fitful slumber.

In her dream she was queen, and Ferdinand had cleansed the face of Spain of the infidel Moors, hurling them back into Africa; bells were pealing and citizens cheering as he returned in triumph from the war, and sons and daughters joined their voices in swelling Te Deums of praise that echoed from all the cathedrals of Spain, a greater, happier, healthier Spain, restored to its ancient birthright of power and prestige.

Beatriz looked down and saw her smiling in her sleep and hesitated. But there was ample reason to wake her. She shook her gently by the shoulder. The dream faded away, but still she heard the bells and the cheering. They were real.

She sat up in bed, wide awake. "What is it, Beatriz?"

Beatriz laughed, her voice high, her black eyes sparkling with excitement. "What could it be, *mi princesa?* It's your wedding day!"

"No, no; the bells, the cheering?"

"All for you."

"But so early?"

Beatriz' face became serious. "The archbishop received two couriers during the night. He is extremely agitated. King Henry is practically at the city gates. Get up, get up, Isabella, Ferdinand is pacing the floor, the archbishop is already vested. The guests are pouring in and by now the candles in the chapel are probably already lighted. Let me help you dress."

"In the *chapel?* What chapel?"

"There isn't time for the cathedral. The archbishop is going to perform the ceremony in the residence of Juan de Vivero. Do, please hurry!"

Decency and decorum! True, the residence of Don Juan de Vivero was large and imposing, but it was not the cathedral,

"It is so close!" Beatriz said.

"Ferdinand is willing?"

"Prince Ferdinand arranged all the details personally."

Isabella made her decision quickly. She was keenly aware of the threat posed by the king's sudden return; the present precarious state of affairs might easily erupt into bloodshed, and some of the blood might be Ferdinand's.

"Run to Carrillo and tell him I shall be in Vivero's chapel in twenty minutes. But tell him *and be sure he hears* that once he has spoken the words of union which cannot be unspoken in this world, I shall wish for a nuptial Mass in the cathedral."

"I will!" Beatriz said, scurrying away.

"And Beatriz," Isabella called after her. "No pretty, dawdling white mules! A horse!"

Beatriz paused, smiled saucily, "Side saddle, Your Highness? Straddle-back is quicker."

"Oh Beatriz, do not be nasty. Of course, side saddle!"

Thus it was that the citizens of Valladolid, who were wont to see their Infantas borne to their nuptials on plodding ceremonial mules, were treated to a novelty as startling as it was beautiful: they beheld their princess with all her attendants in a flutter of old lace and a blaze of sparkling jewels on proud high-stepping horses riding to the most popular wedding of the century. The crowds, who were always better informed than statesmen supposed they were, knew how close and how furious King Henry was. Their Isabella defied him! They took her to their vast plebeian hearts and cheered themselves voiceless. Some of their earthy, intimate, encouraging remarks made even Beatriz blush. Isabella seemed not to hear them; her face was pale and grave.

It was crowded and hot with the press of guests and the heat of hundreds of candles in the little chapel, for Vivero had outdone himself in the matter of illumination and two thousand eager noblemen and ladies wanted to squeeze themselves in. Carrillo was already at the altar, the book in his hand, but his eyes strayed constantly, apprehensively toward the door.

Isabella leaned on the arm of the Grand Admiral, the ranking grandee of her party, who found himself in the anomalous position of being the grandfather of the groom and also *in loco parentis* for the bride, whose own father was dead and whose mother's mind no longer dwelt in this world. He made the responses for her until the time when Carrillo, out of whose mouth the words were tumbling with almost unintelligible rapidity, asked the question that only she could answer, "Isabella, dost thou take this man—"

In a low firm voice Isabella signified her assent.

The ring was on her finger. Kneeling beside Ferdinand, her hand in his, she heard the archbishop pronounce over them the momentous words that Jesus himself had declared no man could unsay.

A trumpet note of triumph boomed in Carrillo's voice. Now the stubborn, tender-conscienced girl could have her nuptial Mass in the cathedral, since King Henry and the

Marqués of Villena and the troops had not appeared.

In fact, the more the archbishop thought about it, the more he fancied the notion, since it is no sin to marry people any number of times provided they are the same people, and all the disappointed notables who had not been able to crowd into Juan de Vivero's little chapel could be accommodated. He resolved to repeat the whole ceremony from beginning to end, with all the pomp and circumstance that had originally been planned before the two couriers had come in the night with their alarming news.

Ferdinand did not object; he knew the Castilian love of splendid ecclesiastical display. And it would strengthen him in Castile to have it repeated on a more public scale. Isabella was overjoyed; she smiled at the idea of marrying him twice, but the nuptial Mass, on which she had set her heart, could now be said with decency and decorum.

When Isabella and Ferdinand emerged from Vivero's palace, amid a confusion of laughter, congratulations and happy tears, a splendid escort was forming to conduct them, in procession, to the cathedral: white mules with silver bridles for the bride and groom, white side saddles for Isabella's attendants, while Ferdinand's caballeros rode their spirited horses whose harness was now decorated with red and yellow ribbons, the colors of Aragón. Before and behind them the guests, who were now sure of witnessing the second ceremony, spread out in a long holiday cavalcade which made its way at a dignified pace towards the great granite pile of the cathedral. Viewing it with interest as he approached it more closely, noting under the maze of scaffolding how massive were its blocks of stone, Ferdinand was struck anew by the stern uncompromising strength that characterized this land of stones and saints: the Castilian were rearing this mighty church to outlast their immemorial mountains.

Towards the end of their progress though the crowd-lined streets, the wind, which had been so curiously absent during the night, sprang up cold and gusty, full of the threat of storm. The brilliant sun blinked out behind a sudden fast-moving cloud of enormous extent that was drawing across the sky like a curtain with an oddly well-defined edge, lacking the fringe of broken cloudlets that usually precede a storm. The city, a moment before so bright, now found itself plunged into premature evening gloom.

Ferdinand said, "That would mean wind in Aragón."

'It means wind here." Isabella smiled. "We're not so different." Ferdinand said, "We are one, mi señora," and this time señora meant wife indeed.

The cavalcade quickened its pace. Even so, some of the ladies near the end of the procession suffered a wondrous destarching of lace, and some of the banners of the caballeros got a wetting in the downpour that suddenly cascaded on the town before the doors of the cathedral closed.

Inside, the odor of incense, the light of the candles, the deep rumble of the organ and the massed singing of the choirs shut out the dark and the noise of the storm, which now began to rage violently around the unfinished towers and new-set bells of the church. One shattering gust of wind started a bell clapper to swinging and brought forth an ominous clang in the midst of a prayer, which caused Carrillo to mutter, "Oh, the devil!" into his book. But Isabella took it for a good omen: the bells could not wait to ring. And Ferdinand dismissed it for the meteorological accident that it was.

The beautiful, satisfying service was long and superbly performed. The archbishop admitted to himself that he had never been in better voice.

Isabella and Ferdinand, now kneeling before the high altar, again heard the sacred words of union pronounced over them. The choir was just bursting into song when suddenly Isabella felt a jolt, as if a monstrous hammer, wielded by a giant in the crypt below, had struck at the floor under her knees.

Later some said it had been a terrific gust of wind, some

said the tremor of an earthquake. Whatever it was, it jarred the deep-rooted structure of the cathedral to its foundations, and the keystone of one of the arches of the northern transept, dislodged from its scaffolding—tomorrow the masons would have set it in place—came crashing down and crushed the life out of a humble spectator of the wedding. He was a noble of no consequence, a grandee of the third class who could address a Castilian king only with permission, only when uncovered, and had to await permission to cover himself again, all in contrast with the grandees of Class II and Class I, for whom Spanish etiquette was different. But still he was a man, a loyal follower, and he was dead. A number of others were injured by flying shards of stone and bespattered with wet plaster.

After the first bad moment of screams and confusion the man's body was decently removed, someone threw an arras over the spot in the pavement and the ceremony continued. Ferdinand, whose expression had not changed, noticed that even the injured preferred to bear their pain and hide their cuts and bruises rather than leave: a proud and single-minded people, these Castilians.

For Isabella the tragedy threw a pall over the few remaining minutes of her nuptial Mass. Perfectly composed, she did not leave her position in front of the archbishop. But neither did she try to hide the tears that streamed down her cheeks. She wanted the ceremony to end.

It never did quite end; the parting benediction never quite left Carrillo's mouth.

Outside there was a sudden distracting noise, starting small and rapidly growing into shaking volume, like the approach of a hurricane. Some of the spectators, now thoroughly unnerved, expected to hear the sickening surge of a greater, more disastrous earthquake. Heads turned in fear.

But then through the uproar they heard the well-known ringing of warhorses' iron-spiked shoes on the cobbles of the street. They smiled, relaxed. Here was no cosmic disaster. Here was only King Henry the Impotent and the Marqués of Villena and the troops, returning from the south, too late.

Sodden and bedraggled Villena and the king burst through the door and rushed halfway down the central aisle of the nave before they stopped in confusion and uncertainty, dripping on the pavement.

Isabella said firmly in a low voice that carried to the farthest reaches of the great church, "Attend me, mi señor." On Ferdinand's arm she left the sanctuary and gravely advanced to meet the king. It was noted, and approved, by two thousand Castilian grandees that Ferdinand bore himself with great composure in a situation that must have been unexpected and trying in the extreme.

A few paces from Henry she halted, curtsied and said, "Your Highness, I present to you *my husband.*"

Ferdinand bowed formally, slightly, as one king bowed to another. Henry's head bobbed in acknowledgment, while he looked helplessly to the Marqués of Villena for guidance. "The King's Highness is delighted—" Villena began smoothly.

"Delighted," Henry echoed tonelessly.

"—and naturally so am I."

"And so am I." Ferdinand grinned. And he, at least, was telling the truth.

The balance of power was now even, the heavy scale exactly horizontal, half the kingdom weighted on one arm, half on the other. Neither side would be able to attack the other till something upset it. Isabella was fatigued and despondent to the depths of her being, the tears still gleamed on her cheeks; but Ferdinand looked as if he understood the political situation thoroughly, and enjoyed it.

The pealing carillon of bells that rang out as they left the cathedral did not sound joyous.

That evening they rode to nearby Duenas, a fortified

town belonging to a brother of Carrillo's. For though nothing overt could upset the balance of power in Castile, a covert thing could—an assassin's dagger, a queer taste in the fish or wine.

Within the week, in the fine clear weather and beautiful Castilian nights that followed in the safety of Duenas, Ferdinand was saying with a confident proprietary air, "Isabella, do you pray that our first child will be a son?"

"If you do."

"Naturally I do."

"Then I do too."

"From the political point of view a prince would be infinitely superior to a princess," he said emphatically.

"I know, Ferdinand."

She did know, and she agreed. The unifying effect of a male heir to inherit the crowns of Castile and Aragón would be an event of first magnitude in the chancelleries of Europe.

But she was perfectly happy for the first time in her life, and the far away chancelleries full of graybeard statesmen seemed unreal and unimportant. Isabella was very much in love.

CHAPTER 13

THE idyllic sojourn at Duenas was short-lived, as is the nature of idylls, else they would not possess the fairytale quality that they do. Isabella remembered an old, old saying: if the stars shone but once in a lifetime, that beautiful night would be set aside for a special remembrance in all intervening years until they appeared again on another miraculous night. But the night when they shone again would be in another generation. Such was her honeymoon with Ferdinand, a little fragment of her lifetime set apart and never to be repeated, since time must march, the earth must spin, and fairytales must end.

The walls of Duenas could not shut out the tide of history that soon welled up against them, and burst in.

The first winter of her marriage brought hard times to Castile from the Pyrenees to Andalusia. Everywhere crops were poor, and in many regions they failed completely. In a better ordered country, with strong and wise management, there might have been enough to go around; but the nobles refused to repair the roads and the peasants were afraid to travel upon them for fear of the outlaws, who seemed to grow in number with every month that nobody bothered to punish them. Transportation, always slow and primitive, ceased. There was nothing to transport, and what little there was the peasant, with his immemorial independence, hoarded and hid for his own use. Even in the comparative isolation of Duenas Isabella and Ferdinand heard the sorry reports, but they were powerless to help.

"Castile could do with a few salutary penal laws," Ferdinand said. He was restless with inactivity; his hand itched to busy itself in the affairs of Castile.

"We have scores of laws," Isabella replied. "Some of them against banditry are positively savage. But Henry is king. He

159

would welcome no advice from us."

"He hasn't even welcomed me," Ferdinand said grimly.

"Nor me, Ferdinand."

King Henry had not once communicated with her since the meeting in the cathedral, though she had sent him a number of letters. They were always respectful in tone, but she steadfastly maintained that in marrying Ferdinand she had only done what he had promised she could do, not once but twice and publicly at that.

"Maybe you ought to be just a bit more diplomatic," Ferdinand suggested, scanning her most recent remonstrance. "This is stiffer than the last one."

"I cannot humble myself without humbling you," she answered. He kissed her for that.

"Stop it, Ferdinand! Someone is coming."

"What of it?" He smiled. "Can't a man kiss his wife in Castile?"

"I just don't think you ought to do it in public."

"This isn't public."

"It will be as soon as you open the door."

He nodded thoughtfully, "Sometimes you frighten me, Isabella. What you say is true, and statesmanlike, and you make me feel like a schoolboy."

He spoke so gravely that Isabella was afraid she had offended him. She put a restraining hand on his arm. "Don't ever open the door, my dearest. Let's always keep it closed and shut out the world."

"*Now* where is my little statesman!" He laughed.

The man at the door was an impudent herald from King Henry. With the curtest of bows he delivered an oral message from the king, who perhaps did not care to commit himself on paper, who perhaps was being calculatedly impolite, since her letters demanded a letter in reply. The King's Highness was vastly displeased, the courier said, and he managed to color his voice and his looks with a sneer that brought an angry flush to Isabella's cheek and set the tendons in

Ferdinand's jaw to working like ropes. The King's Highness blamed Isabella for the deplorable state of the realm, and the King's Highness regretted the necessity of cutting off her revenues from the cities of Avila, Buete and Medina del Campo, Molina, Olmedo, Ubeda and Escalona. And also, said the herald, she need not look to the king when the pinch in her purse began to be felt.

Isabella would have given him a tart reply; Ferdinand saw it rising to her lips. Quickly, smoothly he spoke for her: she remained the king's dutiful subject, he said, but their marriage, sanctioned by promise, duly performed and consummated—Isabella's color heightened—was a subject which neither Isabella nor he would ever discuss. Then he gave the herald a gold florin.

When the intruder was gone Isabella said, "Was it right to say anything about *consummation,* my dear?"

"My dear," Ferdinand smiled, "the whole world will soon know. Why not give Henry something to trouble his sleep and make his coffee bitter? *He* never consummated anything." There was a fatherly strut, a bit premature but amply justified, in Ferdinand's manner. "And it will be very good for Castile and Aragón to have a prince."

"Only God can promise you a prince, Ferdinand. I can only promise you a baby."

Ferdinand said confidently, remembering the Duchess of Eboli, "Pooh, pooh! I know it will be a prince."

"Nobody ever knows."

Ferdinand opened his mouth to say, "I know," but quickly changed his mind.

"Would it be a grievous disappointment?" she asked.

He said, "No doubt there would be another time."

In a curious back-handed way the economic distress of the kingdom worked in their favor, which Ferdinand was the first to grasp. It wasn't fair and it wasn't healthy, since it showed how desperate the common people were in their lives and in their thoughts, but it delighted Ferdinand. "Henry is getting the blame for the famine and the plague."

"Plague, too? Where?"

"Is there ever famine without plague? In Segovia, I'm told."

"But poor Henry can't help that."

"Poor Henry gets the credit; Henry and the Jews. We should thank God. The more the people hate him the more they will love you."

"And you; though the whole thing is wrong."

"If they love me it is only the overflow from the superabundance of love that they lavish on you," he said.

"You are a honeytongue, and I shouldn't trust you out of my sight." She smiled, but she thought of Beatriz. "If there is plague in Segovia Beatriz must come here to Duenas. I shall write her at once."

Ferdinand looked at her sternly, "Would that be wise? Infection? The prince?"

She wavered. Ferdinand thought of everything. But she wished he had included her, too, in his thoughts, even though a new little prince, or princess, might be more important politically.

Ferdinand said confidently, "Beatriz will be safe in the alcazar. Her husband is a Jew; *they* never seem to get the plague."

"Surely you don't believe that old wives' tale about the Jews poisoning the wells. Besides, he isn't a Jew."

"Some mighty queer things happen. There is a definite connection between public wells and the outbreaks of the plague. My inquisitors looked into the matter very thoroughly in Saragossa."

Isabella sighed. "Nobody really knows, I'm afraid." But Segovia's alcazar had its private well, bitter but wholesome. No doubt Beatriz would be safe. For the moment, at least, she decided not to invite her to Duenas. Besides, how could she invite Beatriz without inviting her husband, Andrés de Cabrera; Cabrera, who had refused to desert his post even to

162

come to her wedding? And who knew whether the plague might not strike Duenas itself tomorrow?

"It isn't likely," Ferdinand said. "Not enough Jews in this archiepiscopal city where Carrillo's brother is the seignior. Segovia crawls with them."

"Aren't there just as many Jews in Aragón?" Isabella said. There was a stubborn note in her voice.

Ferdinand recognized it. "I do not wish to quarrel with you on such a subject, mi señora. The fact is, there *are* just as many; but they're not so rich. The Inquisition takes care of that."

Isabella did not wish to quarrel either, though she would have liked to ask him, "Are you any the richer for making them poor?"

She knew how short of funds the Aragonian treasury was. Instead she laughed. "I'm sorry about that florin you had to give to the courier."

"Oh no, no, no. That was an investment. I bought a friend for that florin. Did you see his face? It was the last thing he expected. A florin for bringing us bad and insulting news." He shrugged, sighed. "Anyhow, we'll be living on my 8000 florins for quite a while, I suspect."

"I am terribly, terribly sorry, Ferdinand."

He chucked her under the chin. "Do you really think I mind? I tell you, times will change, times are already changing." If times were changing there was little evidence of it.

As Castile grew weaker with famine, pestilence and the perpetual little civil wars in the south, Portugal grew relatively stronger; Alfonso the African, smarting under Isabella's double refusal, was in a belligerent mood. Queer stories reached his ears that Isabella had married Ferdinand on the authority of a dispensation that had been forged. He fumed. Couldn't Portuguese calligraphers have counterfeited a papal bull as handily as Aragonese? Why hadn't *he* thought of it, and who put the notion into Ferdinand's head? Isabella herself? So brooded Alfonso the African, spurred on by rumor, half-truth, exaggeration and, above all, by jealousy.

Suddenly out of the Dark Continent, from a place with the outlandish name of Guinea on a shore that was soon to be called the Gold Coast, came startling news. A fabulous gold mine, St. George La Mina, had been discovered in territory that Portuguese navigators, in their long push down the African coast, laid claim to, a claim which no one disputed. Portugal was now richer both relatively and absolutely than Castile.

Wistfully Isabella regretted that Henry had so shamefully neglected the Castilian navy; but there was so much that Henry had neglected, Castile had never been a great maritime power; no one should reproach Henry, she supposed, for failing where other Castilian kings also had failed.

"We could have discovered that mine just as easily as the Portuguese" she mused. "Fray Tomás used to tell me how big this round world is. It would have eased the troubles here if Henry had had the foresight to stop the people's hoarding, by building roads, irrigating the waste places, making honest work for the poor peasants whose fields are burnt and barren. Many of them turn outlaw because they're hungry and there's nothing to do, no harvest to gather on their land."

Ferdinand shrugged. "Portugal made a lucky find, that's all. I shall never look to Africa for my gold. The way to wealth is not through gambling, but to save your money and make profitable investments with it." And in this he voiced the unquestionably valid mercantile philosophy of Aragón, a trading nation.

Isabella's views, like the vast uplands of Castile, were broader. "I believe in new wealth," she said simply.

Outrageously, he patted her stomach, whose lines not even her fullest skirts could now conceal. "Make my new wealth a prince," he said.

Not all the news that filtered into Duenas was bad. In

Rome the old Pope died, and Sixtus IV ascended the papal throne. He was no partisan of Henry the Impotent, and one of his first acts was to give ear to Carrillo's entreaties and put right the troublesome business of the Castilian Infanta's marriage to her second cousin, Ferdinand of Aragón. No copy of the dispensation granted by his predecessor seemed to have been made for the Vatican archives.

A herald from the archbishop, the gold galloon on his livery most singularly dull and faded, delivered the new dispensation with all the presence he could muster in his shabby condition. Carrillo, prodigal in the display of his retainers, usually clothed his ecclesiastical heralds in finery that fairly blinded you. Isabella felt sorry for her old friend; the hard times had affected his revenues too.

"What is in the scroll, Ferdinand?"

"Read it." He smiled.

"You know I cannot read Latin."

"There is a translation." Ferdinand could not read Latin either.

Isabella read her permission to marry her husband. She was utterly bewildered.

"But—but wasn't the other one real?"

"This one is certainly better." Ferdinand laughed. It was difficult for Isabella to believe that he could laugh at such a thing.

"I do not understand," she said, and the green flecks flashed accusingly in her eyes.

"On my soul," Ferdinand assured her, "I do not understand either. To the best of my knowledge the other one was absolutely genuine, granted long ago to my father for me. I do willingly confess, however, that I did not inquire closely into the authenticity of a document which, if forged, would have deprived me of my happiness."

"Ferdinand, Ferdinand, Ferdinand."

"Concede that this one, mint-new and just issued by the newly elected Pope, is a great deal better."

"How can I argue against such a tongue!" But it was odd to feel that she might have lived so long, nay worse, conceived a child, in sin.

Ferdinand loosened his purse string, stuck in a reluctant finger and pulled out a florin. "Here, friend," he said to the herald. "You have brought Her Highness and me a handsome present." From the man's appearance Ferdinand, too, supposed that Carrillo must be having difficulty keeping up his grand estate.

Astonishingly the herald bit the gold piece, testing it hard with his teeth. Heralds, who were constantly in the presence of great personages, were usually the soul of good manners.

"Upon my word!" Ferdinand muttered. Things with the archbishop must be even worse than he had suspected.

The herald flushed scarlet. He had made a boor of himself. "Ten thousand pardons, Your Highnesses. Believe me, it is a habit, newly acquired, born of necessity."

"What in the world made you do a thing like that?" Isabella asked sharply.

The explanation tumbled out of the herald's mouth, a jumble of rumor, confusion and hearsay, in a bitter effort to excuse his bad manners. But certain hard facts became clear, even if one discounted the suggestion that the troubled old primate was losing his mind.

The times were hard, Carrillo's revenues had shrunk, and he had continued to expend great sums not only on his usual luxurious style of living but also on the charities that always had sought his help in the past and which now, in the present unhappy state of the realm, he could not refuse. Carrillo therefore lacked gold.

Since there was none to be had through the usual channels the indomitable old warhorse had resolved to make his own. He caused to be built in his archiepiscopal palace at Toledo an alchemistical laboratory equipped with forges, retorts, great green bottles and other necromantic paraphernalia;

166

he laid in a supply of mercury, sulphur, potash, acid and other expensive chemicals; he compiled a foot-high sheaf of unintelligible manuscripts that were supposed to contain the secret formula, if only one could understand the gibberish in which they were written. His astrologer's name was El Beato, for the planets, of course, had to be consulted. His alchemist went by the name of "Doctor" Alarcon. The gold galloon on the herald's tabard was the first-fruit of the labor of these two worthies.

"My poor deluded old benefactor," Isabella said. Often she thought of the shipwreck of her mother's mind, who still dwelt in darkness at Arevalo, forgotten. Was it now to be Carrillo's turn? That which can strike a queen can also strike an archbishop. "But in Mother's case it was sorrow over my father's death."

Not long thereafter she learned that Carrillo, too, had had a private sorrow.

In a man of his temper ambition burned like a fire that could not be put out. He wanted to be more than primate. There was one churchman to whom even the primate deferred. Carrillo wanted the highest ecclesiastical post that the Church could award to a Spaniard: he wanted to be Cardinal of Spain.

But another of the new Pope's early decisions was to give the coveted red hat not to Carrillo but to Pedro Gonzalez of Mendoza, Bishop of Calahorra, the head of the great feudal House whose string of frontier castles had been such a worry to Ferdinand. Mendoza, the unshakable royalist, became Cardinal of Spain.

Isabella wept for her friend. Ferdinand humored and soothed her, speaking of gentle things, knowing from experience that women could be sentimental in certain physical states, given to irrational fits of tears, "But by God!" he thought in his practical mind, "if I were the Pope I would certainly never give a red hat to an old dotard who tries to make gold!" That was even worse than the new wealth

Isabella had mentioned in her dreamy nonsense about ships sailing off to the wilds of Africa!

Beatriz came unannounced, without an invitation, and not to escape the plague. Ferdinand was not with Isabella when she arrived. As his wife's time had drawn closer his fretfulness and anxiety increased, and he had taken to going on long solitary walks about the city lest his mood communicate itself to her. It was not in his heart to hurt anyone to no purpose, and it was easy to hurt anyone so sensitive and deeply in love as Isabella. He neither prided himself nor stood in awe at the daily display of her devotion: it was a fact, like any other fact.

Beatriz laughed at the notion of the plague in Segovia. True, there were a few cases, largely in the Jewish quarter, but by no means an epidemic. Her husband Cabrera thought it might be due to the crowding, for the *Juderías* were always too small to hold all the Jews who were confined in them and who were forbidden by law to live anywhere else. The plague was no worse than in other cities. Beatriz had made the visit only to be present when her best friend presented a new Infante or Infanta to Castile.

"To Spain, Beatriz! He will be the king not only of Castile, not only of Aragón, but of both. Of Spain!"

But the blonde little child who was born in Duenas on October first, just a few days less than one year after her marriage with Ferdinand, was a girl. Isabella gave her her own name, feeling her in a special way her own, since Ferdinand had demanded a prince so often and so insistently. She was afraid he would hate the child.

He did not reproach her; she knew husbands often did; he smiled pleasantly when the midwife presented his daughter to him, pink and lustily bawling in a billow of lace. But he continued his solitary walks, and returned with a polite, well-disciplined face, and spoke in measured, correct and distant phrases such as he might have used with a stranger.

Beatriz said, "If Andres did that to me I'd knife him."

"No, you wouldn't," Isabella said.

"Well, I'd feel like it."

"I have done no wrong. He is disappointed, but he is just. He will return. This will pass. I know him better than anyone."

Beatriz hoped so. Isabella was in agony and would not admit it, even to herself.

But Ferdinand's manner did not change for a long time.

"Perhaps that slow methodical mind of his is working its way through a maze of diplomatic calculations, Isabella; and maybe in a year or so he'll remember that princesses have a certain value, too. He married one."

Isabella frowned and her eyes went green. "I'd a little rather you did not adopt that tone when speaking of my husband."

Beatriz never did again.

"Ferdinand is a man of action," Isabella said more softly. "Inactivity more than disappointment is torturing him."

The winter had passed before Ferdinand's restrained and distant attitude relaxed. One night, returning from his walk, he asked suddenly, "Isabella, who is Gonsalvo Hernandez de Cordoba?"

Isabella was willing to talk on any subject that could bring a light of interest into Ferdinand's lack-lustre countenance. "I know Don Alonso de Cordoba, the lord of Aguilar. He fought for my brother at Olmedo. Gonsalvo—Gonsalvo—I do not know." She looked appealingly at Beatriz, "Do you know him?"

Beatriz' large expressive eyes seemed to widen and melt. "Gonsalvo is the hope and despair of half the ladies of Cordova. He is Don Alonso's younger brother, with the face of an angel, the strength of a bull, the tongue of a poet, the leg of a dancing master—"

Ferdinand laughed heartily. It was good to hear him laugh again. "Before you anatomize him completely, Beatriz, tell me, can he fight?"

"Like a demon, in the lists at least. I believe he has never seen war. The ladies of Cordova call him 'The Prince of Youth.'"

"He seemed very young," Ferdinand said.

"That does not trouble the ladies of Cordova," Beatriz said.

"He hardly sounds decent." Isabella laughed.

"On the contrary," Beatriz said, "that does trouble the ladies of Cordova. He's so chaste they think he thinks he's too good for them."

"Maybe he's just decent," Isabella said.

"He is certainly proud," Ferdinand mused. "I saw him dressed like a duke, with a diamond in his ear and a ruby on his finger. His sword alone was worth a hundred florins—not jeweled, a good Toledo blade. And there he stood with holes in his shoes, hungrily sniffing the smells that came out of a tavern. Not a cheap tavern, either; one of the better ones. I invited him in to take a cup of wine with me. I—I was a little bored."

"Did you tell him who you were?" Isabella asked.

"Naturally I had to, my dear, when he volunteered who *he* was. Politeness demanded it. And I am not ashamed of who I am."

"I only meant—did you think it was safe? You were unattended, perhaps unrecognized."

"Now that is the curious part of it, Isabella. I have always felt safe in Duenas till now. Perhaps I have been careless. The little Infanta will need her father for many years to come."

Isabella smiled incredulously, looking meaningfully at Beatriz. "See?" she said with her eyes. "He has returned."

"I was not hungry, for I had supped; but I could see that Gonsalvo was. I asked him if he would also take a bite to eat. Three times he refused, each time weaker than the last, and ended by finishing off two whole chickens. I never saw a man eat so fast without soiling his fingers above the first knuckle. His jewels were real, and he had not pawned them. That struck me."

"As a cadet he is dependent on his elder brother for every maravedí he spends," Beatriz said. "And not even a grandee like his brother has any money these days."

"You have," Ferdinand said to her.

Beatriz shrugged helplessly. "Andres says it's all King Henry's. I never talk to him about it."

"A pity," said Ferdinand.

But Gonsalvo de Cordoba had paid for his supper in the only way he could. Somewhere in the streets, as he was wearing out his shoes, he had heard vague whispers of a plot against their lives. "My life, Isabella, *your* life and the life of the little Infanta. I should have thought that Villena and Henry and that wicked woman Juana would at least recoil from the terrible crime of murdering a helpless child. It seems not."

Isabella's hand was at her mouth, lest she scream.

Ferdinand continued soberly, "One might discount this as baseless gossip, or the vagary of a romantic mind, which Gonsalvo appears to possess, as is evidenced by his unpawned jewels and emphasized by Beatriz' glowing account of his effect on the ladies. Unfortunately there is other evidence." He pulled a much wrinkled and folded little note from his purse. "Carrillo sends me, through the agency of a monk who plucked furtively at my sleeve today, this cryptic little message: 'The weather is threatening in Duenas.' It is signed in Latin; but *Archiep. Toletan.* can only mean 'The Archbishop of Toledo.' His motive in warning me in this secretive fashion I can only conjecture. Most things can be traced ultimately to money. He may be afraid of offending his brother, lord of this city from which he draws revenue. His brother may be going over to the king. Or Carrillo may be. I do not know. The situation is uncomfortable."

To Isabella it was terrifying. "But he did warn us, Ferdinand."

"Conscience, I suppose. But he was careful to warn us on the sly."

"We must leave Duenas at once," Isabella said.

"And where to, pray?" Ferdinand asked. "Only Aragón, as I see it."

She loved him for that. Isabella, who hated to cry, burst into tears. "Thank you, my husband." She knew what it had cost him to make that proposal. If they should fly to Aragón, discredited fugitives from Castile, it would mean the end of all his dreams of union, all his ambition for power. And very likely it would end in war, and Aragón might lose. And yet he had made the offer. Not, she suspected, so much for herself as for the princess who should have been a prince.

"You must never leave Castile!" Beatriz said spiritedly.

"*Must,* to me?" Ferdinand said angrily.

"Listen!" said Isabella.

"Come to Segovia! Come to the alcazar! My husband will protect you."

"Andres de Cabrera is a king's man," Ferdinand said scornfully.

"Andres de Cabrera is a man," Beatriz retorted proudly.

Ferdinand looked at his wife. Isabella thought rapidly.

"We will go to Segovia," she said.

CHAPTER 14

SINCE the threat was vague and formless Ferdinand stated flatly that no one was to be trusted, and Isabella perforce left most of her little suite behind. "They will serve as an admirable decoy," he said. "Everyone will suppose we are still in residence," and he gave orders that the twin banners of Castile and Aragón should continue to be displayed over their house.

"My ladies at least are loyal," Isabella protested.

"They are the very ones I suspect most," Ferdinand scowled, "because they have access to the nursery."

Where her child was concerned Isabella yielded in everything.

With Cardenas, Valdes, some of his Aragonians and Gonsalvo de Cordoba, whom he had attached to his retinue at a remarkably nominal salary, Ferdinand led his little group to Segovia. They were dressed inconspicuously; one would have taken them for a group of modest burghers. Ferdinand seemed to enjoy the activity; at least he was busy, even if he was leading a retreat. "But even the Holy Family," he said in self-justification, "was not ashamed to fly into Egypt. My family must not be ashamed either."

In Segovia Cabrera welcomed them, warmly as friends of his wife, a little coolly as political enemies. But Cabrera's loyalty had been shaken somewhat by the scheme that Villena, Queen Juana and King Henry had hatched to snuff out the life of a baby in its crib. Cabrera himself had not been involved, of course, because he was in Segovia, and an unlikely accomplice in any case since his wife was Isabella's best friend. It was a public scandal by now, he said, and he could give them the whole story.

A few well-chosen desperadoes, recruited from the slums of Valladolid, had been sent to Duenas. Ferdinand was to be stabbed on one of his walks. Isabella was to be disposed of by a man who would enter by the front door while others went in by the rear and killed the Infanta in the nursery. Payment was to be twenty florins to each assassin, after the event.

"Twenty florins is not a particularly flattering sum," Ferdinand said grimly.

The king's treasurer replied, "Perhaps it was all that King Henry could spare."

"Eh?"

But Cabrera would not disclose the state of the royal coffers. "In hard times when people are starving some men will do anything for twenty florins."

"Murder a baby?" Isabella demanded.

"Alas, yes." He flung wide his white expressive hands, shrugging his shoulders. These gestures, Ferdinand thought privately, display the Jew in him.

Bui there was a comical twist to the murderous business. Queen Juana and the Marques of Villena were all for quick action. But Henry the Impotent demurred. Of late his health had not been of the best. He wanted it both ways, in mortal terror for his soul. He told the whole sordid plot to the Cardinal of Spain and asked for absolution *in advance.*

Cardinal Mendoza broke through all the elaborate rules of Spanish etiquette in as curt an answer as ever was penned to a Castilian king. In a towering rage he not only refused to condone a triple murder; he also gave Henry some sound political advice. "In God's name do not sully your soul with such a deed, for you will have against you the whole realm, and especially the cities, who cleave to the princess your sister and are convinced that the succession to the crown belongs by right to her. And there might follow as a consequence of your act a great deal of inconvenience, nay, even of actual peril to your royal person."

"King Henry," said Cabrera dryly, "is not one to hazard his royal person."

On this the plot fell through, and the unpaid assassins,

complaining among their friends of the underworld, soon set off such a wagging of tongues that everyone knew the story.

"Henry is most delightfully inept," Ferdinand observed. He had not known the king was ill.

Isabella said, "Poor Henry. Poor half-mad half-brother."

In Segovia their stay was long. Ferdinand no longer went unattended on his walks but he was away from Isabella a good deal of the time, hunting, practicing his swordsmanship with Cordoba, who usually beat him, or breaking a lance with one of his Aragonians, whom he always beat. On rare occasions he permitted Isabella to hunt with him, protesting that he felt foolish riding after game fit only for ladies.

Isabella held her peace. Then one day when she could bear his patronizing manner no longer she snatched a hunting spear from one of his men and, spurring ahead of the rest, she personally skewered a wild boar with it, a beast Ferdinand had marked for his own as soon as it came charging out of a thicket.

"That was most unladylike," he said.

"Weren't you frightened?" Beatriz asked.

Isabella said, "To tell the truth, I didn't care what happened just at that moment."

But Ferdinand was moody for weeks. She felt she must have been wrong in beating him at his own game, when all she had wanted was to prove that she was good enough to hunt with him.

At length he said grudgingly, "No man ever pinned a boar more skillfully, Isabella. You didn't break a bone, and the taxidermist found the head in excellent condition to mount, not a scratch on it."

"It was just a lucky thrust, Ferdinand."

"Ah," he said.

"Actually I was terrified, and all I could think of was 'This thing must be destroyed.' Like—like a Moor."

In that at least they could agree.

He was softer in the nursery, and as the Infanta learned to walk and then to talk Isabella saw more of him. But not much. It seemed to her at times that his eyes strayed over to Beatriz more often than was comfortable; but soon he stopped, when Beatriz did not encourage him. Andres de Cabrera, never too cordial, was cooler than before after that. Isabella wondered if ever there would be a prince, and touched her iron cross, which was beginning to acquire a new meaning for her. Padre de Coca had been right: temperate was the word for Ferdinand. Sometimes she wondered if he had found a mistress. If so, she supposed she would never find out. Cautious Ferdinand would be the last to betray himself, and nobody ever tattled on royal princes, whose right to stray was sanctioned by custom as old as the custom of having statesmen choose whom they should marry. The promise she had exacted from Henry, that she should choose her own mate, was a double-edged sword. Doubly it was cutting her, for Henry was irreconcilably alienated and Ferdinand had become almost a stranger since their daughter was born. But she would have beaten her cross into a nail again and thrust it through her heart rather than tell him such thoughts.

The harvest that year was as poor as the last, and with the worsening of conditions came a new and more subtle attempt on their lives by that trinity of scoundrels in Valladolid: Henry, Villena, Juana. This time the plot was shrewdly interwoven with the slumbering anti-Semitism which had always existed in Europe and which in Spain invariably flared up when times were bad.

Queen Juana, alarmed at Henry's failing health, desperately desired settlement of the crown on her daughter La Beltraneja; and the continued existence of Isabella, Ferdinand and their child thwarted and enraged her. The Marques of Villena, confident that he could control La Beltraneja as easily as he had always controlled Henry, thoroughly shared her sentiments. In addition, Villena's revenues had fallen woefully, like everyone else's, and he longed for the keys to King Henry's coffers. King Henry willingly lent his ear, for the new proposal did not imperil his soul. Isabella, Ferdinand and their daughter were simply going to be killed incidentally in the confusion that would accompany a thorough purging of the traitorous Jews of Segovia.

The Jews of Segovia, Villena said, had bought up all the foodstuffs of the realm and were doling out their ill-gotten hoard a dribble at a time to increase their own filthy wealth while good Christians starved. Cabrera himself, the king's treasurer, the son of a Jew, must assuredly remain a Jew at heart; a most unwise appointment. He, the Marques of Villena, would have been a far better choice. Henry said Yes, he thought he would have been. "Your Highness has been ill used by this crypto-Jew," Villena said solemnly.

With the king's permission a strong force of soldiers advanced to Segovia; in the king's name Villena demanded admittance. Loyally, Cabrera admitted them.

They had come, Villena told him, to investigate certain irregularities in the municipal administration. They would not be long. Meanwhile he suggested the billeting of certain of his officers in the alcazar.

"My house is my king's, and yours," Cabrera said. But it seemed to him that the faces of Villena's officers were new, and oddly coarse.

He excused himself on the pretext of ordering a suitable supper for them. Once out of earshot, he whispered to Beatriz, "Take my guests to the tower. Let my personal guard lock the door, and stand watch *inside.*"

"Prince Ferdinand, too?"

"Even Prince Ferdinand."

"Why, Andres?"

"Look at the faces of Villena's 'officers.'"

"Oh, Andres!"

"And you, Beatriz. Lock yourself in the keep also."

"No."

"This is the only time I have ever commanded you."

"It must be very bad."

"It is. But what it is I do not yet know. You will obey me?"

"Yes, Andres."

He concealed a mailed vest under his doublet and ordered a sumptuous repast. He gave certain orders to a captain and hurried back to the great hall.

"Now we shall talk about these municipal irregularities," he said amiably to Villena. "My books are open for your inspection. I am somewhat bewildered by this visitation. For years I have made weekly reports to His Highness, but I cannot recall a single instance when His Highness has reproached me with irregularity."

"No doubt we shall get to the root of the trouble." Villena smiled, nibbling delicately at a bit of pheasant on the prongs of one of Cabrera's silver forks, while his officers, having eaten with their hands as usual, cleaned their fingernails with theirs.

"Men come up from the ranks these days," Villena said.

"Rapidly, I should say."

"Purely on merit."

"And for special services?"

"My dear Cabrera, merit always entails special service."

Outside there was sudden screaming. The cries of pain came from a quarter that Cabrera knew well. It was the *Judería* just under the walls of the alcazar. He set down his glass of dessert wine, his face flaming with anger.

"I see!" he roared.

"Don't you think you ought to go out and investigate?" Villena said. "You of *all* people? The call of the blood, you know."

"You swine!"

"Swine? Oh dear me. Naturally that would offend you."

Cabrera flung himself out of the room.

Villena was instantly on his feet. "Now!"

The officers wiped their mouths and loosened their daggers and ran in separate directions toward all the apartments of the great old castle.

Cabrera was not unprepared. In a court behind the kitchens he knew that his men were waiting, mounted and armed. They had sometimes complained of his strict discipline; now they were glad of it; it was going to save their lives. He ran through the kitchens to the postern door to put himself at their head, smiling grimly. Only one order from his king had he ever disobeyed; only one law of his country had he ever broken. He had never inquired too closely whether some strong young Jew who came asking to be admitted into his service had been baptized as the law required of all who bore arms. Only his iron discipline was holding back some of his soldiers from dashing out and putting a stop to the pogrom in which their relatives were at this very instant being butchered. Beyond the walls a glow appeared in the sky and he smelled the smoke of houses burning.

"The pattern complete," he growled.

At the postern door he felt an unexpected hand on his shoulder. He whirled to defend himself.

"You!" he gasped. "How did you get out?"

"Your wife let me out," Ferdinand said. He had on a steel cuirass and an open-faced helm. "You've an excellent armory up there."

"Beatriz didn't let you out."

"I was forced to suspend her over a drop-hole for a moment to persuade her," Ferdinand said.

"Maria Santísima!"

"I was extremely careful not to drop her. I am most sorry to have had to manhandle your good wife."

"The keep is locked again?"

"All quite secure. A villainous-looking creature in the passage delayed me for a moment, but I killed him. Now, sir? Which way? I shall follow you, since you know the city.
"

"You'll be fighting for a lot of miserable Jews," Cabrera said dubiously.

"Disorders of this sort are highly distasteful to me," Ferdinand said.

"God bless you, mi señor!" And with those words Cabrera called him "lord," a hard-wrung concession from a Castilian to an Aragonian.

During all the anxious hours of that long night the women looked down from the tower, straining their eyes to pierce the darkness, unable to see how the fighting was going in the murky streets below, praying for their husbands while the little Infanta slept peacefully on Cabrera's old army cot. Towards morning the fires burnt themselves out in the *Judería*. The snorting of warhorses, the furious yells of struggling men, the screams of the wounded, the killing noises of steel on steel, steel in flesh, died away, Off in the distance in the first gray light of dawn they saw a column of horsemen forming before the city gate, which presently opened and let them pass out.

"I think Andres gave the king's men a drubbing," Beatriz said.

"Ferdinand did his share!" Isabella said proudly.

"Oof!" Beatriz said, skittering away from the drop-hole, though now its trapdoor was closed. "He terrified me."

Isabella smiled; she would have laughed gaily if Ferdinand had been there, but as yet none of Cabrera's men had come back to the castle. As the light grew stronger they could be seen throwing sand on the blood in the city streets and beating out the smouldering remains of the foes; and carrying off the motionless bodies of many who might be dead or might be only dying. From such a distance all the bodies looked small, of course, but some were much smaller than the rest. Isabella looked over to where her child lay sleeping. How small would *she* look in a *Judería*? About that small, she imagined.

"Oh Beatriz, it's frightful!"

"Andres says pogroms are always like this."

"I will never permit them when I am queen."

Beatriz shrugged. "No sovereign has ever been able to stop them, and some have tried. This one was started by Villena; Andres knows he wants to be treasurer. But usually they just happen. Everybody hates the Jews, especially when everybody is poor. Don't you?"

"I don't really hate anyone; except the Moors, and I don't think I'd hate even the Moors if they'd go back to Africa, where they belong."

"Well always have the Moors and we'll always have the Jews, and as long as we do we'll have trouble," Beatriz said.

She was talking exactly like Ferdinand, Isabella thought. She wondered if boredom or some complex diplomatic motive had caused him to risk his life in a street battle for the Jews of Segovia. She had never heard him say one good word for any Jew. Now he was fighting for them like a Maccabee. Whatever his motive, she was proud of him.

In a short time there was a knock on the door of the castle keep. Cabrera's guard, with orders to open it to no one but him, shouted out that whoever it was had better go away or risk a rock's being dropped on his head. An Aragonian voice shouted through the oak that Prince Ferdinand desired his wife and his little princess to know that he was safe. Isabella thanked God. She told the Infanta that her father had been out for a walk last night and was coming home now.

"It was noisy last night," said the Infanta in the wonderful non-sequiturs of childhood, "and this bed is hard."

"Is Don Andres safe?" Beatriz called.

But the man at the door had gone away.

"Andres never tells me anything," Beatriz pouted.

"He will return. He knows the city, he is surrounded by devoted followers, God will protect him."

It was easy for Isabella to be reassuring now, Beatriz thought. And yet, if God had protected Ferdinand she could hope that God had also protected Andres. He certainly deserved it more.

About noon there was the sound of hooves and Cabrera led his victorious troops into the alcazar. There were very few riderless horses. But his face was troubled as he embraced his wife. Ferdinand glowed with the exhilaration that fighting always aroused in him.

As they passed along the battlements to the living quarters of the castle Cabrera pointed out a heap of about a dozen horribly disfigured corpses in the courtyard. "Villena's 'officers,'" he said. "I told my men they need not be gentle with them."

Isabella told the Infanta to turn her head and see how the broad fields of wheat were green on the horizon, a promise of better times. "Soon they will be yellow, like your hair, and everyone will have enough to eat."

"Let her look," Ferdinand said, "and learn what happens to those who would murder the daughters of kings."

The child looked, and saw nothing remarkable in death. Perhaps, Isabella thought, Ferdinand was right, for a princess would see much of death in a lifetime. She would have preferred such training for a prince, however.

At supper that night Ferdinand was inclined to be jovial and took one of his rare glasses of wine. A good many Jews had been murdered, but far more of the king's men had been slain. The Jews were already nailed up in their pine boxes, the Christians were being embalmed and Masses were being said. Order was restored in Segovia. The fires—nay, The Fire, the great fire of persecution from Valladolid —had been put out once and for all. He was certain of it. His confidence rose to complacency.

But Cabrera was worried. It troubled his conscience that he had warred against his king. "I could not do otherwise," he pleaded, as if justifying himself in a court of law. "I will not permit guests to be murdered. I will not permit defenseless people to be made scapegoats for a national calamity which is an act of God. And I do not propose to stand idly by while a scheming courtier plots to take over my post as the king's treasurer. I could have been a millionaire long since; no one from the court has ever even looked at my books. But I have never diverted a single maravedí to my own use. When a master is incompetent a steward must be doubly scrupulous."

"No doubt the sums are paltry, Henry's habits being what they are," Ferdinand suggested.

He was prying again, but this time Cabrera smiled and was not offended. "I shall never forget how you stood by me today," he said, and he volunteered to the ladies, "Had you seen Prince Ferdinand laying about him with his sword— one caballero's head jumped clean off his shoulders, still yelling!—You would have fallen on your knees and thanked God for such a man!"

"What do you suppose we were doing all last night?" Beatriz asked impudently. *"He* sent his wife a courier. You let me callus my kneebones."

Cabrera raised his glass to her and winked. To Ferdinand he continued frankly, "King Henry is not rich, but he is a good deal better off than he thinks. If he knew what he has, of course he'd spend it all; then I could not meet the demands he makes on me and I should be disgraced. So I do not let him know. The trick is in my books, which are absolutely accurate, believe me, but kept by a Jewish system called 'double entry.'"

Ferdinand used the same system in Aragón. "It isn't Jewish at all," he said. "I know it well."

"I don't," Beatriz said, "and 'double' sounds nasty, like 'duplicity.'"

"Not at all," Ferdinand said. "Merely analytical."

"Assets and Obligations are listed in parallel columns," Cabrera said. "The totals must always balance. To see if you have any money you have to look in the long list of figures *above* the totals and know what they mean, King Henry does actually have sufficient funds to keep the country from going bankrupt completely. But he and his fine friends at court only look at the totals. 'What?' they say. 'Assets and Obligations exactly equal? Then we haven't a penny!'"

Cabrera's shoulders slumped. "Someone must have seized on that detail to reproach me with irregularity. All the personal schemes of ambition and revenge came out into the open. The Marques and the queen sprang into action, with the dismal results that you saw: the pogrom of last night, the outrage that involved the guests under my roof. Victory was fruitless. I shall still lose my post; and how I can protect you after that I do not know."

"No," Isabella said. "That will not happen because it must not."

Ferdinand smiled. "Isabella is right, but as usual she speaks from the sure conviction of faith without bothering about details." He cut to the practical heart of the matter. "Henry has tried twice to kill us and twice failed. Most recently he tried to hide us under a mountain of corpses, like Uriah the Hittite, but that did not work either and we beat off his army. He is ill; for his age he is old, having ruined his constitution with coffee and other Moorish vices; his impotence marches from faculty to faculty, I am talking about your near relative, my dear Isabella, but facts are facts. He will degenerate, and with him the power of his faction."

"The Marques of Valeria did not look well either," Beatriz said.

"Indeed? I did not see him. That is an interesting observation."

"You did not see him because he did not fight," Cabrera said. "His was the glorious mission of leading the cutthroat 'officers.'"

"You let him escape, of course," Ferdinand said. His tone was one of command.

"Naturally, Your Highness."

"Good. Never make martyrs of court favorites. Good, Cabrera, good!"

184

Isabella was learning some of the more practical details of statecraft. They were not attractive. But she would have to be practical. She would have to live in the world. She was not afraid of it; it was a challenging world. It was good, for all its badness, and it could be made better.

"The Jews all over Castile will hear of this and love you," Cabrera said warmly to Ferdinand. "And do not minimize their power."

"I don't."

"On the other hand, some of the Old Christians won't be your friends."

"They will return to him in time," Isabella said. "Times will change; things will be better with good harvests. All this horror will be forgotten. Carrillo's troubles, Henry's troubles, all will pass and ours will, too. I know so; I pray so; and we shall have peace."

Ferdinand shook his head. "Peace will come only when King Henry is at peace, his long last personal peace; and even his death may not bring peace to Castile and Aragón. There is angry Portugal. There is threatening France."

It had been a long time since Isabella had worried over the attitude of neighboring kingdoms.

Perhaps Ferdinand, fresh from his street fighting, was already exhilarated by the prospect of war on a grander scale.

Again and again during the supper Andres de Cabrera said to the prince, "I shall never forget how you stood by me!" Before the evening was out Ferdinand was calling the king's treasurer mi primo.

CHAPTER 15

THE harvest was good that year. The fields of wheat that the little Infanta had seen green on the horizon beyond the heaps of mangled corpses turned from green to yellow, from yellow to gold, under the golden sun and the golden harvest moon of the autumn of 1474, full of the promise of plenty. For even famines must end. With the ending of the long cruel period of hunger the pestilence ended also, and the spirit of the people rose. On the other side of the Pyrenees the ailing, aging king of France read the signs of returning Spanish prosperity and feared a resurgence of Spanish strength, especially if the realm should come under the soft but fearless hand of Isabella, as every day seemed more likely. He had met her; he had sounded her still developing character by one of those feats of intuition for which the crafty old man was notorious: Isabella would be good for Spain. Therefore by definition, according to his lights, she would be bad for France. Therefore she must never be queen, and to that end he bent all the power of his diplomatic and military forces. Both were immense.

To Alfonso of Portugal, still smarting under Isabella's refusal, he sent couriers with costly presents and slyly provocative letters that were calculated to keep open and sore the old wounds of jealousy. The Castilian Infanta must have considered him senile, King Louis intimated; too old to love, too old to fight. Perhaps, suggested the king of France, she was too beautiful, perhaps too sensuous, undoubtedly too headstrong; she would overawe most men. Perhaps also, he implied, Alfonso *was* too old; and, twisting the dagger, he went on to hope in a sanctimonious vein that Alfonso would never suffer the mental and physical decline of their royal cousin, King Henry the Impotent.

In Portugal Alfonso sputtered and fumed, and sent out

a call for his armies.

But even if Alfonso should submit to the crowning of Isabella, King Louis declared, he, Louis of France, would align himself with the true Castilian heiress, the princess whose enemies derisively called her La Beltraneja. La Beltraneja was now thirteen years old, long since ripe to wed, and King Louis reminded King Alfonso that a dumpy figure and a pair of pop eyes were no impediment to royal marriages. Nor was a vast difference of age.

Alfonso reflected that a thirteen-year-old might be a pleasant playmate, to say nothing of the other benefits that would come with marriage with the Castilian heiress. No sovereign in Europe doubted the power of the Spider King of France to achieve his ends.

Alfonso's heralds carried back to France an effusive reply: Alfonso the African was as good as he ever was, he stated proudly, in war *and* in love, and his armies were already gathering against the great Castilian lords whom Isabella had bewitched. He, too, was for La Beltraneja, he stated; he, too, would fight to assure her succession to the throne. Nay more; to make that throne doubly secure Alfonso the African would take her to wife. Her figure might be ample, but so were her lands; and he was of a mind to cherish both.

On this King Louis struck at Aragón, where the mountain passes were low. There Ferdinand could be trusted to rush to defend his homeland and, God willing, get himself killed in battle. Diplomacy would bring Portugal against Castile from the west; a lucky swordthrust would cut off the life of the Aragonian heir, and sunder forever the nations that Isabella's marriage had threatened to unite into a major European power. It was a very good scheme, King Louis mused, one of his best. From the military point of view it was impregnable. Isabella might bewitch the Castilian grandees, but not the Portuguese, not the French, and above all not the Swiss mercenaries in his pay who fought only for money.

Shortly a courier arrived post-haste, grim-faced, from

the field headquarters of the King of Aragón. "The king bade me say—" the courier began.

"I can read," Ferdinand answered, cutting him off. "Kindly remove your hat, and next time be good enough to brush the dust off you before you present me with a dispatch."

"Perhaps it is bad news, my dear," Isabella said. The herald's face was gray with the urgency of his message and twitched with fatigue.

Deliberately Ferdinand broke the seal and unrolled the scroll. "Father is indestructible," he said. It was hard for Isabella to guess whether he meant to convey a compliment or to reproach his aged sire for failing to die and vacate the Aragonian throne. "Father is in no danger."

"But, Sir," the herald muttered, "he is. He is fighting the French."

"Naturally," said Ferdinand, reading slowly, tracing each word with his finger, spelling out some of the harder ones.

"But he fights in person, on horseback, in bodily contact with the invaders."

"That is foolhardy," Ferdinand said. "Please be silent."

Isabella said, "I should call it heroic."

"Please!" said Ferdinand sharply. The courier bowed himself out of their presence. Ferdinand's tone to his wife embarrassed him.

It was an appeal to his son for help. The French, without the formality of a declaration of war, had suddenly attacked in force on the frontier at Roussillon and threatened to burst through. "I can handle the cavalry," King John said stoutly, "and so far we have managed to hold our own. But the French are bringing up guns, our own are ineffective and only you can direct this new-fangled artillery. I don't understand the confounded engines. Come to me."

"You must go, of course," Isabella said.

"Of course," Ferdinand said.

She did not weep but her face was grave. "I shall miss

you, mi señor."

He did not answer.

"And pray for you every day."

"Thank you, Isabella."

It would have been good to hear that he would miss her, too. But it was almost as good to hear him say, "Take care of my Infanta." His color rose, his eyes snapped and he seemed anxious to be off. That, too, was good. For the state. And did not a princess, would not a queen, live for the state? She touched her iron cross.

"You will keep me informed, Ferdinand?"

"That will be most important. I wonder that you ask. Of course I shall keep you informed."

"I mean about yourself."

"If I write," he laughed, "I am alive. And Isabella. About this Jew Cabrera. Cherish his friendship, do not offend him, keep on his good side."

It was not a time to argue that Andres de Cabrera was not a Jew. "I have always been proud of his friendship," she said.

"Good. Good. Good."

He kissed her coolly on the cheek and left Segovia that same day. He kissed the Infanta on the mouth, chucking her under the chin and smiling, "One of my walks, hijita. To blow up some dirty Frenchmen. I shan't be long. Say a nice prayer for me."

"Si, papito," the child said, wide-eyed. Did one encounter dirty Frenchmen on walks? And blow them up?

"You should say *mi padre,* not papito," Isabella corrected.

"For goodness' sake don't be so formal with the child," Ferdinand said.

Those were his last, or nearly his last words, that mild reproach, before he took horse for a war that might easily be the death of him. Isabella supposed he must have said good-bye—he was meticulously polite—before he, Valdes,

189

Cordoba and the rest of his personal suite spurred out of the gate of the alcazar. But how his polite good-bye might have been phrased she could not remember: probably the casual and stilted "I kiss your hands, your feet." If he had been irritated at her correction of the Infanta why had he not barked at her, or cursed, as Beatriz de Bobadilla sometimes cursed? Is it easier to live with fire or ice? But she could not deny he was brave. Cool bravery in a king is better than intemperance and cowardice. Better for the state.

Sometimes in her prayers she prayed, "Maria Santísima, thou who knowest the heart of woman, why was I not born a peasant instead of a princess? It is extremely difficult when one is young to think only of the state."

Then she remembered that Joan of Arc was born a peasant, and she was ashamed; for Joan of Arc had also been young and had also dedicated her entire life to a state and ended that life at the age of eighteen in a fiery martyrdom to her high calling.

Ferdinand's absence was protracted. His frequent couriers brought detailed news of the fighting, couched in formal official language as impersonal as that which the criers proclaimed in the public markets.

Isabella embroidered altar cloths and taught the Infanta to sew and read and worked like a starving sempstress till her eyes were red and her fingers sore on the one thing she still could do for Ferdinand: his shirts. She was an accomplished needlewoman. "Stitches fine as a nun's," she would sometimes say with tight-lipped irony to Beatriz. Ever since putting on the first shirt she had made for him just after their marriage Ferdinand had refused to wear any others. That, at least, was something not for the state.

Ferdinand's dispatches—she could not call them letters—were full of good news. "Our artillery is cutting down the dirty French like a scythe. Soon they will be back where they belong. The king, my father, continues in the best of health.

"Pray let me have private word from my friend Don Andres de Cabrera how it goes with His Highness King Henry, whose health, as I hear, is not good. It elevates the spirits of my troops to witness the mass of dead Frenchmen after every encounter, and also mine. Few of the slain are noble, the French fashion being to fight with peasants and mercenaries. My work has greatly stimulated me."

Death, which Ferdinand found so stimulating among the lowly, struck twice in Castile in rapid succession that winter, with consequences that greatly irritated him.

By one of the exquisite ironies of history the dandified, greedy, arrogant Marques of Villena died in a barber chair while his barber was curling and perfuming his crisp little beard. It was the fourth of October, the day on which the Church commemorated the death of the humblest, simplest, sweetest of the saints, Francis of Assisi, who preached even to beasts and birds and blessed the fire that cauterized a painful wound, calling the torturing element "brother". Cardinal Mendoza, praying for the soul of Villena, sought in vain to find a parallel between him and Saint Francis to take as a text for his funeral oration.

Dutifully Isabella sent a letter of condolence to King Henry, who did not answer. For a few short weeks he languished, sad, forlorn, bereft of the friend who had beggared him, padding about the palace weeping like a woman and refusing to eat or even to drink his coffee. It was noticed that his eyes had a filmy look, like those of a fish too long out of water, and that he stumbled into things as if he could not see them.

On the night between Sunday and Monday in the dead of a cold Castilian winter that was healthy for everyone else, the Cardinal of Spain was called to his bedside. Henry was very low and sinking fast.

All that a priest could do for a mortal *in extremis* Mendoza did; and afterwards, before Henry became quite irrational, he gently reminded him:

"The mystery of your life, my lord, is that you have never said yes or no to the question, 'Is the princess known as La Beltraneja your daughter or not?' This solemn last hour all men must face. Pride falls away, shame falls away as the flesh that has cursed us decays, and the eye glows clear in the glory of God's mercy and promise of redemption. For the good of the realm over which God set you king, speak now and spare many lives as your last good act. For assuredly thousands will perish in bloody wars if you do not speak."

Henry the Impotent turned his face to the wall. Once indeed he spoke, but only to say, "Life has used me ill," and died.

The Cardinal sighed. Life had truly used Henry ill. But it worked both ways. It was no less true that Henry had used life ill, monstrously ill. In his trained ecclesiastical mind Cardinal Mendoza reflected that it was now two o'clock in the morning, the morning of December twelfth, a day on which the Church commemorated the death of no one. No one at all. How pitifully fitting for Henry the Impotent of Castile!

For a moment the nation paused. It was usual for Castilian sovereigns to leave a will, setting forth the broad outlines of the policies they wished continued after their death. Though not clothed with the force of law such solemn documents were always respectfully received and adhered to as far as was practicable. But King Henry, indecisive to the end, left no will to guide his followers. His legacy to his people was confusion, the one consistent element in his nature.

A herald brought news before dawn to Segovia from Valladolid informing the king's treasurer that the king was no more. He was sent, he said, by Queen Juana and the Marques—the young Marques, son of the old—of Villena. And he requested ten thousand florins for current expenses in connection with the king's funeral expenses. Cabrera thanked him cordially for the information and sent him away without a maravedí; then he locked the city gates.

"King Henry's death," Cabrera said to his wife, "was the one, single, unique, irrevocable, positive act that my late unmasterful master was ever able to achieve." He squared his shoulders as if a great burden had been lifted from them, "While he lived I was under the yoke of my sworn oath of fealty. Now I am free. Beatriz, my sweet, how shall we break the news to your friend?"

"That her wretched half-brother is dead? Why, softly, softly, Andres. Isabella will mourn even him."

"That he is dead forsooth!" For the first time in her presence Andres de Cabrera forgot his good manners and spat contemptuously. "That she is *queen,* you silly goose!"

"Andres! You will declare for her? You darling!" She hugged him in front of a server who was giving them a hot pre-dawn breakfast on this exciting day that would be momentous in the history of Castile and—had a magician been able to peer into the future—momentous in the history of the world. On this cold winter day when it lay with the Christian Jew Andres de Cabrera to deliver the keys of the treasury of Castile either to Isabella or to La Beltraneja, and in so doing make a queen, an invisible curtain was ringing down on the last act of the Middle Ages. A Modern Age was about to be born into a world which, through Isabella of Spain, was to double and treble in size. But this was a turn in human affairs that no one living could foresee. Cabrera, like all good men, merely followed his conscience and did what seemed right at the time.

He said to Beatriz, "La Beltraneja is not Henry's daughter. Everyone knows it; the Church has declared it; and twice King Henry, by his actions, himself admitted it. Isabella is therefore my true sovereign and rightful queen."

"And you are still the royal treasurer!"

"If she retains me in my post."

"As if she wouldn't! But, Andres, she must be crowned at once. The old factions will start fighting again unless she is."

"Unquestionably, France threatens. Portugal threatens. The factions threaten, weakening us internally. She must indeed be crowned at once. Today!"

"I don't know how she will take the fact of her husband's absence," Beatriz said dubiously. "She may refuse to be crowned until he returns."

"There won't be time. That would be fatal, Beatriz."

"He'll come scampering home in a frightful sulk," Beatriz said. "He's choleric and greedy under his cold exterior. I don't see how she can love him."

"He's a Jew-hater and a paltry man," Cabrera said flatly. *"Mi primo,* he called me. But that was because I hold the keys to the royal coffers. I admire his bravery in a fight, but he does not fool me, not for a minute."

"And Isabella?"

Cabrera grinned. "You taught me to like her, and then, when I knew her better—"

"She bewitched you? Like everybody else? I'll skewer her with my poignard in her sleep; that I will!"

"She bewitched you, too, Beatriz."

"Nay, that is true," Beatriz said softly. "Even when we were both little girls. Nobody can know her without loving her, neither a man nor a woman."

"Now be off with you to her apartment, Beatriz, and wake her up and tell her she's a queen—at least if she acts quickly."

"I'd certainly act quickly to be a queen." Beatriz smiled.

Isabella's first act was to order the standards of Castile, of Aragón and the city of Segovia edged in black for the dead king and flown at half-staff over the towers of the alcazar. She herself put on a mourning gown and prayed a long hour; and then she pleaded with Beatriz and Cabrera for delay till Ferdinand could be informed and return from Aragón.

"I have already sent couriers to him, to France and Portugal and even to England, with the news of King Henry's death."

"And of your accession to the throne!" Beatriz added excitedly.

Isabella looked at Cabrera reproachfully.

"There is so little time, Your Highness. In fact, there is absolutely *no* time! Please let me try to explain."

Beatriz shot him a warning glance. "Please let *me*, Andres."

Cabrera smiled, bowed himself backward to the door. It was Isabella's first taste of the elaborate royal etiquette that she knew so well but that had never before been accorded her until this moment. She was already queen. The sovereign dies, but the sovereignship never; and coronation is only a formality, though a splendid one with tremendous power to cement a divided nation. That realization took some of the sting, some of it, out of the accident of Ferdinand's absence and the necessity of being crowned alone.

Beatriz talked to her, alternately pleading and warning, and once even skirting the dangerous subject of Ferdinand's enormous personal ambition: how would he value her, she managed to convey tactfully, if, through an excess of devotion, Isabella should lose Castile to La Beltraneja? The shot struck home and Isabella's chin went up in that gesture of determination that Beatriz knew so well.

Isabella did not order the recall of the diplomatic couriers who were now speeding to all the chancelleries of Europe with the news that she had accepted the crown.

In spite of Cabrera's intense desire to bring about Isabella's coronation that very same day he could not quite manage it. The Archbishop of Toledo, whose traditional privilege it was to crown the Castilian sovereigns, sent a courier with a testy message that his Archiepiscopal Reverence was praying for the soul of King Henry and would require a day at least.

Cabrera snorted. "More likely he's still trying to make gold in his laboratory!"

Beatriz answered thoughtfully, "I'm not so sure. Isabella was afraid he might not show up at all. Ferdinand thinks

Carrillo is wavering over towards Henry's side. He used to be her strongest supporter and now she never hears from him."

"Then we will make her queen by simple proclamation. It's perfectly legal."

"That wouldn't have the same effect on the people, Andres. They'd feel cheated if they didn't actually see the crown on her head."

Cabrera nodded. "I know, I know. But every day lost adds strength to La Beltraneja's claim."

Next day, however, Carrillo appeared; he was thinner, far older and somewhat sulky in manner. Privately Cabrera confided to Beatriz that the vain old prelate probably could not resist the temptation to put on the gorgeous ecclesiastical display in which he would be almost as conspicuous as the queen herself. But Isabella greeted him as if nothing between them had changed. Carrillo thawed slightly under her smile.

His was the only stern face in Segovia that day. Everyone else was smiling, and the common people who lined the narrow cobbled streets to watch the procession to the public square were jubilant. Even when a good king died his successor was welcomed in high hope and happy spirit, for an era ended and it was natural to believe that tomorrow would be better than yesterday. But when a bad king died, a king whose rule had brought nothing but misery, the hope for a better tomorrow rose to a passion. Such was the mood that welled up from the sea of faces like a wave and communicated itself to Isabella.

In a gown of white satin and ermine she rode a white palfrey caparisoned in cloth of gold that reached to the animal's fetlocks. On it were embroidered the red lions of Leon and the black castles of Castile in a dazzling and beautiful pattern. Her head was bare, for it was about to receive a crown and no other headdress must cover it that day.

On her right side, holding her horse's silver bridle, Archbishop Carrillo walked in his primate's purple cope, gloved, mitred and ringed, flanked by his crosier bearer. On her left, holding the other rein of the bridle was a smiling Andres de Cabrera in a jaunty velvet cap and his massive chain of office.

A guard of caballeros followed, sword-girt and golden-spurred, the ribbons and crosses and stars of their orders glittering on their breasts; and in the center of the guard walked two young pages of noble birth bearing on a velvet cushion the greatest treasure ever confided to the coffers of Andres de Cabrera: the crown of Saint Ferdinand, three hundred years old. Isabella reflected that Saint Ferdinand also had had to contend with factions, and that the union of Castile and Leon had been the result. In one of those inconsequential bypaths of the mind, where little thoughts wander off when the mind is under the stress of great emotion, she wondered if Saint Ferdinand and his wife were happy. How odd to think about saints' wives, yet countless numbers of them had had them. It did not concern her. She wasn't married to a saint, and the silly notion made her smile till her remarkably white and even teeth shone dazzlingly between her lips, which were especially red that day with the rapid beating of her heart.

Suddenly she was aware how public she was. The brilliant smile, her wind-whipped pink cheeks, the glitter of the cloth of gold reflected in her copper hair, all set off by the flashing whiteness of her gown and the black-flecked whiteness of her ermine—the effect was theatrical, and the people began to cheer and shout as if they had seen a vision.

"Castilla! Castilla por la Reyna, Castile for Doña Isabella! Castile for the queen! Viva la princesa! Long live the Queen Proprietress!" This was Isabella's day. But a few here and there remembered her consort. There were some who shouted for Don Ferdinand also. On these she smiled especially warmly.

In the latter ranks of the long procession were monks, priests, councilmen, soldiers, men at arms, crossbowmen, musicians, trumpeters, drummers and the rabble of common people, rich and poor, mingled helter-skelter as they swarmed in the march to the public square.

At the *very* head of the procession, almost unnoticed because it was a symbol that had lost all meaning in the reign of King Henry, a herald in royal livery carried a naked sword, its point straight up, its hilt at eye level. It was the sovereign's sword of justice and it signified the power of life and death that Isabella traditionally held over every one of her ten million subjects. The day was very bright; the sky was very blue, the same bright blue that deepened the azure of Isabella's eyes and suppressed the flecks of green. On the sword of justice that blue glinted steely cold; never had the weapon looked sharp before.

In the center of the public square Isabella mounted a platform that had been erected, carpeted and draped with banners as soon as news had arrived of Henry's death. She seated herself in a great thronelike chair of state, looking very small and white, her face now grave.

The prayers and invocations were long, and at first Carrillo played his part with tedious deliberation. But soon the cold struck under his cope and chilled his bones and he spoke the words more rapidly, longing for the fires of his laboratory or at least the candles of the cathedral. Beatriz was shivering. She wondered how Isabella could go through the ceremony bareheaded. The odd thought struck her that crowns are not warm.

At length Carrillo took the crown from the velvet cushion, which the Grand Admiral now presented to him. He held it aloft for the people to see. A hush fell over them, silent with awe. Gently he placed it on Isabella's copper-colored curls, which the wind had mussed a little. It fitted perfectly.

"Don't let it fall off!" he interpolated into the solemn ritual of the coronation service. His whisper had something of the warmth of his old familiar fatherly manner.

"I won't!" she replied with the ghost of a smile.

Somehow, he did not think she would; ever.

From the square the procession formed in slow march to the cathedral where a Te Deum was chanted, while all the bells of the city rang out the joyous tidings that Castile had a new queen, and lombards thundered from the walls with a voice that carried far over the countryside.

Spurring south from the border war Ferdinand learned that he was too late, that his wife had not waited for him, and that she had permitted herself to be crowned alone.

He flew into a rage. He devised a revenge. It was intimate, unexpected and exceedingly painful to Isabella.

CHAPTER 16

HAVING heard the news of Isabella's coronation, Ferdinand did not return to Castile, as had been his first intention, but proceeded to Saragossa, capital of Aragón. It had been six years since he had seen his bastard son. Meanwhile the child had been under the care of a court lady named Joanna, of boundless good nature and a vague Catalan claim to nobility, who had served first as his wet nurse and, now that he was a little older, served as his governess.

Alonzo was a stalwart, handsome child. Ferdinand took to him at once when Joanna presented him in the nursery, with its hard little bed and its litter of toy guns, toy swords, toy soldiers.

"Good!" said Ferdinand. "You're making a man of him even if you are only a woman." At the moment he thoroughly disliked all women.

"Your Majesty is too kind," the governess said.

"Eh?"

Ferdinand was doubly a king, now that Isabella was crowned but be was not a "majesty." Only one European sovereign, the King of France, had achieved that grandiose title. "You know how to flatter, mistress Joanna," He looked at her critically.

She was dimpled and pink and petite.

"Your Highness struck me as so formidable and brave, I must have been thinking of how you rescued your dear old sire, the king, when the Frenchmen nearly took him captive." She referred to an incident on the border where the aged paladin had spurred into the melee, grown short of breath and, of course, been surrounded by Swiss pikemen, anxious to share in the ransom of so rich a prize. Gonsalvo de Cordoba had instantly led a furious charge of mailed knights, extricating the king before any serious damage was done, and Ferdinand, quitting his post at the guns in the rear, had rushed in to help. The governess continued apologetically, "'Majesty' just slipped out, since it is so richly deserved."

"I did only what any son would have done," Ferdinand replied in measured tones, "and Don Gonsalvo de Cordoba must be given his fair share of the credit, for he was of great assistance."

"You too will grow up to be a great warrior like your kingly father," the governess said to Alonzo. "He is a spirited young man, Your Highness, as you see, and is already directing his battles." She indicated the toys.

"I have other plans for my son," Ferdinand said. Ruffling the lad's crisp black hair he said, "Well, hombre, how would you like to be an archbishop?"

"I do not know, sir."

"Sire, not sir," Ferdinand said.

"I do not know, sire."

"I have not taught him to say 'sire', because—well, the circumstances of his birth—it would set people to gossiping."

"Everyone will soon know that I am his sire," Ferdinand said. "Sire as sovereign, sire also as father."

"You will acknowledge him publicly? Oh, Your Highness, Your good, sweet, generous Highness!" She permitted a tear of joy to well and sparkle in her eyes, which made them shine very prettily, as she was perfectly aware, and grasped his hand, kissing it warmly and affectionately.

"Tut, tut, lass," Ferdinand reprimanded, vastly pleased with her. But he was by no means blind to the fact that his public acknowledgment of his bastard would enormously enhance her standing at the Aragonian court.

"If Your Highness could only see your way clear to retain me in my position after you do this wonderful thing!" she pleaded, beginning to weep again. "I love the boy so! He is part of me!"

Ferdinand eyed her coolly up and down. She had much

of Beatriz de Bobadilla's dark beauty, but softer, in a yielding sort of way.

"I rather think I shall." Ferdinand smiled.

"An archbishop!" breathed Joanna ecstatically. "To be governess to an archbishop! I shall get candles and books and incense and bells, Your Maj—Your Highness, and raise him up to be a holy man."

Ferdinand grinned. "Put the incense in his cannons to make them smoke. He won't be entering upon his archiepiscopal duties for quite a while."

The Archbishop of Saragossa had recently died, and the richest: ecclesiastical plum of all Aragón had not yet been awarded to a successor. All kings enjoyed tremendous power of nomination to such vacant posts, and the Church nearly always confirmed secular rulers' choices. Sometimes they chose minors, who were duly invested with the titles and revenues but who, of course, performed no ecclesiastical functions, their duties being delegated to genuine prelates. It was one of the ways that the Church, to preserve its universality in an age of growing nationalism, compromised with greedy kings, lest by failing to yield a little the Faith of Christendom break up into a hodge-podge of national churches, and thus lose all. Ferdinand, of course, would personally administer the revenues of the new little archbishop.

Archbishop Alonzo of Saragossa was duly nominated, duly confirmed. A herald rode to Segovia with the news. Isabella discovered that her husband had a bastard son the same age as their Infanta, plus a scant, scant year, and was heaping honors upon him.

But yielding and dimpled as the archbishop's governess was, Ferdinand did not dally with her for long.

His father warned him, "These things have a way of bearing embarrassing fruit, my son. I know from experience, and so should you."

"My wife has chosen to live her own life, and so can I," Ferdinand answered stiffly.

"I think you'd better go back to Castile," the old king said. "Gonsalvo de Cordoba can manage the trouble on the border now; it seems to have let up a bit after they failed to catch me. Good man, Don Gonsalvo."

"For a Castilian, yes."

Ferdinand was still angry. He resented his father's advice and he resented his father's praise of Cordoba. Since he knew that both were justly deserved he sought out the one weak chink in the tired old sovereign's armor.

"I am astonished that you have permitted the municipal administration of Saragossa to degenerate so lamentably in my absence. Taxes are usuriously farmed to Jews, the constabulary are not paid, crime is rampant in the streets and no decent women dare go abroad even in daylight without an armed escort. Why have you done nothing to curb this Ximenes Gordo, who is responsible for the city's order?"

"Son, it's wartime," the king said wearily. "Things always go a little lax in war. Mayor Gordo is no saint, I agree; but in the absence of troops he's the only one who can keep any order at all. The common people respect him because he is one of them. I know that he steals from me."

"I shall have to defer my return to Castile till I can bring him to reason," Ferdinand said unpleasantly.

"I think Isabella misses you, and you'd better bring him to reason fast," King John said dubiously.

"If she misses me why doesn't she write and tell me so?"

"You must admit, son, that you gave her a fearful jolt with Alonzo's sudden appearance on the scene."

Ferdinand scowled.

Shortly Isabella did write. She praised her husband's thorough drubbing of the French. "They are reported to be gathering above Guipuzcoa, however," she warned, and added, "I need you," entreating him to return to Castile, to be received as King Consort and to accept the allegiance of the grandees of their party who were waiting to kiss his hand. "One of them will surprise you, mi señor," she wrote.

"Don Beltran de la Cueva has declared for us! Truly this is a world in which each new day brings new surprises, both pleasant and unpleasant." That was as close as Isabella could bring herself to confess her terrible hurt at the thunderbolt news of the Archbishop of Saragossa.

Still unappeased, he replied that he could not come until one pressing duty in Saragossa could be discharged. He promised her that it would not take long. It did not.

Mayor Ximenes Gordo received a flattering invitation to present himself at the palace. Prince Ferdinand wished, said the messenger, to meet him face to face and show how deeply he appreciated Gordo's administration of the city during these trying times.

Gordo, sensing another chain of office to hang on his shoulders, complied at once. To his surprise he was told by a lackey at the gate that this was not to be a public audience; Prince Ferdinand would meet him alone in his private apartments, a signal honor. Gordos chest swelled out like a pouter pigeon's with pride. He was a Jewish convert, a New Christian. Well might he be proud. Ferdinand was notorious for his aversion to them.

In the private apartment he looked around, bewildered. It was absolutely silent and empty. Then from behind an arras there stepped a priest, and from another, a public executioner, Saragossa's official hangman. Then Ferdinand walked through the door.

"I regret the necessity of this summary procedure." Ferdinand smiled. "Kindly confess your crimes to the padre here, before I judge you, lest you leave this life with your sins still black on your soul."

Gordo screamed and began to run. The hangman struck him down from behind with a small hand axe.

"I knew he was a Jew at heart," Ferdinand said to the priest "He didn't confess a word."

The body was exposed in the public market all next day. There was far less disorder in Saragossa after that; and then, having spent his rage in a whirlwind bout of blood and lust, Ferdinand returned to Castile.

If Isabella had been nothing but a farmer's wife and her husband a mere peasant, all the neighbors for miles around would have been gossiping about her troubles, since nothing is ever quite so fascinating as other people's private affairs. Since she was queen and Ferdinand king the gossip reached national proportions.

"How will she receive him?" Cabrera asked anxiously. "And do stop crying, Beatriz. *I* haven't got any bastard sons up my sleeve!"

"How can I be sure!" Beatriz snapped. Her eyes were swollen and red.

"This isn't a bit good for the state, you know. As if we were not already disastrously divided! If sovereigns cannot live in unity how can you expect the nation to? Now there will be a Ferdinand-faction and an Isabella-faction, added to all the other factions."

"Oh no, there won't! You do not know Isabella. How will she receive him? She will receive him like a *queen*. That is the only way to curb the brute!"

Tight-lipped and dry-eyed, but sickly pale, Isabella had been in conference for several days with the best legal minds and the most loyal grandees of her following, noble, civil and ecclesiastic. Everyone knew the personal affront she had suffered. Not once did she mention it. Since she must live for Spain she resolved to make Spain worth living for, for every Spaniard, and for Ferdinand. Beatriz' warning had struck deep into her heart: How will he value you if you lose?

Ferdinand was not prepared for the kind of reception he received. Having vented his spleen, he was in a sober, defensive mood, with the text on his lips that a man should be master in his own house.

She received him seated on a throne in the great hall of the castle, with a jeweled tiara on her curls, surrounded by a brilliant assembly of the most powerful aristocracy of Castile. Her pallor heightened her beauty; her slender figure seemed almost transfigured in the midst of her retainers; power like a visible glow seemed to flow from her to them and from them to her. It struck him with palpable humbling force that this beautiful, regal woman was his wife, round whom now centered the ancient majesty of Castile, tierra de cantos y santos. He noted with a start that Cardinal Mendoza was there. How had she charmed *him* over to her side? Their faces were grave, but not hostile. Suddenly he felt as if he were on trial.

Yet Isabella wore his ring; Isabella wore his necklace. She wore his cross. If he was on trial the judge at least was friendly.

She rose to greet him and extended her hand, but did not advance. He found himself mounting the dais, kneeling, kissing her hand. Instinctively he had performed the act of homage. Later, to his astonishment, he discovered that that was exactly what had been expected of him as Consort of the Queen Proprietress of Castile. Then, on an impulse, he kissed her cheek, it looked so pale, Isabella colored slightly, and the cheer that went up from the crowded hall was not the cold formal shout of acceptance that it might have been if he had not made his little husbandly gesture.

Isabella held his hand as he seated himself in the vacant throne that stood beside her own. Over all the objections of the College of Heralds she had insisted that it be exactly on a level with her own, though Castilian tradition demanded that the throne of a consort should stand a good three inches lower than the sovereign's. It felt very good, Ferdinand thought.

Good, too, it was to hear the shouts, "Castile for Don Ferdinand, Castilla por El Rey, for the king, por los reyes, for our sovereigns!" He was King of Castile.

Then, beginning with Cardinal Mendoza, the great lords knelt and kissed his hand, swearing their allegiance to him.

These stony-proud Castilians at his feet! At that moment, with all the temperance of his nature, which, like the submerged portion of an iceberg, constituted eight-ninths of it, he greatly regretted some of his recent behavior in Aragón, particularly the nonsense with Alonzo's governess.

Isabella, with a thoroughness that amazed him—he was always discovering new sides to his wife—had fortified herself for a far more drastic rift than now actually developed. Her lawyers had prepared masterful defenses for every one of the provisions of their marriage contract and demonstrated for the benefit of his essentially practical mind how they did not degrade him but, on the contrary, actually worked for his advantage as well as for hers, and above all for the good of a united Spain. As for bearing the naked sword of justice in front of a mere woman, a detail about which he was known to have raged, did he wish the disorderly conditions of Henry's reign to continue into his own? In a realm where all decrees were to be signed jointly by Ferdinand and Isabella, Io El Rey, Io La Reyna, did he not wish his decrees to be received with some weight?

If Isabella could not bewitch him, and she had no hope that she could, she had had faith that she could persuade him. She succeeded in doing both.

"Now," said Cabrera, breathing a sigh of relief, "she can put him to work. There is fighting aplenty for him."

"Maybe he isn't all brute," Beatriz conceded grudgingly.

In the intimacy that followed, born of Isabella's pent-up yearning, born of Ferdinand's heavy conscience and disgust that he had ever neglected her for Alonzo's governess, Ferdinand said, "I am sorry that I had to stay so long in Aragón."

"You were fighting in a noble cause," Isabella said. "I was with you every minute." He knew what she meant, but it made him uncomfortable. Some of those minutes especially.

She did not mention Alonzo, but Ferdinand felt he had

to. "I didn't even know you when I knew the lad's mother. I had to acknowledge him some day, you know. That's only fair."

"I did not reproach you, my dear."

He wished she had. He could have asserted the ancient right of princes to stray. She stole his thunder.

"How did you manage to gain Cardinal Mendoza? Isabella, my little statesman, that was the master stroke!"

"He came of his own accord. Henry wouldn't acknowledge La Beltraneja even on his deathbed, and Mendoza just couldn't stomach her claim. Do you know what is going to happen to La Beltraneja now?"

"I have been very busy," Ferdinand said. "Out of touch. What? A nunnery?"

"She is going to marry King Alfonso of Portugal."

"Oh, *no!*" Ferdinand laughed. His laugh and their intimate talks once again made Isabella's heart sing, "But I'm afraid that's going to prove awkward, my dear," he said soberly on second thought.

"It is. Louis of France won't recognize you and me; he's backing La Beltraneja. Mendoza thinks we're going to have a war on two fronts: Portugal and France. Poor Henry! He could so easily have avoided a War of Succession. Oh my dear, my dear, I am glad you have returned to me. *There is so much to do!* We can only do it together."

Ferdinand said softly, with relish, "Io El Rey, Io La Reyna!" It pleased him that Castilian etiquette placed Io El Rey, I the King, first, even though the king might be only a consort.

"Why wasn't Carrillo here?" he asked. "Making gold?"

"I hope that's all it is."

"Or jealous of the Cardinal?"

"I'm afraid so."

"That is bad, that is bad," Ferdinand said. "Now we shall surely lose him. But it won't matter; I won't let it. I promise."

Isabella too was almost convinced that her old friend, who had publicly snubbed her at Ferdinand's reception, would now permanently align himself with her enemies. But it was good to see Ferdinand's face light up as he talked of their future together. This was as she had first known him and she was happy as she had not been since the early days of her marriage, which seemed long ago. Ferdinand, too, was happy, for now he had a hand in the administration of a kingdom greater than Aragón.

"But our realm of Castile—" he always said "our"—"is unconscionably disorderly. You rode in procession behind the unsheathed sword of justice. Use it!"

"I intend to. In my own way."

"I had a similar situation in Aragón, There was a crypto-Jew in power in Saragossa—"

"I heard about the death of Ximenes Gordo, Ferdinand." Her tone did not imply approval, but she was careful not to precipitate an argument.

"Murders were being committed in broad daylight, streets were unsafe, shops were being looted, corruption was everywhere. But here in Castile the condition is nation-wide. Force is necessary, Isabella."

"Force will be applied. But not yours and mine, or our people will call it judicial murder, murder without even a show of trial. They will say we have begun our reign with bloody hands. We will not permit that," and it was difficult to tell whether Isabella was using the royal "we," which would mean only herself, or the plural "we," which would include Ferdinand. He was reminded that she was the sovereign, he only the consort.

"What do *we* plan to do about it?" he asked, stressing the pronoun a little sarcastically.

There was an old Castilian institution, Isabella told him, formed in a similar time of troubles to keep order in Castile. It was called the Santa Hermandad, the Holy Brotherhood.

Ferdinand broke into a smile. "Like my Inquisition? You

are progressive!"

It was not like the Inquisition at all, Isabella said. It was a body of civil volunteers, recruited from the people themselves, to keep order among themselves. Originally these local policemen had served without pay.

"But I do not believe the Hermandad can be re-established on a payless basis nowadays," Isabella said practically.

"Neither do I," Ferdinand agreed gloomily. "That eliminates your Holy Brotherhood, I suppose."

"No."

There was a way to pay them.

Isabella summoned in Cortes the representatives of all the cities that would obey her and Ferdinand. She proposed that the Santa Hermandad be reconstituted, not as isolated independent units but as a national police force under the single authority of a captain general appointed by the crown. And her method of payment was simple: only those towns which contributed to a small tax for the maintenance of the police would receive police protection, The Cortes approved the measure overwhelmingly. It was the first of her broad-visioned reforms, and because it was simple it worked. And because the Hermandad's authority came from the people themselves, the people did not complain that its methods were sometimes cruel.

"Whom will we make our captain general?" Ferdinand asked.

"Would you like the post?'"

"No, no, I do not think so."

In politics at least they thought alike.

"I do not either. The Hermandad is a plebeian force. The King of Spain is not common-born. The captain general ought to be of the people."

Ferdinand smiled a suggestion. "Isabella—?"

"Yes?"

"Would you take my bastard half-brother, the Duke of Villahermosa? He's an honest and able administrator."

Isabella laughed; Ferdinand breathed a little easier to hear her able to laugh at bastardy. "He is *most certainly* of the people," she agreed. "I think he will be an excellent choice. And it will introduce some more Aragonians into our realm of Castile, and stupid people will stop saying that Aragonians are foreigners. Our people must learn to say *Spain,* not Castile, not Aragón."

The handsome, dashing Duke of Villahermosa proved popular and did an efficient job considering the turmoil, domestic and foreign, that plagued the kingdom. Everywhere that the Hermandad operated crime abated, for the criminal was given short shrift. The mildest penalty for first offenders was the loss of some member: nose, hand, foot, ears. Second offenders were lashed to the nearest tree and shot to death with arrows. Isabella's sword of justice was proving sharp, sharp as it had looked on the day of her coronation. But it was wielded by the people themselves.

As domestic conditions improved, in the palace and in the nation, foreign affairs marched rapidly toward utter disaster.

Alfonso of Portugal invaded from the west. Forty miles inside the border he waited in Plasencia, where he was joined by the young Marques of Villena, who rode from his city of Madrid with all his vassals. With Villena was La Beltraneja and her mother Queen Juana, whose beauty was faded but not her ambition.

In Plasencia, on a hastily erected platform, the portly white-haired king solemnly married his thirteen-year-old niece, to the wild acclamation of all the enemies of Ferdinand and Isabella: "Long live the King of Castile! Long live the Queen of Castile!" For, according to their lights, La Beltraneja was Henry's heiress and carried with her the sovereignty of the kingdom. Thus there were now two kings, two queens in the ancient land that was shaped like a shield to defend Christian Europe.

Down in the south the Moors of Granada stirred, and

erupted over their mountain border, capturing a few towns and filling their dungeons with prisoners, their palaces with slaves.

North of the Pyrenees, tongue in cheek, Louis of France sent a letter of congratulation to the newlyweds, whom he addressed as "Most High and Mighty, True and Rightful Sovereigns of Portugal, Africa, Castile and Leon." Then his armies invaded Guipuzcoa, northernmost province of Castile.

But there was more and worse. Archbishop Carrillo defected. Isabella wept bitterly when she heard that he, with two thousand armed men, had gone over to Portugal's side and made his oath of homage to Alfonso and La Beltraneja.

Isabella did not weep easily, as Ferdinand knew; but her tears seemed not too unnatural, considering her fondness for the friend and protector of her childhood. But her fits of weeping continued, nervously, uncontrollably.

"My dear, things are bad, but not irretrievable. This is not like you. Carrillo isn't worth a single sigh, far less this flood of tears. He'll pay his troops in magic money, it will crumble to dust, and they'll all desert. Come, come! Stick up your pretty chin, the way you always do!" He clenched his big fist and gave it a mock little blow, till up it came and she looked him in the eye.

"Ferdinand, you wanted a prince?"

His eyebrows rose a fraction of an inch in wonderment.

She hid her face on his shoulder. "Let us pray God to make it a prince this time."

He folded her in his arms.

CHAPTER 17

HAD Ferdinand been in a temperate, logical mood he would have realized that the mathematical probabilities weighed against Castile, and given up. But his conscience smarted sorely and he felt the need of a quick dramatic victory to justify himself in Isabella's eyes and restore in his own his habitual smugness. Thus he grew rash.

Isabella, by contrast, cared nothing for mathematical probabilities. Her heart was filled with the steady glow of faith in the rightness of her cause; no room was left for intellectual subtleties. Chroniclers in monasteries, penning her astonishing achievements of the next few weary, disastrous months, did not hesitate to call her a living saint. She was not logical, but her exploits were magnificent.

Money, troops, and above all a spirit of resistance were required to beat back the Portuguese and the French, difficult things to conjure out of a country made cynical by years of corruption, poor, and so tired of war that men were ready to purchase peace at almost any price. There is a seductive security in slavery.

The highway for invasion from the west to the most populous area of Castile lay through the valley of the Duero. Hence Isabella established her headquarters at Tordesillas, a town squarely blocking that highway. It was winter, and fat, old Alfonso, dallying with his child bride at Plasencia, went into winter quarters, as was customary in war, confident that Isabella would make no move till spring.

Isabella disregarded the season. She disregarded her physical condition, which made horseback riding, with its daylong jolting, distressing in the early stages of her pregnancy and acutely painful in her latter months. She disregarded everything but Spain.

Ferdinand protested. The green flecks in her eyes blazed.

"I must do what I must do, and so must you," she said.

"At least take your ladies in waiting."

"They would delay me."

"Then take me."

"You too must raise money, men, provisions, guns. Separately we can cover twice the territory and double our harvest of materiel."

"This isn't proper at all!"

"Neither is the invasion of Castile!" she silenced him.

By-passing enemy towns, she entered every place that would open its gates to her, wringing promises of troops from the lords of the cities, promises of money from the municipal treasurers, and buying supplies from the merchants. For Spain she could haggle like a fishwife. No hamlet was too small to be worth a stop for a public appeal in the marketplace if it could supply four or five mounted men, a handful of foot soldiers or a peasant with a crossbow. No friendly city was too large if a cannon or two could be coaxed off its walls. Slowly, under the persuasion of her prayers, her pleading and the eloquence with which she stressed the peril that faced them, an army began to grow in her train.

Ferdinand was less successful, though he tried hard, for even in deadly danger Castilian pride was slow to accept a foreigner. Hearing of Isabella's growing forces, piqued that a mere woman could do better than he, he threw open the jails for any petty malefactors who chose to win pardon by volunteering to serve under him. And then he had an army indeed! When he joined his forces with Isabella's in the spring she looked aghast at his shuffling assembly of crop-eared, slit-nosed ne'er-do-wells. "It was not a time to be choosy," he said. "I had to do what I had to do. You said so yourself. How are you, my dear?"

"I am well," she said. But her haggard cheeks and dead-tired eyes belied her brave words.

"Isabella, I forbid you to ride any more! You have accomplished miracles. No one is quicker to give credit

214

when credit is due than I. But enough is enough. For the sake of the prince, you must rest; rest here in Tordesillas, and leave the rest of the war to me."

"I'm afraid I really must, Ferdinand."

He had expected less ready an acquiescence. In her such a symptom was alarming. More than ever he resolved on a quick victory.

Sensing his impatience she warned, "A two-front war may be long, trying the patience of the troops. You must drill them, Ferdinand, that they may be restrained in their victories, high in resolve if victories elude them at first." That was as close as she came to reproaching him for the raw, undisciplined condition of his troops or voicing her doubt of their effectiveness.

He patted her shoulder. "You agreed to leave the rest of the war to me."

Isabella sighed. And yet, she reflected, she had no reason to doubt her husband's prowess in war. His record was long and brilliant.

"First I will squash this fat, incestuous worm of an Alfonso! Traitorous Toro, which opened its gates to him, shall be given some salutary lessons in hanging."

The Castilian city of Toro, on the river that lay like a highway to invasion, had declared for Portugal. Thither Alfonso had retired with his bride to spearhead and consolidate the conquest.

"Hang only the traitorous leaders, Ferdinand."

"Why, of course, you silly goose! You don't make a martyr of a sheep when you can hang a scapegoat. What odd notions you have nowadays." He kissed her cheek. "Never mind. I know why. God bless you, and keep you off horses. The good Lord is probably the only one who can. A cushioned litter is the safest thing for you for a while, Isabella."

"I will *not* be carried about like an old woman or an invalid! There is nothing abnormal or sick in having a baby."

"Then at least ride a slow-gaited, comfortable mule."

"Oh very well," she promised.

But she was ill at ease when he bade her good-bye that same week, after only a few casual hours of drilling with the troops, most of whom were more skilled with a dagger at night than with a sword in the daylight of battle, more accustomed to inflict wounds from behind than before.

"I have promised them the spoils of Tirol!" he said as he led them away. "That is all the training they need."

She hoped he was right. But she wished he had taken the artillery her loyal cities had given her. But Ferdinand complained that the cumbersome pieces would only delay him and that powder was scarce and extremely expensive, a fact which she could not deny. Cabrera's coffers in Segovia had never been lower, not even in King Henry's reign. Dutifully, weekly, the treasurer sent her reports of her dwindling resources. It had been difficult enough to collect taxes in peacetime; with the country invaded on two fronts it was virtually impossible. Some money indeed continued to trickle in from Don Abraham Senior, Grand Rabbi and Collector-General of the Taxes of Castile, a wizard at finance and a loyal supporter. But from Andalusia, always chaotic with private war and now terrorized by the menacing attitude of the Moors, nothing could be collected at all.

At the sight of the walls of Toro, the last of Ferdinand's illfounded mood of victory evaporated. Once parted from Isabella he recognized the true character of his shabby troops. Toro was half surrounded by the Duero, a natural and impregnable water defense. The battlements on the land side were sheer; he saw at a glance that his coterie of jailbirds could never scale them. Isabella's better troops very probably could. But even if they should sacrifice themselves to the last man, would his tatterdemalions follow them up the dizzy ladders and complete the job? He very much doubted it. All the temperance of his cautious nature now reasserted itself, and he sent back a flying herald for artillery, powder and shot, with orders to buy them even if Cabrera had to empty the royal coffers. He was convinced, he said, that Cabrera had more in reserve than the startlingly small funds he would admit to. He had deceived King Henry. Very likely he was deceiving King Ferdinand and Queen Isabella also by some new Jewish trick.

Meanwhile he sent a courier with a flag of truce to the great gate of Toro with a personal proposal for King Alfonso which, he said, should prove a great boon to both Portugal and Castile, since it would save countless lives and end the war in accordance with traditional canons of chivalry, which kings still pretended to believe could declare the divine will of God. Alfonso courteously admitted the messenger and, flushing an apoplectic red to the roots of his thin white hair, he read Ferdinand's invitation to personal battle! Whichever won would win the war.

"He's more slippery than my good friend King Louis of France!" Alfonso cried in dismay. He called his advisors around him and begged them to find a way out of the difficulty, and above all not to let his bride know that he did not feel quite up to a duel with the lean and fit young King of Castile.

Yet neither could he refuse.

On the advice of his ministers he sent back the herald with a reply that he was willing to meet Ferdinand at any time, but that Ferdinand must agree to an exchange of hostages. "For I doubt not," Alfonso said, in a vein that was intended to insult but actually paid high tribute to Isabella, "that when I kill Your Aragonian Highness your wife will still continue the war, without you, and in defiance of the manifest will of the God of Battles."

Ferdinand grinned. He would be happy to exchange hostages, he replied.

Alfonso's next herald named them: their queens. Isabella for La Beltraneja! It was Ferdinand's turn to flush beet-red with fury. "Isabella will be most courteously cared for," Alfonso's message ran smoothly. "Doña Beatriz of Portugal, her maternal aunt whom she has not seen since the days of her early youth, will welcome her into her own house and see to her every comfort with love and affection. As for my own queen, I know that you will treat her with distinction."

When his rage had abated Ferdinand replied with icy correctness that Queen Isabella's condition did not permit her to travel. He would send, however, his daughter the Infanta as hostage.

Alfonso refused the Infanta, and there the tragi-comedy ended. The negotiations had consumed many days. The war continued and Ferdinand settled down for a protracted siege, with troops unpaid and supplies running low. Every day came discouraging word of the leisurely depredations committed by the French, who were almost unopposed in the north. Isabella wrote that the guns and powder could be procured, not to lose heart; the only obstacle was now the rains, which had caused many washouts on the roads. She was having them repaired.

She was having them repaired indeed! She was personally supervising the transport of the guns, exhorting the workmen to speed their efforts, on horseback from morning till night. They labored like Guinea slaves for her, but before the work could be finished she returned to Tordesillas in a cold panic of physical fear.

There she miscarried. She swore the surgeon to secrecy, not to tell Ferdinand that it would have been a boy, the prince he had longed for, demanded. The surgeon kept his word, but of course Ferdinand found out.

At once he abandoned the siege of Toro. His mutinous troops had long since abandoned it, straggling off in the night, deserting by twos and threes and then by the score, muttering curses against the foreigner who never had paid them and now would not even feed them. Many went over to Portugal; many joined the private armies of robber barons whose dark castles infested the hills; many turned outlaw, terrorizing the roads and pillaging the countryside. The Hermandad was busy hunting them down for months, till a man could not travel a league without becoming accustomed to the sight of corpses pincushioned with arrows, rotting, lashed to trees.

"I told you, I implored you, not to ride," Ferdinand reproached her. "Nay, I commanded you."

The green smouldered ominously in Isabella's eyes. One did not command the Queen of Castile, not even the King Consort. But she held her peace.

"A prince!" he muttered gloomily. "A King of Spain! You foolish, foolish woman. I do not deny it was intrepid. But it was mad, mad."

"There will be no Spain if we do not conquer Toro," she said; and then, more gently, laying her hand in his, "Perhaps God will send us another, to take the place of our little lost prince." It was more of a prayer to Ferdinand, pleading with him not to withdraw from her as he had done after the birth of their Infanta, than a prayer to God.

"Perhaps," Ferdinand said.

Then, in the very midnight of their fortunes, help came like a miracle from an unexpected quarter.

Cardinal Mendoza performed the most extraordinary Act of Faith in his long ecclesiastical career, an act of faith in a mortal. All Europe buzzed with it. Nothing like it had ever been recorded in Christian history since the Crusades.

CHAPTER 18

"THIS land of Castile," King Ferdinand mused, not very happily because it was all so illogical, "is most difficult to understand." Here was a land that had bred a Carrillo, the archbishop who tried to get something for nothing, tried to make gold. This same strange land, however, where nothing came in half-measure, had also bred a Mendoza, the cardinal who now poured the treasures of the Church into Isabella's lap in one tremendous, unasked-for, unexpected heap.

Knowing how poor she was, he approached her with the offer of a loan. Not of money; indeed the church was as pinched in its purse as the state. But of silver and gold to melt down into money. The term: three years. The interest: none. The security: her bare word.

"This act is unprecedented, Your Eminence," Isabella said. She was awed, humbled, but uplifted and encouraged beyond measure.

The cardinal replied that the peril of the times, too, was of an unprecedented character, and the menace of the Moors, the Portuguese and the French combined could be met in no other way. For if Christian foes should mortally weaken Spain the infidels of the south would resume their march up the peninsula towards the northern nations, sweep over the Pyrenees and capture, perhaps, the whole of Christian Europe as once they had nearly succeeded in doing. From Valladolid to Paris, from Paris to London, from London to Scandinavia, like a river growing in volume, the hordes of Mohammedans would stream up in an overwhelming tide; and everywhere before them the Cross would go down before the Crescent. Simultaneously in the Eastern world the conquering Turks, already embarked on a wild and seemingly unstoppable wave of conquest, would march upon Poland, Austria, Hungary, Italy, the Holy Roman Empire, eventually to join their Moslem brethren the Moors, blotting out Christendom from the face of the earth. In the face of utter extinction, what, asked Cardinal Mendoza, would it profit the Church if she hoarded her treasures and lost her soul? The silver and gold that he offered was the talent buried in the earth. It was time to dig it up and put it to use. God's use, And, incidentally, Spain's; since only with the invaders thrust back and Isabella firmly on the throne of her ancestors would peace and prosperity return.

Had she accepted immediately he would have been pleased. Since she hesitated he was delighted, confirmed in his faith in her.

"It is an act of great daring, Your Eminence. It is also, as I see it, somewhat arbitrary. Not all of your clergy will co-operate. Some may even bury their treasures."

"I have the authority."

So had Isabella authority for punishing malefactors. But she had used the authority of the Hermandad.

"Would it not be equally wise to convoke the bishops, archbishops, abbots, priors, and ask them for their vote? Then if they decide to help me—"

"They will, Your Highness. Not for a Henry. But for an Isabella, yes!"

"—then the opinion of their peers will be against any reluctant prelates, and none of them will *dare* bury their treasures, and your measure will be universally effective."

The cardinal smiled broadly, "I was not deceived in my estimate of Your Highness. A Convocation will certainly take some of the sting out of the procedure, and relieve me from bearing the burden alone." She could mingle kindness with consummate statecraft, he learned.

The Convocation assembled. Dissident voices—for there were a few just as Isabella had foreseen—fell silent, shamed by their brethren of broader vision and greater faith. And the very ones who might have hidden their treasures were the ones who were most frightened by the picture of Europe in peril, when once they clearly understood it; and they were the ones who came forward with even more than the cardinal requested, which was one-half of all the objects of silver and gold that had been accumulating for centuries in every church in Castile. The unprecedented action was taken, the unprecedented vote was cast. It was almost unanimously favorable to the queen. Carrillo voted against it by proxy, being at Toro with the King of Portugal.

The result was a great outpouring of crosses, ciboria, platens, chalices, aspergilla, pyxes, crosiers, vessels for holy water, vessels for holy oil, baptismal ewers, and all the costly and beautiful Christian things that the Church had elaborated during the course of centuries of growth to enrich and dignify Christian worship. Many were of venerable age and irreplaceable artistry. Ruthlessly they were melted down to make gold and silver Castilian coins. If they were the purest, most honest and fullest weight that had ever been minted, they were merely consistent with the history of the metals of which they were so strangely and wonderfully made.

To protect the new coinage Ferdinand and Isabella issued at once a *pragmatica,* a royal decree without parliamentary sanction, restricting the coinage of the realm to the sovereigns alone, a drastic and daring step. Other European rulers, who claimed the same right of edict by fiat, wished that theirs could be obeyed as thoroughly as the young Spanish queen's. With some embarrassment their chancellors pointed out that Isabella had somehow managed to win over both the people and the Church to her side. How else, by one sweeping autocratic act, would she dare to deprive scores of feudal grandees of their hoary right to mint and debase their own baronial coins?

The answer, like all of the answers to Isabella's challenging acts, was simple. Her people's representatives, the Hermandad, and her clergy, in Convocation, had backed her. There were only five authorized mints in Castile now, and they were all royal mints. The stately tree of royal authority, withered and diseased in the past, had taken on new strength and was growing. The wind of war still lashed it, but its roots were firm, for now they struck deep into the hard Castilian soil and drew their sustenance from the people. Thus from the heart of the shield-shaped land, where the queen had begun her work, the nation began to grow strong, though the edges were still weak with foreign and domestic strife.

The solid new coins brought immediate changes in the army. The troops were paid; a better class of fighting men presented themselves to enlist in the forces of the queen, la reyna. But she would not suffer that term to gain currency. It was the army of los reyes, she decreed, the Army of the Sovereigns, whose titles were coupled on every royal writ, Io El Rey, Io La Reyna, and whose throne was jointly shared, In time, she knew, everyone would get used to it.

She purchased more guns, powder, shot, buying only those that could fire farthest and fastest. Artillery was Ferdinand's special field, but the purse strings were hers; he watched his wife add a competent understanding of ballistics to her accomplishments. Grudgingly, for he was still moody over the loss of the prince, he came to admit that a woman could become expert at something bigger than sewing buttons on shirts.

Metal foundries sprang up around Valladolid. The air was full of the martial music of hammer on steel as weapons and armor multiplied. Isabella broke all the rules of Castilian etiquette that prescribed a certain distance from the common people, walking among the forges, touching with her finger a spear point some sweaty craftsman would say was especially sharp, handling an unfinished sword, inspecting a granite rock that a mason was chipping into a cannon ball. To Ferdinand this was unladylike behavior and he reproached her with it, but the workmen worshipped her. "I do not believe I demean myself by watching over the weapons that mean life to Spain," she said, "or the Spaniards who make them. Precious reliquaries were destroyed to pay for these things."

"You're certainly getting your money's worth," Ferdinand said. Never had he seen men work so hard.

She purchased food for men, fodder for beasts, warhorses, pack mules. She rode indefatigably inspecting the roads. Her interest in roads amounted to a passion, since her failure to get the guns to Toro in time.

"Is there blood of some old Roman road builder in the House of Trastamara?" Ferdinand smiled.

The tiring work exhilarated her. She laughed more. "The blood of Trastamara is *very* mixed, I'm afraid," she said. Isabella was always in good humor when she could joke about the illegitimate origin of her House, though the scandal was now a hundred years old.

By the winter of 1475, five months after the failure at Toro, Ferdinand and Isabella had a superbly equipped army of 15,000 picked men, fewer in number but vastly superior to the one that had disintegrated in the spring.

There was a change in the temper of cities and men also. The little town of Villena, from which the marquisate took its name, revolted against the young Marques, declaring for Isabella. She accepted its homage at once, riding there to receive the oath in person from the governor of the alcazar, wearing a crown and an ermine robe for the occasion, as dazzlingly beautiful in her gown of state as she had been earthy and practical among the forges. Then prudently she salted the garrison of the place with some of her most trusted officers.

In Madrid the loss of the smallest, but first, of the great estates of his House, proved a great worry to the slippery young Marques. In a changing world was he not, perhaps, serving the wrong master? Queen Juana, Henry's widow, La Beltraneja's mother, who had long been his guest, reproached him, "You could recapture your town of Villena in a day if you'd spend less time hunting."

"Madame," he replied with the elegant sarcasm of his father, "I believe I have come to love hunting almost as much as I love beauty," and he placed the faded belle in protective custody, wrapping the bars at her windows with beautiful red velvet.

Good maps, large and clear, were a tool of war that Isabella demanded; and when some detail was obscure she sent out scouts to survey the place. Long into the winter nights she and Ferdinand pored over these maps by lamplight, sitting in armor, she as well as he, after an inspection of the troops where they always appeared together. Red lines on the maps spidered out towards Portugal where the roads had been smoothed for the passage of men, horses, munitions wagons, guns. Around Toro the line was especially broad and heavy.

Together they planned, together thought, prayed, schemed, neglecting no detail of the campaign they would launch in the spring. Their minds worked smoothly, remarkably in accord, suggesting almost in the same breath a feint against Portugal that would disrupt Alfonso's rear, and approving Gonsalvo de Cordoba for the venture.

"This time your wife will get you your guns," Isabella promised him smiling warmly. She had thought they were growing closer again. It was a long time since he had referred to her miscarriage.

"From the appearance of the map their safe transport would indeed seem to be certain," Ferdinand said, tracing the red line with his big hard finger, not looking at her.

She remembered wearily that it was a long time, too, since he had referred to the possibility of another prince. The ice in him was still uppermost. Yet his tone had not been harsh. Just businesslike. Sometimes when she was tired the little iron cross seemed mysteriously to have grown heavier, but that of course she knew, was nothing but an illusion brought on by fatigue.

"Everything is easy when you have money," He shrugged. "Remember that I had none the first time at Toro. Your

225

treasurer, that Jew Cabrera—well, never mind."

"He accounted for every maravedí!" Isabella said with spirit. "You looked at his books for days after Toro."

"One set, anyhow."

"Oh Ferdinand, Ferdinand. Can't you tell when people love you and trust you? I can. I *feel* it."

He patted her shoulder politely.

Queen Juana in her velvet jail was frightened, angry and bored. Intimate knowledge of many men had trained her to know when her charms had ceased to charm. In addition, she sensed a change in the political wind; young Villena would swivel with it like a weathercock. Already her status had slipped from honored guest to protective custody. Soon she would become an impossible political burden and finally a prisoner of war, if Ferdinand and Isabella's progress to power continued. In her mind's eye she pictured herself shut up in a drab, narrow cell of some nunnery—it would be under a strict Rule, too, if she knew Isabella!—cloistered away from the world she had loved, and in which she had loved so widely, imprisoned for the rest of her life, which would not be worth living. But in Portugal she would be free.

The gloomy forests around Madrid moaned in the winter winds, the sad sound breathing through the mocking velvet bars. She cursed King Henry, she cursed Villena, she even cursed Don Beltran de la Cueva, who had deserted her for Isabella, Isabella the untouchable! She cursed all men and could not look in her mirror, ate little, she who had loved to eat and drink, and longed for her daughter, who was now Alfonso's queen. She wrote long letters to La Beltraneja, advising her tenderly with the wisdom of hindsight how to be a good and virtuous wife. But La Beltraneja never answered and Queen Juana wondered whether Villena had not burned the letters. Probably, since he was wavering, waiting to see who would win before he threw his weight to one side or the other. Sometimes from her window she would see him riding off with his men. But they were all in hunting costume. He was not taking sides now; the House of Villena was observing a strict and impartial neutrality. She wondered how many other powerful grandees were doing the same. Probably many.

In her boredom and loneliness she observed that her only attendant, the jailor who brought her her meals, was handsome in a dull, brutish way, and far too young to have learned very much. In a moment of inspiration she realized that here was the key to her jail, here was the magic carpet that would whisk her through the velvet bars, over the moaning forests to Portugal. Through this stupid peasant she would smile her way to freedom.

One did not approach such a confederate with subtlety, however. She dipped deep into the rouge pots; her mouth glistened wet and red. Her mirror chirruped, "Not bad, not *bad!* Good enough for better than he."

"Sit down and sup with me," she said one night. "There is far too much for one."

"Already et, ma'am, thank you ever so!" answered her magic carpet, beaming at the honor.

"Then sit and chat with me. I get lonesome here never seeing anybody. Nobody ever comes here, day or night, not even in the hall. Why, if somebody started to walk down that long hall we could hear him two minutes before he could get to the door!"

"It's mighty deserted all right. Safe, though."

Apparently Ferdinand and Isabella had not yet won. The Marques was still telling his servants that her imprisonment was protective custody.

"Safety is the nicest thing about it. Here I am safe from intrusion by anybody, anybody at all."

"You like that?"

"With you as company I do."

And another night: "It's cold in here."

"Let me fetch you more wood for your fire."

227

"No, I was just thinking, could you possibly move my bed over to the corner? It's not so drafty there."

"Sure, ma'am."

"Oh no, don't. It's terribly heavy."

"That light little thing?"

He moved it in a trice. Was she right in suspecting that he moved it ever so cautiously so as not to make a single telltale scratching noise? A look at his face told her she was.

"You're amazingly strong."

She ran her hands knowledgeably over his arms, murmured at the power of the muscles, caressed the broad shoulders that had borne the weight of the bed.

"Oh, I dunno," he said, feet shuffling.

"Amazingly!"

"Oh, I guess I'm pretty strong in *some* ways," he said with heavy humor.

The widowed queen of Castile and Leon giggled. "I'll just bet you are!"

During some weeks, in the comer where it was warmer, they hatched her scheme of escape. He knew the peasantry all around the countryside. He did very well, she thought, even arranging the hayrack in which to conceal her after he let her down over the walls. In it she could trundle comfortably to Alcalá, where Carrillo had a residence and she could find men of her party to speed her to Portugal.

All that was needed was one long rope and one stout farm basket; these and those arms, which now had come to cherish the queen, could be trusted to lower her safely over the battlements to the ground. The hayrack and the other trusted peasant would accomplish the rest.

The rope was strong. But twenty feet from the ground the basket handle broke, and the unfortunate Juana crashed to the stony earth at the foot of the wall, fracturing her leg. She did not cry out, though the shock was severe, but dragged herself to the cart, where the dismayed accomplice was sweating in a panic of fear.

"Your Highness must see a surgeon at once!" he whispered, recognizing the severity of the wound with his countryman's hand in the darkness.

"I will do nothing of the sort! Drive me to Alcalá."

"But, Your Highness, when a cow breaks her leg and the bones stick out—"

"You dolt! You pig! I am not a cow."

Softly under the hay she wept, first in anger, then in agony as the pain began to pound.

Next morning the Marques of Villena found Juana's disconsolate lover with the broken basket in his room, blubbering that he had murdered the woman he adored. Villena clapped him into a dungeon, waiting to see if he would execute him for high treason, if Ferdinand and Isabella should win, or reward him for patriotism, if Alfonso won. Shortly, in Alcalá, Queen Juana died, but her lover did not know of it till Villena appeared at his dungeon to tell him his fate, which had been decided by the course of a war beyond the infatuated lad's power to change. That war now took a momentous turn.

South of the Duero, the Tagus, another invasion highway, swept out of the highlands of Castile to puncture the frontier of Portugal. Here the river ran in a relatively narrow valley below the level of the adjacent country. Great masses of troops could have passed unnoticed by anyone standing on the higher ground. Ferdinand and Isabella dispatched Don Gonsalvo de Cordoba with a considerable force to this strategic corridor, which was shaped as if an engineer had specifically fashioned it for a surprise attack. Riding at night, hiding by day, Cordoba crept up to the Portuguese border, and then burst through. Systematically he ravaged the unsuspecting country, taking a dozen towns and abandoning them quickly, provisioning his army with the spoil, suffering almost no casualties and causing consternation among the inhabitants who never knew where he would turn up next.

In Toro Alfonso received a succession of heralds with reports of the wildest confusion and havoc in the heart of his own domain. Each ravaged town begged him to return and protect his homeland.

He did not return, but he sent back La Beltraneja to safety; and then he split his forces and sent half of them galloping south to the Tagus to repel the Castilian invaders. When they got there the Castilians had disappeared. They were flying toward Tirol to join Ferdinand. The feint had succeeded brilliantly.

Ferdinand now struck at the weakened Portuguese king with all the efficient engines and men that he and Isabella had been grooming during the winter. Rather than be slowly hammered to death under the hail of heavy artillery, Alfonso elected to defile his forces out of the city and fight in the open. On the first of March, 1476, a Friday, always a fortunate day in the history of Castile, Ferdinand fought the great battle of Toro. It was bloody and long, but the issue was never in doubt. Alfonso fled with only four or five attendants and made his way back to his bride. Archbishop Carrillo flung off his armor and redeserted to Castile, slinking by cowpaths and byways back to his town of Alcalá, dispatching a vague and meandering message to Isabella begging her forgiveness. She stripped him of seven towns, sequestered his revenues, sharply admonished him to behave himself, and forgave him.

Ferdinand captured eight Portuguese battle flags, including the king's, and two thousand prisoners, who were valuable for ransom purposes. But thousands more of the Portuguese were slain and floated down the Duero. Some, it was said, before they rotted and sank, actually reached their homeland.

In Tordesillas, though it was March and cold, Isabella walked barefoot over the freezing cobbles to the church of Saint Paul to kneel in thanks for the great victory, and directed the preacher not to mention her in the triumphal sermon that he would almost certainly preach. Surely, the priest demurred, that would hardly be fair. The queen had done as much, nay more, than the king to assure the fall of Toro. Everyone knew it.

"I am not a theologian, mi padre, and cannot divine the will of God, but it is evident that God meant King Ferdinand to win since He gave the battle to King Ferdinand, and it is most important that my people love my husband, even as I do. Therefore praise him, not me."

It was important; and the fulsome eulogy that was heaped on the king did much to soften Castilian resentment of his foreignness.

No treaty of peace resulted from Toro, but the war with Portugal languished and all but stopped. Isabella wondered why Ferdinand did not come home.

Had she forgotten the French? he wrote in a tart reply. He was marching north with all his guns at top speed.

In order to see him again before he embarked on another campaign Isabella begged him to let his men return to their wives and children, at least for a short rest, to enjoy their triumph and restore their spirit.

Their spirit was very high, he replied, and if he were willing to forego family pleasures for Castile, so should they.

She sighed. It was maddening to be forced to treat a husband as if he were some elusive grandee who had to be coaxed over to your side. She wrote in a carefully worded dispatch that she had assembled a considerable store of muskets and some light field guns, easily transportable, capable of being mounted on wagons. They could dash into enemy ranks like the war chariots of ancient times, and the muskets would be invaluable in the guerrilla warfare in Guipuzcoa, far more effective than the siege artillery which he had. Actually, she said, she needed his heavy guns; for she was of a mind to turn them on Madrid if the Marqués of Villena did not soon come to make his homage. It would be wise, she said, if Ferdinand should be at hand also to receive the allegiance of so great a vassal. She thought Villena might declare for the Sovereigns soon, she said, for he had sent her word that he had executed a traitor who had aided in the escape of Queen Juana just before she died.

The lure of the mobile guns brought Ferdinand back, but only long enough to get them, and to appear at a tremendous victory celebration that Isabella arranged in his honor.

Then he left. Ferdinand traveled fast; her calendar told her he had been away but a short time, but the few reasonable weeks were interminable to her. Then heralds began to arrive with good news from Guipuzcoa. The French were flying like leaves before an autumn gale, he informed her.

Searching the glowing reports for some personal word, she found that he had been good enough to thank her for the muskets, but the gun wagons, he said, were not fitted for the rough terrain and should have been equipped with the wider-rimmed wheels. But he inquired tenderly after the Infanta.

Queer news had just reached Isabella about the Infanta. She did not answer Ferdinand's inquiry. She took horse toward Segovia with a sinking feeling in the pit of her stomach that once caused her to retch in full view of her embarrassed escort. The proud Castilian queen did not seem to care; she did not even stop. She bloodied her mount cruelly with sharp spurs; she had never worn sharp spurs before. Nowhere along the way did she halt her wild gallop to acknowledge a single cheer. The people who turned out to greet her stood in bewilderment as her escort thundered through town after town. She was riding like one possessed, and her face was a white mask of fury, but fury sick with fear.

CHAPTER 19

THE trouble in Segovia was simple on the surface, but extremely complex underneath, like a mysterious disease in its crisis. The crisis could be treated empirically. To cure the underlying disease might be beyond the skill of mortal wisdom.

Isabella, riding like the wind to her child in danger, could see only the crisis. A large portion of the citizenry of Segovia, taking advantage of Cabrera's protracted absence while he was supervising the minting of the new money, had revolted against his strict rule. They had penetrated the outer defenses of the citadel itself. Only the great old keep still held out. In the fastness of that high tower, with a few faithful guards—and with Beatriz de Bobadilla; how she thanked God for Beatriz' presence of mind!—her daughter was besieged.

As she rode, Isabella's mental vision was tortured with vivid pictures of all the disasters that could happen to her child: she might peek through a slit in the battlements and be killed by a chance missile while she stared innocently, uncomprehendingly down at the milling rioters below. Or fall. Or the populace might break in. When a child is killed by the violence of a faceless mob how can the culprit be singled out and punished? No punishment could be too severe, not even the horrible tortures prescribed by law for high treason. Isabella, with a hardening heart, began to understand how such ferocious laws had come to be framed. Or if the keep of the alcazar held firm, the Infanta might starve, as children always starved in famines and in sieges. But this was *her* child; what a difference that made! Hers, and Ferdinand's too, of course, but always in a very special way her own.

"Isabella, your mother will not let you die!" she muttered

over and over again to herself, while the straining warhorse under her dropped blood and froth as she spurred it to its last ounce of endurance and beyond, for the animal was good for nothing after this last supreme effort.

Later, she knew in the back of her mind, she would try to cure Segovia's disease, whatever it was. There was time now only to treat the crisis. She was ready to do anything, promise anything to get through the city gates—she knew they were locked—to get through the gates of the outer citadel—they too would be locked—and through the great oaken door of the keep, which of course would be locked also, and fold her daughter into her arms. "If I cannot get through to you, if anything happens to you, I will wreak such a vengeance on Segovia that the hated memory of Peter the Cruel will fade from men's minds, and the memory of Isabella the Cruel will take its place!" She meant it with every drop of her heart's fierce Spanish blood.

At the city gate a tipsy guard, who expected anybody but her, leered at her little escort and told her to go to the devil.

"Let her in! Let her in!" some officer commanded. "Now we've got both of them!"

The gate swung open; Isabella spurred through on her foundering horse, her escort white, their hands on their swords. In the streets the people made way, some moved to compassion by her pale face, most merely confused and scurrying out of the path of the horses' clattering hooves.

The outer gate of the alcazar remained shut for some minutes, though she had been spied from the walls and recognized. A soberfaced officer slid aside the wicket, "Your Highness will enter at your peril, if you enter at all. We have grievances, sore grievances. We cannot answer for your safety."

"You are my vassal, and I am your queen, and you will obey me!" Isabella answered, her chin up, her eyes hard as green jewels.

Her imperious demeanor, or perhaps the small size of

her escort, caused the guard to shrug his shoulders. "Very well, Your Highness." The great gate grated open. Isabella ran through.

'The gate of the keep was clear, for bloody rocks lay all about where they had crushed a number of ruffians who had attempted to storm it. But gangs of armed men stood at either side, spears poised, swords naked, arrows fitted and drawn.

Voices from behind the door cried, "Shame! Shame! Let the queen enter!"

"You will not go in," an officer said, barring her way.

"Traitor, I will go in! You will step aside for your queen!"

She advanced till her face was very close to his, and slowly, very slowly, he stepped aside; but the other men closed in, as if to rush the door the instant it opened a crack. Isabella grasped the terrible danger; her presence might bring about the fall of the keep.

Far overhead a drop-hole opened. "Stand clear, Your Highness!" a voice shouted down in warning. A dozen rebels were clustered directly underneath, where the rock would fall.

"Fools! Fools! Hold back, and close the drop-hole! These men have a grievance, and I will hear them, and I will give them justice!" They had not expected that. Indeed, they did not know what to expect after their treatment of her, but certainly not that.

"We demand the removal of Andrés de Cabrera, Your Highness," the man in command said, his manner slightly changed.

"Then I shall remove him," Isabella said promptly.

"Do you swear to that?" the leader asked, his eyes narrowing.

"Sir, who dares ask me to swear, when I give my word?"

"Nay," he muttered, "everyone knows you have never broken your word."

"Then I swear," she said, smiling.

She was winning.

In the keep above, Beatriz heard the public disgrace of her innocent husband and felt anger against the queen, then promptly forgave her. Isabella was desperate.

"Would you and your men wish to accompany me inside? Kindly sheathe your swords. There is no enemy of Castile in our midst."

She won them. Their volatile spirit changed. No Spaniard could witness beauty and bravery unmoved. And she had sworn to give them the thing they demanded.

The leader led a cheer that echoed throughout the courts of the castle, astonishing the rest of the rebels who came running to see what had happened.

"No, Your Highness," the leader bowed, "there is no need for us to accompany you now."

The last gate opened. Isabella ran up the long steep stairs and swept her daughter into her arms, laughing and weeping, kissing the child again and again, "Isabella, dear Isabella, my little Isabella!" The Infanta's fair hair, exactly the same color as hers, mingled with her own in indistinguishable curly disarray.

"Mamita, what is the matter?"

"Nothing, child, nothing now."

"Auntie Beatriz wouldn't tell me anything, and cried a lot."

Beatriz, tight-lipped, stood by. "Your Highness could not help doing what you did," she said.

Without releasing the Infanta from her embrace, Isabella reached out to grasp Beatriz' hand, which was cold and forlorn.

To her daughter Isabella said, "Do not call Doña Beatriz 'auntie' any more. You do have an Aunt Beatriz, a very nice old lady in Portugal, your great-aunt Beatriz. But from now on we shall address *this* Beatriz as Señora Marquésa!"

"Why?"

"Because I am going to ennoble her husband and make him a marqués."

Later, when she was rested, there was time to meet a deputation of citizens who came with their grievance and to ponder the deeper reasons for Segovia's wild and irrational revolt. She noticed that the deputation was composed entirely of Old Christians, whose family names dated back to the Crusades; proud, provincial, poor.

They resented Cabrera's unrelenting enforcement of every law on the books, they said, even ancient outmoded ones that had long since lost their usefulness.

It was a temperate approach, Isabella thought. They were no longer irrational; their anger had spent itself. And their grievance might be just. In the vast and conflicting accumulation of Castilian laws, which had never been properly codified, there must be much that was only a nuisance nowadays. A successful administrator had to be an artist, imaginative, not scrupulously accurate like Cabrera.

She resolved one day to codify and simplify the laws, When she had time. There was so much else to do now, and always in a crisis.

However, the deputation continued, there was one law, one law that was dear to the people, which Cabrera was known to break consistently, It was the universal law of Christendom, especially cherished in Castile, that forbade unbaptized Jews to bear arms.

Isabella frowned. That law indeed she deemed honorable, just.

"We believe, Your Highness, that Don Andrés is a crypto-Jew. True, we can find no evidence of it. We have examined his personal garbage thoroughly, for many of his kitchen servants are Old Christians like us. They find pork, like in everybody else's garbage. They do not find onions or garlic cooked in oil, or other Jewish delicacies; nor does he eat meat cooked in oil like a Jew, but in lard, like any good Christian. Nor does he wear his best clothes on Saturday.

And on Friday he does not eat meat, and on Sunday he goes to church."

How closely these common citizens had spied on the personal habits of her treasurer. There was not a caballero among them. These were her people; theirs was the voice of Castile. She heard the voice in her own heart, too, for she could not imagine an age in which a crypto-Jew could be tolerated. A Jew, yes. But a crypto-Jew, one who had been baptized and still practiced Judaism secretly? Nay, that was a relapsed heretic, and the law burned them everywhere in Christendom.

"Since there is no evidence that he is a crypto-Jew, by your own admission, it is not fair to call him one," she told the deputation, and she reminded them that another Castilian law provided red-hot tongs to tear the living flesh from the limbs of false witnesses.

"Nay, nay, Your Highness! We do not accuse him. We only remember that his father was a Jew."

"What was your father, my friend?" she asked one of them.

"Why, a tinker, ma'am."

"And what are you?"

"I am a butcher by trade."

"Nay, I think you are a crypto-tinker. And you? Your father?"

The man smiled uneasily. "My father was a baker, Your Highness," He saw where the queen's questions were leading. Straight into absurdity. He did not like it. "And I am a mason. I am not a crypto-baker."

"But your hands are covered with white. Is it marble dust? or is it flour? Yet I believe you. I will always uphold the law, but I will not apply it without evidence, for that is tyranny. As for Don Andrés, if he has permitted Jews to bear arms he should be removed. Nay, I shall remove him anyway, since I promised to. Nay, he is already removed, and Don Gutierre de Cardenas is already appointed treasurer and governor of this alcazar, though the papers are not yet published."

Gutierre de Cardenas was an Old Christian of one of the most honorable Houses of Castile.

She did not tell the satisfied deputation, as it bowed itself backward out of her presence, that a patent of nobility was also in preparation to create Don Andrés the Marqués of Moya, with increased revenues drawn from his new estate. She resolved also to make him Master-General of the Mints, under the new treasurer. There his intense scrupulosity would insure the continued honesty of the coinage.

She wrote Ferdinand a full account of the happenings in Segovia, defending herself on the grounds of necessity for "something that troubles my conscience and something which I do hope, my señor, you will not consider double-dealing. I refer to the equivocation of which I was guilty when I promised to remove Don Andrés, did so, and then gave him a much better post."

Ferdinand was already riding hard for Segovia. He had already heard the news; she did not yet know how. His herald arrived only a few hours before he did. Ferdinand's scribbled note was the warmest he had ever sent her, the first that ever began mi señora, my wife. When no one was looking she kissed it.

"You handled everything exactly as I should have done." Was she growing like him, or he like her? she wondered. It continued, "You kicked the rascal upstairs, a little too high but understandable under the circumstances. God bless you. I kiss the hands and feet of both my Isabellas."

"Is the business with the French in Guipuzcoa still progressing satisfactorily?" she asked the herald.

"Highness, that business is ended. There are no French in Guipuzcoa. Only dead ones."

She had scarcely had time to greet Ferdinand, who arrived from the north, wind-burnt and handsome, without a battle scratch anywhere from his numerous engagements, when the Marqués of Villena rode unexpectedly into Segovia at the head of a dazzling escort of cavalrymen. He sent her a noble young page dressed in velvet fit for a duke, requesting an audience. She asked his intentions. "My master desires to present the keys of Madrid to Her Highness Queen Isabella," the young caballero replied.

"The king and I will receive them tonight." She thanked him, smiling so warmly with happiness that the youngster's eyes began to pop in adolescent appreciation. Then, remembering his manners, he blushed, and tripped making his exit. He reported that this queen was far prettier than the last one to whom Villena had made his homage.

"That isn't why I'm making it, you imp," Villena said.

Isabella ran with the wonderful news to Ferdinand. He looked perplexed. "My agents usually keep me well informed," he said slowly, "But this was not reported." Then laughing, "How did you manage it? Did you actually level the big guns from Toro on Madrid? I should have heard about *that!*"

"No, he just appeared."

"He probably heard how you put down a riot just by staring people in the eye. He didn't dare hold out after that."

"I'd rather think he was loyal all the time; just weak."

"You don't, though."

"No, I'm afraid I don't. He heard about your victories."

"Yours too, Isabella."

"My dear," she said excitedly, "I have utter faith that we are unconquerable together."

He answered slowly, "I rather think so myself." He did not put on his business-like face when he stressed, unconsciously, the word "together."

That night Villena came to make his tardy homage to the king and queen, who went to great lengths to honor him, as if this were the first chance he had had to declare his allegiance. He was visibly impressed with his reception, Villena, like his father before him, loved display. But this display was charged with meaning. The great hall of the alcazar was hung with captured Portuguese and French battle flags, awesome symbols of success and sovereign power. It had been a long time since a King of Castile had captured a battle flag. And the hall was crowded with notables of Segovia, the city that had been so recently in revolt, all now loyal, smiling and united around Ferdinand and Isabella. The Infanta stood beside them, a slender circlet of gold on the fair high brow that came from her father and the copper curls that came from her mother. The three presented as startling a contrast to the former royal family as could be imagined; this was so right, the other had been so woefully wrong, for themselves and for the realm. Kneeling before the queen, whose tactful courage had quelled the Segovians, kneeling before the king, whose hard hands had won the battle flags, Villena wondered why he had waited so long. As he swore aloud to be faithful he swore to himself to keep his word.

Villena's allegiance added more strength to the strength that Isabella had already established in the heart of Castile, and as the heart grew stronger the outer members of the body politic began to feel and respond to its quickening pulse. Andalusia, the beautiful, the chaotic, now turned to Isabella for relief from its perpetual feudal wars, which had ravaged the province so long and so cruelly that she had not been able to get either men or taxes from the area to support the Crown against either the Portuguese or the French.

The first request came in secret from a deputation of merchants from Seville in the very heart of the disturbed district. They painted a somber picture of houses burned, crops destroyed, towns besieged, warehouses plundered and ships putting out to sea halfmanned, half-provisioned, half-laden, whenever the troops of the two great feuding Houses appeared. They pleaded with her to throw the weight of her armies against the Duke of Medina Sidonia or else the

Marqués of Cadiz. It did not matter which. Only when one or the other was crushed would peace and prosperity come to the south, and a man could live in security in his own house, and a merchant could thrive.

"Which is in the right, Medina Sidonia or Cadiz?" Isabella asked. The deputation hemmed and hawed and would not take sides. Ferdinand smiled wryly. He pondered the fact that they had come in secret. What could that mean but that they were afraid to risk reprisals?

"Well, then, my friends," he said, "which has the better chance of winning? The Duke of Medina Sidonia or the Marqués of Cadiz?"

On that they were a little more communicative, but only a little. The Duke, they said, had more men; the Marqués, on the other hand, was a better general. They were only merchants; they did not know who would win. For years neither had won.

"We promise to do all we can, God helping us," Isabella told them, agreeing, at their urgent request, to keep secret the interview. They scurried back to Seville at once lest their absence cause comment.

"And what are *we* going to do this time?" Ferdinand asked. "Be sure you pick the winning side, my dear."

"Neither side should win; and we are not going to fight Castilians."

He was glad to hear that, he said. He reminded her that there was yet no peace with Portugal. It wasn't wise to split armies. He liked to finish one thing at a time, neatly. "There is too much of the artist in you, mi señora. Artists in government—I am always a little uneasy."

"I cannot help being as God made me, and I am far too simple a woman to be an artist."

"My dear, I did not mean it as a reproach."

Isabella remembered Medina Sidonia with fondness, in spite of his lack of cooperation in the war with Portugal. The Marqués of Cadiz she had never seen, and reports of him

242

were not good, a brash, emotional illegitimate son of the Count of Arcos. But apparently gifted also, since his father had preferred him over his legitimate sons and left him all his titles and estates when he died, an exclusion not uncommon in Castile. The northern nations were somewhat more strict in this matter. Some day, Isabella supposed, some day far in the future, the world might improve so that bastards would not inherit; they would certainly not be made archbishops at the age of six.

The second request for help came in the form of a herald from the Marqués of Cadiz.

"He is scared," Ferdinand said. "Not enough men."

"I'm going to try to think that his heart has changed, that this is the beginning of loyalty. Remember, he is married to a sister of Villena's."

"Wives don't have any influence over their husbands' politics."

Isabella could not repress a smile.

"Oh, maybe a little." Ferdinand was in a much better mood these days. "Especially if they're queens. But the Marquésa of Cadiz isn't a queen and she isn't an Isabella."

The Marqués, tentatively and cautiously, offered to tender his oath of allegiance to Isabella if she would agree to help him against Medina Sidonia.

She sent the herald away with a friendly but noncommittal reply, promising to do what she could regardless of his oath, "which is a sacred union between sovereign and vassal mutually given for mutual good, and not to be bargained for." Thirdly, a haughty demand came from Medina Sidonia himself, reminding her of his offer of support when Henry had tried so hard to marry her to the king of Portugal, reminding her that he had sworn homage whereas Cadiz had not, reminding her also of his service to Castile in wresting Gibraltar from the Moors. All the fault, according to Medina Sidonia, lay with the Marqués of Cadiz. As a loyal vassal he sought the aid of his sovereign.

"Now we've got them!" Ferdinand cried. "Play one against the other till they exhaust themselves."

"That's what King Henry did, and they only exhausted Castile."

"Louis of France succeeds at it; it is the keystone of his policy."

"Castile is not like France. Castile is not like any place else in the world."

"I grant you that," Ferdinand muttered. "What will you do?"

"I shall have to go to Seville, I suppose."

"And what will you do there, pray?"

"I really do not know."

"Nonsense. I will not permit it. There is too much danger." But he knew from her face that nothing could stop her.

She sent Medina Sidonia's herald back to Andalusia with a cordial, but also noncommittal, response, saying that she planned to visit *her city* of Seville shortly and would give her answer then.

Ferdinand, thoroughly worried, enlisted the help of Cardinal Mendoza, who added his voice to the king's in an effort to dissuade her. "Even Daniel did not enter the den of lions of his own free will, Your Highness. If I remember my Scripture, he was cast in most forcibly, whereas nothing forces you to go to Seville."

"At least take me," Ferdinand begged, when she refused to follow even Mendoza's advice.

"You and the army are needed to keep watch on Portugal. You were quite right in reminding me that there is still no treaty of peace, and until there is Alfonso may strike again."

"I do not like being ordered away from my wife by my wife!"

"We are not really away from each other any more, Ferdinand. Not this time. Only distance separates us."

Grudgingly Ferdinand took up the watch on the

Portuguese border, organizing it so thoroughly that not even a mouse could slip through without being caught by one of his spies. Isabella took horse for Seville.

CHAPTER 20

SPRINGTIME in Seville was a lush and beautiful season, when the herons flew over from Africa to strut pink-legged and proud in the marshes along the lower Guadalquivir. Eagles circled and shrieked out of sheer exuberance in the crystalline depth of the blue Andalusian sky. The sun was warm on endless groves of fruit trees, coaxing their winter-drab branches into a luxuriance of fresh leaves, each of a different shade of green, full of new life and the promise of all their colorful fruits to come, red of the pomegranate, gold of the peach, purple of the olive, yellow of the orange like captured suns flaming in the trees. The fame of the Seville orange, after centuries of Moorish cultivation on Spanish soil, had spread back to Africa, whence the Moors had brought its sour barbaric ancestor. Some of the Granadine Moors read in the orange the past and the future of their race and were afraid. For the orange was the typical fruit of the Arabs. They had given it their Arabic name, *naranj.* In their sweep of conquest through Africa and across the Pillars of Hercules into Spain, everywhere they had taken it with them. Even as they had been rude and hard in the days of the Prophet, so had the orange been thorny and tough. Now both were civilized, too civilized perhaps, civilized into decadence. Whereas the Spaniards under their vital young queen seemed to stand on the threshold of something new and strong and big, and to the Moors very dangerous. Thus the orange; thus the musings of some of the Moors of Granada, for the Moor was a sensitive creature.

Riding the Roman road to Seville, remarkably smooth considering its fifteen centuries of continuous use, Isabella saw the promise of fertile Andalusia and felt the sadness a Queen Proprietress ought to feel that the promise was not fulfilled. In great stretches the rich red earth shone through unplanted, unworked, between sparse little cultivated fields. Farmers would not plant where robber barons would only sweep down on the crops as soon as they were dry enough to harvest, dry enough to burn.

Evidence of the waste of war was all around. Centuries-old olive trees, still in their prime, lay dead where battle axes had hacked them down. Mighty oil presses, with millstones three feet thick and eighteen feet in diameter, fit to provide food and delicacies for thousands with surplus left over to export, stood motionless, their running gear dismantled; they had not turned for years. Orange trees, too, were mutilated and the mulberry groves, on which the silk industry depended, were ill-kept. Signs of lassitude and hopelessness were everywhere, even in the faces of the people. The queen, with growing impatience, reflected that it was no wonder she could collect no revenue from this sick Andalusia, which could have, should have, contributed so much.

Seville had a Moorish look about it, its narrow streets snaking in labyrinthine confusion, grilled balconies overhanging, almost touching the houses on the opposite side. It owed allegiance to the Duke of Medina Sidonia, its immediate feudal overlord. He rode out to meet Isabella in considerable pomp.

"Welcome," he said, "to my city." The voice was friendly enough, but he lacked the warmth he had displayed at Gibraltar. He looked older and harder.

"Welcome," she said, "to mine." She supposed she was older and harder, too. At least she was not a frightened little girl any more.

He smiled slightly. He admired spirit, especially in men but also in horses and women. "It is my hope that Your Highness will enjoy your stay in Seville. I had expected, indeed I should have been happy, to pay the expenses of your entertainment out of my own revenues, though my quarrel with the bastard of Cadiz puts a strain on them. But for some reason—" He paused perplexed.

"Yes?" Isabella smiled.

"For some reason," Medina Sidonia answered, "the Council of the Twenty-Four got ahead of me and voted a special city tax all of their own accord."

"They must have sensed in their loyalty to us that you would request it," Isabella said; and here again, in the subtle Castilian tongue, it was difficult to tell whether Isabella meant "us" to mean her and Medina Sidonia, her and the king, or her, the queen, alone. But in the special tax Isabella saw the secret wily hand of the deputation of merchants who so desperately wanted peace, The tax was paid without stint by the little people of Seville, who trusted the queen who had already done so much for Seville.

The town put on its gayest dress, spring flowers festooning the balconies, heirloom tapestries hanging colorfully from the windows. Don Alonso de Solis, the venerable bishop of Seville, took the queen with pride to show her the new cathedral, the biggest church in the world, now rising on the spot where a Moorish mosque had been demolished in the reign of Saint Ferdinand, who had wrested the town from the Infidel. "Here we shall erect such a monument to the Faith," exulted the bishop, "that posterity will say we were mad!" The arches of the nave soared a hundred and twenty feet, striving for heaven in stone. Nothing was left of the mosque but its soaring minaret, so beautiful in its Oriental architecture and Eastern ornamentation that even Peter the Cruel had not had the heart to tear it down. No steps led to its lofty summit, which now voiced its call to prayer not with an Arabic chant but with a carillon of Christian bells. One reached the top by a series of inclined planes straight out of Babylon.

He preached her a sermon of welcome on Sunday. Before the high altar a choir of chorus boys danced a slow, solemn figure, accompanying their steps with the clicking of castanets. This custom, not found in the north, was very old, as was the image of the Virgin whom it honored. The statue was exquisite Byzantine work. It was made of ivory, its hair was spun gold and it had movable arms. Saint Louis of France had brought it from his Crusade and given it to Saint Ferdinand of Castile. Kings *could* be saints, Isabella remembered, though her Ferdinand was not; Crusades still *could* be made.

Everyone tried to please her, since everyone wanted something and she had promised nothing. After a little time she was not sure whether she had the power to promise much. The character of her Andalusians like their customs, she thought, was wild and indecorous, though warm and expansive.

And they were fiercely touchy of personal slight, as soon she learned. Because she had gone to Seville without first going to Utrera, the cutthroat lord of the place, which was little and out of the way, had sent a gang of ruffians to steal some horses which he seemed to need at the moment from her own stables and killed her own groom who tried to defend them.

"I should have thought it unnecessary to post a guard over my property in your city," Isabella said sharply.

Medina Sidonia answered, "Seville is Your Highness's city, as Your Highness reminded me only the other day. I keep what order I can. Utrera, I regret to say, does not lie in my jurisdiction. King Henry gave it to its present lord, the Marshal Saavedra. Perhaps I should add that Utrera is very small, but very strong."

"Marshal Saavedra shall be punished for his murder and his thievery."

"Madame, he certainly should." But Medina Sidonia did not offer to help with the punishment.

Isabella sent a herald to Utrera with a stern demand that the marshal return the horses, make his oath and deliver the assassins of her groom for trial. The marshal's lackeys beat the herald senseless, stole his gold embroidered tabard and sent him back on a mule. Isabella held her peace, but her chin went up and she wrote of these things to Ferdinand.

To the delight of the Sevillanos a gala bullfight was held in her honor in the thousand-pillared amphitheatre that the Romans had built when they built the road. Like the road, it was in a remarkable state of preservation. How soundly they had wrought, those ancients, their mighty architecture, their mighty empire! How stern, to accomplish all they did, they had had to be. Sobering thoughts for a queen who was fitting herself to rule the descendants of those Romans.

Isabella had always looked away from the cruel ape-on-horseback spectacles. She cared for bullfights scarcely more. The Moors, who also fought bulls, at least gave the beast a sporting chance, standing delicately on the sand in the arena and slaying it with a skillful thrust of a sword as it charged. But the Spaniards skewered it from horseback with a spear. Invariably there was wanton slaughter of valuable horses and sometimes the fighters, borne down by the snorting bulls, were unhorsed and gored to death. Anxious to please her on this festive day, a toreador took needless chances and lost his life.

Her groom, the bullfighter, her beaten herald, her stolen horses—she had brought only death and suffered disgrace in Andalusia. She suspected that the bickering grandees secretly enjoyed her discomfiture; it proved her helplessness and left them wild and free, in chaos.

Ferdinand's herald rode down from the north with his thoughts on the Marshal Saavedra's treasonable behavior. "I am sleepless with apprehension, mi señora. I did not want you to go; I prayed you would not. But you went. God gave you tact; use it now, and keep alive for me. You gave me guns. I will use them."

It was a somber note, a little disjointed, but she treasured it as she did all his letters, locking them in a silver casket. She wore the key on the chain with her cross, which seemed feather-light now.

But she was startled by what he did. So were Medina

Sidonia and the Marqués of Cadiz. The king marched south with two hundred knights, a thousand troops and twenty heavy lombards. Without entering Seville, where he too would have been lavishly entertained, he laid siege to Utrera and bombarded it relentlessly for forty days. "Since Utrera is Crown property," he said when she protested, "no one can object if I damage it a little, not even your Andalusian grandees." He almost blew it to pieces. At the end of the forty days the shattered citadel surrendered. Marshal Saavedra bent his quaking knees and made his oath of allegiance, glad to escape with his life. Ferdinand demanded the assassins of the groom and the horse thieves. Saavedra delivered them at once. Ferdinand gave them a drumhead trial out of deference to Isabella's sense of propriety, and hanged them all, twenty-nine of them, before the ink was dry on their death warrants. Then he entered Seville.

Isabella cried on his shoulder. "I wish there had been some other way. But, oh my dear, how happy I am to see you!"

"I wish you would come home again," he said, "at least till Medina Sidonia and Cadiz patch up their feud."

She wanted to say, "All Spain is my home," but she did not think he had used the word in quite that sense; she preferred his warmer meaning and merely whispered, "I wish I could."

He said, "Since you won't, then I will stay here. Portugal is quiet."

"I want you to. I need you here."

She did not use the royal "we."

"I want to, too," he said.

The Duke of Medina Sidonia shrugged off the surrender of Utrera. He was powerful enough not to resent the Sovereigns' one little nugget of power in Andalusia. It worried him only slightly more when Ferdinand and Isabella forbade Saavedra to rebuild his castle and confiscated most of his revenues to the Crown, for the lawless vassal did not escape retribution entirely.

The impetuous young Marqués of Cadiz, however, reacted in a way that made Ferdinand blink with disbelief. "I was only just beginning to understand the Castilians. The Andalusians seem mad."

"You did the same thing when you came in disguise to wed me." She smiled. "Have you forgotten?"

"Cadiz didn't come to wed you, my dear," Ferdinand said primly.

"He swore to be faithful!"

"He didn't even look Spanish," Ferdinand said, less prim.

Cadiz had the olive complexion, the coal-black eyes and the lithe elegance often encountered in the south, where everything smacked of the Moors.

With a single servant he had ridden into Seville, the city of his mortal enemy, and suddenly presented himself to the queen. The hour was late, and she was so astonished that she summoned a secretary to take down his words. Without that statement she might not have believed what had happened; posterity assuredly would not have believed it.

Cadiz had come, he declared, to place himself in her hands unescorted, unprotected even by a safe-conduct such as he might have demanded. Enemies of his, especially Medina Sidonia, had spread rumors about him which were not true; his innocence was his safe conduct. The wicked Duke, he protested, had warred against him for years, despoiled his lands and even, once, driven him out of his own house. "He will say, Your Highness, that my cities of Xerez and Alcalá are garrisoned against you. But I know how magnanimously you treated my kinsman, the Marqués of Villena. Send therefore, Your Highness, to Xerez and Alcalá and take them for your own if you need them in your great designs, for I deliver my patrimony to my queen as now, here in this room, I deliver my person!" Kneeling he swore his oath of homage, to her and to Ferdinand.

The pen of Fernando del Pulgar, Isabella's most trusted secretary, a converted Jew, crackled over the parchment pages.

"The queen," Pulgar noted, "was muy contenta, since he spoke briefly and to the point."

After a moment she answered, "It is true that I have heard bad reports of you, but your loyal action this night assures us that much is to be said for your side. We like to hear both sides, and we thank you for coming." Then touching the sensitive spot where all Andalusian pride melts if you only know how, she said, "We are equally the sovereigns of Medina Sidonia and you, and you are equally our subjects, and we shall mediate your quarrel with honor and justice to you both, retaining you both in our esteem and all such estates as are rightfully yours."

His black eyes misty with gratitude, the happy vassal bowed himself out of the room. She had saved his self-respect.

"*We* will also take possession of Xerez and Alcalá instantly," Ferdinand said.

"Of course. But no guns. Only a few troops."

"Quite a few, I should think. But I agree, no guns. Guns do not bewitch, Isabella. I'd have thought this impossible! This is a far greater victory than the surrender of Utrera. Now Medina Sidonia won't have anybody to fight but us, and he won't dare do that."

"He might, except for your terrible lesson of Utrera."

"No, no. You bewitched *him* long ago at Gibraltar. Mi señora, you scare me sometimes with your power over men. It's a pity I'm a man."

"Oh no, it isn't!"

Medina Sidonia sulked when he heard of his enemy's submission. The evenly balanced scale of power now tipped hopelessly against him. But he was loyal. He would no more have gone over to Portugal than he would have gone over to the Moors. Ferdinand and Isabella published a *pragmatica* forbidding both him and Cadiz to enter Seville till they should make up their quarrel. Both stayed away.

But the king and queen remained.

Word reached Medina Sidonia that order was being rapidly, drastically restored in Seville, where criminals had run riot, unpunished for years, knowing that one or the other of the warring feudal lords would welcome them into his army. Isabella had just instituted a startling innovation, tremendously popular with the people. But no, he remembered, it was centuries old, born in an era when kings and queens were closer to their subjects.

Isabella had revived the Friday audiencia, as she had revived the Santa Hermandad. Each Friday she and the king would sit as judges in the Hall of the Miradors, to hear any case of law that any citizen of high or low degree might care to bring before them. Anyone could approach them; no one was turned away; no grievance was too petty, no crime too heinous for the sovereigns' ears. Usually she would whisper briefly with Ferdinand before giving judgment, but the voice of decision was always hers.

These audiencias, with their free and easy procedure, might have degenerated into undignified public brawls. But the Sevillanos loved a spectacle. Even those who were not in litigation crowded into the great Hall as miradors, spectators, unconsciously continuing the function for which it was named in the days when the Moors had built it. The slender, lovely queen, wearing her crown, her ermine robe of state and Ferdinand's flashing necklace of rubies gave them their spectacle. Ferdinand, hiding his boredom behind his handsome, gravely expressionless face, seemed to double her strength. It was immensely flattering to the citizenry of Seville that the supreme court of the kingdom should sit patiently week after week and give personal attention to their problems.

Once, as the sovereigns leaned toward each other and seemed to confer at the end of a particularly involved case,

Ferdinand was whispering, "You're not a lawyer, mi señora. This was a tricky one. Better postpone judgment,"

And Isabella was whispering, "I know who's right; I'm going to pronounce for him. There are so many laws that the lawyers will surely find one to back me up."

"Artists in government!" Ferdinand muttered. They drew their whispering faces apart. The queen gave her judgment. And sure enough, there was a law. Isabella's reputation as a legist grew greatly among the learned *jurisperitos,* who never knew and could not guess that she had acted from instinct and sterling good sense.

But, above all, the audiencias were successful and decorous because the people of Andalusia wanted security; their feudal lords had not given it to them; only their sovereigns could; the people were anxious to help. Like the Hermandad the audiencias were popular because the populace backed them.

Like the Hermandad, too, the audiencias produced quick results, Isabella's judgments were always in accord with the laws, but the laws were ferocious. The garroters' wrists grew weary throttling the lives out of murderers; the arrows of the Hermandad whistled through the bodies of hundreds of highwaymen. Seville's merchant vessels suddenly had more convict rowers than they could use.

"This is the way to rule!" Ferdinand said. "If only we didn't have to spend so much time at it. You should delegate your authority."

"That wouldn't be the same."

"It works very well in Aragón. My Inquisitors do all the work and get all the blame. And I get all the fines."

"We will not be blamed for punishing criminals." Fridays in the Hall of the Miradors had proved an intense education in human depravity. She had heard things she did not know existed. "Ferdinand, I thought only Hell could house such evil as Seville. I want to sweep it clean!"

"You will require a very large broom, mi señora, and

wield it into eternity, till men are no longer men."

"I suppose you are right," she said, looking at him.

He was uneasy under her glance. "What have *I* done?"

"My dear, I was only thinking how much wiser you are than I."

She was asking too much.

She was asking too much, Don Alonso de Solis warned her. He came in a purple cope on a pale Andalusian mule in all his Episcopal pomp to pay her a special visit. Only the City of God would be wholly sinless, he said; the city of Seville was far, far down on the long steep ladder that reached up to Heaven's perfection. Hundreds were fleeing Seville for fear of her quick and inflexible justice; nearly everybody in Andalusia had a guilty conscience after so many years of civil war. He begged her in the name of Christian charity to temper her severity; the wicked city had had its lesson, he said.

Isabella could compromise. As suddenly as she had laid siege to the evil in Seville, she now raised it, granting a general amnesty for all crimes committed during the days of the feudal war. That too now ended, for she sent a herald to both the Duke of Medina Sidonia and the Marqués of Cadiz, warning them that, grandees though they were, they would be excluded *by name* (among all the common malefactors!) if they did not make friends at once. To salve their pride she invited them to a bullfight; their boxes, with silken awnings of exactly the same degree of splendor, were side by side, conspicuously, intentionally.

Both appeared, both smiling. At the show of friendliness between the two great authors of their misery the jamming crowds in the old Roman amphitheatre cheered themselves hoarse.

Unnoticed at first in the general excitement was another of Isabella's reforms. She was weary of the killing of brave young men, who ought to be fighting for Spain; she was weary of the slaughter of spirited horses, which ought to be carrying them to battle.

For the first time in history, since humans first fought bulls in Crete as long ago as the pharaohs, the horns of the bulls were sheathed in leather to blunt their horrible attack. "This I will never change!" Isabella said, and formalized her will in a pragmatica.

"The people won't stand for it," Ferdinand said, shaking his head as he signed Io El Rey before her Io La Reyna.

But they did, balancing the spoil-sport edict against all the blessings she had brought them. Ferdinand puzzled it over and over in his neat mind. It was the most autocratic act of Isabella's career as queen to date. Not at all like the Hermandad or the audiencias; those he could rationalize, this he could not. He concluded she must have spies. How else could Isabella, a blueblood to her fingertips, so deftly place those fingers on the pulse of the people and read it so unerringly? The notion of his wife having spies disturbed his thoroughly masculine sense of personal privacy.

"Isabella," he said uneasily, "how could you be sure that the ordinary men and women, who love a bloody show, wouldn't riot when they found out you'd blunted the horns of their precious bulls?"

"I wasn't sure. I just hoped. I didn't *think* they would."

He eyed her narrowly, unconvinced.

"I'm afraid I'm a very ordinary woman myself, Ferdinand. Maybe I know how they feel."

He did not find her ordinary. The big Andalusian moon through the tufted palms of the alcazar gardens, where they strolled in the evening, lent a magic to the soft silk gowns she wore in the summer heat; and she, he told her often, lent her magic to the moon, her fragrance to the flowers.

"Thou'rt a honeytongue!"

But she could not remember him so attentive.

"Does your ordinary woman of a wife please you?"

"I would never call you ordinary, Isabella." He spoke with conviction. He knew.

257

The guards who guarded them, the minstrels who sang and guitarists who played to them, the dancers and jesters and acrobats who entertained them, down to the maids and lackeys and cooks, whispered and winked and made broad Andalusian gestures among themselves: the king and queen were lovers. The Sevillanos adored them.

As the city and province grew calm and safe Beatriz de Bobadilla brought the Infanta to join her parents. Beatriz, always her husband's best ambassador, had some news from the Master-General of the Mints. It was a large sheaf of neat, closely written figures. "I do not pretend to understand it Your Highness."

"Hija Marquesa," Isabella said, prefixing a "darling" to Beatriz' impressive new title of Marquésa, "I'm sure I shouldn't understand it either." She knew she would, but Ferdinand would sulk if she didn't give it to him first. She gave it to him, glad to be free to spend time with her daughter. Ferdinand studied the figures for many nights, looking gloomier every day.

"Cabrera goes into greater detail than your Treasurer," he said finally. "Have you any notion how much the war with Portugal is costing?"

Isabella admitted that she had not. She had been far too busy and happy with her husband to fret about a war that had been inactive for a long time.

"Andalusia will do its share to help now," she said.

"I do not think that will be enough. The reason Portugal hasn't attacked is because I've a wall of cannon and men from Xerez to Toro; that costs a great deal."

Now she too read the figures, and was dismayed by them. Her Treasurer had sent her sketchy reports; Andrés de Cabrera's figures, showing how every one of the fine new coins had been spent, presented less sanguine a picture. The war, for all its inactivity, was a cruel drain on the treasury.

"We are not bankrupt, anyhow," Isabella sighed.

"We soon will be; that is the road to ruin for princes."

She knew it was.

He proposed an extraordinary war measure. In Aragón there had long been an Inquisition. There, as in Castile, there were many New Christians, secretly still Jews, who, to protect their wealth, had been baptized and made a convincing show of practicing their new religion. "The beauty of an Inquisition is that it is a self-perfecting, self-perpetuating organization. Not only does it root out heresy but it requires almost no supervision on the part of the Sovereign. The people do it all. No one hates rich crypto-Jews like poor Old Christians. It is thus also self-purifying, from the bottom up, like the Hermandad; and, important to us now in our present need, the property of convicted heretics becomes the property of the Crown. It is an almost bottomless, as well as legitimate, source of revenue."

"I hate spies," Isabella said.

"Don't you hate heresy more?"

The green eyes blazed. "I hate heresy more than anything else in the world!"

"Well then?"

Ferdinand was relentlessly logical. He brought over his Grand Inquisitor from Aragón, who pleaded with the queen to complete the great work of purification she had begun in Seville by striking at heresy, which he said was the root of it all. "I still hate spies," she said. Did she not, he asked blandly, employ spies in war? And was not the extirpation of crypto-Jews a war in behalf of God Himself?

Ferdinand enlisted the local clergy of Seville, who agreed with the Aragonian. It would certainly complete the pacification of the province, they said.

Isabella sought the advice of the deputation of merchants who had come to her with their secret appeal for help. Their eyes glinted greedily. "Above all things, Your Highness, the secret Jews of Seville must be rooted out." Nothing, they protested, was so injurious to the legitimate profit of merchants as the loathsome competition of the crypto-Jew, who, they said, ought to be boiled in his own heretical oil in which he cooked his heretical meat. She remembered the Segovians who had spied on Cabrera. The feeling against the Jew was strong and deep and fifteen centuries old.

"You have shown strength that verges on recklessness in enforcing all the other laws," Ferdinand said impatiently. "Why do you always shy away like a skittish colt when I so much as mention the enforcement of this one? Everyone wants to enforce it but you. But you would not change the law, would you?"

"No, I wouldn't."

"You couldn't," he said flatly. "Not even you. It's far too popular." She did not want to quarrel with him. All her advisors, all her own most logical thoughts agreed with him. All her traditional training was on his side. Only a voice in her heart whispered that spying, even for God, was wrong. But that voice was little and weak, and its whisper wasn't logical. Maybe it was the Devil's voice. She stilled it.

Ferdinand congratulated her when she showed him a letter to the Pope in which she requested the Pontiff's authority to establish an Inquisition in Castile. Ferdinand nodded approvingly. "Now you will wield such a Sword of Justice that the one you had carried before you when you were crowned will look like a little boy's toy." He still had not forgotten that.

"Ferdinand?"

"Yes?"

"There may be a little boy."

"Then for goodness' sake stay off horses, will you?"

He had taken her disclosure rather temperately, she thought. Perhaps Cabrera's alarming figures or his enthusiasm for the Inquisition was on his mind, drawing him away again just when she thought he was closest.

Shortly he left for the north to keep an eye, as he said, on the Portuguese border and not let the war grow too costly.

In Seville, keeping off horses, she busied herself with

a strange new invention, in which she saw a great future. A German craftsman named Theodore, called Teorodico Aleman, printed the first book in Spain.

It was the Bible. If the crypto-Jews would only read the Bible perhaps she would not have to institute an Inquisition after all; for after Ferdinand left, the little voice of conscience, or the Devil, began to nag at her again. There was always her silver casket. She felt its key, and resolved that if, in the slow deliberation that characterized Rome's response to its correspondence, the papal bull should ever come, she would lock it up. She also felt her cross.

Meanwhile she asked Cardinal Mendoza, who wanted an Inquisition no more than she did, to prepare a very simple catechism that would wean the heretics away from their error. This the good man did, and preached it from his heart, with an eloquence that was not to tire for two years.

Ferdinand's letters lapsed into their old formal diplomatic style. Something was worrying him. But he referred only to his hope for a prince and warned her to take care of herself.

"Of the prince, he means," she thought wearily.

CHAPTER 21

EARLY in the morning hours of Tuesday, June 30, 1478, the bells in the great old Moorish tower that served as the belfry for Seville's cathedral began to ring so long and loud that startled citizens leapt out of their beds. Church after church took up the ringing, swelling the sound with their thousand-voiced bells, till the city trembled under an ocean of brazen music in tribute to Isabella.

Behind the bed curtains Isabella heard the bells through a fog of pain. She had not yet spoken. Some of the grandees who crowded the room were concerned for her; women usually screamed at such a time. They resented the curtains, since their privilege, old as their titles, permitted them to witness the birth of an Infante or Infanta of Castile, to witness actually with their eyes, not symbolically with their presence. But Isabella had demanded the curtains. Proud and fastidious nonsense, most of the men agreed. No screams had passed her lips, because she had bitten them back.

"Is the queen all right?" Ferdinand asked.

He had come spurring down from the watch on the border when a herald advised him that Isabella's time was very near.

The midwife beamed, nodded; then opened the infant's lacy little garments to show the proud father how great was the gift his wife had given him. Ferdinand grinned majestically. The grandees clustered round,

Isabella whispered to the midwife, "Is our child a boy?"

"A beautiful boy, Your Highness."

"Please do not lie to humor me. I am awake. I am strong."

"Wait till you see! A beautiful, beautiful boy!"

Ferdinand parted the curtains, kissed her damp brow. "There is indeed no doubt about the matter, my dear. I could

262

scarcely tear my eyes away for pride and rapture." Isabella wept and thanked God. "Give him to me, darling."

He was a tiny baby, but spotless and perfectly formed. He had pale yellow hair.

"Blue eyes, like yours," Ferdinand said.

"Silly, all babies' eyes are blue."

"Look at those arms!"

Isabella smiled. "Strong, like yours." But they did not look exceptionally strong. She was just a trifle worried about the Infante's hint of frailty. But mothers always worried, she reassured herself; and how can you tell so soon!

"What shall we christen him, Ferdinand?"

It was Saint John the Baptist's Day, Ferdinand said, His father was John of Aragón. "I want him called John."

She nodded, pleased.

"Give him to me."

She took the prince and held him close to her, glad to hear the strong high-pitched bawling that came out of his pink searching little mouth.

"Good lungs," Ferdinand said.

"Will you leave me alone with him a little while?"

"Eh? Oh, all right, all right." He grinned.

The grandees hushed and tiptoed about the room, and went off to drink the health of the new Prince of the Asturias, as if the feeding of a baby were something that had to be done in absolute silence. The midwife, a jolly fat woman of the people, known as la Herradera, the Bucket Biddy, shook with silent laughter and touched her forehead. "Men!"

The queen kissed the child's brow—it was Ferdinand's again—and softly stroked his hair, where she could feel the heart beating on top of his head. So tipsy, so helpless a head on its weak little neck; her hand had to support it. But one day the neck would be strong as a bull's, like Ferdinand's, which had always been somewhat thick; and the head would hold itself proud and erect. It would have to be strong. It would have to bear the weight of three crowns. "Little

263

prince, little prince," she murmured, "King of Castile, King of Aragón, King of Sicily." Nay, perhaps four crowns. One day Prince John would marry. What more likely than a Portuguese princess? King of all the Spains; united, one, under one crowned head, now so small as it nestled against her breast.

"But at the moment Your little Highness does not look as if you had many political ambitions." She smiled.

Seville and the whole kingdom celebrated the birth of the Prince of the Asturias for three days and three nights. When he was ten days old a high-born nurse carried him on a red brocade pillow in the midst of a gala procession to be baptized in the cathedral. There, in a forest of granite pillars that had been hung with velvet and silk and draped with battle flags, Cardinal Mendoza christened him John. Outside, among the throngs that could not crowd into even that mighty church, Ferdinand's midget jester, scarcely three feet high, carried a massy silver dish on top of his head so they could look down into it and see the baptismal offering that the sovereigns had made: it was an enormous gold *excelente* for which fifty golden ducats had been melted down to supply the precious metal.

At the feast that followed the king was in a jovial mood; he drank a glass of wine, applauded the dancers loudly, and pinched Beatriz de Bobadilla when once she passed close to him. She danced quickly out of reach. "Prude!" muttered the king. But Isabella's eyes were fixed on him, green; he set down his glass, put on his grave face and conversed with the Papal Legate concerning Italian affairs.

"I think you had better sit beside me, Señora Marquésa," Isabella said when the music stopped.

Beatriz sat down gingerly. Ferdinand's fingers were strong.

"Will you come to me alone tonight? I want to talk to you about something."

"Your Highness! I could not help it. I'm sure it was a

mistake, I bumped into him. Everybody does that."

"Sh-h-h!" whispered the queen, smiling. "That was nothing," Then, with a catch in her voice, "Rather you than somebody else. For you, Beatriz, I know and love and trust. It is about something that I heard by chance on the street today."

During the procession to the cathedral she had caught the words of a couple of tipsy revelers. "Why does he fool around with that Aragonian bitch when he can get a legitimate prince in Castile?" one asked.

The other, whose wine had made him philosophical, replied, "Hell stop, hombre, he'll stop. He has suffered a great disappointment in the Aragonian bitch. Virgen Santísima! Hold your tongue!" He began to cheer wildly. "Viva la Reyna! Viva el Principe! Viva...." The queen passed by.

That night she asked, "Beatriz, what does everyone know that I do not know?"

"I do not understand Your Highness."

"Please, Beatriz! I have known you so long."

"Truly, I do not understand."

She would not cry, but her eyes were very bright. "Who is the Aragonian bitch who has disappointed my husband?" Such a word from Isabella's prim tongue rocked Beatriz like a thunderbolt.

"Your Highness forbade me to speak of the king."

The tears welled over in spite of all she could do. "Drunkards on the street know; only his wife does not know. I beg you to tell me what everybody knows that I do not."

Beatriz knelt at Isabella's chair and threw her arms around her. Beatriz was crying too. "He couldn't help it. All men are like that. Kings are even worse. He doesn't see her any more. They say he shut her up in a nunnery. He hardly knew her a week. Oh my dear friend, how sorry I am you found out. She was a nurse of some kind, a nobody."

"It is now clear what the king did," Isabella said. Her voice was so low Beatriz could hardly hear. "Did he acknowledge the child?"

"Ye-es."

"Publicly?"

"Yes."

"There is great honor in him, Beatriz. It took courage to do that."

"Yes."

Isabella hesitated. "Is the child a boy?"

"A girl."

"Ah!"

She was raking the ashes for sparks of hope. There was a little spark in this for she had given him a *prince.*

"What is his child's name?"

"Joanna."

"Joanna was his mother's name. The king has strong family feeling."

"Yes."

"How old is the king's little girl?"

"Two, I think," She thought back. It must have been about the time when Ferdinand was resentful of her being crowned alone. She did not say any more because there was nothing more to say. She rested her head against Beatriz' shoulder. Beatriz dressed extravagantly, as always; the velvet shoulder was soft and warm.

Beatriz said, "Can I get you a glass of milk?"

"I wonder if you would fetch me a sip of brandy? No, rather more than a sip. Do not let the maids see you."

Beatriz ran to her room. With a shaking hand she poured a little glassful of brandy from one of Cabrera's Venetian decanters. The Marqués of Moya turned over in bed. "What in the name of all the saints are you doing?"

"Go back to sleep!" she snapped at him.

Isabella did not mention the matter to Beatriz again, nor did she mention it to Ferdinand. But she could not hide her feeling of hurt, of shock and, oddly, of shame like a personal shame.

Cabrera said to his wife, "What were you doing with my brandy in the middle of the night?"

"The queen wanted some," Beatriz said.

"Isabella? Wanted *brandy?*"

"She heard about the king's second bastard."

"Who was cruel enough to tell her?"

"Not I, be assured. She picked it up on the street."

"What miserable luck. What damnably miserable luck. Still—" he shrugged—"she was bound to find out sooner or later after the public acknowledgment in Aragón."

"Ferdinand is a beast."

"In the finest tradition of sovereigns. At least he acknowledges them."

"Isabella said she thought that was brave of him. She is the brave one. I'm glad I'm not married to him."

Cabrera rubbed his chin reflectively. "It can't be easy."

Though Isabella did not reproach the king he sensed a deep change in her. He tried to joke with her, but she did not laugh. He grew angry; she did not ask why. He overwhelmed her with attention, mixing in his mind the dynast with the lover, for since she had given him one prince he was convinced she could give him another. She was dutifully, distantly submissive.

"Isabella?"

"Yes?"

"What is troubling you?"

She looked at him. It pained her a little to see him wince and drop his eyes. She did not like to watch her idol crumble.

"I knew you'd find out about Joanna," he blurted out. "I couldn't face you after I acknowledged her, and I stayed away as much as I could."

He was being honest, she thought.

"It was hard to endure," she said, "that you and I were married when Joanna was born, whereas you did not even know me when you had your first illegitimate child." His

267

defense was ingenious. If he did not deeply love her, he said, would he have feared her finding out about the child? Did not kings flaunt their mistresses in their queens' faces all over Europe? Nay, did they not proclaim national holidays when their bastards were born, just as they did for legitimate princes? He had done no such heartless thing, he said, because he loved his wife.

He sounded sincere. His handsome face was pale and in deadly earnest. What he said about other kings was notoriously true, even of the ugly ones. How much greater Ferdinand's temptations must be.

"But if," he said emphatically, "I dallied with a wanton in a moment of pique, that does not mean that I shall not love my innocent bastard child."

How infinitely more difficult it was to know one man than a nation of men! Perhaps, as the Bishop of Seville had told her, she was asking too much. She supposed she always would, and often not get what she asked for. By a curious transference of her own great pride it hurt her to hear him apologize. She was so much a part of him that she felt herself degraded by his degradation of himself.

"I didn't scold you, Ferdinand."

That wasn't enough; he wished she would. "It would be easier if you did."

"It is not in my heart to. You see, I love you too."

"I am forgiven?"

Formal Ferdinand! He wanted his ego te absolvo, neatly, that his conscience might be purged and he might get on with his work.

"From my heart," she smiled.

"On my sacred honor, Isabella, I'll never hurt you again!"

To the Sevillanos nothing had changed, and the royal lovers still strolled in the alcazar gardens, though summer wore into autumn, the flowers faded, the golden fruits dropped to the ground and the year went into its colorless winter rest.

The conviction that she asked too much and would not get it simply by asking bore in upon her heart. Her chin went up. If she could not get it by asking, then she would earn it. She was not vain but she was far too honest with herself to deny that she had more than her share of beauty. Reports of Ferdinand's mistresses attributed no great beauty to them. Since he seemed to demand more than beauty she resolved that she would force him to respect her as no man had ever respected a woman before. She had read more widely than was common among the highborn, even the stories of Boccaccio, though she hid the naughty volume because she knew Ferdinand would not approve of it. It had always struck her as strange that the great enchantresses of men were extraordinary first, beautiful as if only by an afterthought. "I shall not lose him if I accomplish things."

Outside the little world of her heart the great world spun, full of its great affairs. That winter most of them were sad.

In Barcelona, at the age of eighty-three, in full course of majestic good health, King John of Aragón suddenly died in his sleep. Ferdinand had to go at once to Aragón, to bury his father in stately pomp and assume his father's crown. "I am reluctant to leave, my dear. It will be a tedious lengthy time. But I am determined that every one of my father's vassals must swear me homage in person." She knew he had a complete list of them, in alphabetical order, neatly packed in a saddle bag. As each one swore a secretary would check off his name with a heavy red pencil.

"I'll ride with you part of the way!"

He looked at her searchingly. "Are you quite sure it's all right for you to ride?"

"I never felt better in my life." Isabella laughed.

"I'll have to travel fast."

"I can too."

To Spaniards, who loved the spectacular in their reverence for death, there was nothing inconsistent in the behavior of the long royal cavalcade that thundered towards the north on horses caparisoned in mourning through towns draped in black to the tolling of funeral bells. The crowds solemnly cheered the king who was galloping to pay his last respects to his dead father, the queen who bore him company.

As they passed the Sierra Morena and entered the cold Castilian uplands the wind whipped Isabella's cheeks so pink that Ferdinand compared them with the peaches of the south. She called him honeytongue, and shared his quiet laughter.

Out of earshot behind them Beatriz de Bobadilla said to her husband, "I'm frightfully worried. She is three months with child, and the king does not know."

Isabella accompanied him as far as Toledo.

"I wish you could go on," Ferdinand said. "Aragón has never seen my queen."

"Aragón will welcome me more warmly when we can bring them their Prince," she said practically.

"At any rate," he said, "I suppose one of us has to stay behind to watch the border. Portugal will surely strike again, now that I am away."

Isabella smiled. "I don't think so."

"Your instinct is sometimes right."

Her confidence was based on more than instinct, but she could not tell him what it was without offending him. Isabella was engaged for the first time in her life in some highly secret diplomacy.

The cavalcade separated, the king and his escort pressing on towards Barcelona, the queen and her suite remaining as guests of Cardinal Mendoza.

Beatriz approached her diffidently. "Do *rest,* Your Highness."

Isabella was in great bodily discomfort. "I shall have to, Beatriz, for a while."

But it was only for a while. She was saddened by reports which Mendoza gave her of Carrillo's rapidly failing health. He was in retirement in Alcalá de Henares only a few miles away. She sent him a warm invitation to come to see her. He replied peevishly that he could not afford to travel, being beggared, as he put it, by the confiscation of his revenues. She did not want to quarrel with the sick old friend of her youth and increased the amount she allowed him, which had always been enough to live on comfortably but not enough to pay a private army or to waste on costly alchemistical experiments. Then she rode to see him, since he would not come to her.

The archbishop was pitifully changed, greatly aged and broken in spirit. He was too weak to rise from his couch to greet her. His necromancer and his astrologer padded back and forth outside his door. There was a suspicious smell of chemicals in the air. He spoke of her youth in a rambling old-man's way; he did not speak of the future. It was a painful interview and she wondered why she had made it. But in a few days she was glad she had, for Archbishop Carrillo died.

Then it was that she discovered why the odor of chemicals still hung about the house. He had gone deeply into debt to continue his futile experiments. She paid his debts and prepared an order of banishment for Doctor Alarcon and El Beato; but the wolves that had preyed on the old man's greed and foolishness had disappeared, their purses well lined with real gold that they could not make for him.

While heralds sped over the roads between Portugal and Toledo, between Toledo and Rome, Isabella rode to Arevalo to see her mother. At very infrequent intervals she had paused in her crowded career to make this pilgrimage of duty, preferring usually to provide for the Dowager Queen's comfort and care through subordinates whose kindness and training she trusted. Isabella could visit the tomb of her father with joy, in the calmness of faith; but to visit the living sepulchre of her mother's mind filled her with dread. Yet she was impelled to the visit. Carrillo had died; Ferdinand's father had died; the mad die too.

But she knew there was another reason; none of her love but much of her idolatry of Ferdinand had died also. She wanted to run to her mother, as often when a child she had run to her to be comforted when she hurt herself.

It was a mistake. The river of time could not be turned back. The woman could not become a child again. Nay, the roles were reversed, and it was the mother who had become the child. The old queen, though still alive, had traveled the wheel of life full turn, from infancy through stormy active years and back again to infancy. She was perfectly well. She was pink and fat, and cooed happily like a baby.

Isabella bent and kissed the thin white hair of her mother's head, half-expecting to feel with her lips the heartbeat there.

It was impossible to exchange a single thought. Faces, gestures, words, all had lost their meaning.

Isabella tiptoed out of the room as she might have tiptoed out of a nursery where a tired child had just fallen asleep.

Had the helpless invalid been anyone but her mother, Isabella would not have been distressed. Everything was being done that affection and money could do. But once she had lain in that madwoman's womb; another child now lay in her own. Far, far in the back of her mind, thrust down by a fierce effort of will, there was always the fear that her body might be a carrier of madness.

CHAPTER 22

IN Portugal there lived a quick-witted old lady with royal blood in her veins, sister of Isabella's mother, who had also been a Portuguese princess. Sometimes it seemed to Isabella that Nature was cruelly capricious, prodigal of gifts to one sibling, niggardly with another; for Aunt Beatriz, whom Isabella had called "Aunty Portugal" as a little girl, was as sharp as her mother was childish. It was as if Nature had exhausted itself in endowing Aunty Portugal's mind and found no intelligence left over for Isabella's mother. There were frightening overtones in that.

By a quirk in the complicated intermarriages that characterized royalty, Aunt Beatriz of Portugal was also the Portuguese king's sister-in-law. Beatriz did not like him, and she considered his December-May marriage with little La Beltraneja the height of undignified nonsense. Moreover, she was careful how she spent her own revenues and she was outraged at the cost of the war between Portugal and Castile, for it was a drain on the Portuguese treasury also.

She had written to Isabella in secret, forthrightly expressing her disgust with the war and asking for Isabella's views. "My brother in-law, the king," she said, "has gone up to France to solicit the help of that rascally Louis. Louis has put him off for months, saying neither aye nor nay, entertaining him lavishly but never once committing himself. This can only mean that Louis considers our war a stalemate, for he always jumps in on the winning side. Meanwhile Portugal and Castile both pay huge amounts to armies who do nothing to earn their keep. Even as a girl you possessed wonderfully good sense. Give me your thoughts, my dear niece. You can write me in complete confidence on this matter through my herald, who, to my eye, with his harp and his motley, presents the picture of a *most* convincing minstrel.

"No doubt," she continued, "you will want to consult Ferdinand. Yet I wish you would not. He would only construe this missive of mine as a confession of Portugal's weakness. Believe me, we are as strong as you are. That is the pity of this war; that is why it is a stalemate. That and the stubbornness of proud men."

Since Aunt Beatriz had pointedly by-passed Ferdinand, Isabella could not show him the letter without offense to his pride. Nor did she particularly want to. For here was a chance to end the war. Ferdinand would respect her for that, if she could end it on terms sufficiently favorable to Castile.

Noncommittally she replied that Ferdinand too would shortly be away, the death of his father requiring his presence in Aragón. No doubt, she said subtly, he would raise a great army there to fight Portugal. That would be sad, she said, since she too wanted peace. She would not concede to her aunt that Portugal was as strong as Castile.

There were other secret dispatches, but the big beginning had been made, the ice had been broken.

Early in May in advancing pregnancy she rode the hundred and forty miles from Toledo to Alcantara on the Portuguese border, taking with her no one but Pulgar her secretary, Beatriz de Bobadilla and a small escort of caballeros. One would have supposed the little group some minor gentry from some inconsequential estate.

The motion of the horse no longer made her feel sick, but the child had grown heavier and she could not ride fast because of the jolting.

Aunt Beatriz of Portugal was already there, waiting for her. How exactly she looked as Isabella's mother should have looked!

She greeted her niece with affection and more than family admiration. "What a beautiful creature you grew up to be, sobrina mia! I too had hair like that once. It's the blonde English blood in us, you know." Then her sharp eyes traveled downward. "Maria Santísima! I had no idea! You have not announced this. I should never have dared suggest that we meet if I had known."

"Even Ferdinand doesn't know."

Aunty Portugal did not ask why. She was far too shrewd to pry into their personal lives, especially after Ferdinand had acknowledged two bastards.

But she was glad Ferdinand was away; she knew she could have wrung no concessions from him, The absence of men, with their touchy pride and their interminable bickering over details, would enable her and her niece to cut to the heart of the matter quickly.

"You will not want to stay long, I expect," she said. "Fortunately you can speak with authority for Castile. As for Portugal, I flatter myself that I can convince Alfonso, the silly old goat."

"I shall stay as long as I must, dear aunt. We will try to convince our men."

Aunty Portugal settled down to a duel of wits in which she knew herself to excel, confident that Portugal would profit by any negotiations in which she took part.

"Alfonso should never have married that poor little girl," Isabella said. "'It's unnatural."

Beatriz of Portugal shrugged. "I told him not to, but now the damage is done."

"I think it can be rectified," Isabella said, smiling ingenuously.

"Over his dead fat body! He will never give up his bride."

"Then you must persuade him to. That dreadful marriage is the biggest obstacle to peace."

"My dear, there are limits to my persuasive powers."

That marriage was also Portugal's biggest diplomatic advantage.

"Then I must help you persuade him."

Not for nothing had Isabella's heralds been flying to Rome

as well as to Portugal. Her representatives at the papal court had vigorously protested the bull that permitted Alfonso to marry La Beltraneja, pointing out that it had brought on a war between Christian nations when all Christendom ought to be fighting the Turk, whose conquests continued in the East, and the Moor, who was increasingly restive in Granada.

Now Isabella had received a reply, which she showed to her good but thoroughly Portuguese aunt. It was couched in cautious language but it left no doubt that the Pope would reconsider the matter and annul the troublesome marriage.

Beatriz of Portugal's face fell.

"This is heavy artillery, my dear. Like your guns at Toro. I was not quite prepared for this."

"Aunty Portugal, is it *right* for an old uncle to marry a teen-aged niece?"

"The Holy Father seems to agree that it isn't." She sighed. "You leave me very little to bargain with, Isabella."

Isabella had left Portugal even less than Aunt Beatriz realized. In France the wily King Louis learned, through his network of spies, what was afoot in the papal court; he guessed who would win and made a quick turnabout in his foreign policy. He withdrew recognition from Alfonso and sent him back on a slow ship to Portugal empty-handed, with many pious words on the wickedness of marrying youngsters. At the same time he dispatched letters to Isabella and Ferdinand addressing them as Most High and Mighty, True and Rightful Sovereigns of Castile, León, Aragón and Sicily. Slyly he congratulated Isabella on the expected Infante or Infanta and expressed his hope that she and her aunt would come to terms on a peace treaty.

Shortly the Pope issued the bull declaring Alfonso's marriage with La Beltraneja null and void *ab initio*.

From Aragón Ferdinand wrote, "How is it, mi señora, that I must learn from the King of France that my wife is expecting a baby? How is it that you are engaged in diplomatic matters of which I know nothing? Nevertheless, God bless you in both your glorious endeavors and bring them to happy fruition. I long to be at your side. Only the stubbornness of some factious vassals keeps me from you. I will crush them. Do thou do likewise. Crush Portugal, preferably by marrying our children with Portuguese Infantes. I kiss your hands and feet. God keep you. Ferdinand."

Beatriz of Portugal too favored intermarriage among royal families; it was traditional and it offered the best means yet devised of keeping a peace once made.

Soon Isabella was able to write to her husband, "I send you the terms of a treaty, mi señor, which lacks only your signature (and Alfonso's, of course. He is still at sea.) to become effective and end this profitless war. I am well in body and spirit. I love you. Your wife."

It was a treaty that years of war could not have wrung from Alfonso the African.

Alfonso gave up all claim to the throne of Castile, and agreed even to stop quartering Castilian arms on his personal standard, a stinging rebuke to his pride.

Little La Beltraneja, now on the marriage market again with her dangerous claim to Castile, agreed to marry no one but Prince John, Isabella's son, thirteen years her junior, Or else go into a nunnery. Ferdinand laughed heartily at that. Isabella had effectively blocked La Beltraneja's alliance with anyone except a prince too young to accept. With her withered pretensions to Henry the Impotent's crown, La, Beltraneja elected the nunnery, as Isabella had known she would.

There was to be another royal marriage: their daughter the Infanta Isabella would marry a younger son of the Portuguese king. This had good chance of success, for the children were about of an age.

Ferdinand wondered what security Isabella had given shrewd Aunt Beatriz that this marriage would be performed when the children were old enough. So far the treaty gave nothing to Portugal. Running his eye down the list of provisions he found the security, the sop to Portugal's pride. At first he was startled. Prince John and the Infanta Isabella were to be delivered into the custody of Beatriz of Portugal. It did not seem like Isabella to part with her children. Then he smiled. There would be no separation. True, the Infantes were to live with their great-aunt, but not in Portugal, not even in some frontier city. Beatriz of Portugal agreed to set up residence in the city of Moya, a stone's throw from Toledo in the very heart of Castile! "It is difficult to tell," Ferdinand wrote, "who are the hostages, the children or your Aunty Portugal. From the geographical point of view the hostage is most certainly your aunty. Alfonso would be a fool to sign. But then, of course, he is. Do not tarry too long in Alcantara. If you do not take a litter home I will poison all your horses."

"No one is actually a hostage," she answered. "It only appears that way. The children will have their own tutors as usual and Aunty Portugal will simply run the house. She is charming, cultivated and reasonable. We shall spend much time there. The children will learn Portuguese; I was always glad I knew it. As for my journey home, I promise to take a litter. You need not poison horses; there are far too few of them in our realm. Why is it that so many men prefer to ride mules in Spain? I think strange thoughts these days." She was extremely tired. Her greatest worry, she told Ferdinand, was that Alfonso might refuse to sign, "though I really do not see how he can help it."

When Alfonso, who had been seasick on the voyage, disembarked at Lisbon, he found his marriage annulled, his bride in a convent and his capable sister-in-law in Castile. The forces that Isabella had marshaled against him were so strong that the treaty—it already had a humiliating nickname—was in effect without his signature. He saw with a sense of frustration that nobody cared whether he signed or not.

He was beaten; by women. In a rage he affixed his name to the document he hated, calling it by the name that everyone called it in secret, *The Portuguese Treaty*, cursing all females, especially Isabella of Castile.

Then he did an astonishing thing. He abdicated. He tore off his sword and crown and exchanged them for the rope girdle and russet cowl of a monk. He retired to the monastery of Varatojo on a bleak and wind-swept promontory near the ocean where he could watch the restless waves over which, when he was young, he had sailed to fight the Moors and win for himself the name of Alfonso the African. His eldest son, Dom João, ascended his throne.

To create the treaty that ended the Portuguese War of Succession, driven as she was to accomplish it almost singlehanded, had cost Isabella dear. Her body had pleaded for rest, her mind for repose. Instead, she had ridden hundreds of miles and spent weary sleepless nights reading and dictating complicated diplomatic correspondence, every word of which would be scrutinized by shrewd and self-seeking statesmen. Men were not so constructed, Isabella thought wryly, that they needed to conserve some part of their strength to bring children into this world. The mental and physical strain had been severe. But, reading Ferdinand's glowing praise of her as she made her way slowly back to Toledo in a litter, she thought that her effort had been worth the cost. The crowds were encouraging too. At every crossroad they turned out to cheer her, especially the common soldiers who were trooping back to their homes from their long watch on the border, which now was at peace.

In Toledo she bore a daughter. The baby looked strangely, eerily old. It was sluggish and unresponsive. Its forehead was bulbous and high, too high to look like Ferdinand's.

Ferdinand was still in Aragón.

She christened it quickly, not knowing how long it would live. "I have named our daughter Joanna, after your mother," she wrote.

She could not in honesty say the child was beautiful. "She is very quiet and sweet."

CHAPTER 23

SHE watched Ferdinand's first warm flood of admiration subside into chilly impersonal approval of her statecraft. True, he admitted, she had ended the war on astonishingly favorable terms for Castile. True, he could not have won such terms without an enormous outpouring of blood and treasure. And true, he said, he would have done exactly as she had done if he had been a woman, if he had had an Aunty Portugal

She had forced him to respect her. But she was left with a weary feeling that somehow she had stolen his thunder.

His tight lips and formal manner whenever he spoke of the ugly little princess were also significant, and disheartening. He did not reproach her; he did not say, as some men might have said, "You rode horses in your last months and that is why our child acts like an idiot."

"But next time," she vowed to herself, "*he* shall win the war." For Ferdinand, to judge by his attitude, was jealous of her.

He was also suspicious. She had done too much by herself.

"What else are you hiding, Isabella? Diplomacy is a sticky oil, and once it wets you, you never dry."

She admitted that the Pope's reply had come from Rome and that an Inquisition to root out heresy from Castile would have the sanction of the Holy See.

He leapt like a tiger at her disclosure.

"This is momentous news! This is the Sword of Justice we should have wielded long since. But I see no Inquisition in Castile."

"I locked the Pope's reply up in my casket."

"You sheathed your sword," he accused her, "How, pray, do you propose to pay for the war? How will you pay back your debt to the Church? Unless my memory for figures fails me, and I assure you it does not, you owe thirty million maravedíes, and the sum is now due."

"The Church has not pressed us."

"It will."

"We will pay."

"You have a most disconcerting way of saying 'we,' my dear."

"That is because we share in everything."

"It makes me extremely uncomfortable to share a debt of thirty million maravedíes."

"We will manage."

"How will *we* manage thirty million maravedíes without an Inquisition? Be reasonable, Isabella."

The thought struck him that the papal bull might be limited in scope. Or perhaps she was only pretending to have received it. "Is the King of Castile permitted to read the queen's correspondence?"

"Ferdinand, please don't be sarcastic."

She detached the key from the chain that held her cross. He lifted the lid of the silver casket and found himself gazing down at a somewhat disorderly hoard of all the big and little personal things that Isabella treasured or kept secret from the world: the first milk tooth shed by their daughter; his own letters that began mi señora, these much fondled and worn; the jewels he had given her when he came disguised to wed her. There was also a heavy parchment scroll.

He said in a softer voice, "I did not mean to be sarcastic. I was only afraid you had stretched the truth a bit to please me." He pulled out the scroll and settled back to read the Pope's reply. Presently he found himself whistling in astonishment.

"Señora mia, you must have bewitched the Holy Father himself! In Aragón I enjoy no such sweeping power as this will give me in Castile!" His face shone with satisfaction; nowhere did the bull mention Isabella alone; her name was coupled throughout with his; this was something he was delighted to share with her. "The beauty of this," he exclaimed, tapping the parchment till the leaden seals of the Apostles on their colored ribbons gave out a doleful little rattle, "the surpassing beauty of this is that you and I appoint the inquisitors. The Church abdicates all control over our Inquisition. This is something entirely new in authority for kings. You are thorough, Isabella."

"I try to be," she said. It was enough that he praised her. She did not tell him how stubbornly she had argued for the right to name the inquisitors. Rome was far away and full of the whole world's affairs; she was close at hand and could temper the zeal of her Spanish inquisitors, for they would hold office only during her pleasure. She might even, if she chose, never appoint any at all.

"We must publish this at once," Ferdinand said positively. "We will pay all our debts in a week, *and* win many souls to God."

She answered him evenly, "It seems to me you are putting the cart before the horse." Her chin was up and her eyes were green, and Ferdinand knew he must walk warily, on this of all subjects. She took the bull and locked it up again; the lid came down with a decisive snap. He shrugged, smiling. He could not publish it alone. But he was a patient man.

"If that is not your way, my dear, what is?"

"Cardinal Mendoza's catechism is being preached everywhere. It is making many converts."

"Not many. I've followed it."

"Even a few, won without fear, are good at the start."

"They are all poor."

"More will follow, rich as well as poor."

"Slow, slow, slow."

"Such work should be slow."

"And our huge debt?"

"That indeed must be paid at once."

He looked at her.

She said, "I am going to repossess all the Crown Lands that Henry gave away."

Slowly the enormity of her simple statement sank into Ferdinand's neat and orderly mind. Henry the Impotent, who could never say no to a suitor, had flung broadcast the patrimony of the Crown, a castle to one, an estate to another, rents, revenues, titles, privileges, all with witless extravagance. Over the years he had beggared himself to enrich his rapacious vassals. All that he had squandered Isabella was now proposing to take back. It would be an uncompromisingly autocratic act.

Ferdinand frowned. "You are right, of course," he said slowly. "I had to do the same thing in Aragón, on a somewhat smaller scale. I'll help all I can. We shan't be popular, you know. There will be a great deal of spilt blood. It means war against your great nobles. It will take all your guns."

"We are going to try to do it with votes."

"Votes?" He burst out laughing. "Votes!"

It could not have happened in Aragón, which faced a sea and breathed soft air and had learned to compromise with its soul. But it happened in Castile, the land of stones and saints, where nothing came in half-measure and miracles were common. Isabella convoked the Cortes of 1480, a parliament that immediately became famous throughout Europe for its unprecedented acts of devotion to her.

It was the most brilliant assembly Castile had witnessed for many years, composed of gold-mitred bishops, the Knights of Santiago de Campostella in their white mantles blazoned with the lily-hilted sword of Saint James, the Knights of Calatrava in their green ribbons and crosses, of dukes, marquises and counts in their ermine and jeweled coronets; and, outnumbering all the grandees and prelates, the sober, proud Castilian representatives of the towns. These burghers were dressed in velvet, for the realm was prosperous and at peace. It seemed to Ferdinand, looking down from his throne at the great assembly, that Castilian faces were remarkably alike, as if everyone were everyone else's first cousin. No such family resemblance characterized the Aragonian assemblies over which he had presided. But perhaps, he mused, this odd similarity was merely the result of their all thinking the same thoughts.

They were not looking at him. Their eyes were fixed on the slender beautiful woman who was their queen, queen by right and by war, a war she had brought to a victorious end. The crown that King Henry had tarnished shone like fire on her copper hair, Ferdinand's rubies blazed at her throat. The budding Princess Isabella stood beside her, her double in exquisite miniature. Behind her, white-haired and regal, sat Aunt Beatriz of Portugal, living symbol of Portuguese friendship, with the other Infantes. Isabella had restored order where before there was anarchy, justice where before there was lawlessness, prosperity where there had been poverty, peace where there had been war. Now she wanted something from them. Nay, she wanted a great deal, for her work had only begun.

With utmost candor but without a trace of diffidence she told them what the Crown desired, not as a favor but as a right, to right a wrong. "For if you had come to us, instead of the other way round," she said, "and told us that our predecessor had unlawfully deprived you of certain estates, you must believe our word that we would have restored them to you."

She had never broken her word. They believed her.

Even if some of the grandees had not, Ferdinand suspected, they would have had to pretend to. The clergy, the commons and most of their peers were solidly against them.

The result was a massive disgorgement of revenue by the richest feudal Houses of Spain: the Grand Admiral resigned 240,000 maravedíes of his annual income; the Duke of Medina Sidonia, 180,000, Cardinal Mendoza lost heavily, and Don Beltran de la Cueva, in a romantic burst of loyalty, cheerfully forfeited more than any of the others, the enormous sum of 1,400,000 maravedíes. All told, the restoration to the Crown was more than Isabella's debt. She paid back the Church.

"You got your thirty millions," Ferdinand said, "not for a year but for life! Carrillo could not make gold with all his magic, but you can, by some black magic all your own. Isabella, Isabella, what are you made of?"

"We had the votes," she said.

He shook his head. "First you had their hearts. That is an art I shall never possess."

"You have mine."

"You know what I mean," he smiled.

Isabella and her consort Ferdinand emerged from the celebrated Cortes of 1480 as absolute monarchs. She began to spend her great revenues in ways that at first he judged foolish. Why should she pension widows and orphans of fallen soldiers at her own expense, or settle disabled veterans on little farms donated by the Crown? No one had ever done that before, at least no one since Caesar.

But she also spent herself. She gave him a gift as much to his taste as cream to a cat. Far to the south in New Castile beyond the Sierra Morena the Knights of Santiago assembled in solemn conclave. The Grand Master of the Order had just died. Like cardinals electing a new Pope the leaders of the Order were voting behind locked doors to elect one of their number his successor. Unlike cardinals they could not hold their tongue. The succession was in dispute and the secret leaked out. Here was something that only she could give Ferdinand, and it was difficult for her to imagine how he could possibly be jealous or moody afterward—if only she could get it. It was bad that the Knights were bickering. They only did that in peacetime, when no natural leader arose to win the honor for himself by his own fighting prowess. But she almost hoped that the bickering would continue till she could get there.

She took horse at once from Valladolid and rode almost as fast—lacking only the sharp spurs—as she had ridden to Segovia to save her daughter. She arrived in a pouring rain, drenched to the skin. She knocked at the great locked door and asked to be admitted.

Utterly astonished by the sudden appearance of their queen, the Knights let her into the secret Chapter where no woman had ever set foot before.

The sight of her touched their hearts and tipped the scale of the election. She was weary and travel-stained; her wet clothing clung to her slender body. The Knights were comfortable and dry, their flowing mantles immaculately clean. She had wanted something so terribly, not for herself but for her husband, that she had ridden forty leagues to request it. She could not command the honor. But she shamed them.

"We were rather wavering towards Don Alonso de Cardenas, Your Highness," one of the officers said. Don Alonso was a famous grandee of the great House of Cardenas.

"The king should rightfully lead the Knights as he leads all other fighters for Spain," she replied. "Elect the king, and I promise he will resign in Don Alonso's favor, provided only the Grand Mastership rests in the Crown."

Isabella's gift to the king stretched far into the future, beyond Ferdinand, beyond little Prince John, reaching out to touch all the other kings of Spain to come, in whom her blood would flow with Ferdinand's.

The Knights elected Ferdinand. She had solved a difficult problem, breaking a deadlock with hurt to no one's pride, for at once, in Ferdinand's name, she appointed Alonso de Cardenas.

She had come with the wind, she was gone with the wind, for she could not rest till she presented Ferdinand with one of the most coveted privileges in Castile, the right to appoint the Grand Master of the greatest of all the Military Orders.

Later the Knights wondered whether she might not have been some beautiful witch borne in on the dark wings of the storm. But by then there was nothing they could do about it and shortly a herald appeared with a gorgeously engrossed scroll signed Io El Rey, Io La Reyna, confirming Don Alonso de Cardenas in his exalted post as Grand Master of Santiago. He was a good man and he was immensely grateful to Isabella.

"You should appoint the heads of the other Orders, too," Isabella said to Ferdinand. "That should be easy now."

Nothing had given him so much pleasure since, the birth of Prince John. "I think you flew down on a bat," he said, kissing her.

"Ferdinand?"

"Yes, my dear?" He was all smiles.

"I want something from you."

"Anything."

"That horse was unconscionably slow."

"It was the fastest one in the stables."

"I want a better breed of horses in Spain."

"So do I," he reflected. "But I do not believe anyone, not even you, can ever coax the Spaniard off his mule."

"We can try."

"Hm-m. Spanish horses used to be the best in the world, before the Crusades ended."

"I don't believe they're finished yet, any more than Spanish horses. The blood is still good; all they lack is speed. Would you be willing to encourage horse racing among the grandees? That will better the breed."

"Slowly, slowly, Isabella! You think too fast. Better the breed of what, the horses or the grandees?"

"You are purposely confusing me," she laughed. "Of the horses, naturally. The English king races horses all the time."

He saw she was serious. "I'll try," he said.

But the Spaniards did not take to horse racing. It was colorless compared with bullfighting and it seemed rather pointless. One caballero said to her, "It has already been established that one horse can run faster than another. Why prove it further, Your Highness?"

"They love you," Ferdinand said, "but I think they resent your sheathing the horns of their bulls."

"Then we must try something else. I am not a spoilsport, but I do not like waste. There are other sports."

She threw open great areas of royal hunting preserves, inviting scores of nobles to hunt her game. The occasions were festive. She and the king would often compete with their guests. It was difficult to beat Ferdinand to a kill. But the royal prizes were so substantial and bestowed so graciously that she made fast horses fashionable.

The grandees vied with one another to coax even greater speed and endurance out of their hunters. She sent ships to the Barbary Coast for Arab stallions, an experiment so successful that it gave a name to a powerful new breed called the Spanish Barb.

During one of these hunts two fiery young caballeros, the Conde de Luna and the Conde de Valencia, had a quarrel over something trivial. Since the queen was nearby, vividly beautiful in a green hunting costume, a jaunty green feather in her pert little cap over her wind-blown curls, they were anxious to distinguish themselves. Their voices rose and their swords leapt out. A circle gravely formed to watch them kill each other.

"Stop them, Ferdinand."

"My dear, nobody stops a duel."

"Stop them, I say!"

Blushing furiously Ferdinand rode his horse between them. "Gentlemen," he said sternly, "perhaps you have not heard of our pragmatica. I remind you that the winner of a duel is a common murderer and shall be hanged as such."

They sheathed their swords, their honor equally saved,

and bowed to the queen, glad to be alive. No, they protested, they had not heard of the new edict.

"Thank you for saving those foolish brave men," she said in a tense whisper. "If they want to fight, let them fight Turks or Moors."

"Now I suppose we shall have to publish a pragmatica forbidding dueling," Ferdinand grumbled. "You are taking all the joy out of life."

"I think your terms were exactly right," she smiled. "I could not have phrased them half so well."

On other hunts she noticed the balding hills in many parts of Castile. During Henry's lax reign lazy peasants had cut down the trees for firewood. The soil had eroded badly with no roots to hold it in place. She hired hundreds of peasants to plant thousands of trees at a cost that made Ferdinand wince. No one had ever had the vision to plant trees on a national scale before.

"You're wasting your money."

"Would you rather waste Spanish soil that can be made fertile?"

It was a period of happiness for Isabella, when she consolidated her victories in the world of affairs and in the little world of her heart. But victories could erode like Castilian hills, she knew; happiness was an elusive possession. It had a tendency to slip away like water unless one were vigilant. Perhaps, in happiness, there was an indwelling principle, as the professors said there was in the element water, that caused it simply to evaporate. She was acutely conscious of her happiness. Honest with herself, she knew that it centered in Ferdinand; therefore, self-avowedly, she was jealous of him, and saw no reproach in it as long as she did not nag, which her great pride would not have permitted her to do in any case. She wanted to though, sometimes.

He had always liked to play cards. She disapproved of card playing on principle, since it led to gambling. Grandees had been known to lose their estates on the turn of a card or a throw of the dice. Then they would quarrel, then they would duel, then gloriously, proudly, with a quip and a prayer on their lips, they would die. Gambling had been one of the gay tragedies of Henry's reign.

Oddly, the best card players at court were pretty young ladies in waiting. She suspected they practiced in secret so Ferdinand would seek them out as partners. His record was not such that she cared to have him exposed to too high-calibre feminine charm too long. The accomplished ones, like a certain Magdalena Perez, were especially dangerous. She had great respect for Doña Magdalena, whose intellect was superior; that made her all the more formidable. True, Doña Magdalena did not throw herself at Ferdinand as some did; he had always been handsome—a king did not even have to be! —and now he was one of the most powerful monarchs in Christendom. There were others besides Doña Magdalena, however, of easier virtue. With a husband and scheming intruders who have mutual inclination and ample opportunity, how can a wife prevent the inevitable?

Isabella refused to believe that anything was inevitable.

One day she presented Ferdinand with a pragmatica that she proposed to publish. It already had the Io La Reyna of the queen. He read it with some surprise.

"You will prohibit card playing? My dear, you *are* cleaning house, aren't you!"

"It leads to gambling."

"I certainly never gamble. Not a maravedí."

"I know you don't, but people can't help trying to do as the king does, and *they* gamble."

Ferdinand laughed good-naturedly. "Oh very well," and affixed his Io El Rey to the edict.

He obeyed it too; the wicked cards disappeared from the court and dropped out of fashion. Unfortunately for Isabella's peace of mind he was equally fond of chess, which was not a gambling game.

Now Doña Magdalena was even more adept at chess than she was at cards. Worse, chess was a game that only two could play at a time, with long intervals of silence while they studied the board, or each other's faces, to guess their opponent's next move. Doña Magdelena's calm intelligent face was extremely attractive. So was her conversation, to a factual mind like Ferdinand's. Chess came, she explained in her musical voice, from the fabulous East; it had been invented by a queen of India, who was so rich she had nothing else to do. Then it had traveled to Persia, to Arabia and into the Western World. Even now it was a favorite game of the Moors of Granada. She knew the Moorish names of the pieces: the bishop was not shaped like a bishop, of course, in the Infidel version of the game. It was shaped like an elephant; and elephant, she explained brightly, was called *aleph-hind,* or Indian ox, and from *aleph-hind* came the Christian word, *elephant.*

"How perfectly fascinating," Ferdinand said.

Isabella had always shown a marked interest in the welfare of her sex. She had pensioned widows and provided schools for the rehabilitation of wayward girls. These were great innovations, made in her deep conviction that women had rights as well as men. In her own life she had experienced the misery that can come from the double standard. And now, she thought, if a woman could be a queen why could not a woman be a professor? She took the matter up with Fernando del Pulgar, her learned secretary.

"Indeed, women once *were* professors, Your Highness, and delivered lectures under the elms in the academy of Athens in ancient days, and in no wise were they inferior to men. But I do not believe there have been any since the time of the Greeks."

"I think there is going to be one in Castile," Isabella smiled. "Doña Magdalena's talents are wasted at court."

Shortly there was a new chair of History in the University of Salamanca. Magdalena Perez filled it capably and with dignity, very beautiful in her doctor's gown. The academic world was rocked to its foundations at this shattering of tradition, but scowling professors who dropped in to her lecture hall found their fears melting away and smiled; her learning was sound.

Her lectures were certainly popular.

"I am happy here," Doña Magdalena wrote to the queen, "and I should be less than candid if I did not avow the pride I feel at being Castile's first female educator. The only embarrassment I ever experience is that I cannot, in decency, accept the gifts my students bring me." Isabella looked into the nature of these gifts. She found it was customary for students to bring their masters offerings of food.

"That is odd," she said to Pulgar.

Pulgar replied, "Professors' salaries are low, Your Highness. Under their gowns their clothes are patched and threadbare. They do not starve, but they are very poor."

Isabella immediately raised the salary of every teacher in every institution of learning in Castile. There were not many, and the added drain on the treasury was not great, but it was another expenditure nonetheless. Ferdinand complained vehemently.

She saw he was bored. He was also bored at the audiencias, which still continued each Friday. He did not understand Castilian laws, he said. They were contradictory, there were too many of them, and he could not feel his way among them by instinct as she could. She saw he was also idle. That was bad.

She wrote to Doña Magdalena at the University of Salamanca, asking, "Who is the greatest living authority on Castilian law? We should like to see him."

"Without question the man you seek," Doña Magdalena replied, "is Doctor Alfonso de Montalvo. A broad-minded, kind and immensely erudite scholar, he treated me with much courtesy when first I came here."

Isabella summoned him at once with a proposal close to

his heart. She said she desired him to undertake a great work, nothing less than the codification of all the mass of edicts, pragmaticas, ordinances and laws that comprised the corpus juris of Castile; to throw out those that were obsolete, to simplify those that were obscure and to reconcile those that were contradictory. And when he should finish, she said, she desired that the new Code be printed from types, for she wished to encourage that new and beneficent art.

There was an important stipulation which included Ferdinand. It would keep him occupied at something in which he was expert. "Since Castile and Aragón are now united," she said, "we must be very careful that the laws of the two kingdoms do not conflict. I do not know Aragonian customs. Therefore you should consult closely with my husband the king, that he may give you the benefit of his great knowledge and experience. You will wish, I expect, to see him daily in conference. Request his permission. But do not, I charge you, represent this suggestion as coming from me."

Doctor Montalvo smiled, with wonderful human understanding. "I shall weary him with my pleas for guidance, Your Highness."

Ferdinand threw himself into his new work with all his tremendous energy and infinite capacity for detail, Montalvo supplied the scholarship. The result was imposing. The celebrated *Ordencas de Montalvo,* duly "printed from types" and distributed throughout the Spanish peninsula, were so just, so clear and understandable that they were destined to endure unchanged for a hundred years, long after Ferdinand and Isabella had crumbled to dust in a tomb in a place that as yet was not even part of Spain. She also ordered the printing of hymns.

In the midst of these peaceful constructive pursuits in Castile the climate of the whole Christian world abruptly went black with a deadly threat to its very heart. On a vehement east wind like the wind that smote Jonah the conquering Turks surged across the Strait of Otranto and landed in Italy in Ferdinand's domains. These Aragonian lands were part of the Kingdom of Sicily, of which he was king. They lay in the heel of the Italian boot. It had become an Achilles' heel.

CHAPTER 24

ISABELLA was glad that her husband's shoulders were broad; they were about to bear a heavy load. Otranto had been a great seaport, populous and rich with trade. Now courier after courier reached him with reports of the catastrophe that had befallen it. A fleet of Turkish ships armed with heavy cannon and engines for hurling the unquenchable Greek Fire had suddenly appeared in the harbor and bombarded it furiously. Walls crumbled, great fires started and spread. The people panicked. Then, howling the name of the Prophet, hordes of the turbaned Infidels had swarmed ashore. Slaughter among the inhabitants had been dismal and indiscriminate. The corpses lay about the streets. An accomplished Turkish janissary could swing his razor-edged scimitar so deftly that one stroke could cut a human body into two halves from crown to groin, whether it were the soft body of a child, the somewhat more resistant body of a woman or the bony hulk of a strong fighting man.

Ferdinand read the reports grim-faced. Some of them he tried to keep from Isabella. He had seen much of war; he knew that in the sack of a city there were always grisly details. She insisted on reading all, however, and shuddered when she discovered that some of the sundered Christian bodies had been placed together again with obscene humor, male with female, so as to appear half — man, half—woman.

Her hatred of Mohammedans, already great, deepened to passion, diamond cold, diamond bright, diamond hard; and as everlasting.

Ferdinand saw some hope in the very excesses committed by the Turks at Otranto. "When soldiers behave that badly they are usually on their own, out of touch with their commanders. The Sultan's campaigns are less wanton as a rule, though of course pretty girls and handsome youths always have a hard time, ending up as eunuchs and concubines in harems. That is part of Turkish economy; I do not hold it against them."

"I do."

"Bear in mind that Otranto is far from Turkey though close to us. Let us pray that this was merely a raid they made on their frontier. Perhaps it will not be followed up. We may have time to plan; God knows we need time."

"I will help, Ferdinand. Every ship I have will join yours from Aragón, and I will build more."

"God bless you! I wish the Italian princes would help, too, but of course they will not. They are too busy quarreling with one another."

In this he was right. Italy was divided into a hodge-podge of independent republics and principalities, of city states and papal states. The map of the long peninsula resembled a patched old stocking far more than it did a boot. Italians were so intent on maintaining a balance of power among themselves that there was no power left over to repel the invader. A thousand years before, in the twilight of Imperial Rome, the Barbarians had burst in from the north and darkened the twilight into a long night, in which Christianity alone preserved the light of civilization. Now, after a lapse of a thousand years, a new and more fanatic breed of infidel was threatening that civilization from the south, and had already secured a foothold on Europe's oldest Christian soil. But since Otranto happened to lie in Ferdinand's kingdom of Sicily Europe considered the Turkish invasion Ferdinand's personal responsibility and looked the other way.

Once again the shield-shaped land of Spain took up its historic burden of defending Christendom. Having lived seven centuries with the Moor always just over the mountains, Spaniards were the most fiercely Christian Christians in the world. Isabella had been born in the very heart of the shield.

"Portugal will help, too," she said. "I know it."

"I hope so," Ferdinand replied.

She prevailed upon Beatriz of Portugal to return to Lisbon and plead with the young Portuguese king for ships. Beatriz said, "Dom João is Alfonso the African's son. I know he will want to do all he can. But his hand is still inexperienced and he may be slow."

"I know *you* will not be slow, Aunty Portugal."

The valiant old lady kissed the Spanish Infantes farewell, bade them remember their manners, and, scorning the litter that was offered her, set out on a strong white mule for Portugal accompanied by an escort of caballeros. Shortly she was able to write, "Dom João has agreed to help, as I knew he would. Work is hampered here, however, by a sickness among the ship builders. I hear grave reports of a similar sickness in Andalusia, and I pray that they are exaggerated."

Reports of a sickness in Andalusia were not exaggerated. It would have been difficult to exaggerate the sudden outbreak of the plague that struck and crippled the southern provinces. It happened during a summer that was suffocatingly moist and hot. Milk soured quickly; a queer red mold appeared on bread as if it were bleeding. Smoke rose languidly from fires and sometimes returned to the earth as if it were heavy. Water rose to unprecedented heights in wells though there had been no more than the usual amount of rain. In the Marismas at the mouth of the Guadalquivir, eerie blue lights flickered over the swamps, and foul odors bubbled up through the turbid waters. The cranes deserted Spain and flew to Africa before their usual migration date. Some saw in that a hopeful sign, since it meant an early winter with cleaner, colder air; but autumn brought no relief and winter was slow in coming.

In Seville, the greatest port and center of Castilian shipbuilding, 15,000 people died. Shipbuilding was halted, as was all other normal activity. As always in a time of great fear, travel was disrupted, commodities disappeared from the market, people hoarded food, prices rose fantastically. As always in the plague, everyone blamed the Jews. There were vicious pogroms in Seville.

Ferdinand lived in fear of another Turkish landing and could scarcely believe his couriers when they reported week after week that no, the invasion had not as yet been followed up and no, it had not spread beyond Otranto. But now that he had time to assemble a mighty armada against the Infidel he was unable to build or man the ships. His soldierly mind resented the missed opportunity to smite the enemy; all that was neat in his nature hated the disrupted economy; all that was cruel in him blamed Isabella.

"This is your fault. God gave you a sword, and you sheathed it in a jewel box. What good is faith without acts of faith? God is punishing you because you have not acted. I see His punishment everywhere: in the Turk, in the plague, in your crazy daughter!"

Isabella cringed as if he had struck her a physical blow. He had never reproached her for Joanna before. "She is slow, but she is not insane. The doctors say she will grow out of her little oddities in time. I will never believe she is insane, Oh Ferdinand, Ferdinand, do not say she is crazy!" Isabella wept uncontrollably. He did not like to see her weep.

"Time will tell." He shrugged.

Seeing Isabella so shaken he did not pursue the subject of Joanna, but pressed home relentlessly his plea that she implement the bull that authorized an Inquisition in Castile. It would be better, he argued, if a few crypto-Jews were executed after a fair trial than for thousands to be murdered in pogroms without any trial at all. Would not hoarding then cease and prices come down? Would not the plague abate? Could he not then build his ships and beat off the Turks?

"I do not know. I do not know. Cardinal Mendoza does not think an Inquisition would help."

"I remind you that you and I, not Cardinal Mendoza or any other Churchman, are specifically charged with responsibility for a Spanish Inquisition. Why are you afraid?"

"I do not know," she repeated weakly. Against his thundering arguments the little voice in her heart, which might be the Devil's voice, did not prevail. It was unquestionably true that a criminal would be treated more fairly by sober judges than by wildly fanatical mobs. As for spies, it was absurd with the Turk in Italy and the Moor in Granada for her to say that she preferred not to use secret agents in a holy war.

She took the Pope's bull from the casket where it had lain for two years. Firmly she wrote her Io La Reyna to the edict that implemented it; Ferdinand wrote his Io El Rey.

"We will confine it to Seville and it shall be a temporary war measure," Isabella said; and the edict as published so declared, in unequivocal words.

"Naturally," said Ferdinand.

Six weeks after the landing of the Turks in Otranto, to the excruciating complacency of the wretched Sevillanos, who massed to behold the new spectacle, six crypto-Jews, being duly tried and convicted, were burned in a public square on the outskirts of Seville. Many in the crowd fainted with excitement. Others, similarly fallen to the cobblestones, could not be roused and were found to be dead of the plague.

Ferdinand and Isabella now traveled to Aragón.

CHAPTER 25

TO hurl the unspeakable Turk from the holy soil of Italy was an enterprise that aroused the crusading spirit in Isabella. In her mind's eye she saw the Infidel beaten back into the sea. In the church towers of Otranto, where impious hands had cast down the bells and triumphant muezzins now chanted the hated Arabic call to prayer, she saw the bells restored and heard, in imagination, their sweet Christian music. She saw the Cross set up again where the Crescent had replaced it and altars purified where the Turks, as the stories went and as she firmly believed, had defiled them with human filth to show their contempt for the faith she loved and lived by. To this great end her Castilian ships were sailing to join Ferdinand's in harbors up and down the coast of Aragón.

But it was not to be her war. This was the war she had sworn to herself that Ferdinand must have the glory of winning, with all its victory parades, its stately presentations of titles and honors, its festive celebrations, its gala bullfights and tourneys and music and feasts. After the battles there would be solemn toasting of warrior by warrior, grandee by king. Ferdinand would preside at the head of the banquet hall as he made and listened to long congratulatory speeches in that masculine air of good fellowship which, to Isabella's way of thinking, was just as silly and windy as the chatter of a bevy of women at their needlework. She had learned a great deal about men in her marriage with Ferdinand; above all, she had learned not to steal a man's thunder. This was to be his war.

Aunt Beatriz was with her in the great cavalcade of knights and troops, grandees, burghers, lawyers and ladies who were riding to Aragón to witness the *reconocimiento* of little Prince John, his formal recognition by vote of the

Cortes as heir to the throne of Aragón. He already was heir, by birth, to the throne of Castile. Aunt Beatriz, with an acid old tongue, was never at a loss to express her low opinion of men. Item: they would rather be right than happy. Item: they are ill at ease with a woman of virtue. Item: they think they are strong and silent, but give them a chance and they gossip like fishwives. Item: any giddy, painted little trollop can make a fool of the best of them.

Isabella laughed. "Only for a while, Aunty Portugal. The good ones always return."

"Do you call that a consolation, sobrina mia?"

The Infanta Isabella was within earshot, riding a small but spirited pony that she handled with easy grace, her hair like her mother's golden in the golden sun of spring, her big eyes greedy to hear more and green at the wonders of what she had already heard spoken between her elders.

"Drop back a little to the Prince's litter and see if he is asleep," the queen said.

Reluctantly, the Infanta wheeled her mount and cantered back to another part of the long procession where her brother lay in a purple litter slung by silvered leather straps between two snow-white Andalusian mules, surrounded by a retinue of condesas, marquesas and other highborn ladies in waiting.

"A beautiful seat," Isabella said, turning her head and watching her proudly.

Beatriz of Portugal said, "A beautiful princess."

"As for your question, Aunty Portugal, the answer is Yes, it *is* a consolation that the good ones return."

"But soiled, my dear, so dirty and soiled."

"Dear Aunt," Isabella said earnestly. "When God made man in the Garden of Eden, what did He make him of? Was it not soil? And when man was tempted in the Garden, who tempted him? Was it not a woman?"

"For goodness' sake, whose side are you on?" Beatriz of Portugal asked.

"Ferdinand's."

"I shan't argue with you," the old lady sighed. "The last time I argued I lost a treaty at Alcantara."

Isabella was about to protest that that treaty had resulted in a lasting beneficent peace and that that peace had now united Portugal with the rest of the Spanish Peninsula in an effort against the Turks, which this journey to Aragón would strengthen; but her aunt smiled, "I was only joking, Isabella. I am the true winner, since I won the companionship and affection of the Infantes."

Princess Isabella rode up and said, "John was wide awake and howling like a wolf—"

The queen smiled.

"Factual mind, like Ferdinand's," Beatriz of Portugal said."—till the Marquésa de Moya gave him a sausage to munch on."

"Give him an orange, too, lest the sausage bind him."

"I did," the Infanta said, "and some prunes and a Moorish fig. He'll be a sticky mess in no time, but by the saints, he won't be bound!"

"Factual, but coupled with your imagination," Beatriz of Portugal said. "One day Portugal will be happy to have such a queen, and I shall be happy to have had a hand in her upbringing."

"That was my real victory in The Petticoat Treaty," Isabella said.

They both laughed.

At the border, some rotting timbers were all that remained of the customs shack where Ferdinand had smuggled himself and his jewels into Castile when he came disguised as a merchant to marry Isabella.

"By God!" he said, riding up and smiling, "I could wish it back again, so I could show the guards the treasures I take back to Aragón!"

"It's better this way," Isabella said. "No line cuts through the heart of a country that is one."

"But I want to mark the place. I want it to be remembered. I shall erect a great church here."

Isabella nodded her approval and looked at Beatriz of Portugal, who read in her eyes, "You see? This is my consolation."

"On the other hand," Ferdinand reflected, "the population in this arid region is probably too small to support a church. A wayside shrine of local stone and wood would be more appropriate. Far cheaper, too, a consideration not to be lightly dismissed in times like these." He turned and spurred back to the head of the cavalcade, muttering, "Or any other times."

"He doesn't look a day older than he did at nineteen," Isabella said.

Beatriz of Portugal glanced at her tolerantly out of the corner of her eye. "*You* certainly don't," she said.

It would serve no purpose to call Isabella's attention to Ferdinand's hairline. Each year it had crept a little higher. The King of Castile, León, Aragón and Sicily was getting slightly bald.

To Isabella, reared in the rugged uplands of Old Castile, where the climate was sudden and violent, the gentle breeze that wafted the early Aragonian spring from the warm blue Mediterranean Sea was almost wickedly seductive, like a not quite respectable lover. As the cavalcade progressed towards Calatayud she passed castles swathed in a silver mist each morning, bathed in the liquid gold of each night's dusk; and everywhere these mighty fortresses of her husband's vassals dipped their standards and fired salutes in honor of the king and queen. And of little Prince John in his purple litter, who drowsed or bawled as the fancy struck him, oblivious of the extraordinary activity for which he was responsible.

At Calatayud, in the Church of San Pedro de los Francos, the representatives of Aragón, assembled in Cortes, acknowledged the child the true and rightful heir to the throne and swore him their homage. The setting was solemn and magnificent, the sovereigns in ermine on thrones before an altar surrounded by battleflags, the prince in a little robe of scarlet on a scarlet cushion snug on Beatriz of Portugal's lap. But the ceremony was simple: each vassal knelt to Prince John and swore his oath, then kissed the sovereigns' hands, first Ferdinand's, then Isabella's, and retired.

One very young nobleman, about the age of Princess Isabella, made his obeisance with exceptional grace. His face was manly, handsome and frank. It was also startlingly familiar.

"Who is that charming caballero?" Isabella whispered.

Ferdinand flushed scarlet with pleasure.

"Mi señora, that is Don Alonso de Aragón. Naturally he won't be wearing his archiepiscopal vestments for some years."

Isabella's heart missed a beat, but the lad was looking at her with Ferdinand's eyes, pleading to be accepted. He retired quickly, with modesty that did him honor. Some royal bastards would have swaggered.

"We must receive Him soon, at some suitable occasion," Isabella said, knowing that her words must sound outrageously stilted. But she did not know what else to say.

Nothing she might have said could have affected Ferdinand so deeply. "God bless you for that, my dearest," he whispered so fervently that he was heard. The rumor spread like wildfire, through all the balconies where fine ladies whispered behind their fans and all the marketplaces where commoners gossiped, that the prudish foreign Queen of Castile had a heart as warm as any Aragonian's. Don Alonso was immensely popular.

Ferdinand wanted to leave at once for Barcelona, to see to the manning of the fleet. He was still plagued with bad dreams of another Turkish landing in Italy. But the Cortes was still in session.

"You will have to preside while I am gone," he said.

Isabella knew enough of Aragón's law to be aware that Aragón's queens were only consorts, No woman could rule the country in her own right. In Castile and England a woman could rule; in Aragón and France the ruler had to be a man.

"I don't think they'll have me," she said.

"Will you try it?" He was smiling. His attitude was that of a man with secret information.

"It is true that you are needed to gather the ships," she said hesitantly.

"Darling, you bewitched them. Nobody knew how you were going to treat my son. They hoped you would not be contemptuous. Naturally I made enquiries before I asked you to preside, however, since my Aragonians are a touchy, turbulent lot. There isn't a single dissenting voice!"

When Isabella mounted Ferdinand's throne, grave, pale and very small in the massive chair that had been built for fighting men, she was the only queen in history who had ever presided over an Aragonian Cortes. For a day or two the hall was full of florid oratory. The addresses of welcome were long and warm, for a woman in their midst, and a beautiful one, and spring in the air, proved so novel that the dullest deputy suddenly felt the urge to be a poet. But at the end of the session it was noted that an astonishing amount of business had been accomplished, particularly the arming and provisioning of the fleet. Isabella of Castile, they discovered, was much more than decorative. She was thoroughly experienced in the recruitment of armies. The Aragonian representatives dispersed having gained a new and respectful measure of their queen.

In May, through a blossoming, prosperous countryside, she rode to join Ferdinand at Barcelona. Evidence of her husband's industrious administration was everywhere. The roads had been smoothed for her passage by praedial serfs, a species of peasant unknown in Castile. They could be sold with the land; they were little better than slaves; yet they paid taxes. Town walls were in good repair, the serfs being required to work on them also. Peasants labored in fertile fields, pausing only long enough to pull off their sweaty caps and straighten their backs and cheer the queen, then bending their backs again to their toil, for the king's tax collectors pressed them hard. Every hamlet had its gibbet, every gibbet had its corpse, whose open mouth and hanging tongue still spoke the warning of Ferdinand's swift and inflexible justice. She would have liked to pause and give orders that some of the older corpses be buried, but she was anxious to see Ferdinand again and she knew he would not thank her for interfering in Aragonian affairs.

Barcelona was wholly unlike any city in Castile. It was even unlike Seville, though Seville was also a seaport, with a seaport's wicked, noisy and cosmopolitan waterfront. Barcelona lived by trade, as it had since Bible times when some Greek merchants from Phocaea had landed there, fallen in love with the beauty of the place and remained to colonize and do business. Isabella disliked seaports.

Trade, to a highborn Castilian, was contemptible. Even to Isabella it was a tolerated necessity, reminiscent of the Scripture, "the love of money is the root of all evil."

Barcelona faced the East and traded with the East. It was full of exotic odors of pepper and spice and dyewoods from Trebizond, of oil from the Barbary Coast and salted hides of Russian furs from ports in the Putrid Sea beyond Crimea. There was an unsavory district around the wharves on the waterfront, crowded with sailors and merchants from distant lands, wearing outlandish clothes and speaking outlandish tongues. Cheap taverns served food prepared in strange ways: Syrians ate salades of sheep's eyes; Arabs smacked bearded lips over a confection of sour milk that went by the name of yoghurt and belched to signify their approval of its taste; Egyptians ate fried locusts. Throughout the district black-eyed girls of the town with painted faces and gaudy scarves skin-tight around swiveling hips, walked like harpies among the men, selling themselves.

None of this was new to Isabella, for she had seen similar things in Seville. But in Barcelona it was exaggerated. Since she could do nothing about it she drew from it what consolation she could, for Barcelona helped to explain Aragón and Aragón explained Ferdinand. Judged by his background— how else can you judge a man? —he was an exceptionally good husband, and for some time past he had been close and kind. The days of the bastards, please God, dear God, were over and gone. He and she were now embarked on a mighty endeavor, common to their Christian hearts.

From a height above the city Ferdinand showed her, with considerable pride, an armada of fifty ships riding at anchor in the harbor. Many were sleek narrow galleys, propelled by oars, the ironbeaked warcraft that scarcely had changed since Roman times. But some were new sailing ships with three masts, with high forecastles and poops. These full-bottomed vessels were built to carry heavy cannon, and each could transport three hundred armed troops.

"Ten thousand men are ready to sail the instant I give the command!" Ferdinand declared.

"Are they in the ships now, Ferdinand?"

He laughed tolerantly. "There speaks the Castilian highlander in you! No, my dear, when a ship is in port one never looks for a sailor aboard her."

"When will you give the command?"

He rubbed his chin reflectively. "I want to be absolutely sure of victory. I am waiting for Portugal's fleet. All Europe is watching me, Isabella. Since I am designated Commander in Chief of the allied fleets I do not propose to lose this war. I shouldn't care to be made a fool of. I must wait for Dom João's ships. He is very slow."

"Aren't ten thousand men and fifty ships, all ready and fit, enough for the enterprise?"

"Perhaps. But I won't gamble."

"Aren't the men actually more fit now than they will be after weeks of idleness in that unpleasant waterfront quarter?"

He raised his eyebrows. "Eh? Oh *that!*" He laughed heartily. "By the time they reach Otranto they'll be fit enough again. What a beautiful apostle to the heathen you would have made, Isabella."

He had his way and waited. Isabella did not press him; she too would be glad of Portuguese reinforcement. Meanwhile the seductive spring passed into a delightful summer, for the Mediterranean that tempered the cold of the winter months also tempered the summer heat. The soldiers and sailors who crowded the town grew bored with inactivity; street fights flared up occasionally along the waterfront. "At least they're not eating up the ships' provisions," Ferdinand grumbled.

Late in August Dom João sent word that his fleet of twenty ships had finally cleared Lisbon harbor and was ready to join Ferdinand's and Isabella's. The combined flotilla met at sea. It was a formidable force.

On the second of October this mighty armada bore down on Otranto, with giant crosses painted on their sails and twelve thousand warriors, blessed for a crusade, eager to do battle with the heathen Turk in the name of God and King Ferdinand.

But a little boat rowed out and met them in the harbor of Otranto with a message.

The unspeakable Turk was gone.

CHAPTER 26

FERDINAND'S war against the Turk, which Isabella had resolved he should win, had ended in victory indeed but in victory by default. There were no Turks in Otranto to fight. They had slipped away over the Strait as suddenly as they had come, leaving the city a mass of rubble. Reading the dispatches from the Grand Admiral, Isabella thanked God that Italy had been purged of the Infidel without bloodshed. But a king did not win military laurels through victories by default. "They evacuated Otranto because they feared you, mi señor," she said.

Ferdinand answered calmly, "They evacuated Otranto because the Turkish Sultan happened to die just before the fleet arrived. You have read the dispatches announcing his death, and you know that as well as I." He smiled rather grimly. "Thank you anyway, Isabella."

"If he had not died at that crucial juncture you would have won just the same."

"Unquestionably. I was well prepared."

But the fame of the battle that Ferdinand would have won, if it had been fought, was lost in the larger news of Mohammed the Second's death. The evil genius of Islam, the Sultan who had conquered Constantinople, the Grand Turk whose name frightened Christian children to sleep in their cradles, was now no more, and Christendom might reasonably expect a respite from the Turkish menace, at least till such a genius arose again, an unlikely prospect for many years.

"What will you do with the fleets, Ferdinand?"

"Disband them, naturally. Dom João has already called his back to Portugal. I'll need mine for trade, as usual."

"I have a feeling we ought not to disband them so soon."

"You have a feeling indeed! Pray, founded on what? Your instinct?"

"The Turks may return."

"Never."

Unnoticed among the massive news of the world was a little note from the Duke of Medina Sidonia, complaining that his old enemy, the Marqués of Cadiz, had trespassed on his estates, "foraging for fodder, Your Highness, in a hunting preserve that I especially prize. True, he apologized handsomely, excusing his foragers on the grounds that he had given them orders to lay in a large supply of grass and hay. He is building up his stables against the Moors, who raid him as usual. But they raid me, too, and I do not have to trespass on the estates of the Marqués of Cadiz to feed my horses."

Isabella persisted, "Even if the Turks do not return, the Moors of Granada are showing more truculence than I like. We could use the fleets to awe them into a more respectful attitude."

Ferdinand read Medina Sidonia's dispatch and tossed it aside with a chuckle. "Your two Andalusians still hate each other at heart, don't they! Except for their promise to you I dare say they'd still be fighting each other, just for the fun of it. Cadiz used the Moors as an excuse."

"The Moors were never so belligerent before at this time of year. It's too late in the season."

"I'm certainly going to disband *my* fleet and refit it for trade," Ferdinand said positively. "The Otranto expedition has been a woeful expense."

"I think I may keep the Castilian ships in commission for a while," Isabella said. She said it gently, as if she had only half made up her mind, not wishing to differ with her husband on a matter of policy. But privately she resolved to give orders to the Grand Admiral to maneuver in mass formation close to the Granadine ports, in a mighty demonstration of strength.

Ferdinand shrugged. "It's your fleet. I am quite aware that I do not command it."

He was in a sensitive mood; she reproached herself for irritating him; her lip trembled ever so slightly.

He clenched his fist playfully under her chin and brought it up, and looked questioningly into her eyes. "When these are misty," he said, touching them, "and this quivers," touching her mouth, "I always wonder what you are hiding from me."

"Nothing, Ferdinand, on my honor."

"Nay, then you are hiding nothing indeed, and it's all right for you to ride horses. We have a great deal of riding to do." Isabella's appearance at the Cortes of Calatayud had so enhanced his popularity that he planned more appearances for her. "There will be a Cortes at Saragossa, another at Valencia, and receptions all along the way, with bullfights and suppers and audiencias..."

"Will you grant some pardons at the audiencias?" Her mind went back to the hanging corpses decaying in chains.

"I always grant a few, to make sure the King's mercy is adequately talked about. But to pardon too many criminals would reduce my mercy to a commonplace."

There was hard sense, as always, in what he said. Very hard.

"Could you give the hanged a *little* quicker burial, Ferdinand?"

"The length of time that they hang, as a salutary warning to other malefactors, is influenced by local conditions and fixed by local judges, not by me."

From Barcelona to Saragossa the road measured 160 miles; from Saragossa to Valencia, 200; and from Valencia to Castile, to which they returned at the end of the year, the distance was 300 miles more. Everywhere along the road the king and queen were feted extravagantly. But the banquets lost their flavor for Isabella as the long royal progress drew to its end, and during the last three hundred miles she knew, but forbore to say, that it was no longer quite safe for her to ride horses. It was wrong, perhaps, to keep her condition secret from Ferdinand, and she felt a little guilty. But he had won no military acclaim. She was glad that, in place of it, he had won at least the acclaim of his people, and that she had been able to help. He seemed to have enjoyed it immensely.

In Cordova she joked, as she might by now since it was the fourth time, "I think I shall put my horse out to pasture till June, mi señor. No doubt he will get very fat for a while, but then, so shall I."

Ferdinand counted slowly on his fingers, back to October, and thought of the hundreds of miles she had ridden, the dozens of public appearances she had made without a murmur of complaint "You should have told me. We could have cut short the progress. Nay, I should have preferred to. The people would have understood. They would have gone wild with joy—they always do, I find. Oh Isabella, you foolish woman!" But he did not reproach her severely, nor could he in conscience bring up the subject of Joanna, for that little princess seemed, very slowly, to be growing out of her sluggishness.

In June she bore him another fair-haired blue-eyed princess. Ferdinand, hearing from a lackey that the child was a girl, retired to a private room, called for one of his rare glasses of wine and sipped it a whole hour in thought, controlling his disappointment. And having thought, he emerged from the room and received the congratulations of his courtiers with an air of Olympic detachment, as befitted a king whose dynasty was safe. Nay, he said earnestly to Isabella, perhaps it was not her fault that most of their children were girls, in spite of all medical knowledge to the contrary; perhaps God in His wisdom had decreed it so. Too many princes warred among themselves for their father's crown, like the sons of Charlemagne, who dismembered his empire; whereas princesses could marry abroad and make friends for the state and bring unity.

"He is changing, and softer, and at great pains to excuse us for not being men," Isabella whispered happily to her baby, which was exceptionally pretty and, better still, as bright and responsive as poor little Joanna had been dull and queer. Cardinal Mendoza christened the child Maria, to everyone's delight, since it was the name of at least half the girls in Spain and the second name of many a fiercely mustachioed fighting man. Isabella had chosen it out of devotion; Ferdinand had gravely approved it as a democratic gesture.

He would have liked to leave for the north to escape the Andalusian heat, which was severe that year. But the doctors advised Isabella not to travel so soon after the birth of the princess; it had been a difficult one, and Isabella's recovery was not as rapid as usual. Seeing Ferdinand idle, restive and getting a little fat, she would have disregarded the doctors' advice and gone hunting with him in the cool forests around Madrid except for disturbing reports that the Marqués of Cadiz continued to send her. Over the mountains, he warned, the Moor of Granada was prowling like a caged panther.

"Nonsense," said Ferdinand. "This is the season. I'm tempted to make a few forays across the border myself, since it seems inadvisable for us to go hunting right now."

"When the war comes," Isabella said, "it won't be sport."

Ferdinand chucked her under the chin and smiled. She was still in bed and a wetnurse sat at the other end of the apartment nursing the new little Infanta. "Prone and helpless and already fighting a battle! My dear, I think you have a fever." He kissed her brow; it was cool. "No, no fever." But he respected her instinct even when he made fun of it. "Can you possibly be serious?"

"It's exasperating to be forced to lie in bed so long."

He nodded thoughtfully. Apparently she was serious. "I think we can expect only the usual border raids during the summer," he said, "and when winter comes they will dwindle out. That has been the pattern for seven hundred years. Why should it change?"

"Things do."

"Not much."

"I think things change."

"Wars don't."

"Yes, they do."

He laughed. "You are the most stubborn, most illogical, most delightful creature I have ever met!"

"Ferdinand, will you recommission the Aragón fleet for war?"

"Now I am positive you have a fever," he said.

But he took pains to examine the state of their kingdoms and he was satisfied with what he found. The plague in Seville had abated; harvests that year were good; there was peace at home and abroad; taxes were paid on time and in full; the roads were safe and few brigands had to be hanged. At length Isabella arose from her sickbed, almost too slender for Ferdinand's taste and pale after repeated bleedings.

"I wish the doctors would change something, too," she said. "That horrid treatment. I always feel weak after a bleeding."

"Good heavens, Isabella, how would anybody ever get well?"

He ordered Cardinal Mendoza to sing a Te Deum of thanksgiving in the cathedral on Christmas Day, and joined his own prayers heartily with those of every other Spaniard that the queen was safe. During her long convalescence the odd thought had struck him that it was possible for Isabella to die before he did. He had always assumed that he would be the first, probably in battle, a hazard he coolly accepted. But the hazards of childbirth, it seemed, could equal those of battle. He shook the gloomy notion out of his thoughts, for he knew that if he were to analyze it, step by step as he analyzed everything else, he might come to a conclusion involving the relative bravery of women and warriors: for whereas a warrior in battle had faithful comrades to help him, a woman in childbed had to fight her battle alone. "There is something grossly illogical with any such conclusion," he muttered and quickly thought about pleasanter things. Come spring, he and Isabella would have their hunt at Madrid and then the Castilian roses would bloom again in her cheeks.

While Cardinal Mendoza was chanting the Christmas Te Deum the Moors of Granada accomplished a feat of arms that astonished even themselves by its complete success. They raided Zahara; they took Zahara.

Zahara was a Castilian frontier city that was deemed impregnable. It sat on a granite mountain; the roads to it were so steep that steps had had to be cut in them; the walls of the citadel were sheer and the place was so high that at times the watchmen in the towers could actually look down on clouds drifting below them. Zahara was so unapproachable that women were sometimes compared with it. If a man tried to flirt with a beautiful girl and found her to be of cold, unassailable virtue he was likely to shrug and say, "Chaste as Zahara!" and go on to easier prey.

Beautiful, impregnable Zahara fell, humbled on Christmas Day to a daring surprise attack. Under cover of a howling storm, in a blinding rain, the Moors, unheard and unseen, slithered up the mountain and scaled the dripping walls and found no watchmen there, for who would stand watch on the walls of such a city in such a tempest on such a day when the castle was feasting?

Isabella's eyes blazed green with fury when a herald came spurring with the totally unexpected news from the Marqués of Cadiz. She touched her clenched hand to her breast, like a priest at the *mea culpa,* and murmured, "My fault! My fault! I have failed to be watchful over my inheritance." She crumpled the dispatch and threw it into the fire, where it burned brightly for a few seconds and disappeared into ashes. "So perish all infidels! So perish all enemies of the holy faith!"

316

"Exactly," said Ferdinand, amused. "A sentiment I thoroughly approve."

She walked rapidly up and down the apartment, her skirts billowing and rustling like a wind, her heels clicking over the flagstoned floor. In a corner, like an unused dress, her armor hung beside Ferdinand's. She went over to it, touched it, and drew her hand away. "Dusty," she said in a tone of reproval that sometimes she used to a negligent servant. But this reproach was addressed to herself. "Oh Ferdinand, I am so ashamed." Her cheeks were scarlet.

"I must say, it becomes you. Viva el Moro!"

"Ferdinand, for shame!"

"Nay, my dear, I am only joking. Yet if this is the tonic to bring back the roses to your cheeks I could find it in my heart to declare that the loss of Zahara is not an unmitigated disaster."

"But it is, it is, it is!"

He dropped his bantering tone, "I wish you would calm yourself. Even a man, if he's sick in bed, cannot be expected to attend to every single detail of his duties in person."

"Zahara is no detail."

"I do not minimize the loss of Zahara," he said soberly. "But it certainly wasn't your fault. No one could have foreseen the attack, which was foolhardy in the extreme from the Moorish point of view."

"It was successful."

"Only because some lazy sentinels were stuffing themselves with Christmas dinner instead of keeping watch. If I could get my hands on them I'd teach them a lesson."

Isabella's anger subsided, for she remembered that by now all the garrison of Zahara were in Moorish dungeons. One of her childhood memories, a sight she had never forgotten, was the white, scarred wrists, still disfigured and swollen, of Pedro de Bobadilla, father of Beatriz, her friend. He too had languished a prisoner in a dungeon in Granada until he was ransomed.

"Nay, they are learning their lesson now, this very night, groaning under a weight of cruel chains that are biting into their flesh," she said. "They are being punished enough. And as for the women, pray God that He will solace them in their shame."

Ferdinand nodded slowly. He would pray. All Spain would pray. But through the centuries such prayers had very seldom been answered. Some women, indeed, accepted Islam and rose to high estate. The Sultana of Granada herself had once been a Christian captive. She was so beautiful that the Moors named her Zoroya, the Morning Star, and she rose from slavery to marry the sultan and bear him his firstborn son, now heir to the infidel throne.

In a calmer mood Isabella directed her secretary to write to the sultan and negotiate for the ransom of the prisoners, as was customary on both sides, both Moor and Christian alike, after border raids. Abul Hassan, the sultan, replied with a beautiful scroll of flowing Arabic script, itself a work of art, that he was quite willing to follow traditional procedure. But he was old and capricious and flushed with unexpected victory. He demanded an exorbitant sum.

"I'd let the traitors rot before I paid such a price to get them back," Ferdinand said.

Isabella answered, "We're going to need those soldiers," and ransomed them all. She would have liked to ransom the women, but those the Moors never gave up.

"Perhaps I shall get the women back in the spring," Ferdinand said, "if their husbands will have them and if they want to return." He had given up his plans for a spring hunt and looked forward to some border raiding as far more exciting. He could not take seriously Isabella's foreboding that a long and exhausting war might already have begun which would end in the total defeat of one or the other of the belligerents. Such a dream, indeed, most Spanish caballeros cherished in their youth, but always abandoned as only a dream by the time they reached Ferdinand's maturity and wisdom.

The difficulty of conquering the Kingdom of Granada was almost unimaginable. It had taken seven centuries for the Spaniards to roll back the Moorish frontier from the northern provinces to the line of mountains in southern Andalusia where now it lay and had lain for many years. Throughout all the reign of Henry the Impotent only one advance had been made, the spectacular capture of Gibraltar, and that was achieved by the Duke of Medina Sidonia.

But the Marqués of Cadiz did not wait for spring. A man of strong passions, twice married, childless—at least as regarded legitimate issue—chivalrous beyond the ordinary demands of chivalry (he even released captive Moorish women) and fiercely jealous of his personal honor, he took the rape of Zahara as a personal insult. Zahara lay close to his city of Xeres, where the wine that the English called "sherry" was made, close to his capital city of Cadiz, from which he took his title,

Within the month he approached the king with a plan for immediate action. He had learned from his scouts, he said, that a certain Moorish city was almost as carelessly guarded as Zahara.

Ferdinand nodded approvingly. "Nothing is so useful in war, nay, in government itself, as an efficient body of secret agents. Pray proceed."

The city of Alhama, said the Marqués of Cadiz, could be captured in a day with a little luck and a little daring!

At the name of Alhama Ferdinand stared incredulously. Cadiz was proposing a wildly impractical adventure. Alhama lay squarely in the geographical center of the Kingdom of Granada, fifty miles from the Castilian frontier. Except that distances were shorter in the Moorish kingdom the plan was very much as if a Moorish captain were proposing to capture Toledo in the heart of Castile.

"If you captured it you would be cut off, surrounded by enemy fortresses. Then what would you do?"

"Why, hold it, Your Highness, till the places in between could be reduced."

Ferdinand repressed a smile. He did not like giant leaps in life; he did not like giant leaps in war. They left one with no avenue of retreat.

"I think you should take your plan to the queen," he said. "In my judgment the venture is not sufficiently sure of success to warrant the risks; but the queen should decide, since her troops are involved. Whatever she decides, señor marqués, your plan does you honor and exhibits superlative imagination." Ferdinand smiled graciously.

The Marqués of Cadiz left the king somewhat crestfallen, convinced that he was being put off with fair words and that Isabella would give him a soft but definite refusal.

Isabella did nothing of the kind. She was elated with the plan. Her face lighted up like a clear sudden dawn. She called at once for a map and followed it enthusiastically as Cadiz pointed out hidden ravines and mountain passes high in the clouds where a powerful force could make its way secretly to the city and surprise it as Zahara had been surprised.

"God prosper your glorious endeavor," she said, "and return to me safely so faithful and daring a vassal!"

He left her presence as high in spirit as he had been low when Ferdinand dismissed him.

Ferdinand said to his wife, "A soldier ought to make war the way he eats a piece of meat: first chew around the edges, then devour the heart."

"That is certainly one good way," Isabella said.

"It's the only way."

"Cadiz spoke like a poet, so inspired he was by his plan. But it's practical too. He should have explained it to you more thoroughly."

"I suppose I didn't give him the time," Ferdinand laughed. "Artists in government, and now poets in war! I just naturally distrust them, Isabella."

"He will be slain if he fails," Isabella said gravely.

"Nay, a man can hazard no more than his life. I do not say I do not admire him. But it's no way to eat meat and it's no way to capture Alhama."

In February the Marqués of Cadiz placed himself at the head of his troops. Hiding by day, marching at night through rocky gorges, over barren mountain ridges, the long line of Spaniards snaked its way through enemy country unnoticed towards Alhama and fell violently upon it. A scout who had been left behind for the purpose observed the action from a neighboring height, and turned and made his solitary perilous way on foot, back to the queen to report that Alhama had fallen. The plan of the Marqués of Cadiz had achieved complete success.

But immediately the surrounding countryside began to swarm with alerted Moorish troops. Cadiz had penetrated deep, like the head of a spear; but the shaft of the spear broke off. Ferdinand scowled, "Now he is isolated, just as I knew he would be. I warned him, but he would not listen."

"There was more to his plan," Isabella said. "We will support him, and reduce the places in between."

"We means *me* this time, I suppose," Ferdinand said, and grimly set out to organize a relief expedition. "Cadiz traveled light; he can live on the supplies he found in Alhama only a month or two at most. I don't want him to starve, of course, but it will take time to reach him, Isabella, it will take time."

Isabella hoped it would not take too long. "I'll help all I can," she said.

It was difficult to recruit soldiers out of season, but slowly they gathered, yielding to Isabella's eloquence and Ferdinand's unremitting industry. A mountain of arms and supplies began to pile up. But months passed and still Ferdinand was not satisfied that he had enough.

"I wish Medina Sidonia would offer his troops," Isabella said wistfully.

Ferdinand snorted in disdain. "Medina Sidonia is

thoroughly enjoying the discomfiture of his enemy, I *told* you he and Cadiz still hate each other at heart."

"That is wrong," Isabella said.

"It's a fact," Ferdinand said. "Why won't you ever face facts?"

Quietly Isabella summoned the Duquesa de Medina Sidonia to Cordova and pleaded with her. "The duke is Cadiz' closest neighbor," she said, "and could be his closest friend! How shameful, how pitiful for Spaniards to stand aside and continue a personal feud when Spaniards are starving in Alhama!"

"I truly think," the duquesa smiled, "that my husband awaits only an invitation from Your Highness to offer his help. I know how much he loves you, but he loves his honor too."

"He will lose no honor fighting the Moor," Isabella said.

Somewhat stiffly the duquesa replied, "The duke has fought the Moor before, Your Highness, if Your Highness will only remember his present of Gibraltar to your brother Henry."

Ferdinand grumbled in private, "Command the old fool! She's your vassal, isn't she?"

It was hard to command a highborn Andalusian lady, and it was impossible for a wife to command a husband. Isabella could only persuade.

Medina Sidonia, his punctilious pride assuaged, roared into action. He addressed a loyal letter to Isabella, thanking her for the opportunity of fighting the Moor again and promised to lead his men at once to the relief of his good neighbor the Marqués of Cadiz.

"One would think he had just heard of the predicament at Alhama," Ferdinand muttered. "I am half-inclined to hurry my plans a bit and go to the relief myself. I am almost ready to march anyhow."

By the time he marched, however, Medina Sidonia had

forced his way through the Granadine territory and arrived with a fanfare of trumpets under the walls of Alhama, The beleaguered Christians within threw open the gates, and a long line of heavily laden sumpter mules filed in with great quantities of arms and provisions for the defenders. Then, in a demonstration of mutual forgiveness that brought tears and wild bursts of cheering from their troops, the marqués and the duke publicly embraced. In Alhama, the city that the one had stormed and the other relieved, the two former enemies buried their ancient hostility and swore to be friends for life, united in a greater, a common cause. No one could doubt the sincerity of their reconciliation, for the isolation of Alhama lent an awful solemnity to their meeting. Alhama was still surrounded by miles of unconquered country; beyond the walls the bell that now called the Christians to prayer would fall on furious infidel ears.

Ferdinand, hearing of Medina Sidonia's exploit, gravely turned his column about and marched back to Cordova in perfect order. Isabella greeted him affectionately and went to great lengths to praise him. "I do not doubt that Medina Sidonia would have had a much more difficult time if you had not followed him so closely with such a powerful force." For once again a battle had eluded her husband and the laurels of war went to Medina Sidonia and Cadiz.

"If you imagine for one moment that I am jealous of your wild Andalusian grandees, mi señora, be assured that I am not! It would be gratifying, however, if they would deign to coordinate their military affairs with their king's."

Leaving Alhama strongly garrisoned and provisioned, the duke and the marqués returned to Cordova accompanied by an escort so small that some said a host of guardian angels must have sat in their saddles. The cheering populace who greeted them attributed their safe transit through infidel country to the skill and romantic good luck of the born Andalusian frontiersman. Ferdinand's sensitive nose sniffed the political wind from the south and his keen analytical mind suspected something far more mundane. He did not know what it might be, but the Moors seemed astonishingly unobservant.

Cadiz and Medina Sidonia presented themselves to their sovereigns, who feasted and feted them royally and invited them to sit in their presence.

In spite of Ferdinand's fierce denial that he was jealous, Isabella knew that he was. The conquerors of Alhama would have been glad to return to their estates for a while for a rest; but if they should, Isabella foresaw a mood of protracted gloom in her household. "There was another important aspect of your plan, señor marqués," she said pleasantly to Cadiz.

"The reduction of the places in between. Which place shall be first?"

Cadiz said at once, "Loja, Your Highness."

She looked to the Duke of Medina Sidonia for confirmation. "Loja, unquestionably. But for Loja cannon will be required. It is massive rather than high, with powerful defenses in depth. The Moors of Loja never sleep."

"We have cannon in abundance," Ferdinand said.

Medina Sidonia persisted. "The state of the roads is extremely bad. It would be difficult to transport cannon without extensive road building, and that would absolutely eliminate whatever small chance of surprise still exists."

"I do not think cannon are necessary. My instinct tells me," Ferdinand said, glancing slyly at Isabella, "that all is not well in the high councils of the enemy. Without in the least detracting from your successes, mis primos, I think we should storm Loja at once; for there is some weighty reason why thousands of men can slip through fifty miles of Moorish territory, not once but twice, without a major battle."

"I will follow Your Highness anywhere," Cadiz said to the king, but he looked at the queen.

"The king shall lead you," Isabella said. "And yet, my dear," she said, turning to Ferdinand, "is it truly wise to go without cannon? Our experts counsel caution."

"I abhor unnecessary risks. I was the first to legislate against gambling; I dare say I am the only man in Spain who still obeys the pragmatica; also I am thoroughly conversant with the value of artillery, which I have used with some effect against the French. But I am persuaded that something is happening in Granada which renders the Moor unobservant, off his guard."

"We did have phenomenal luck," Medina Sidonia admitted.

"It would be a glorious victory to take Loja," the marqués replied, warming to the venture.

Ferdinand led them to Loja, but either his instinct had been wrong or whatever was amiss in Granada had now rectified itself. At Loja the Moors were alert. Cannon fire raked the Christian troops from the walls and inflicted heavy loses. Then the Moors sallied forth and gave battle. Ferdinand charged deep into their ranks, enraged at his persistent ill luck and furious at having guessed so wrongly. The crown on his helm and his gold-inlaid armor marked him a special prize. He was surrounded by screaming fanatic assailants, greedy for a king's ransom. His sword crashed and whined like a thunderstorm among the bodies of his attackers, and Cadiz and Medina Sidonia were astonished at a novel sight, as Andrés de Cabrera had been: a swordsman so strong that men's heads jumped off their shoulders when his blade struck their necks. If Ferdinand had died at that moment he would have died happy.

He did indeed come perilously close to death, for the supply of Moors was endless, and he was only one. Seeing him surrounded, knowing that he could not retreat if he wanted to, the Marqués of Cadiz and seventy caballeros cut their way to him through the howling melee. They could not see his face, but through his steel vizor they heard him shouting curses at them, He did not want to be saved. For those curses, in that perilous instant, they forgave him all his bad judgment, from their hearts.

He was amazed to find how these wild Andalusians respected him after that, when they retreated, when they were safe again, when they could talk to him. For of course the Christians had to retreat. The attack on Loja was a dismal failure.

Ferdinand swore solemnly, "I will go back and take Loja if it is the last thing I do in this life."

Cadiz and Medina Sidonia said, "So will we, Your Highness, any time you give the command."

The year and the war went into their winter rest, but the life of the Spanish sovereigns was more crowded than ever, not only with military preparations for the spring but also with multifarious administration duties both foreign and domestic.

To speed up her foreign correspondence Isabella learned to write and speak Latin, a feat which astonished her secretary, Pulgar, who taught her, and awed her Andalusian grandees almost as much as the heads that Ferdinand sent spinning to the ground with his sword.

Everywhere in Spain men blessed their king and queen. The devil had sent them Henry the Impotent, but God Himself had sent them Isabella and Ferdinand.

Alhama, however, remained isolated.

CHAPTER 27

THE failure at Loja nagged unceasingly at Ferdinand's mind. He could not rest until he explained it away. It seemed illogical, and he disliked illogicalities.

Isabella soothed him, calling his failure the fortune of war. She praised his bravery in battle; everyone was talking about it, she said. She dwelt at length on his service to Spain in bringing Cadiz and Medina Sidonia together, "closer than I ever could," she said, "and in addition you won their deep personal devotion, a thing these southerners do not give easily."

"All that may be true, Isabella, and I love you for saying it. But I still think there was something wrong, for a time at least, with the Moorish high command."

"Please don't take such chances in a melee again, Ferdinand."

'Tut, tut, Isabella! I am not old yet, in spite of this." He ran his hand over his receding hairline, laughing. "Forehead like a Salamanca professor's, haven't I!" One of the best things about him was his absolute lack of vanity. "Perhaps I should act like one and get me a big fat mare and stay judiciously to the rear while a battle is being fought."

"Kings do, and are not called cowards. You have won your spurs long since."

"Isabella, I'd die."

"Then I should too."

"The truth is, my dear, I was furiously angry in that fight and I didn't much care what happened."

"I cared."

"Now, of course, I am grateful to Cadiz for coming to my rescue, though it was humiliating at the time."

"Cadiz and seventy others, Ferdinand! It took seventy-one brave caballeros to beat off the Moors you fought singlehanded.

Please be more careful, my dear one. I do not wish to be a widow."

"Hm-m," Ferdinand said. He was thinking again about Loja.

Ferdinand's political instinct had not been wrong, merely a little slow in operating. Something had indeed been amiss in the Granadine high command, something that had spread great confusion among the Moors. A swift palace revolution had brewed, burst and been settled all in the space of a few weeks in the capital city of Granada.

Old Abul Hassan, the sultan, had fallen in love with a luscious young concubine and married her. Zoroya, the Morning Star, whose beauty was somewhat dimmed in her middle age, was furiously jealous. Zoroya's son, who was impatient to rule, plotted with her against his father, the sultan.

"You see the evils of polygamy," Ferdinand said, when the news came out.

"I do indeed," Isabella replied, not joking, as he had been.

Zoroya and her son Abdallah, the crown prince, had recruited a substantial following. Fighting broke out in the palace and spread to the streets. It ended in a draw, but with hatred still strong in both factions.

Rather than give up his young new wife, Abul Hassan gave up his capital, retiring to Malaga on the beautiful Mediterranean coast. Young Abdallah was promptly proclaimed sultan of the city of Granada, while Abul Hassan remained sultan of the rest of the Moorish kingdom. Thus the Moorish realm was split in two, as Castile had been during the reign of Henry the Impotent.

"This is wonderful news for Christendom, Isabella!"

Isabella thanked God, not only for the weakening of the foes of Spain, but also for Ferdinand, who could see how marital discord could work to the detriment of a whole kingdom. Not, indeed, that she worried so much any more.

His behavior had long been exemplary. In closest unity they had worked and thought and planned together. She felt sure of his love, and the torturing visions of rivals had all but faded. Sometimes she was even a little glad that he was getting bald, for however handsome he might remain in her eyes, she did not suppose other women would find him quite as irresistible as he had been in his twenties. But then she would remember that it did not matter what a king looked like. He could be hook-nosed and toothless and ugly and old as sin, nothing mattered so long as he was king. And when she remembered that, she would touch her cross and smile and pray God to preserve Ferdinand from the wiles of scheming women as well as from the perils of battle.

Isabella's thoughts were bent on the prosecution of the Moorish war; Ferdinand's on paying for it. Help came again from the Church. Pope Sixtus dispatched a ship to Spain with a magnificent present, not a loan but an outright gift, of one hundred thousand gold ducats. But the papal legate who brought the gold brought something else that annoyed Ferdinand exceedingly: a letter from the Pope protesting against the Inquisition in vigorous terms. "Many baptized Jews of your city of Seville have come to our court," the Holy Father said, "complaining that your Inquisitors do not accept the sincerity of their conversion and threaten them as crypto-Jews, with the result that these converts, who ought to be welcomed into the shepherd's fold like lost sheep, fear for their lives and have left their homes and their country." In Rome, the Pope declared, he would give them sanctuary until such time as the Spanish sovereigns should change not indeed their zeal for the faith but the reckless haste of their Inquisitors in Seville.

The Seville Inquisition had been Ferdinand's special interest since its inception. He longed to extend it to other cities. "Just when it is beginning to pay, this confounded letter has to come!" he grumbled to Isabella. The temporary war measure was more than ever necessary, he said, now that war had become chronic. But the supreme head of Christendom condemned it! Ferdinand found himself in a quandary that tested his wits to the uttermost.

His wits were equal to the test. He schemed to extend the Inquisition quietly, logically and legally; but he knew he would have to approach Isabella warily on a subject she always found distasteful. "There has been an alarming increase of crime in the last couple of years," he said.

"I'm afraid there always is in wartime."

"Too many of the Hermandad are now soldiers in the army."

"We've got to have soldiers, more and more of them."

"But they neglect their police duties, especially during active campaigns."

Isabella sighed. "I know."

"It has occurred to me that in a good many cases the Hermandad does not have proper jurisdiction anyhow. Many lords of great estates are feudatory to abbots, bishops and other churchmen. Could not crime in such places be curbed more effectively by Inquisitors than by the Hermandad, which is usually absent? It would take a heavy burden off them and it would certainly contribute to orderliness."

"I suppose if an estate is an ecclesiastical fief the Inquisition could claim jurisdiction in heresy cases."

"What's fair for one place is fair for another, isn't it?"

"I never liked it in Seville, and neither does Cardinal Mendoza and neither does the Holy Father."

"Nay, wait a moment, and do not let us quarrel. The Seville Inquisition has not claimed wider jurisdiction. I merely suggest that we *ask* our ecclesiastical prosecutors to assume certain additional responsibilities when crimes are committed on church fiefs—murder, bigamy, rape, arson, theft, usury, divination, mixing of love potions, a host of civil offenses now dealt with by the Hermandad, too often inadequately since the forces of the Hermandad simply cannot be in the army and at the same time attending to their local police duties."

It was a reasoned argument and he saw her wavering. He pressed his advantage.

"I know, of course, that you dislike spies," he said, "but 'spy' is just an unpleasant word. A better word is 'informant.' Trusted informants are necessary in government. England has its Star Chamber, Louis of France is famous for the accurate intelligence of his network of secret agents. Are the Inquisition's methods so different from those of our able and respected cousins abroad?"

Isabella hesitated. The fiefs of the church were extensive. He was asking her to make an important decision... "I cannot deny your logic, Ferdinand, but I feel in my heart there are seeds of future trouble in this."

"No one can legislate for the future," Ferdinand said, "which will doubtless have troubles of its own."

"Would you let me choose the Chief Inquisitor?"

Ferdinand saw he was winning, and beamed, "My dear, of course! No matter how soft he may be."

"I do not want a soft man, but a soft man, fearless, hard-working, broad-visioned. I know such a man, but he is so retiring that he will probably refuse the appointment. He was my tutor when I was a girl at Arevalo."

"Anyone you please, my dear."

She summoned Fray Tomás de Torquemada from his priory of Santa Cruz in Segovia. He was now sixty-four years old. He walked barefoot the two hundred and thirty miles from Segovia to Cordova. Having washed his habit and patched it with a needle and thread that he always carried for the purpose, he presented himself to Isabella.

"You sent for me, *mi princesa?*"

Ferdinand was not easily awed, but Torquemada had the air of a Roman emperor and feet like a beggar's. Even in Castile, the land of stones and saints, Ferdinand had never seen such imperial assurance coupled with such abject heedlessness of self. Yet the man was not putting on a show of saintliness. He was not ostentatiously ragged; his leathery feet were clean; he seemed indeed to have been at some pains to look his best. It was astonishing for Ferdinand to hear the queen addressed as *mi princesa,* as if she were still a little girl. "This man won't impose many fines," Ferdinand thought as he looked at him, "but those he imposes he will not steal. Here is the incorruptible, if ever I saw it.

Isabella told her old tutor that she wished him to accept a newly formed post; she asked if he would become the Inquisitor General for Spain. "I am afraid you will be very unpopular," she said honestly, "since the king and I, influenced by the rapid increase of crime during this war, shall add a number of purely civil offenses to your jurisdiction. Thus, some offenders who would have accepted their punishment without complaint at the hands of municipal judges, will probably protest that they are being persecuted when the same offenses are punished by religious judges, but crime must be put down."

Ferdinand assured him, "A prosecuting attorney can never really be popular, Fray Tomás."

"I do not in the least care what the world thinks of me," Torquemada replied, "so long as I do my duty."

To Isabella's surprise Torquemada proved not at all unpopular. People in districts that could not conceivably be classed as church fiefs actually asked for (and Torquemada refused them) the establishment of an Inquisition in their towns. Like the Hermandad, like martial law, it would give them civil security in wartime. On occasion, of course, in the places where it operated, it would put on spectacular burnings of relapsed heretics, like the French, who burned Joan of Arc, and the Germans, where, said the German ambassador, a lamentable outbreak of witches had just occurred, requiring the slow roasting of thirty thousand of the creatures, a figure that Ferdinand halved in his mind, knowing how Germans exaggerated. Nowhere in Spain did it equal the exquisite entertainment afforded by the Hungarians when they tortured John Huss, nor the elaborate ritual of boiling in oil, which was the fate of French traitors; for Isabella, in a pragmatica that found its way into the chronicles, required strangling to death before burning, a spoil-sport edict which disappointed the crowds like her sheathing the horns of bulls during bullfights.

"Your fear for the future," Ferdinand said to her with great satisfaction, "must have envisioned a very far future indeed."

Shortly Pope Sixtus died, and the new Pope was soon so embroiled with secular affairs in Italy among contending factions who were fighting The Barons' War, that Rome, like Spain, lost sight of the infant Spanish Inquisition among current events of far greater moment.

The Moorish war now gave Ferdinand another if somewhat backhanded, source of satisfaction. It purged him of much of the shame that he felt for his failure at Loja, but he savored it only in secret, since it was a bitter reversal for Spain. The indomitable Marqués of Cadiz, it developed, could also lose battles.

There was a fertile valley winding among the mountains north of Malaga. It was superbly farmed by the Moors, rich in grain fields, vineyards, cattle and sheep and thriving little towns. It seemed to offer rich spoil, especially of provender for the army. Into this winding valley Cadiz led a large foraging expedition, expecting an easy victory. His knights and troops were in a fiesta spirit and sang as they marched.

Then the Moors, who had hidden on the heights in a place where the valley was narrow, swooped down on them from both sides in the dark when the Christians had camped for the night. Cadiz barely escaped with his life. Five hundred Spanish troops were captured and enslaved. Two hundred Spanish knights were herded into the dungeons of Malaga, to wear chains instead of beautiful Toledo armor, till Ferdinand and Isabella could ransom them. Reluctantly Isabella agreed that the ransom of so many titled caballeros would have to wait, for Abul Hassan, in whose territory the disaster had occurred, demanded an impossible sum for their release.

"Unchivalrous, untraditional, unethical old scoundrel!"

Ferdinand fumed. "Either he is fabulously rich and doesn't need the money, or else he is desperately poor and hopes we can meet his demands."

Isabella shook her head; her face was grave and troubled. "He's neither, Ferdinand. He simply doesn't want Spain to get back those fighters. He knows, as I do, that we are engaged in a war of extinction!"

"But kings have always ransomed fighters, titled ones, anyhow."

"Not in a war like this."

"This war is like any other war," he said. But little by little she was edging him over to her belief that the character of war could change, and had changed and involved the heart of a nation, not only its edges. He finally yielded to her entreaty that he supply at least a few ships from Aragón to reinforce hers, which had begun to blockade the entire Granadine coastline. When the Grand Admiral of Castile captured several profitable prizes Ferdinand sent more Aragonian ships. But on land he continued the traditional border tactics of raids and forays, leading them often in person, bravely as always.

One such raid, which he did not have the luck to be commanding, met with spectacular success. In a minor engagement a tall and handsome Moor, fairer of complexion than most, had his horse killed under him. As the animal fell he leapt to the ground and continued to fight on foot. He was instantly surrounded by a ring of Castilian infantrymen; he cut them to pieces with a jeweled scimitar. But they were too many for him and at last, fainting with fatigue, he shouted his name, lest he be killed, and surrendered to a totally undistinguished soldier named Martin Hurtado. The brave and handsome light-skinned Moor was Abdallah, the young Sulla of the City of Granada. He had gone into battle with a rash high heart to win glory and renown; he had succeeded only in getting himself captured by a peasant.

The peasant took him to a captain, the captain took him to the king, who said, "Well, Isabella? What have you now to say for your silly theory of war! You had almost persuaded me that you knew more about fighting than a man."

"Pray God that such miracles continue in the future," she answered.

"It is very disconcerting the way you evade a simple question," he said.

Taking advantage of the general confusion among the Moors that followed the capture of one of their sultans, the Marqués of Cadiz led an attack against Zahara so daring in concept as to be absurd. He recaptured the city in the clouds in broad daylight without the loss of a single Spaniard.

"Well, Isabella?"

She was beside herself with joy; Alhama was now no longer isolated and could probably be held.

"The miracles continue!" she murmured.

"Perhaps. Or else we have proof that chewing around the edges eventually eats into the heart."

"Or that Zahara, the virtuous lady, having once lost her virtue, was an easy conquest thereafter."

"Do not let Cadiz hear you say that."

"I thank God for these victories, and it does not matter on what theory they were won."

"My dear, the war is all but over."

"I hope so."

They summoned a Cortes to deliberate what should be done with the sultan, whether he should be offered for ransom or held prisoner. But even before the Cortes convened, Ferdinand sent a herald to Abul Hassan in Malaga, threatening death to the young man unless all 200 of the caballeros still imprisoned in Malaga were released. Abul Hassan had no reason to love the son who had revolted against him, but neither did he wish to see him killed, and he knew Ferdinand's record. He released the Spanish knights.

"Well, Isabella?"

She merely asked, "Would you really have executed him, Ferdinand? His mother was once a Christian. He might have been converted."

Ferdinand laughed heartily.

Then, in France, King Louis suddenly died and upset the equilibrium of Europe.

"Since the war is all but won," Ferdinand said, "this is a golden opportunity for me to go back to Aragón and raid Roussillon and Cerdagne, those two cities that Louis stole from my father."

It appalled her that he was willing to divert strength to a border fight against Christians when she did not believe that the war against the infidel was won, or anywhere near.

"We cannot afford a war with France," she said.

"Not a war; just a raid."

"It would lead to a war, and that would involve all Spain. The Moorish war needs you."

"Nonsense."

"I'm afraid, Ferdinand."

"You afraid? Then you are sick. Why, if we never win another Moorish victory we'll still have done more for the Reconquest than any other Spanish sovereigns."

"Ferdinand, I need you too."

"Eh?"

"A wife wants her husband near her at times."

"What on earth are you talking about?"

She looked at him. In other years he would have understood.

"I shall remain until the Cortes decides about Abdallah, of course," he said. "I shall want to be there to advise them."

"We are going to have another prince, or princess," she had to explain.

"Tut, tut, you won't need me for that. After all, it's the fifth time, isn't it? And it will probably be another girl."

She was suddenly furious at him; her eyes flared big and green. "The Mother of God was a girl!"

"I consider such a remark highly irreverent," he said primly, "and not in the least applicable."

336

"Perhaps it is, but it's still the truth," she said in a lower voice. Her spasm of anger had passed, but her heart and her cross were heavy. She had been bedridden for months after her last confinement; she was frightened of what another might do to her. She wished Ferdinand had not forgotten so quickly.

"I know you have a great deal on your mind," she said; but he did not accept the little peace offering she was extending to make amends for her anger. He was counting on his fingers.

She smiled. "If you remain to advise the Cortes and then conquer Roussillon and Cerdagne quickly enough, I dare say you'll be back in time."

His attitude altered slightly, but it was too diplomatic and persuasive to be warm. She saw that he wanted something from her. "Quite true," he said in his best king's council voice. "Naturally I shall want to be with you. However—" and she knew that next would come the demand; she knew him so well!—"you admit that Roussillon and Cerdagne will have to be captured very quickly. I shall need money, brave captains, troops. Nay, do not look displeased. I do not ask for Castilian money. I can get money in Aragón. But some Castilian officers and men, added to my own, they indeed would speed up the venture immeasurably. And then I could be back at your side to greet the little new one!"

"Ferdinand, Ferdinand, fighters cannot be spared from the Moorish war." She wanted to plead with him not to mix their private and public lives. It was ominous that he should use their unborn child as a political weapon to bribe troops and generals away from her for a border raid that he knew she did not approve. It betrayed the trader in him, from which her proud Castilian nature instinctively drew away. Nor was it very kind. But she did not plead. She could not. She, who had begged cannon off castle walls for war, could not beg one word of kindness for herself.

He continued daily to press her; daily she refused his demands. Talking to each other grew more and more painful. The unpleasantness that had started as a disagreement over policy degenerated into a bitter personal quarrel.

Everyone sensed that the king and queen were not getting along. A pall of gloom settled over the court. Generals tiptoed in and out of their presence as if they were walking on eggs, guarding their tongues, avoiding mention of the war; and thus all war planning came to a stop. The court physician, noting the tense aspect of the sovereigns, would have prescribed a sedative for the king, to calm his angry bilious eyes, a draught of Oporto for the queen, to give her strength, for her cheeks were wan—but he was not consulted, and he dared not intrude. In the palace kitchens the cooks complained that Their Highnesses were eating nothing at all, and speculated unhappily what might be the cause. *Maria Santísima!* Oughtn't a woman to build up her blood for a baby, especially after that sickness with the last one?

Beatriz de Bobadilla said to her husband, "It breaks my heart that I cannot take her into my arms and comfort her, but I learned long ago not to criticize that cruel cold fish she married!"

"Sh-h-h! The Marqués of Moya whispered. "Do not say it aloud. But the king is hopelessly wrong, of course, to fight the French instead of the Moors."

"I'd garrote him!"

"She'll have her way in the end. She always wins him over."

"This time I'm not so sure," Beatriz said.

Ferdinand lingered a while to address the Cortes and advise them. They debated the fate of Abdallah lengthily. Some of the deputies were in favor of executing him; others advocated a tremendous ransom.

Ferdinand's solution was shrewd and superlatively calculated. Let the young Moorish sultan be released, he said, without any ransom at all. Let him be sent back to Granada, to rule as before. But first let him swear homage to the Spanish Sovereigns and hold his city in fief, like any other vassal, swearing by Christ or the Prophet—Ferdinand would accept either—never to bear arms again against Spain. "Thus," said Ferdinand, "Sultan Abdallah will be neither a good Moor nor a good Spaniard, which is good for us, since the capital city of our enemy will be immobilized. Confusion and discord will spread throughout all Morisma, and when the time comes the whole kingdom, rent by internal dissension, will fall to us!" And, lest Abdullah be tempted to make war again, Ferdinand proposed to keep his infant son, whom Abdallah adored, as a hostage whose life would be forfeit the instant Abdallah broke the conditions of his release.

The Cortes overwhelmingly adopted Ferdinand's proposal. Abdallah, who had no choice, signed the humiliating treaty that released him, swore his oath of homage and tearfully left behind in Spanish custody the small bright-eyed boy who was his son. The other sultan, Abul Hassan, and the rest of the Moorish kingdom continued the war.

Shortly thereafter Isabella announced that Ferdinand would leave for a visit to Aragón to attend to some business that the death of King Louis had brought to a critical stage, requiring His Highness's personal attention. She was at pains to explain that his sojourn in Castile had been long, beneficial to the nation and invaluable in the Moorish war; his stay in his native Aragón, therefore, might be expected also to be a little protracted. She was confident, she said, that all Castilians would pray for the speedy accomplishment of his mission while he was away and welcome him back, as would she, when he should return.

Ferdinand left with an escort composed entirely of Aragonians. The queen and some ladies in waiting rode with him a little distance. He was silent until they parted. Then, in a well-considered speech of farewell, as if he were reading a scroll, he kissed her hands and feet and assured her of his high esteem in many a formal phrase, and turned his horse's head, dug in the spurs and disappeared.

At once she called a council of war. All her trusted Castilian fighters were there; the Marqués of Cadiz, the

Duke of Medina Sidonia, Gonsalvo de Cordoba, the Grand Master of the Knights of Santiago, the Grand Admiral; men who loved and owed her much. With Ferdinand gone, her listless manner changed; she was crisp and efficient, consumed with a zeal for war, for this war was the reason for her quarrel with Ferdinand. She hated it; and since she could not hate an abstraction, she merely hated the Moors a little more. Never had the high resolve to crush the entire Kingdom of the Infidel burned so fiercely within her.

It was difficult for her generals to keep up with her rapid-fire orders; guns to be bought, roads to be constructed, troops to be recruited, powder to be manufactured, marble cannon balls to be chiseled, iron chain shot to be fabricated—it was new, she said, and extremely effective against enemy personnel, whom it simply sliced to pieces. It was also good to rip the rigging of enemy vessels to shreds; let the Grand Admiral see to it! He nodded, amazed at her. Since often she presided over the war council after a review of the troops, they grew accustomed to seeing her in armor.

But armor was steel, and steel was not flexible like a gown. Shortly she could wear it no longer.

She still gave orders, but they were gentler ones. Her own condition recalled to her mind the sick, the wounded, the suffering that war always produced. Why was it that no one had ever thought of assuaging the pain of the wounded in war? Yet no one ever had.

She summoned her court physician, who thought perhaps he should bleed her, her activity having been feverish of late. An assistant was ready with the knife and the little brass dish. She said No.

"I want you to organize a system of hospitals to follow the armies," she said, "and staff them with apothecaries skilled in the treatment of wounds."

"But Your Highness," he protested, "hospitals are great solid buildings and cannot be moved!"

"A tent can be moved, señor physician. Why cannot a tent

be a hospital? Let tents be used. Erect them and take them down as the armies advance, that many brave men may not suffer needless agony and many precious lives may be saved. See to it."

"This is a totally new departure from traditional medical procedure," he said stiffly. She saw he was preparing a host of objections.

"I am confident that my own trusted surgeon will manage to solve the details," she said quietly, but her eyes were stern. "Or do you suppose I ought to choose someone else?"

He could not tell whether she meant someone else as the Queen's Surgeon in Chief, or someone else to organize her entirely new concept of a mobile medical corps. His post was lucrative and honorable; he did not want to lose it.

"I feel certain that I can handle this great humanitarian undertaking myself," he replied, and at once advanced not objections but assurances that the plan was feasible: "A few extra tents, some light wagons for instruments, drugs and stretchers, some strong young apothecaries who can carry the stretchers and stay cool under fire— Your Highness, the soldiers will bless you for this!"

As Isabella organized her realm alone, without Ferdinand, without even hearing from him, it seemed to the world that the Queen of Castile was content to be a warrior. But one day, speaking to Beatriz de Bobadilla about a mountain road she was building to transport certain heavy guns, she broke off in the middle of a sentence and said, "He didn't even ask me not to ride horses. He always did before." Then she went on and finished the sentence about the mountain road.

CHAPTER 28

FROM Tarazona, where he had summoned the Aragonian cortes, Ferdinand at length wrote a letter to Isabella and chose Francisco de Valdes to deliver it, as the most likely person to make a good impression on her. She had always shown favor to Valdes, whom she had spirited across the border away from Henry's wrath and unnatural affection when he was a mere page boy in Henry's court. Ferdinand's letter was a clever mixture of diplomacy and domesticity. Though addressed to her and beginning mi señora, it was obviously intended to be read by her generals also, and to influence them.

Ferdinand had had, he confessed, some slight difficulty with his parliament: it refused point-blank to vote funds for his raid against the French. "But I have no doubt that were you here to address them, as you were once before, you would sway their votes and make possible this venture which I consider so vital to the interests of both our kingdoms." Since he realized, he said, that it was not possible for her to appear in person, he suggested that she send them a message which he could read to them, "that they may see that our minds and our hearts are in all things one, wherein lies the strength of our great and united realm of Spain." It would also help him immeasurably, he said, if her Castilian generals were to signify their approval of his action against the French and recommend for it a substantial appropriation of funds to her Cortes. "I hasten to add," he assured her, "that such funds need never actually be paid. Merely a promise is enough to change the stubborn resistance of my vassals." He suggested a parliamentary maneuver. When asking her Cortes for the money, he said, she could quietly let it be known that a favorable vote would not cost them a maravedí; it would just be an expression of confidence, made with the intention of swaying the Cortes of Aragón.

Isabella sighed. That was not the way to influence Castilians. Such an approach would have infuriated her Cortes, since it would have commercialized their pride and reduced a solemn parliamentary promise to an empty gesture. "He will never understand Castilians," she thought. "Perhaps, since I too am Castilian, he will never understand me."

She had taken good care of her health since Ferdinand left. Recently she had rested a few hours each day, and for several months she had used a litter when it was necessary for her to travel. She received Ferdinand's courier in a chamber adjoining her private apartments; she was seated in a large chair with a cushion under her feet and a velvet robe thrown over her knees, for the weather was cold. With her were Cardinal Mendoza, Beatriz de Bobadilla and a few servants. She sent the servants away after she read Ferdinand's letter.

"The king keeps well, Don Francisco?"

"Madame, His Highness enjoys the best of health."

"Is he ruddy of face? Are his spirits good? Does he hunt?"

"He is much in the saddle and his color is good, but his appearances before his Cortes leave him little time to hunt."

"Does he eat his meals with good appetite?"

"More than I have ever seen him," Valdes replied, anxious to say the right thing.

"Is he calm in his mind?"

"That is hard to say, Your Highness. His mind is full of great plans against the French."

"Does he still play chess in his moments of leisure?"

"Oh yes, Your Highness."

"He works so hard. But he does allow himself a little leisure, away from his duties? He isn't lonely?"

Valdes said, "I assure Your Highness the king is not lonely."

Beatriz de Bobadilla glanced sharply at Valdes, who had smiled involuntarily. Cardinal Mendoza was frowning. But Isabella was not prying.

"I shouldn't like him to be lonely," she said. Her own loneliness was speaking.

Valdes smothered his smile and hastened to add, "I often play chess with His Highness, and so do many other men of his suite."

"Good lad!" Cardinal Mendoza said gruffly.

Beatriz said, "Almost everybody plays chess nowadays. I've even taken up the game myself, though it taxes my wits."

Suddenly it seemed to Isabella that her loyal friends were protesting the harmlessness of chess a little too strongly.

"We will answer the king's letter at once," she said to Valdes, who knew that he was dismissed and bowed himself to the door. When he had gone, Isabella said, "Get good enough at the game, dear friend, for the king to choose *you* as a partner when he returns."

"I will!" Beatriz promised.

"I too occasionally relax over the board," Cardinal Mendoza said, but he was still protesting the harmlessness of chess, beating a horse that was dead, for Beatriz knew that Isabella had also noted, and read what she had read, in Francisco de Valdes' smirk. Assuredly King Ferdinand was not lonely in Aragón.

Knowing that his letter was intended for the eyes of her war council, Isabella submitted it to them without comment. They condemned in vigorous terms any Castilian participation in Ferdinand's French adventure, and implored her not to summon her Cortes to consider Ferdinand's scheme to appropriate money with no intention of paying it, a slippery tactic that left them speechless with indignation.

She wrote him a letter softening their refusal but stating unequivocally that the temper of Castile was not friendly to anything that might divert strength from the Moorish war. Ferdinand lapsed into his former silence. He did not answer. Angry he had left her; angry he remained. He was still in Aragón in December when their baby was born, still struggling with his Cortes, who still refused to finance an expedition against the French. The border had been quiet for many years, they told him; they preferred to leave it so. Their dogged refusal to support their king, of course, was common knowledge; Isabella heard of it and, though she agreed, she felt the humiliation that she knew Ferdinand must feel.

Rumors of a private nature, however, which Isabella did not hear, filtered back to the ears of Beatriz de Bobadilla. Ferdinand had found a way to forget his troubles in the arms of a giddy little wench from Barcelona, who danced a seductive Catalan dance with bells on her toes and a rose in her mouth and, so went the rumors, very little else to encumber her motions except a pair of castanets.

"That is a lot of filthy gossip!" Beatriz snapped, and she threatened Isabella's ladies in waiting that if a single one of them should so much as breathe a single word of it to the queen, she, Beatriz de Bobadilla, the Marquesa de Moya, would personally see to it by fair means or foul that the talebearer lost her place at court. They knew she could and they knew she would. They held their tongues.

"But I'm sure it's true, every nasty word of it!" Beatriz said to her husband.

"How will you quiet the men?" he smiled. "I've heard the rumors, too."

She tossed her elegant head, "They won't talk. You men always protect one another. I was only afraid of the women."

"You'd have made quite a queen yourself, Beatriz."

"And have a king for a husband, like Ferdinand? No thank you, Andrés!"

"Not quite like him, I hope," he said. "But it isn't fair to mix 'the king' and 'the husband.' He's not at all a bad king. He's a wizard at foreign diplomacy; witness the treaty that released Abdallah."

"Well, he's a very bad husband, and you can't separate the two."

"You ought to try."

"The queen can't."

"That's because she is a woman."

"For goodness' sake, what else would a queen be?"

The Marqués of Moya laughed. "You're a scatterbrain, actually, Beatriz. But it was right of you to stifle those rumors, which after all may not be true."

"Would you wager me a new gown they're not true?"

"Hm-m, no; no, I don't think so."

"Then I'll buy it. You lost!"

When Isabella could summon the strength and the courage she wrote Ferdinand that their child was indeed only another girl, "but a bright and pretty one," she said, "to join the others one day in contracting good marriages for Spain." She had christened the new infanta Catalina. Ferdinand answered that he had already heard the news and excused himself for not congratulating her sooner on the grounds that Aragonian affairs kept him busy night and day. "Night and day" was an unfortunate phrase, and Isabella wept. "But it should comfort me," she told herself, "for Ferdinand, of all people, would never have used it if it had had a double meaning."

She was extremely anxious to see him again, she wrote, and if his business kept him away much longer she planned to come to Aragón as soon as her doctors permitted her to travel. "The birth of Catalina was an easy one," she said, "but they make a great fuss over many silly little symptoms, as if such things were new to them and to me."

"I marvel at your change of heart," he replied, "for I can only construe your letter as an offer to address the Aragonian Cortes in behalf of my plans against the French. But it is too late, mi señora; I am beaten, and it would be ill advised for you to be involved in my failure. Therefore remain where you are and do as the doctors bid you, for it comes to my ears that you have had a difficult time. It was wrong of you not to tell me."

Isabella said happily to Beatriz, "The king will soon return! He does not say so, but I know he will." She sensed that he had already returned in spirit, the way she cared for most.

Beatriz said, "My husband says my chess is still bad, but it's getting better all the time." She had kept her ears cocked for gossip about the king's affair, but it had suddenly stopped just after Catalina was born, stopped with a story of the dancer in a nunnery, as usual. Ferdinand's lightning amours never varied.

"I do not think chess will be necessary," Isabella said. "I was jealous for no reason, and now I am ashamed of the wrong I did him in my thoughts."

"Yes, Your Highness," Beatriz said dutifully.

Isabella smiled, "You do not deceive me, Beatriz. Do you know how I know I was wrong to be jealous?"

"Frankly, I cannot imagine."

"He actually believes I meant to come to Aragón to back his plan against the French! Clearly, he has been thinking politics and nothing but politics all the time he has been away."

Beatriz nodded and smiled and tried to look as if she believed the queen's words, and since the queen so fiercely and defiantly believed them herself, she succeeded.

From her sickbed Isabella had planned with her war council a mighty thrust against the Moors. It involved nothing less than a strike across the entire infidel kingdom, clear to the seaport of Malaga, which Abul Hassan had made his chief stronghold. In advance of her land armies, her fleet had already concentrated its blockade against Malaga, neutralizing its shipping and forcing it to procure supplies by difficult overland routes. The Marqués of Cadiz had at first hesitated, pointing out that the blockade betrayed her plans and precluded all chance of surprise.

"We shall not count on surprise," Isabella said. "Let the Moors know our high resolve! Let them behold our massive preparations! Let them learn that each city to which we lay siege is doomed, for having encamped before their citadels we shall never turn back until they are battered down or starved to their knees!"

This was the war of attrition, of relentless sieges, the war of total conquest that had always been her dream: its goal, the utter extinction of the Kingdom of Granada. In Ferdinand's absence she had planned its grand strategy and, with the blockade of Malaga, actually begun it. The magnitude of her concept inspired her generals; her absolute faith in its success communicated itself to them and swept them along. The Grand Admiral, an old and deeply religious man who could remember Joan of Arc, sometimes wondered what angel had brushed her with its wing and prayed that God, who saw fit to send twice in one century to Christendom women who out-warriored the warriors, would not let her fall into the hands of the Moors, who assuredly would deal with her more harshly than had the English with Joan.

The Marqués of Cadiz, fearful that his first hesitation might seem to reflect on his honor, begged to be allowed to lead the army to Malaga.

"The king will be home shortly," Isabella said. "The King shall lead us all."

Meanwhile she left her bed, first to a chair, then to a litter, then to a mule, then to a warhorse, till finally she rode again in armor, recruiting, inspecting, encouraging, and purchasing materiel in quantities never amassed before. The cost was high. But so was her dream. She wearied her escort with the speed of her travel. She was hours each day in the saddle. She would appear unannounced in distant cities, dispensing with ceremony and protocol in order that she might visit more places, preaching her Crusade. Wherever she went the citizenry thronged into marketplaces and church plazas to hear her. And when she left, she left with them her dream of conquest; for men could not forget the queen in steel, astride her snowwhite charger, her green eyes blazing with faith in her cause, her hair like fire in the sun, who called them to battle with words like victory bells.

Ferdinand heard of these things and dismissed the Aragonian Cortes in disgust. He returned to Castile, chastened, beaten by his parliament, secretly smarting in conscience and hot with a rage to distinguish himself.

Outwardly he was calm.

"I shall seriously attempt your way of making war," he said.

"Malaga?"

"Soon."

But when she presented him with his new daughter his face went grim.

"No one can help having a girl when God sends her a girl," Isabella said spiritedly.

"How well I have learned that lesson," he said, quietly, as any husband might; but then he repeated the words in a voice so charged with mysterious emotion that he frightened her. "How damnably, damnably, damnably well I have learned!"

"What is it, Ferdinand?"

Suddenly he crushed both her hands to his lips and kissed them again and again, then pressed them hard against his cheeks.

"What *is* it, Ferdinand?"

"I have had a trying time," he said. He was himself again; his face and his voice were under control.

The queen's hands were moist where his eyes or his lips had touched them.

"Dear husband, I never saw you weep before."

"Weep?"

"These tears." She held out her hands.

"Not tears, you silly goose. It's so long since I've kissed you, I kissed a little too hard. That's all."

The incident troubled her spirit, but she did not refer to it afterwards; there were dark depths in Ferdinand that she did not wish to plumb for fear of what she would find.

More understandable was his attitude toward the Moorish war. Casting his eye on the superbly successful results of her preparation, he threw himself into battle with fury. The zeal of her troops was high, and there were fifty thousand of them. Field captains had always admired him. He placed himself at their head and cut a swath of destruction through the Kingdom of Granada up to the very walls of Malaga, ravaging the countryside all around it.

"I could take it if I wished," he sent word to the queen, "but it would be a pity to waste such beautiful fighting weather in a long siege, which even the Marqués of Cadiz will tell you Malaga will require." She did not press the matter, happy at his success.

His spirit was soaring in action. Isabella concluded that his odd behavior on first seeing their daughter could not have been resentment, for the herald brought a little present for Catalina. It was a Moorish sweetmeat of colored sugar crystals, beautiful as a string of jewels, costly and rare. "I am instructed by His Highness," the embarrassed herald said, "to request Your Highness not to let Her Highness swallow the string, which is not edible."

"Tell the king I'll be very careful," she smiled, "and please thank him fondly from both of us."

In quick succession Ferdinand took the powerful cities of Illora, Setenil and Ronda and seventy other towns. Before the year was out the heart of Morisma resembled a fabric that moths had begun to eat, spotting it with holes and every hole a Christian garrison, well-provisioned, well-manned. No longer was he chewing around the edges.

One place revolted after he had conquered it, the little Moorish town of Benamaquex. To revolt was an act of treason since Ferdinand, like any feudal lord, always exacted an oath of homage after a surrender. He marched again upon

Benamaquex and fell on it like a storm. He leveled it to the ground, forcing the Moors to perform the labor of tearing down their shops and homes. Then he mined the walls and blew them up, with the bodies of one hundred and eight persons whom he had hanged from the battlements as an example.

Ferdinand's victories, for all their speed, took the better part of a year, since even a small town (and there were seventy of them) required a few days to capture, to garrison with occupation troops and to reorganize; all of which he did thoroughly. He would not go on to his next objective till he had exacted an oath of homage and set up a system of tax collecting in each place. The taxes were moderate, lest the conquered towns revolt like Benamaquex; and he seemed further moderate in allowing his new subjects to keep their own Moorish laws and religion. Thus there arose an odd juxtaposition of Crescent and Cross that looked as if Ferdinand were tolerant. It would happen that a new Christian church would ring its bell at the same hour that the town's muezzin would climb his minaret and chant his Moorish call to prayer. But the tongue of the bell was iron, the tongue of the men was flesh, and no one could doubt which would win in the end.

The king, proud of his victories, greedy for more and pleased with the queen's method of waging war, was willing to keep the army in action all winter. He would now advance, he said, upon Loja, the place that she had asked for before Malaga. It had humbled him at his first attempt, but he had sworn to capture it if it was the last thing he did in this world. He had learned, he said, that war could change. So the ancient custom of disbanding an army each winter could also change.

Isabella too would have liked to wage war both in and out of season. But springtime and harvest did not change, and her very success in recruiting so large an army called a halt to the king's campaign: fifty thousand troops, most of them farmers, could not be spared from their winter chores and spring plowing. Nor would the great lords whose land they worked have permitted it. Famine would have been the result. Even as it was, the garrisons of seventy conquered towns, who must of necessity remain, would constitute a strain on the agricultural economy of Spain.

Reluctantly Ferdinand left the field, where he had won so much distinction and where he had buried some memories that troubled his conscience. He returned to the queen in Cordova; he burned with ambition for Loja; he wanted her plan for the best and most certain means of its capture.

He found Isabella listening with interest to a sailor from Genoa with a wildly impractical scheme, which seemed to be based on the notion that there was no difference between east and west.

CHAPTER 29

KING Ferdinand was a realistic man, and took some pride in so being. Born in a nation of seafarers he assuredly knew east from west. He was familiar with the compass, an ancient Oriental device which, in crude form, had originally been used by Chinese merchants to lead their caravans across the trackless, empty, featureless steppes of central Asia, so similar in every respect except wetness to the sea. Now, in perfected form, the compass was used aboard ship by all Western nations. The compass, if not one's own good common sense, should have provided incontestable evidence that east and west were diametric opposites. The impoverished sailor now pestering the queen was trying to persuade her that they were the same, for he said that by sailing west one could arrive at the Indies. This struck King Ferdinand as no less absurd than that one should travel to Barcelona in Aragón by way of Lisbon in Portugal.

He excused Isabella good-naturedly in his mind, however. She was only a woman, reared in the uplands of Old Castile, far from the sea; she should not be reproached too harshly for being a dreamer. But he was irritated that she, who had refused to help her own husband against the French, had now fallen under the spell of this foreign adventurer and seemed actually on the point of helping him with funds for his queer navigational scheme, funds, of course, with which he would simply skip off and never be heard from again. Sovereigns were continually plagued by such charlatans.

This man, though, seemed to have wormed his way into the good graces of many highly placed persons, including Beatriz de Bobadilla and Cardinal Mendoza. Beatriz, being a romantic creature, might be expected to fall prey to any fabulous story. That Cardinal Mendoza had permitted himself to be imposed upon was less easy to understand, till the king remembered that the cardinal in his youth had made a translation of the *Odyssey* from the Greek of Homer and of the *Aeneid* from the Latin of Vergil. Some of the love of poetry and nonsense must linger in the grave old cardinal still.

Despite his irritation, Ferdinand had reasons of his own for wishing to avoid any unpleasantness just at that moment between himself and Isabella, especially over a minor nuisance. He resolved to get rid of the Italian beggar by discrediting him. He had him thoroughly investigated.

Colom was his name, some said, and Ferdinand pricked up his ears. A relapsed Jewish heretic named Colom had been burned some time before at Seville. But further reports disclosed that this Colom was not Jewish. His parents had been middle-class burghers of Genoa, perfectly good Christians for generations, too poor and hardworking (at the wool dyeing trade) even to parade their piety. Colom was simply a Spanish attempt to pronounce his Italian name. He was also called Colomo and Colombo. At court most people simply referred to him as Cristobal Colon. In his letters, however, the fellow had the effrontery to Latinize himself into Christopher Columbus, as if he were some figure of international importance.

In appearance he was as tall as Ferdinand himself, with a good head, a clean chin, a high brow, a deep persuasive voice and an insufferable assurance of manner that went ill with his threadbare cloak and patched shoes. His Castilian was laughable, but his Italian was good, better than a common sailor's. He claimed to have been educated at the University of Pavia. He looked a young forty.

He had with him a six-year-old boy, who he said was his son. Ferdinand naturally looked into that matter also, but could find nothing wrong with it. Columbus was a widower, the child was lawfully born, fruit of a marriage with a Portuguese lady of no means but respectable rank, Felipa Moniz de Perestrello. "His marriage at least explains where he got his ambitions," Ferdinand grumbled to himself, "crack-brained though they are." For Columbus' wife had been the daughter of a sea captain named Bartholomew Perestrello, who had risen from the ranks in the navy of Prince Henry the Navigator of Portugal and become the first governor of the newly discovered islands of Madeira, far out in the Western Ocean. Not quite so far indeed as those other Portuguese islands, the Azores; but all practical men knew that the Azores stood on the rim of the world, and beyond them was nothing but fog and whirlpools, sea monsters, storms and disaster.

Columbus seemed not to be practical, for he was not afraid of these things. He had visited the Azores and found the ocean there no different from any other. He had worked on the fortifications of Saint George La Mina in Portuguese Africa; there too the ocean was the same. He found it the same in eastern waters, too, for he had sailed to the Greek isle of Chios from which could be seen the Turkish mountains of Asia. He claimed also to have sailed to England, which Ferdinand considered likely enough, since England, though far away, was well known; and to have made a voyage to Iceland, which was highly unlikely indeed. In Iceland, Columbus said, he had heard legends of an ancient Viking who had found land a few days' sail to the west. This land must assuredly be Asia. Asia could be reached by sailing west round the sphere of the earth!

"Legends indeed!" Ferdinand thought.

When not at sea Columbus earned his living by making maps and navigation charts for use by sea captains. Ferdinand saw some of them and was forced to concede that they were accurate (insofar as he was able to recognize the places depicted) and beautifully, even artistically drawn. "Artists in seafaring, too?" he smiled. "No wonder Isabella likes him." But even more than government or war, navigation was the business of a practical man, not an artist.

Ferdinand's agents turned up more about the visionary

Italian sailor. They discovered something that Columbus had tried to keep secret from Isabella. She and Ferdinand were not the first sovereigns to whom he had come with his plan. First he had gone to King João of Portugal. King João had rejected him, for his demands were as bold as his dream. But without Columbus' knowledge the Portuguese king had sent a ship to the west to test his theory; it was a secret voyage in which Columbus had no part, and had it succeeded, he would have had no reward. It did not succeed. A little distance beyond the Azores the ocean turned black and menacing; the sailors refused to go on, and the captain, as terrified as they, turned back and crowded on sail till he reached the safe waters of Lisbon harbor, where he penned a report to King João that the wealth of the Indies was not to be had by sailing west; far better sail round the tip of Africa, if Africa had a tip. At least that would lie in the right direction. King João agreed, and so did King Ferdinand.

Armed with these facts Ferdinand approached the queen and told her all he had found out about Columbus.

"Even so, won't you listen to him?" she asked.

"I shall take it amiss, mi señora, if you finance him when you wouldn't finance me!"

"He asks very little, Ferdinand."

"Nothing can be spared from the Moorish war. You said so yourself. I have not spared myself."

"No, my dear. But if he can actually reach India by his plan he will reopen a trade that the Turks have completely cut off. The profits will pay for his voyage a thousand thousand times."

"Your appeal to my base commercial nature is well directed," Ferdinand said, not unkindly, "extremely skillful and absolutely useless. His plan has already been tested. It failed."

"I think rather the Portuguese captain failed. He was afraid of his crew and afraid of the sea, Columbus is afraid of nothing. Please hear him with me."

"You are singularly taken with this visionary."

"I believe in him."

"What about Loja?"

"I believe in you, too. You will conquer Loja."

"I will conquer Loja; but I want you behind me, not squandering money and ships and attention on chimerical voyages of discovery. I respect your theory of war, Isabella; wear them down, starve them out, then smash them! It works. But above all I want the strength of your spirit, undivided, all to myself; for you still bewitch me, my dear, like any other soldier."

He rather startled her. It had been a long time since she could laugh and say to him as now she did, "Honeytongue!"

"At least do not finance his voyage till the war with Granada is won."

"You are probably right," she said gravely, "Nay, I am sure you are right. But Columbus has come with a splendid dream, he offers it for sale and I wish we could afford it."

"When we march triumphant into Granada and open the treasure chambers of the Alhambra, I dare say we shall be able to afford even Christopher Columbus. I understand that his terms are a little high."

"You know them?"

"Title of Admiral, title of Don, title of viceroy and governor-general of all islands and continents he may discover in the western ocean; ten percent of all products and profits to come therefrom in the future, including *gold*, if you please! And as if that were not enough, he demands that all his titles and revenues be settled on him for life and, after he dies, vested in his heirs forever."

"Maria Santísima! He made no such sweeping demands on me."

"He will. Those are the terms he demanded from the king of Portugal. No wonder cousin João sent out an expedition on the sly!"

"Columbus does not seem like a man who will easily give up anything he sets his heart on," Isabella said dubiously.

"Neither a dream nor a maravedí," Ferdinand said.

Isabella laughed. "I am always surprised how thoroughly you inform yourself on the smallest details of everything. I never learn anything till the very last minute."

"Hm-m," said Ferdinand, rubbing his chin, thinking it was just as well. "It is downright admirable in you, Isabella, that you never employ spies. Not practical in a queen, perhaps, but lovable in a woman. Spying is a dirty business."

"We shall certainly have to wait till the war is over to employ my ambitious sailorman," Isabella said positively.

Ferdinand had won; he had got rid of the nuisance; he could afford to be generous. "Of course, if it will please you, which is always my desire, I am quite willing to listen to the fellow. Nay, a man with such faith in himself deserves a hearing, provided we promise him nothing now. Loja is closer than India, and to Loja I know the way."

"God prosper you, God keep you, Ferdinand. That is my dearest prayer."

"I think you have His ear," Ferdinand said without a trace of flippancy. He was a little superstitious about Isabella's prayers. In seventy battles he had received not one wound, shed not one drop of blood. "Continue to pray for me."

"My darling, as if I wouldn't!"

"I suppose I've been difficult at times. Perhaps I'll always be. Maybe I'll never change."

"Neither will my love," she said in a very low voice. He was in a strange mood; it was not like him to disparage himself; but she loved him for what he said. The iron cross at her neck felt warm, like the glow she fell in her heart, and her heart sang.

On a Sunday afternoon during a momentary rest from his military preparations for the great assault on Loja, Ferdinand told the queen that now would be a good time to hear Columbus if he were still wailing for an audience. "Or has he sailed off to the moon?"

"No, Beatriz took him in, him and his boy. They looked hungry, she said."

"She's an extravagant, emotional woman. She always was. The Marqués a de Moya would take in any poor stray and feed it, just to see its tail wag."

"On the contrary, Columbus stuck out his chin and declared that he had no need for charity. He threatened to go up to France and interest King Charles in his project."

"Splendid idea! I'll give him a mule, free."

"I wouldn't sign the *permiso,*" Isabella smiled.

A special permit was now required for men to ride mules. Ferdinand and Isabella, as an extraordinary war measure, had actually succeeded in pushing the Spaniard off his mule.

"And I doubt if you would give him a horse," she said.

"Certainly not," said the king. "Who is feeding the beggar who refuses charity? You? Probably."

"No, Beatriz soothed his pride—"

"Por Dios! Now we sooth his pride!"

"—and employed him to teach her chess. Poor Beatriz is still trying to improve her game."

Ferdinand laughed heartily. He had played a match or two with the marquésa out of politeness. "Columbus has permanent employment," he said.

"She says he's a wizard."

"I'll take him on and see."

"The king shall not sit at chess with a common sailor!" Isabella said in genuine alarm.

Ferdinand shrugged and smiled. "Oh, all right, all right. What a mixture of steely pride and soft heart you are."

"It wouldn't do at all, Ferdinand."

"A man who plays good chess may not be a *complete* fraud," Ferdinand said thoughtfully.

Isabella looked at him oddly. "I thought the very same thing."

She sent word to Beatriz that she and the king would

grant Columbus an audience at once. Delighted and excited, Beatriz ran to a clothes press and took out a rich velvet cloak of her husband's. "You're going to see the queen!" she cried. "For goodness' sake make yourself presentable."

He thanked her gravely, but refused. "One day I hope to see not merely a queen but God Himself," he said, "and what I am, not what I wear, is what will count."

"The king, the Grand Admiral, the cardinal—everybody will be there."

"I am glad of an opportunity to present my offer to so many distinguished persons," Columbus said, and went as he was, threadbare, patched and grandiose.

Ferdinand had presided over many assemblies as king, sat as a judge in many a court of law. He was accustomed to oratory with a purpose. An excellent speaker himself, he admired a skillful advocate. Columbus was one of the best he had ever heard.

Columbus did not labor the argument that the world was round. Most people of education believed that. The queen did, having been taught so as a child by Fray Tomás. Ferdinand himself was more than half-convinced. Instead, Columbus argued that his plan was feasible. His manner was earnest; his deep voice rang with cathedral sincerity; no one could doubt that he believed in his plan with a passion amounting almost to worship. But his approach was not visionary, It was more like that of an able lawyer, who sees before him several judges of differing interests, each of whom must be persuaded.

To the queen and the cardinal he stressed the opportunity of spreading the Gospel. India was peopled with hordes of poor heathen who never had heard God's word. But once Columbus had led the way, whole fleets of ships would follow. The voyage that now seemed unprecedented would become a commonplace. After the explorer would come the missionary, with multitudes to convert and glory undreamt of for Christianity.

It was a clever opening, Ferdinand thought, for the queen's crusading eyes were green, and Cardinal Mendoza was nodding his head in approval.

To the king, who sat impassive, Columbus painted a glowing picture of flourishing trade. The old routes were closed: the route through the Red Sea, the route through the Persian Gulf, nay, even the caravan route from Trebizond overland to India—everywhere in the East the unspeakable Turks with ships and armies lay in wait for Christian merchants, whom either they taxed so exorbitantly that no profit was left, or mercilessly slew. But he, Columbus, would demonstrate a way to bypass the infidels: sail west and avoid them completely. Sail round the globe, and by so doing, arrive at the same goal, India, from behind.

"It is true," said the king, "that a clever peddler will sometimes go round to the back door of the house when he finds the front door locked. But in this case the house is very large."

Not so, Columbus said. The world was relatively small; far smaller than was commonly believed. The Azores were close to Asia. He had proof. A Portuguese pilot named Martin Vincent had been caught in a gale that blew him four hundred leagues west of Lisbon, and there in that spot (where the Atlantic Ocean was no more formidable than any other) Vincent fished out of the water a piece of strangely carved wood that was like no European workmanship. Another Portuguese pilot named Pedro Correa, Columbus' own brother-in-law, had discovered an astonishing object that Columbus had seen with his own eyes. In Porto Santo in Madeira, Correa had found floating on the sea a stick of bamboo of enormous diameter. It had been worked by man and seemed to be a container for liquid. Columbus measured its capacity. It held four quarts, wine measure, between the joints. Such giant bamboo was known only in Asia. From Asia it must have floated to Europe. Europe and Asia could not therefore be far apart.

"Is not bamboo practically indestructible?" the king asked. "Might not this man-made object have been floating for many years?"

Columbus was prepared, "Assuredly, sire, that is a possibility, though I saw it and it looked freshly wrought. But other objects of a more perishable nature have also been found, objects which the evidence of our eyes no less than the words of the holy apostles themselves teach us are prone to corruption, quick to decay when the spirit goes out of them, namely, the frail human body of man." At Flores in the Azores, Columbus said, the bodies of two men had been washed ashore. They could not have been shipwrecked sailors, he said, "for they were very broad of face, lank of hair and different in color from Christians. Those who found them said that they looked like Asiatics." Surely human bodies would not float for years before they rotted and sank.

For the benefit of the Grand Admiral, Columbus stressed recent technical advances in shipbuilding, which now made long voyages practicable and safe. For a thousand years the shipbuilder's art had slumbered, Ships had but one mast, fitted with either one big square sail or one big fore-and-aft triangular sail. Thus one ship would be good for sailing before the wind, one for tacking against it; no ship was good for both, and the practical difficulties of combining the two types of sails baffled ship designers for ten centuries. Then in the space of a single lifetime everything changed. A technological revolution occurred. Ships took on a sudden, beautiful, new and entirely different aspect. The thousand-year-old problem was solved, just when Christendom most needed the solution. A way was discovered to combine the two dissimilar types of sail. The big square sail and the big triangular sail were broken up and placed on separate masts. These smaller sails could be individually controlled, furled to temper the fury of a blast, unfurled to take advantage of the slightest breeze. The same ship could now run before the wind or tack against it. As for oars, which vessels had always carried, they were no longer necessary at all. God had placed at man's disposal the inexhaustible energy of the wind and taught him how to control it. It is fixed in my mind," Columbus said, "that the same divine wisdom which sends us the scourge of the Turk in the East now bids us look West, to the strengthening of our faith and the conversion of countless heathen souls and to recompense us for our material losses in trade, for He says to us in His Holy Word that He will not suffer us to be tried above that which we are able, but will make a way to escape in order that we may bear our trials. It is quite impossible to explain the astounding advances in shipbuilding on any other grounds."

Thus, one by one, all but the king, Columbus won over his audience. Ferdinand sensed their approval. He was a skilled parliamentarian. One could always lose a project in committee.

"The queen and I are impressed by the scope of your proposal," he said. "It offers large promise, both spiritual and material. It should be examined most thoroughly." He would appoint, he promised, a committee of experts to examine it.

Columbus retired, to wait and to hope.

Months passed. At length the committee reported adversely.

Columbus disappeared.

CHAPTER 30

NOT even a minor nuisance now stood in Ferdinand's way. He advanced again upon Loja, fulfilling the vow he had sworn in the dark hour of shame and defeat that attended his first assault. Ferdinand always returned.

This time he was well-prepared. Isabella's big guns and abundant supplies, her military roads and the spirit of her captains, coupled with Ferdinand's own furious resolve to purge his honor, sealed the doom of the place. Under a hail of artillery fire the city lost heart. Marble cannon balls whistled against the walls, breached them and mingled their flying fragments with shattering masonry; the defenders went down before the lethal shards like a harvest before the scythe. Throughout the nights the Christian guns belched red-hot iron cannon balls. Flaming parabolas arced up against the black sky, and death crashed down with a fearsome whining sound like high-pitched cries of pain into the heart of the city. Uncontrollable fires burned themselves out. In a week Loja surrendered, but not before Ferdinand had had a particularly gratifying personal satisfaction. The impulsive Marques of Cadiz carelessly let himself become surrounded, much as the king himself had done. Ferdinand led an overwhelming party of knights through the melee and rescued him. Cadiz was beside himself with gratitude.

"It was a debt, and I dislike debts," Ferdinand said. "The Conde de Escalas, Señor Stantum and many others deserve credit also."

Englishmen would not have recognized the name "Conde de Escalas" as their own Lord Scales, nor Irishmen "Señor Stantum" as their own Hubert Staunton. But many highborn foreigners had flocked to Isabella's service to win glory and excellent pay in the war against the Moor, especially now that it seemed certain of success.

At Loja Ferdinand left Gonsalvo de Cordoba in command of the occupation troops. Both Cordoba and Cadiz spoke Moorish, like many nobles of Andalusia, but Cordoba was more diplomatic and would prove a better administrator for the Moorish population.

From Loja the king led his host to Moclin, and pounded it with two thousand cannon till stone dust rose like smoke from the walls as if the stones were burning.

In a high good mood he wrote to the queen,

> *Moors called Loja "the right eye of Granada." They call Moclin "the shield." I blinded the eye. Come, watch me now shatter the shield of the enemy's capital city, for your presence always cheers your troops no less than it cheers, - Your Ferdinand.*

Isabella sensed that he needed her. He had kept the army a long time in the field and driven it hard. Another spring was all but spent; fifty thousand peasant soldiers longed to lay down their spears and grip their plow handles and smell the peaceful, healing smell of fresh-turned earth instead of gunpowder. True, they gloried in their victories; but war was perpetual now, and another year would always bring more victories. Meanwhile behind them their wives and children and land were alone and neglected. They wanted to go home, lest there be no food.

She sent word, "Of course I shall come. But are your forces well-positioned against surprise? Are the outposts alert? Is the camp absolutely safe from all sudden assault by the Moors?"

Those were strange questions for Isabella to ask. "My dear, I have bottled them up," he replied. "Have no fear. You could not be safer in Valladolid. Come."

Then Isabella surprised him. She surprised everyone. She came, and she did not come alone. She brought with her two of the royal children of Spain. Princess Isabella rode beside her mother on a high white charger that looked like the twin of the queens own mount. Their bridles were crimson satin, their side saddles flashed with silver and gold decorations. This was not a time to appear in steel; both Isabellas wore full flowing skirts of green velvet over rustling petticoats of fine scarlet brocade and pert feminine black hats trimmed with pearls and gold embroidery.

Behind them, in bright yellow chamois breeches and a short black cloak, rode little Prince John on a pony. He was too young for spurs and he had no sword, but his hand rested solidly on a jeweled dagger at his belt; he scowled as furiously as he could at Moclin. Cardinal Mendoza rode beside him on a mule so as not to tower above him. His eyes twinkled as he glanced at the sober-faced lad. "Patience, Your Highness. Next year, or surely the next at the latest, you too shall fight the Moor."

Behind the cardinal a group of hooded friars marched barefoot, two by two, holding aloft a great silver cross on the tip of a gilded spear. The cross was a gift from the Pope, sent to Isabella and Ferdinand from Rome, blessed for the Crusade. Below the cross hung a broken chain that once had fettered a Christian prisoner in a Moorish dungeon.

Next day the king and queen, with their children beside them, reviewed the troops on the sunny plain outside Moclin in full view of the Moors, who watched and howled from the walls. Battalion after battalion dipped its colors to the royal family in salute as it marched by. The horses were curried to silken sheen, armor and weapons were burnished fire-bright, the spirit of the troops now soared. For the sight of their queen and her children, here so close to the enemy, symbolized in a special way their own families and the Spain for which they were fighting.

From Moclin the black eyes of the Moors glittered in hate. They hated the silver cross. They hated the massed Spanish banners fluttering so proudly around the queen, castles of Castile, lions of León and the crimson bars of

Aragón, so ominously like prison bars. They hated the fifty thousand troops. But most of all they hated the greenskirted figure of the woman just out of range of their guns, who was responsible for this formidable military array, Isabella herself. She had unified Christian Spain in her person as no one had been able to do since the century of Charlemagne. She was so contemptuous of them that she did not once glance at Moclin. She was so certain of victory that she had brought her own children with her. Her genius had introduced a wholly new concept into the longest war in human history. After seven hundred years a Spanish fighter, incredibly a woman, had arisen who scorned surprise and advertised her military plans in advance. They were not prepared for that. It smacked of the supernatural, like the foreknowledge of an angel, or a devil, or Allah's awful impersonal will, *qismah,* predestined doom. Exactly as her coming had raised the spirits of her troops, so now it plunged the Moors into deepest gloom.

The day after Isabella and the Infantes returned to Cordova Ferdinand smashed his way into Moclin.

Malaga was next, Isabella had determined on its capture at the very beginning of the war. To reach it her armies would be required to march from the Castilian frontier to the Mediterranean Sea, traversing the entire width of the enemy kingdom from north to south. Ferdinand had called her plan a magnificent dream at first; but by now many places had been conquered in between. They could be used as steppingstones in the line of march, as one might cross a dangerous torrent by leaping from rock to rock and arrive at the other side of the stream. Now, he agreed, it was time to take Malaga, and cut Granada in two. But first he and the queen sent the army home—excepting always the occupation troops—to raise another crop of grain. For the increasing number of men who had to remain to garrison the conquered towns was each year an added strain on the economy of Spain. The margin of safety between plenty and scarcity was extremely narrow now, and only miraculous good weather had insured adequate supplies of money and food. What one bad harvest might mean was a possibility too ominous to contemplate.

Meanwhile the Christian victories against Granada alarmed the entire Mohammedan world. Islam stretched from Turkey to Tangier and, like Christendom, was torn by internal dissension. Tangier and Tunis were at odds over water rights, Cairo and Tripoli bickered over trade, while the conquering Turk at Istanbul, mightiest of them all, stood proudly aloof and let them quarrel, scheming to extend his sway in his own as well as the Christian world. But the threat of the Spanish queen was so great that Islam began to patch up its feuds. All along the north coast of Africa the word was passed that Allah had sent a scourge to try the faith of the Faithful: Let us make peace among ourselves, lest the beautiful, brazen, *gavour* witch destroy us all! In Egypt the Caliph of All Islam, speaking from behind the black veil that hid his holy face from view, pronounced a solemn pontifical decree: Let the green banner of the Prophet, inscribed in gold with the thousand names of Allah, be unfurled! Isabella's Crusade had begotten a counter-Crusade. Even the Turks agreed to help their Mohammedan brethren in Granada, and promised an assault on Ferdinand's vital and sensitive island of Malta.

In Granada the Sultan Abdallah repudiated his oath of homage to Spain and made peace with his father. His father was on his deathbed, old, infirm and exhausted; but he was happy to be reconciled with his son at the last. Conscious that life was ebbing away, fanatically fearful lest Malaga fall to the relentless Christian queen, old Abul Hassan dispatched a mule train of treasure and a long shuffling column of Christian prisoners of war in chains to his son, admonishing him never to relinquish them and blessing him in his dying breath as "beloved prodigal, thou cherished son of my loins." Thus the Kingdom of Granada was once more united. Its heart and its temper were hardened, for now it was fighting for its life.

Isabella grimly tightened the sea blockade on the coast of the enemy kingdom, concentrating on Malaga. Ferdinand willingly reinforced her with Aragonian ships, since by now he was completely won over to her grand strategy of watch, wait, starve and smash. When another harvest was reaped and still another seeded, he led another army, swollen to sixty thousand, from stronghold to stronghold across the width of the Kingdom of Granada, scorching a broad path of destruction as he went, sundering the enemy territory, till he reached the sea and camped round Malaga. Simultaneously the fleets bombarded the city from the harbor.

Malaga was a breath-takingly lovely place. Its streets were shaded with rows of palms. Bamboos and giant eucalyptus trees, thickly entwined with flowering vines, beautified its parks and plazas. Its air was a perfume, the poems of the Moors said in their florid Eastern hyperbole, "like an opened flask of musk," and the warm blue sea that washed its shore was clear as an amethyst jewel and flecked with waves that were white as the pearls in the ears of the houris of Paradise.

But for all its beauty its aspect now was grim and warlike. Elaborate hanging gardens that had adorned its walls for centuries were ruthlessly destroyed, lest they afford a foothold to scaling parties of the enemy. Forbidding stone rose sheer and high, bristling with cannon, defying the Christian hosts.

Ferdinand smiled craftily. There were other ways through walls than scaling. Hoarding his men as he hoarded his money, he wrote to Isabella, "Malaga presents certain difficulties, and I do not wish to protract this siege. Send me some heavier guns. But above all send me much extra food—it need not be of good quality—as much as you can spare. I have a special reason for this. Fail me not, as you love God and me!"

She sent him the guns, seven enormous lombards, whose deeper, throatier roar could be heard above the ceaseless cannonade of his other artillery. Watch towers toppled in cascades of pulverized stone. Holes were blasted through the walls, gaped, grew and finally yawned in broad breaches that could not be repaired.

She parted with food less readily, however, for she was reluctant to draw upon her critically valuable reserves. But she sent him some shiploads of grain, which Ferdinand successfully unloaded on the beach out of range of the enemy, who watched the operation hungrily. Their supplies were low. They were consuming food at a rate that only the dread of starvation can stimulate. Ferdinand counted on that. The grain was a weapon more lethal than the guns, not only against Malaga but Granada also.

In the tenth week of the siege the sick and hungry inhabitants revolted against their city governor. They elected one of their number to approach Ferdinand with a deputation under a flag of truce and ask for terms of surrender. Ferdinand refused to admit the deputation. They did not look quite hungry, quite desperate enough; they might haggle over the terms.

On another and later day they returned with threats: they would place their old men and women and children in the citadel, they said, set fire to it and the town and sally forth to the field and die fighting.

"Pray do," Ferdinand said amiably, "though it seems a pity to burn your helpless loved ones. I had planned to feed them, as well as you, as soon as you surrendered. But of course—" he shrugged—"that is your decision, not mine." He fed them a sumptuous meal and sent them, sick with food in shrunken stomachs, back to Malaga. The instant they entered the gate the seven lombards riddled it with cannon balls.

At length, rather than starve, rather than burn, lusting after the promised food, the deputation returned and surrendered the city unconditionally, hoping for nothing.

It was then that Isabella's supplies became a weapon of war. Ferdinand rushed quantities of bread, fresh from the ovens and baked in the sweet Moorish fashion, into the fallen city and fed the starving populace. The rumor spread throughout Morisma that the stern Spanish king could be merciful in victory.

"Your grain," Ferdinand wrote to Isabella, "was worth its weight in gunpowder!"

The fate of the Malagan Jews was even better. There were four hundred and fifty of them. Their Spanish brethren, headed by Abraham Senior, Grand Rabbi of Castile and one of Isabella's most trusted ministers, ransomed them all and they were as free as Spanish law allowed.

But the fate of certain Christian renegades in Malaga was melancholy. Twelve captives had turned Moslem. Ferdinand buried them up to their necks in sand, and companies of caballeros practiced marksmanship on their heads in a whole day's victory celebration. In the hot bright sunlight they thundered past at a gallop hurling pointed reeds the size of an English longbow shaft at the round and ridiculous targets, which were as hard to hit as melons but much more amusing because these moved and screamed.

"Nothing now stands in the way of the conquest of the city of Granada!" Ferdinand exulted.

"Doesn't it?" Isabella asked.

CHAPTER 31

MUCH stood in the way, a pestilence bred in the misery of Malaga swept beyond the walls of the fallen city and infected all the southern provinces. Thousands died. Fierce storms raged throughout Andalusia that winter. The rivers rose over their banks and flooded the fields; the harvest failed. The French raided the frontier of Aragón. Troops had to be diverted from the Moorish war to repulse them. Most threatening of all, a Turkish fleet was gathering in the African port of Tripoli with the avowed intent of seizing Ferdinand's island of Malta. If Malta should fall Italy once more would lie open to invasion. The king and queen journeyed to Aragón to block the new danger from the East, The Crusade against Granada paused.

But it was only a pause. The momentum of victory was strong. The habit of winning was deep in the blood of a fierce new generation of Spaniards who could not remember the evil days of Henry the Impotent.

Isabella could remember those days and was sometimes forcibly reminded of them. One evening as Ferdinand labored over a sheaf of depressing accounts, all ending in deficits, and reports of supplies, all dwindling, he came across a small white paper written in Latin that some busy secretary had failed to translate for him. He handed it wearily to the queen.

"My dear, will you read this for me?"

She glanced at it; she read it through twice. Then she said in an icy voice, "The Mother Superior of the Convent of Santa Magdalena in Barcelona reports that the king's daughter, Maria, has suffered a bout of the croup." She looked at him. "Maria? I do not know the king's daughter, Maria."

He swore and snatched the letter out of her hand; then

slowly gave it back. "It happened three years ago," he said angrily, defensively, guiltily. "I was having trouble with my parliament. They refused to help me against the French. So did you. I was alone against everyone. I was angry. I snatched at any solace. But I swear on my sacred honor it shall never happen again! I beg you to believe me, Isabella."

"Have you acknowledged this Maria?"

"I shall."

She sighed. But since she could not make him over she must love him as he was.

"I always used to use an onion plaster on the chest for croup," she said in a tight and strangled voice, Then after a silence, "Will you wish my ships for Malta?"

"Will you give them to me? You refused to help before."

"I refused against Christians. Against Turks I refuse nothing."

"I do need ships. Scores of ships! But not for Malta. It is not necessary to defend Malta." His face took fire with a larger plan. "With the help of your ships I will smash the Turk in his African base before he has a chance to sail! If I have learned nothing else, Isabella, I have learned to strike at the heart!"

"How well, and deep, and coldly," she murmured.

"Eh?"

"Strike in Africa," she said. "You are quite right."

She withdrew fifty ships from the fleet that continued to blockade the Granadine coast. Under her Castilian Admiral, son of the old who was now inactive, they joined a flotilla of Ferdinand's and crossed the Mediterranean in overwhelming force. In the harbor of Tripoli they blasted the Turkish ships out of the water. Tripoli was a famous Christian victory; the Turk retired to the East; the Islamic Alliance was disrupted; Malta was safe; Italy was safe.

In recognition of their repeated defense of Christendom, Christendom's head bestowed upon Ferdinand and Isabella the title of Los Reyes Catolicos, the Catholic Sovereigns, with the style of "Majesty," giving them pre-eminence over all other Western kings except the king of France. In the short space of one woman's reign that had not yet reached its peak, Spain had risen from impotence to rank with the mightiest of European powers, and the end of its glory no man could foresee. The queen was still young. One could hope it would never end.

During the pause in the Moorish war while the action against the Turks was in progress Ferdinand and Isabella went on a long pilgrimage to the shrine of the patron saint of Spain, to fast in that season of scarcity with their hungry subjects, and pray for victory. The shrine was remote, Saint James of Campostella, on the bleak shore of the Atlantic in the gray granite hills of Galicia. The somber place matched her somber mood and the perilous times. Ferdinand accompanied her willingly and exceeded her in his show of devotion, praying at the shrine in a black penitential robe.

They were met at Valladolid by a herald with the news of the complete success of the African expedition, and a papal nuncio who bore a scroll that confirmed their majestic titles. They had encompassed the whole extent of their united Spanish realms in their pilgrimage round the peninsula. Everywhere they had shown themselves, exhorting, encouraging, recruiting soldiers and guns and supplies. The Spanish people took heart again and braced themselves for the supreme effort against Granada, for now indeed nothing stood in the way.

Ferdinand now placed himself at the head of an army of 80,000 troops, the most that had ever been mustered, and pitched his camp in the vega of Granada.

Though the rest of the kingdom had fallen, the Moors of Granada determined to fight for their beautiful capital city to the end. Seven centuries of history protected it; in Moslem eyes Granada shone as a priceless jewel in Islam's crown; so long as the Moors retained it the Mohammedan world might hope that the conquests of the Prophet in

Europe were not irretrievably lost. The tide might turn, the Christian queen might die; sovereigns like Henry the Impotent again might sit upon the Spanish throne, and once again, as had happened so many centuries before, the green banner inscribed with the thousand ineffable names of Allah might lead the hosts of the Faithful northward and onward to the final humbling of Christendom.

But more than faith and tradition protected the capital city. Hidden defenses had been constructed in vineyards and orchards outside the walls in anticipation of the siege: waterfilled trenches to block a cavalry charge; pits with sharp spikes at the bottom to impale horses and men when they fell through a thin concealing curtain of brush; peaceful-appearing farm buildings that actually held hidden guns and water mills with lookouts and sharpshooters lurking in their tops. Much of this construction was the work of Christian captives, for along with thousands of Moorish refugees that swelled the population of Granada great numbers of prisoners of war had been brought there to labor on the defenses.

Ferdinand systematically, unhurriedly, hacked down the fruit trees and destroyed the vineyards and groves which the Moors, most excellent of husbandmen, had assiduously cultivated for centuries. After a few disastrous accidents with mantraps and water mills he burned every structure, razed every building, filled every pit and depression even though it were only a harmless irrigation canal. Nothing remained that might conceal a trap or an enemy marksman. He destroyed everything. From the Christian camp to Granada's red walls the land lay level, scorched and featureless. And there, for seven months, while the fleets blockaded by sea, he besieged the place, waiting for hunger and sickness and failing hope to take their inevitable toll.

When he judged that the will to resist might have softened he dispatched a herald under a flag of truce with an offer to treat with Abdallah, recalling his liberal treatment of Malaga, promising the same for Granada.

The time was not yet ripe.

For answer Abdallah sent him a vicious starving dog. Ferdinand shrugged, ordered it fed for a week, and when it was tamed and fat, sent it back again to Abdallah with a note: "No one need starve. All you need do is surrender." On which Abdallah returned the unfortunate animal's severed head. The episode of the dog was much talked of, for it seemed to signify that Granada would rather starve than surrender.

The Marqués of Cadiz then led a large force of picked men in a determined assault on the city. The defenders on the battlements overturned the scaling ladders with long hooked poles. A screaming company of Moors with drawn scimitars issued from a hidden sally port and fell upon the attackers, who were floundering disorganized and confused among the broken ladders at the foot of the wall. Many had fractured arms and legs in their fall. Ferdinand at once sent a relief party, but not before some hundreds of Cadiz' men were butchered.

Each morning the walls of Granada were repaired, despite the heavy cannonade. A thin, disdainful Moorish officer, captured in the sally, declared, "You Spaniards are excellent masons. What better way for Christian prisoners to die than by Christian guns? Would Your Highness prefer that we starve them?"

Ferdinand's mouth hardened into a grim white line. "Señor Marques," he said to Cadiz, "pray order the firing continued."

Ill luck continued to dog the Christians at first, as indeed it always did when Ferdinand led them. A disastrous fire broke out in the Spanish camp and destroyed acres of tents. Seven months was an unprecedented length of time to remain in the field. Ferdinand's army was almost too large; tax receipts were low, owing to the famine of the previous year; he could not pay his troops. He wrote to the queen, who was at Cordova close to the scene of war, "Not only I, but the

Marqués of Cadiz, the Duke of Medina Sidonia, Gonsalvo de Cordoba and all my captains advise a postponement of action for another season. The shortage of money is particularly embarrassing. Give me your thoughts."

She wrote, "On no account give up the siege. Victory rises before us!"

He answered, "Eventual victory no doubt is certain, since God and guns and hungry bellies fight on our side; but it does not seem close. Do not, I charge you, visit my camp; it is not safe; the enemy may sally at any moment."

At the same time he said to his council with a smile, "Gentlemen, I fancy Her Majesty will shortly join us here. Pray, prepare a comfortable place for her."

He was right. Isabella appeared at the camp unannounced, with a suite of distinguished retainers and with something else that was shortly to prove a strange new weapon of war: she brought with her forty silver bells. Bells were forbidden by the Koran; they infuriated the Moors. But over the hideous noise of the cannonade their music, associated in the minds of Christians with the holiest moments of worship, carried a message of hope to the prisoners in Granada.

There followed in her train the Cardinal of Spain, Prince John, Princess Isabella, Aunt Beatriz of Portugal, Beatriz de Bobadilla with her husband Andrés de Cabrera, Master of the Mint: her friends, her children, her power, her faith. There was also a heavily guarded mule, plodding under the weight of two chests of coin that were strapped to its back. Round by sea went shiploads of supplies: more guns, more munitions, more food for horses and men.

Ferdinand, who had no money to pay his troops, questioned her sharply. "This is a strange and unexpected influx of plenty, my dear."

She had pawned the crown jewels of Castile.

"There was no other way," she said simply.

"My emerald coronet?"

"Yes."

"My balas rubies?"

"Yes."

"My sapphire brooch?"

"Yes."

"At least not the crown of Saint Ferdinand!"

"That too. Andrés de Cabrera arranged everything for me with some Valencia bankers."

"I know them. They're Jews."

"Well?"

But Isabella's white throat was not entirely stripped of her jewels, She still wore the iron cross that Ferdinand had given her when he came disguised as a merchant from Aragón to wed her.

He touched it speculatively, "This could have been pawned for more than all the rest combined."

"Never," she said.

Isabella's silver bells rubbed raw the nerves of a Moorish holy man named Ibrahim Algerbi. He was a dervish from Tripoli. He had come on a ship from his African desert to preach to his brethren in Granada, feeling a call from Allah. He asked for four hundred volunteers to follow him in the night to the Christian camp and there, he prophesied, Allah had shown him in a dream how the Christian queen would die at their hands, which he said were mystically blessed for the liberation of Islam.

Prepared by fasting and prayer they followed him; they were promptly cut to pieces by a detachment of Cadiz' men. At dawn Ibrahim Algerbi was found kneeling by a rock, his green turban bowed to the dust in prayer. The took him to the Marqués of Cadiz. Cadiz questioned him in Moorish.

Ibrahim Algerbi claimed to be one of Ferdinand's secret agents with information relative to Granada's capture that he would divulge only to the king and queen. Cadiz shrugged; Ferdinand had many agents; the fellow's story might well be true. He sent him under guard to Beatriz de Bobadilla's tent, to wait, for it was now noon and the king was taking his siesta and could not be disturbed. The queen was in one of her field hospitals.

Beatriz' tent was the most spectacular of the entire camp. It was pink canvas with green silk cords. Over it waved the Moya coat of arms on a large banner. Ibrahim Algerbi thought they were the royal arms of Spain and breathed his thanks to Allah.

Inside a beautiful woman sat at chess with an imposing personage whose chain of office and gravity of countenance matched descriptions Algerbi had heard of the king. So lovely a woman must unquestionably be the queen. He requested a drink of water. His guard obligingly went to fetch it.

Beatriz and Dom Alvero of Portugal looked up from their game to see the black-faced, turbaned fanatic rushing upon them with a dagger he had drawn from the folds of his burnoose. The blade flashed over Beatriz' head and came down between her shoulders. She screamed and fell to the floor, while Ibrahim Algerbi, uttering a loud cry of triumph, turned on Dom Alvero, whose neck and shoulder he wounded severely. Then the guards rushed in and stabbed the Moor with a hundred mortal blows. He died praising Allah, thinking he had rid the world of the king and queen of Spain.

The Marqués of Moya, aroused from his siesta, ran into the sitting room of his tent and raised his fainting wife. The gold galloon at her neck had turned the assassin's point; she had merely swooned, unwounded. "I shall never again complain how much you spend on your gowns!"

Dom Alvero, however, nearly died. He was attached to the Spanish court as a military observer for the friendly power of Portugal. His death would have been embarrassing.

Ferdinand's wrath was terrible. Ibrahim Algerbi's dead body was placed in the sling of a catapult and hurtled over the walls of Granada. The Moors retaliated by flaying a noble Spaniard and stuffing his skin with straw. Lashed to the back of a mule the caballero's grisly shell trotted into the Christian camp. Hardened veterans retched at the sight of the limp and boneless thing that had once been a man, for its limbs writhed like serpents with every step of the mule, Ferdinand swore a frightful oath: "What the Moor has devised I shall improve upon, so help me the Father of Evil in Hell!"

But Isabella called a halt to the mutual atrocities. There were more than a thousand Christian captives in the dungeons of Granada, not only prisoners taken in the present war but many others, victims of old border raids who had languished in chains for years. There was danger that the Moors, in growing desperation, might slaughter them all.

"There are better ways to show our faith and put the Infidel to shame," she said.

Evidence of the disastrous fire that had ravaged the Christian camp was all around. Ferdinand had neatly cleaned up the debris but great blackened areas still yawned among the serried rows of tents and the troops were severely crowded in those that remained.

Ferdinand had complained, "The men bicker over trifles when they are quartered too closely together."

"I don't think it's healthy," Isabella had said, "and if they bicker it's because they are idle."

"Idleness cannot be helped, I'm afraid. We spend a week doing nothing for every hour we spend fighting. That is the dull mathematics of your kind of war, my dear. The fights of the future will probably be very stupid."

"We arc certainly not going to quarter them in tents any more."

Idleness ceased abruptly now. In place of the thin inflammable tents a solid city of stone and mortar structures began to rise on the vega before Granada. The soldier turned craftsman, the caballero turned overseer. The whole plain rumbled with the strangely incongruous noises of building, as blocks were chiseled, iron was wrought, lumber hewn and carts creaked all day long carrying loads of finished construction material to preplanned and carefully laid out sites. Not only substantial dwelling places but stables, smithies, armories, kitchens, laundries, storehouses and a church arose and took shape before the astounded eyes of the Moors. In place of tents, that could fold in a night and disappear before dawn, here was a permanent city for eighty thousand inhabitants who would never, never go away. Isabella's demonstration of absolute conviction that she would conquer did more than the loss of a dozen battles to crush the spirit out of the Moors.

To add to their discomfiture, and because it was an excellent plan for a city built new on unencumbered ground, two broad paved avenues formed the principal thoroughfares. They met at right angles. Thus, whenever the Moor looked toward the hosts of his enemy, he saw the Christian Cross, in everlasting stone.

Three months after she arrived construction was complete, the last stone in place, the last roof tiled. She actually began to plant flowering trees along the avenues.

"We'll hardly need those." Ferdinand laughed.

"This is the only city in Spain that the Moor has never defiled by his presence," Isabella said. "The trees will shade future generations, and remind them, and keep them on their guard. Let the city live, and blossom, and grow, forever."

"The army wants to call this place Isabella," he said. "I rather agree." But she named it Santa Fe, for the Holy Faith that built it.

Santa Fe was costly to build. Laboring over accounts of expenses, which he audited as sharply as any Valencian banker, Ferdinand came across a bill "For Cartographical Services: 10,000 maravedíes." It was signed, "Christopher Columbus, in the suite of the Marqués of Moya."

"Here, here!" he said. "What is this?" He handed her the paper.

"Truly, I do not know."

"Your Italian sailorman is back?"

"Beatriz hasn't mentioned him."

"Well, he seems to be, and I won't pay. Let the Marqués of Moya pay him. Por Dios! Ten thousand maravedíes! For *cartographical services!* Not out of my pocket!"

"It does seem unconscionably high," Isabella said, "I'll ask what he did to earn it."

"If anything."

Columbus had returned, sensing as did all Europe that the end of the war with Granada was very near. With the end of that war, he knew, would come a golden opportunity such as never before had presented itself and never again would occur to press his personal suit upon the Spanish sovereigns. Beatriz de Bobadilla once more had taken him in.

Columbus had not stood idly by, dreaming of his voyage. It was not in his nature to be idle, especially in the midst of the bustling activity that surrounded him on all sides as the sturdy buildings of Santa Fe took shape and rose from the ground. He applied to the Marqués of Moya for employment. Skeptically the Marqués asked him, "What sort?" It was good that the Italian navigator was willing to earn his keep, but he wondered how he planned to do so.

Columbus's qualifications were impressive, and he did not minimize them. Did the marqués remember, he asked, the Portuguese port in Africa, Saint George La Mina, where fabulous treasures of gold bullion were stored till Portuguese ships could load them for Lisbon and pour them into the coffers of the Portuguese king? Assuredly, the marqués replied, he remembered the port; it was safe as the keep of Segovia; cunningly protected by rings of walls and bristling with guns that pointed to all quarters of the compass, guarding the sea approaches as well as the jungle paths on the land side. It was impregnable.

"I, Christopher Columbus, laid down those fortifications," Columbus said; and from a voluminous sea chest drew forth maps of his own making to document his assertion.

The Marqués of Moya commissioned him to execute a series of charts for the builders of Santa Fe. They proved of great value, for they were beautifully drawn, in clear understandable detail, showing buildings and streets and even a system of drains.

"But his price was high," Beatriz admitted. "I slipped his account into a big sheaf of others that Andrés was preparing for the king."

"Why, hija marquésa?"

"Andrés would never have approved a sum of ten thousand maravedíes."

"Neither did the king."

"He found the bill?"

"Like a hawk."

"Oh dear. I hoped he wouldn't notice it among so many." A pleading note slipped into her voice. "Columbus must not go away! He plans to. He threatens to. He has approached the king of England, who has written showing some interest, and talks of taking his project up to present in person to him. The English king is a shrewd and grasping man. Columbus would never come back to Castile."

"I won't let him go, and I won't pay ten thousand maravedíes," Isabella said positively. "Tell the marqués to give him three thousand maravedíes a month from my funds." It was almost as much as the salary of a Salamanca professor; it would support Columbus comfortably. "Tell the marqués to continue the payments till the war is over. Then we shall see."

"You have spared me a bitter argument with my husband," Beatriz said. "He'd have been furious at what I did."

"Now I shall have to go and face mine," Isabella smiled.

Ferdinand grumbled, "You're wasting your money." But it was her money, and it would not reach the amount that Columbus had demanded for his cartographical services for some months.

Columbus accepted his stipend and did not leave Castile. He had peddled his dream to four Christian princes: King João of Portugal, King Charles of France, King Henry of England. Only Queen Isabella of Spain, in the final exhausting hours of a terrible war, had listened, and demonstrated her faith by granting a regular salary, sufficient to keep him in dignity, paid from funds which he knew she had raised by pawning her crown jewels. Her faith strengthened his, and he waited, thankful and full of hope.

In the autumn of the year of Our Lord 1491 the city of Granada, bottled up and beleaguered by land and by sea, began to starve. Internal dissension seethed and erupted in revolt against the Sultan Abdallah. From their red walls the Moors looked out across the vega toward Isabella's magical city of Santa Fe. Endless mule trains of supplies were snaking their way across the plain and unloading their plenty into Isabella's storehouses. A bountiful harvest had replenished the granaries of Spain; but the Moors, reduced to a diet of boiled cats and scavenger dogs, of palm leaves beaten to flour and baked into a semblance of bread, hungered and sickened and died. It was observed that the siege sickness in Granada did not spread to the Christians. Santa Fe was too clean, too airy, too sanitary, too well policed for the infection to take root. Its hospitals, marked with the red cross of Santiago, were empty.

The Sultan's sad and hungry subjects approached him first with suggestions, then requests, then demands for peace. He looked into their haggard faces; he said he would give them peace. A Moorish herald disguised as a peasant rode out of Granada at dead of night carrying concealed in his turban a piece of parchment on which Abdallah had stamped in green ink the impression of the palm of his own right hand: the emissary's credentials, the Sultan's royal authority to treat with the enemy.

Thus opened the secret negotiations for peace. Gonsalvo de Cordoba, with his fluent Moorish and great diplomatic skill, met often at night with Abdallah's representatives. Sometimes the meetings took place in a hamlet outside the city, sometimes within the walls of the Alhambra itself in the heart of the city of Granada.

Step by step, one by one, night by night the terms of capitulation were negotiated. On its face the treaty was moderate; the fierce Arab pride of the Moors was salved. They retained their laws; they were permitted the practice of their religion. But there was never a doubt who was victor.

For seven centuries forty Spanish kings, each in his turn, had striven against the Moor and faded, humbled, into history. Now, after the passing of so many centuries, so many kings, the Moor surrendered to a woman, Isabella.

On the twenty-fifth of November, 1491, the last of the Sultans left his capital for the last time to meet his conqueror and sign away his crown. His last command was an order to wall up the portal through which he passed. The command was obeyed; the gate was walled up; walled up it would remain. No Moor would ever touch the stones that sealed the Sultan's shame; no Spaniard would ever disturb the monument that commemorated so glorious a victory for Christendom.

In a tent on the banks of the river Xenil in the midst of the Christian host Abdallah wrote his name in flowing Arabic script in golden ink on the treaty that delivered the sovereignty of the entire Kingdom of Granada to Spain, and wept as he wrote. Isabella affixed her Io La Reyna, Ferdinand his Io El Rey. His signature on the document of surrender was one of the last things Abdallah ever saw in this life. He fled to an African kinsman, the Sultan of Fez, who offered him sanctuary when Granada fell. Then the Sultan of Fez put out Abdallah's eyes as a public reproach for the loss of Arab Spain, and banished him, blind, to a country estate where shortly he died.

Immediately on the signing of the treaty a powerful detachment of troops under Cardinal Mendoza entered to take possession of the city, to pacify and feed the starving populace, to render Granada orderly and safe for the entry of the king and queen. Soon the great banner of the Crusade with its enormous silver cross was unfurled in the sunlight from the highest tower of the Alhambra. Eighty thousand Spaniards, waiting anxiously for the signal, set up a victory shout of joy, kneeling, prostrating themselves, kissing the ground that now was Spain. Some had grown gray in the Moorish war; all were now entitled to be called *conquistadores*. Not only a long war, a long era had ended. An era of alien domination by an alien culture had come to a close. With a solemn sense of a mighty mission accomplished Ferdinand and Isabella entered into their new kingdom.

Dragging their chains the yellow emaciated prisoners crept out of their dungeons and kissed the feet of the king and queen, watering the ground with their tears. Compassionate comrades hammered the fetters from their limbs with armorers' tools, a slow and painful task for Moorish iron was tough. But the joyful prisoners did not wince when the hammers struck, and when the weights that had burdened them so grievously finally fell in a growing heap to the ground they waved their gaunt arms and lifted their legs and danced, singing and shouting for joy with tears streaming down sunken cheeks into long unshaved beards. Isabella sent their chains like precious relics to hang on the walls of churches throughout Spain. God, king and queen were equally praised in that sunny hour of deliverance.

In the quiet gardens of the Alhambra Isabella walked hand in hand with her husband; it was her first moment of relaxation from danger, trouble, toil and war she had ever enjoyed in her long and not yet finished reign.

The air of the gardens was sweet with the perfume of myrtle and orange. At their feet cinnebar-hued fish glided and flashed in the limpid waters of Moorish pools. The quiet of the evening was broken only by the liquid plashing of many fountains and the distant sounds of Christian bells.

386

The year was at its Spring, the soft and beautiful springtime of 1492, full of the promise of plenty, prosperity and peace—peace after generations of war.

The queen wore silk and her collar of rubies again. Ferdinand had opened the treasure chambers of the Moors and caused a concise inventory to be made of their almost incalculable riches. The towers of the Alhambra had yielded their seven centuries of plunder in gold and priceless objects of exquisite Moorish art to the Christian conquerors. Isabella had redeemed her jewels from the Valencia bankers.

Following at a little distance as the sovereigns strolled among the fountains and flowers in the gathering dusk, Beatriz de Bobadilla said to her husband, "I like her better in silk than steel, don't you, Andrés?"

"She's dazzling in both," the marqués replied.

"You made her queen, Andrés."

"Oh, come, come."

"Yes, you did. The day you declared for her, and gave her the keys to Segovia, and financed her very first war."

"Perhaps I helped."

"Spain lay in your hands that day. You could have made anyone king, anyone queen. Anyone. Weren't you uncertain whom to choose?"

The Marqués of Moya rubbed the stiff little tuft of beard on his chin. "To tell the truth, I never even considered anyone else."

"Then you see very clearly, my Andrés."

"I was certainly blessedly right."

"Her armor will grow rusty now."

"I suppose so."

"She won't like that."

"It is better so."

"There is a touch of sadness in it, though. There is nothing left to conquer. She used to say Spain was shaped like a Christian shield, and only the tip was foul. Now the shield is purged of the Infidel; from Gibraltar to the Pyrenees every foe has fallen. Now she has everything."

"Hm-m," said the Marqués of Moya.

Beatriz laughed softly and slipped her arm through his. "No, she hasn't everything. I have more than she. I have you, and she has only Ferdinand, and only part of him. I could never have endured his infidelities, not once but thrice, with her patience."

"Kings are different, I suppose."

"Then I am glad you did not make me a queen!"

Her husband smiled. "I had other plans for you, my dear."

"Isabella's life will be dull and empty now. Her dream for Spain became reality, but dreams end in reality. There is a loss in that."

The Marqués of Moya placed his finger on his lips. "Hush, Beatriz; we shall be overheard." Their footsteps had carried them within earshot of the king and queen.

They heard Isabella saying to Ferdinand, "Do you not think, mi señor, that now, without gambling, we can undertake the venture of my patient, persistent Italian sailorman?"

Ferdinand snorted contemptuously, "That Christopher Columbus? That visionary? That ragged, impractical dreamer? Certainly not."

Her chin went up a fraction of an inch in that gesture of determination which Beatriz, Ferdinand, the Moors themselves, knew meant that Isabella of Castile had made up her mind. The westering sun blazed fiery red on her rubies.

"I'd pawn these again to help him!"

"Oh very well, señora mia," he agreed grudgingly. "I suppose we can afford him now, and you seem to feel strongly about him. Sail him away, for all I care, out of this world. At least he'll quit pestering me."

"How do we know," Isabella smiled, "that he won't bring back another?"

Beatriz whispered happily to her husband, "No, her life

will not be empty. She has exchanged one dream for another. She will never grow old or pine or fret so long as she cleaves to a dream."

"Knowing Columbus," the marqués said soberly, "I have a feeling this new one will never end."

Lawrence Schoonover, successful author of highly popular historical and biographical novels, passed away in 1983 but left a legacy of exceptionally readable and thoroughly researched works of great interest to lovers of history, adventure, and romance.

Schoonover was born in Iowa and graduated from the University of Wisconsin before moving to New York to work for a large advertising agency.

In the spring of 1948 he began research for what was later published as *The Burnished Blade*, the novel which immediately won him critical accolades and was chosen as a Literary Guild selection. This success allowed Schoonover to continue his writing. Many editions and millions of copies of his works have been printed and translated into eight languages including Spanish and Norwegian.

Among his highly acclaimed works are *The Spider King*, a novel of King Louis XI who united France, *The Queen's Cross* about Ferdinand of Aragon and Isabella of Castile and their reconquest of Spain, and *Gentle Infidel* which tells the story of the son of a Venetian merchant who grows up to become a Turkish Janissary during the Turkish conquest of Constantinople.